Monstrous Guidebook Volume 1

VAMPIRE SURVIVAL GUIDE

an Anthology
for Cautious Immortals

I0678048

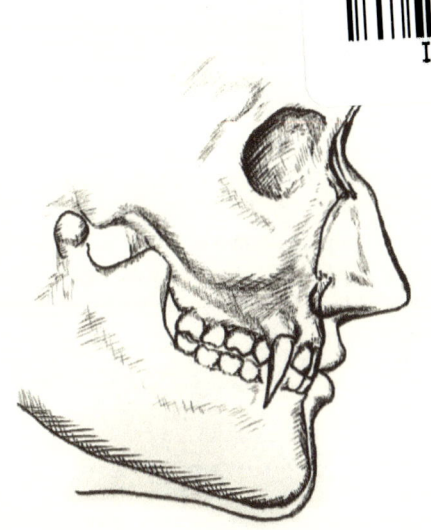

Edited by Mike Jack Stoumbos
Published by WonderBird Press, LLC

ISBN: 979-8-9875384-4-9

TABLE OF CONTENTS

Acknowledgements

This publication was a community endeavor, pulling from author education and support groups for submissions, sections readers, and Kickstarter promotions. As the groups continue to grow, it becomes harder to single out individuals apart from something like the Kickstarter list below. That said, I'd like to express appreciation for Morrigen Stoumbos and N. V. Haskell who really helped to make this anthology possible.

Kickstarter Supporters

Adam Goldstein ♦ AJ Benson ♦ Alex Harford ♦ Alison Diem ♦ Amanda N ♦ Angelia W ♦ Angelique Fawns ♦ Anne Larsen ♦ Ashara T. ♦ Ashley F ♦ Aysha Rehm ♦ Becky Lyle ♦ Bess Turner ♦ Beth Lobdell ♦ Bill Emerson ♦ Brandon Layton ♦ Brendan Pease ♦ Bryan Z ♦ C&H Stoumbos ♦ Candice R. Lisle ♦ Cat Girczyc ♦ Cathy Green ♦ Chad Bowden ♦ Cheri Kannarr ♦ Cherise P ♦ Chris Mandeville ♦ Christina Fernandez ♦ Cody L. Allen ♦ Colleen Feeney ♦ Dagmar Baumann ♦ Darren Lipman ♦ David Hankins ♦ Day Leitao ♦ Dead Fish Books ♦ Diana Bringhurst ♦ Dione Basseri ♦ Dodie Sullivan ♦ Dylan Humphreys ♦ Elesa Hagberg ♦ Frog & Esther Jones ♦ Gary Phillips ♦ Grace Stewart ♦ J. O'Donahue ♦ Jacen Leonard ♦ Jake and Becky Holt ♦ James S ♦ Jared Nelson ♦ Jeanna Simmons ♦ Jennifer Flora Black ♦ Jennifer L Collins ♦ Jenny Perry Carr ♦ Jessica Meade ♦ Jim Cebulka ♦ JL George ♦ Joe Monson ♦ John K. Patterson ♦ Jordan Theyel ♦ Joshua McGinnis ♦ Joshua Palmatier ♦ K. Z. Richards ♦ Kaden Koba ♦ Kat & Paul ♦

Kathleen Allman ◆ Kathy P ◆ Kelly Lynn Colby ◆ Kestrel369 ◆
Kevin A Davis ◆ L. D. Burke ◆ L.A. Selby ◆ Lauren Nicolette Colie ◆
Ligia de Wit ◆ Lily G ◆ Lily Raven ◆ M. L. Hutchins ◆
Margaret S. McGraw ◆ Marie W ◆ Mark E. Phair ◆ Martha E. Pedersen ◆
Martin S ◆ Mary Jo Rabe ◆ MGK ◆ Michele Hall ◆ Mike Wyant Jr. ◆
Morgan J. Muir ◆ Mustela ◆ Nick Mandujano III ◆ Paul & Laura Trinies ◆
Piet Wenings ◆ R. Hunter ◆ Rebecca ◆ Richard O'Shea ◆ Robert Brown ◆
Robert Claney ◆ Robert F. Lowell ◆ Rosamaria Cirelli ◆ Rosetta ◆
Ruth Ann Orlansky ◆ Ryan Cole ◆ Samantha R ◆ Savana St. Aubin ◆
Seamus Sands ◆ Shannon Fox ◆ Shelley Swift ◆ Stace Johnson ◆
Steve Pattee ◆ Tanya Hales ◆ Tara Henderson ◆ Terry Gene ◆
The Creative Fund ◆ Timothy Hankins ◆ Timothy VanKleeck ◆
Tracy "Rayhne" Fretwell ◆ Tracy Hughes ◆ Travis H ◆
Trip Space-Parasite ◆ Tyler Hulsey ◆ Venessa Giunta ◆ Victoria Dixon ◆
Vitale Family ◆ Wingnut ◆ Wulf Moon Enterprises ◆ Zack Fissel

...and several other anonymous supporters.

Thank you for the vote of confidence. Please enjoy the book.

CONTENT WARNINGS

The *Monstrous Guidebook* series is largely PG13, but due to the nature of vampires, some elements of monster behavior, gore, and language may cross into the R-rated category. While this anthology's content could appear in episodes of *Angel* (especially with tactful camera angles), reader discretion is generally advised.

Stories for which the main or only trigger warnings are violence or blood are not directly mentioned on the list below. Story-specific content warnings may contain spoilers.

- "Whitechapel" by N. V. Haskell is set during the terror of Jack the Ripper, and as such involves notes about prostitution, sex, and murder; no graphic sexuality is directly depicted.
- "Just a Nibble" by Jason P. Crawford contains strong language, as well as gore, animal attacks, and crude commentary about a vampire's lust for and treatment of thrawls (humans under vampiric influence and used for food).
- "Dawn of the Lizard Prince" by Fulvio Gatti contains strong language and a sex scene.
- "A Different Ideation" by Jennifer L. Collins is about mental health, depression, and suicidal ideation; it does end on a hopeful note and depicts finding something to live for.
- "Leeches" by C. L. Fors depicts mental illness and includes violence within a (vampire) family unit; there is also a dissection scene from the point of view of a historic physician.
- "Stakes" by Mia Dalia includes a character's reflection on "mercy killing."

for Dracula

Preface

Just One Old Soul's Advice

Trust me when I say that I tried to be as clear as possible:

**This book is written for vampires,
trying to survive a world run by mortal humans.**

That disclaimer doesn't necessarily dissuade the wannabe "slayers" who have watched too much *Buffy*, or the would-be objects of fascination, hoping to become the mortal lover of one with far more experience and prowess. By all means, read ahead if you do wish to know how the other kind live; hopefully further exposure will aid your understanding and empathy. (As an avid reader through the centuries, I laud the practice as the best method for stepping into unfamiliar experiences.)

For the fanged members of my audience—whether you have newly clawed your way out of a coffin, or are entering your second century of unlife but still struggling to fill out last decade's tax forms—I acknowledge that you too may be resistant to pausing for shared knowledge. After all, your blood would have you believe that you are a perfectly omnipotent lone hunter, too good for not only humans but your elders. And though no one wants to listen to a stubborn old fop brag about *that one time* for the umpteenth time, I maintain that there is wisdom to be gained from tales of vampires come before.

My long life is a testament to this fact—a survival by application of others' learned lessons and past mistakes, largely communicated by word-of-mouth or stumbled upon. After reading several self-help volumes, (including a handbook by one Mister Brooks, which describes *human* survival of zombies), I realized how lacking such literature was for our kind. I had been lucky enough to gather the right advice at the right moments, but I am vampire enough to admit that could have just as easily slipped into a drunken sleep on a rooftop patio or tripped and fallen on a number-two pencil.

So I set out to assemble the best collection of such wisdom: lessons, rules, the occasional quick-tip or "life hack," if you will, each bound in an anecdote. Knowing little of human publication, I conscripted an editor, who—once he'd stopped screaming and climbed down from the furniture—believed the truth of my nature and agreed to help me compile this volume, which I devoted to the four most pivotal components of survival: power, connections, stealth, and (oh, yes) duty.

The names and places have been altered to protect the hidden dens of still thriving urban vampires, including myself, but I pray you take these lessons and use them well. In lieu of a true title, you may think of me as Virgil to your Dante or Obi-Wan to your Luke, an avuncular elder acting as your mentor.

Your most humble and obedient servant,

a Vampire Survival Guide

PART 1 - UNDERSTANDING YOUR POWER

So you survived the turning. Congratulations! You are now stronger, faster, sharper in your instincts and senses.

You are also vulnerable in entirely new ways—and not just from fire or stakes to the heart, which could have just as easily dispatched your mortal body.

Your place in the food chain and natural order has dramatically shifted. There will be hungers and drives, the likes of which you've never known. The blood that makes you mighty could quickly become your biggest threat. And, though brazen youth would wish to deny it, you will never be the most powerful being on the planet.

It is therefore crucial to long, comfortable vampiric existence to understand the extent of your power.

A Day in the Unlife

by Jentina Grey

Devon startled awake at the sound of a high-pitched wail, loud enough to penetrate the walls of his thick wooden box. He stretched out his senses, seeking the source of the sound. A smallish creature in its last moments of life, a death scream. He felt the spark of its tiny consciousness flare and then meld into the great sea of spirits that surrounded them.

Devon rubbed at his eyes, then reached for his phone to check the time, but pulled up short as it tugged against its cord. He was reminded, yet again, that he really needed to drill a hole in the bottom of the coffin to run a charger through. He unplugged the phone and squinted against the glaring light of the display screen. It was six hours before nightfall. He groaned, unlatched the lock on the coffin's inner lid and lifted it open to peer over the rim. Beez wasn't anywhere in sight, but the growling coming from the kitchen downstairs told him that the small creature had been her kill.

"Beez, are you okay?" he called. The cat's hearing was sharp; he knew she'd heard him. His annoyance grew as the growls continued and she didn't reply. The thing, whatever it was, could have bitten her—she could be bleeding all over the living room, but he'd never know if he let himself fall back asleep.

"Beez!" he shouted. "If I have to come down there, you're not going to like it!"

"Fiiiine," Her reply floated up to him from the kitchen.

"Details, Beez," he prompted her, switching to telepathy. *"Did you catch something?"*

"Priiiiiize," she yowled back, ignoring their mindlink. She sounded extraordinarily pleased with herself, and very clearly *not* injured.

Devon rolled his eyes and went back to sleep.

Devon's alarm jolted him awake at nightfall, and he dragged a comb through his black hair before stumbling blearily down the stairs. He'd completely forgotten about the noises until his feet met with the soft fur of a dead rabbit as he entered the kitchen. It had been gutted, and there were the usual fang marks on its neck. Beez was demurely grooming one sleek black paw in her usual spot on top of the fridge.

"How many times have I told you, Beez? Keep your kills outside!"

Beez only twitched her whiskers at him, which he was positive meant 'whatever' in cat.

"So I don't need to give you your bloodfeast for today?"

She growled and put her ears back in response. Her scarlet-rimmed silver eyes tracked his movements as he glided over the dark wood floor to the coffee machine.

"You really only need to eat every two weeks or so, you know."

Another low growl brought a satisfied smile to his lips. He hit the button on the espresso machine, and the grinding of beans drowned out her grumblings.

Mug in hand, Devon finally felt alive enough to tackle his correspondence. He floated back upstairs to his office, where stacks of letters on actual vellum were piled up, waiting for his reply. He wished, not for the first time, that the council would join the brave new world, and just email him next time.

As he settled himself into the ancient velvet throne that he'd mercilessly upgraded with sturdy office chair wheels, he saw that Beez had done far worse than dragging in a corpse: Splashes of rabbit blood and blackened paw prints covered his writing, drying black ink deeply saturated the surface of the rare antique.

The papers he didn't really care about, but the beauty of the desk was tragically ruined. His gaze shifted up to dwell upon the hand-carved rosettes and enchanted tray. It had been a core fixture in the house for generations, but he could barely stand to look at it now. Devon sighed with frustration, and hastily began clearing out the drawers in preparation of tossing it out. He didn't want to think about how much a good replacement desk was going to cost, or whether the magic tray that delivered his handwritten missives to the council would still function when he seated it upon its replacement. Before long the contents of the drawers; the photos, knick knacks, and ghosts of times past, began to tear at his heart, and he had to walk away.

The night passed slowly, with the mess waiting for him upstairs haunting his thoughts. Beez seemed to sense his mood and nuzzled up against him, demanding his attention.

"Still mad at you," he said, but obliged by scratching under her chin.

Her purr was a deep rumble in her chest and had the intended effect of lifting him out of his brooding—for now, at least. When she grew bored, she placed a paw on his shoulder and looked into his eyes. "Death to the sun," she hissed.

Devon snorted. "You're a better daywalker than I am, with that thick black fur of yours." But he fed her a quarter portion of one of his anti-UV gummies, and she left to do her regularly scheduled neighborhood terrorizing.

Devon busied himself well into the early hours of the day, but found himself walking disconsolately past the door to the office for no other reason, save to cast mournful eyes upon the travesty of the desk. The third time, he walked inside to glare at the mess.

The ink had dried. It wasn't that the desk was unusable, but rather that he liked nice things, and now it was no longer nice, with the black ink pooling across its length like a spreading bloodstain. He didn't want to think about food when he was tending to business, he was already terrible at following up with any actual work as it was.

He wandered over to the window and squinted against the sunlight streaming in. Could he just push the entire desk out the window? It would shatter into a million pieces, but it might clip the porch and take the deck out with it too. Would that be better than calling someone to come dismantle the thing and carry it away? He shuddered at the thought of letting strangers… noisy, stinky mortals, into his home. Caught in indecision, he stood and stared at the stain long enough for him to feel his heels digging into the floorboards. He shook himself out of his fog, and pulled a new sheet of vellum. The fountain pen had been knocked over too, its nib resting in the ink next to the inkwell's displaced stopper. He fixed it with a new nib and wrote a quick note to the council's facilitator, Felix. He was on casual terms with the old vampire, they shared a love for sarcasm and fine art. He kept the letter brief and to the point.

Dear Felix,

Desk broke, tempted to toss the whole thing in the trash. Care to talk me out of it? If you ask me, we're best rid of the ancient things. Will its splinters help kick the council into the future? Electronic communication is encrypted nowadays, might be for the best...

Devon

He stared at his flowing script before folding and sliding it into an envelope, which he affixed with red wax. Finally, Devon pressed in his personal seal, a bat in flight suspiciously similar to the logo of a certain brand of rum.

He deposited the envelope into the box marked with a number five and flipped closed the lid, which sealed the teleportation magic. Before he set the dial for Felix's desk, he thought better of it, and went to fetch a tiny pot of honey from the store of gifts he reserved for special occasions. Felix lived in Vienna, but the honey was made from the wildflowers that grew on Devon's estate in the sprawling hills above Los Angeles. It was sweet and savory, with a pleasant herbal bite from the wild rosemary and sage. Devon felt somewhat of a kinship to bees, they produced venom just as vampires did, and likewise their saliva had healing properties. But unlike vampires, he wouldn't turn into a bee if one of them bit him. He penned a smaller note to accompany the jar:

A little bit of honey to sweeten the tone of my missive.

All my best,

Devon

He placed the honey carefully in the tray, closed the lid, and dialed the arrow to twelve for Felix. The smell of ozone wafted up from the box, and when he lifted the lid, it was empty. Devon smiled, pressed the carved wooden rose in the bottom of the tray into the ready position, and closed the lid again.

The old thing still held its charm, despite the horrible stain across its face. Pity that the desk hadn't been dyed black, else there would never have been a problem.

An idea formed in his head, and he went to find a squeegee.

Ten minutes later, he upended what remained of the inkwell's contents and pushed it across the rest of the desk. One bottle of ink wasn't able to cover the entire thing, so he opened another.

Before the ink had dried, the magic tray crackled with energy, and the lid flipped open of its own accord. In the tray lay a single piece of white computer paper, scrawled with Felix's narrow handwriting in splotchy ballpoint pen.

Devon smiled at Felix's blatant defying of council tradition, but his grin faded as he read the letter.

Devon:

Firstly: Guard your tone, fledgling. If I thought for a minute that you truly intended disrespect, I would send a member of our esteemed council over there to have your teeth dulled.

Secondly: As much as I would love for the council to welcome in this frightening new era, I am under strict orders to preserve every tiniest bit of history that we have left to us. If your desk is truly unusable, I will send a team to collect it from you and have it restored. They will give it to someone who will show such a brilliant piece of our heritage proper reverence. Please respond at your earliest convenience.

P.S.,

Thank you for the bee spit. My sweet tooth abandoned me centuries ago, but I will feed it to one of my flock before dining upon them. I'm certain it will make the occasion that much the sweeter.

Yours,

Felix

Devon's fangs retracted deep into his gums in chagrin. He had spoken to Felix in the letter exactly as he would have spoken to him in person, with the same sort of sarcastic wit both he and Felix appreciated. Perhaps the council was scrutinizing his paperwork now? Or maybe he simply hadn't thought too hard about how he sounded before sending it. He wished he could go back to his letter and comb over it to see where he had made the misstep, but the only copy was in Felix's possession. Which, Devon thought sourly, was just another reason to fully transition to email.

He scrunched up his nose, considering how to word his reply respectfully, with just the right amount of baring his neck to the old bat.

Taking his fountain pen in hand, he flattened Felix's ugly letter upon the desk and wrote his own addendum upon it.

Felix,

My apologies for any perceived disrespect on my part, I hold you and the council in the highest esteem. Regarding the desk, I have had a change of heart. Its looks may have been marred by ink and countless cat scratches, but I have done my best to repair it myself. It was maybe not the most beautiful restoration ever performed, but I love it again. Thank you for your kind words. I hope to see you at Yule.

My best,
Devon

Not a minute later, Felix's reply arrived in the tray.

Devon:

Am I to understand that your cat has been using the desk as a scratching post? Need I remind you that sharing one's immortality with a pet is against vampiric law?

The council is dispatching a delegate to evaluate you. I am sending you this letter as a courtesy. Please prepare for their visit.

Felix

Devon's anxiety rose as he felt the hole Felix had punched into the paper at the end of his angrily scrawled signature. He crumpled the paper and tossed it in the bin. "One badly written letter," he muttered, shaking his head.

A visit from the council was the last thing he needed. He scanned the room with a critical eye, and panic seized him as he imagined anyone seeing the place as it was. He would need to clear any traces of the cat in residence, or they might try to take Beez from him. He could lie and say a raccoon left the marks on the desk, but Felix knew the truth. Aside from that, the whole house needed cleaning.

First, the council's delegate would inspect the desk. Devon tried applying wood cleaner to the entire surface, which lifted a fair portion of the ink, leaving a pleasing deep grey. There was a thin wavy line between the edges where the ink had spilled and where he had applied new ink, but it flowed in a manner that seemed intentional. Artsy, even.

Beez, however, was not as enraptured with it. Devon pulled himself back from the desk in startled dismay as she landed beside him, and her clawed bracelets put another line of scratches in the desk. Beez had requested the sterling silver claws to, quote, 'fight werewolves'. Devon had regrettably indulged her by commissioning a set. They had finger-loops for Beez to slide her toe-beans through, and straps to secure them around her wrists.

"Hi!" Beez said, applying her own vampiric powers to work the mechanism on the window. She sprang through it in one fluid leap, not bothering to close it behind her. Devon darted over to lean out the window as she floated in slow motion down to the front yard below.

"Lazy little beast!" he shouted down to her. "You could at least shut it when you leave!"

A dismissive flick of her tail was her only response. As soon as her paws hit the lawn she darted away.

◆ ◆ ◆

Devon was polishing the desk when he heard Beez push open the front door. He listened closely, but didn't hear the click to confirm she'd shut it. He rushed downstairs to give her a proper scolding, but skidded to a halt when he saw her trotting into the sunlit kitchen carrying a gigantic fish.

"Where did you get that from?" he asked.

"Freeeee," Beez said, around the fish in her mouth.

By the looks of it, it was a deep sea fish, its eyes bulging out from the expanding internal pressure when reeled up from the depths below.

"It's bigger than you are! The lake is two miles away, how far did you go?" Devon asked as he moved to shut the door. He quickly forgot his question as his gaze fell upon a stranger in a white apron, running up the winding path while brandishing a cleaver.

"Oy! Is that your cat?"

Devon scowled, and his instincts defaulted to shutting the door. He winced at the click of the deadbolt that would have been audible from the path. A second later, there was a rapid pounding on the heavy wood.

"I saw him come in here! He stole one of my fishes, the little monster! Let me in!"

Devon stayed silent, angry at the intrusion upon his peace, and half afraid that he would have a corpse to dispose of if it came to a fight. And yet the man continued to pound his fat fists on the door.

Every vampire expected to one day walk out to torches and pitchforks, but not like this. Devon spared a glance for the ancient stained-glass panes, rattling above the lintel. He had traveled to Italy himself to bring them home after winning them on an international auction site. Three red roses in full bloom, set by hand in the 1300s. He'd knocked out the entire porch wall to house them, and the massive door below had been carved to match. The pounding turned into kicking. The doorknob clanked as the brawny fellow put everything he had into kicking the lock free. One of the leaded glass panels gave an ominous crack.

"I'll show that little devil whose path he crossed!" Another kick, and the doorframe splintered, while the third panel of glass shifted downward. It was more than Devon was willing to take.

"Hold up!" Devon shouted. "I'm in my pajamas, give me a minute!"

It was absolutely true. In fact, Devon hardly ever switched out of pajamas anymore—only when he went out, maybe once or twice a week, to grab a bite. He heard a stuttered apology, and the sounds of labored breathing. Devon pulled a trench coat over his black with bloody hearts pajama set and buttoned it most of the way up, but his white exposed legs made him look like a flasher. He slipped on a pair of shoes, took a deep steadying breath, and opened the door.

The man was downright burly, with arm hair so thick and red as to make him seem half animal himself. The scent of old meat wafted up from his blood-splattered apron. Devon held his breath with distaste and automatically scanned the yard beyond to make sure he hadn't been followed, in case the situation devolved. He wasn't in the habit of disappearing people, but that option was always in the back of his mind.

The butcher must have seen a glint of the predator in Devon's eyes, because despite all of his earlier blustering, he took a step backward, crossed his hugely muscled arms against his chest, and regarded him with something akin to trepidation. There was a certain robustness to him, but Devon had plenty of cleaner, tastier victims available who would fall all over themselves to feed him, and who didn't smell of bad meat.

"You would clearly win against me in a fight, sir, so let's skip that part," Devon said, using both an honorific to appease the man's ego, and a reply that would give him the victory he wanted, without going through the physical test of it.

The butcher was caught off guard, but only for a second. He drew himself up and raised his voice too loud for Devon's sensitive hearing. "I asked, is that your cat?"

"And I would ask for you to keep a reasonable distance," Devon said, restraining the urge to simply take his head off.

The man pointed his chin belligerently at the rooms beyond. "I saw your cat run inside," he said, searching over Devon's shoulder for any sight of Beez. "I'll assume you pay your debts. You owe me for a very good fish that he stole from my seafood counter. And also for the cleaning charge, and for my needing to toss out all of the other fish in the counter, for the unclean state he left them in. He pranced through the refrigerated cabinet with his dirty little feet, sniffed each fish, and then picked the exact one he wanted."

Devon waited for him to run out of air, it wouldn't do to anger him further.

"She," Devon said, when he finished.

"Aha! You admit that is your cat!" He poked him in the chest with one thick, meaty finger.

"Please do not," Devon said, not moving an inch, despite the uncomfortable pressure. He wondered idly if anyone would miss the man.

"Yes, she is my cat. I am sorry for her theft and for the unfortunate need to toss all of your fish. Yes, I will pay you for each fish. In fact, I want them all, and I will put them in my freezer and let her have them at her leisure."

The butcher's jaw dropped open. "Hundreds of dollars, is what we're talking about. In fish." Devon nodded. "What's your name, sir?"

"Chuck."

Devon blinked. "Is that a nickname? For the cuts of meat you chop?"

"Sort of," Chuck said. "Yeah. It's a running joke at the shop."

"I will accompany you to see what sort of damage my Beez has caused, but first allow me to apply some sunscreen. If you'll wait for a moment?"

Chuck looked up at the cloudy sky. "It's not that hot out. Guess you don't get out much?"

"Irish blood," Devon said, grimacing at the lie. "I burn easily."

He left the door open as he found the tube of zinc on the hall tree beside the door. Beez stared at him from atop the balcony. He glared back at her.

"You did this on purpose, didn't you?" he asked her silently, through their vampiric connection.

"Fish," she said back, with a mental hiss. She preferred speaking aloud to keep her thoughts secret. He got the impression that she thought he should get out of the house more often, and that her tolerance of him being around all the time had grown thin. Which might explain why she had let the butcher keep pace with her, all the way to his front door.

"How far did you run?" Devon asked while rubbing the thick white paste all over his face and hands.

"Few blocks," Chuck said, averting his gaze. "Nice to get outside, if I'm being honest. Cooped up in the shop all day, this is almost a treat. But I don't trust the place to my assistant, so the sooner I get back, the better."

Devon opened the closet while he talked. He could have just glamoured Chuck to forget he'd ever seen the cat, but Beez would probably do it again, and black cats already got a bad rap. Sometimes it was as if the cat was glamouring *him*, he thought ruefully, as he selected a pair of pants and pulled them on one leg at a time. He stuffed his wallet in a pocket, then motioned for Chuck to lead the way.

"You could drive us," Chuck suggested. "You might have a problem toting all that fish back with you, if you're serious about not letting it go to waste."

"Wonderful idea," Devon said, pointing to the 1969 Camaro parked in the roundabout driveway. "Right over there."

Beez waited beside the car, head held high so that her collar, resplendent in its bars of rectangular cut garnets, sparkled in the sun against her black fur. Devon glared at her as Chuck walked to the passenger side, seemingly oblivious of the cat. Before he could leave, a black rental car appeared on the long driveway. It stopped midway up, as the occupant saw that Devon had company. Devon shook his head minutely at the car, and covered the action by trying to shoo Beez away. Beez, of course, would have her way regardless of what he wanted.

Chuck got in and Devon followed, wincing as he heard her silver-clawed bracelets dig into the roof. He closed his eyes and sucked in a breath for strength before starting the engine. The other vehicle pulled forward to follow him through the circular driveway. He couldn't be sure who the council had sent, but whoever it was would no doubt require an explanation as to why he'd left the scene just as they pulled up. It didn't take long to drive to the shop, but to Devon the minutes felt like hours. His tension rose as the other car kept pace behind him.

"You ran all this way?" Devon asked Chuck, who growled with disgust before answering.

"She picked the most expensive fish in the cabinet, it was three times her size! I figured she had to drop the thing at some point. Once I'd started chasing her, I couldn't just give up. That's why I was so blasted angry when you finally answered your door!"

Devon smiled fondly. That was his Beez. "Valid," he said.

"Here it is." Chuck pointed at a little white storefront with a green awning, shaded by trees. The words Farm Fresh Grocery and Meats were painted on the storefront windows.

Devon pulled up to the curb, and the tailing rental parked a safe distance behind him. Chuck exited the Camaro, but Devon hesitated. Instead of opening his own door, he pantomimed reaching into the back of the car to grab something, so he could peer through the back window.

Devon was immensely relieved when he saw Felix himself exit and then lean casually against the vehicle. Felix had dyed his hair grey and let it grow long, to where it almost reached the shoulders of his tweed suit. He had lived through nearly three centuries, though he looked to be only in his mid-thirties.

Devon stepped out of the car. Felix shot him a brief but pointed stare, and Devon returned a pained smile.

"Bad time?" Felix asked, mind-to-mind.

"Extremely," Devon sent back. *"Cat's gotten me into trouble yet again. Can we talk in a bit?"*

"Not now?" Felix sent, with a taunting cast to his mindvoice. *"Not like this?"*

Devon cast Felix an apologetic grimace as he followed Chuck to the shop's entrance.

"Just a minute while I unlock the door," Chuck said, proceeding to fumble with his keys. "Left my apprentice in there alone, he can't work the register yet."

Devon shuffled his feet in embarrassment, feeling Felix's eyes on his back while he waited for Chuck to open the shop.

"It's just an ink spill," Devon continued to Felix, *"The desk is still functional. I should have worded my letter better. It was really just me having a minor meltdown and lashing out like an absolute brat. I'm sorry you had to fly all the way from Vienna."*

Felix replied with a mental harrumph. *"I was in fact already in Los Angeles, bringing my own desk in to be 'upgraded'. The council has installed a device to copy them on any transmissions I receive. I'm sure they have the* very best *intentions in doing so,"* Felix said with no little bit of sarcasm. That was the vampire Devon knew. *"Lady Letricia herself read your letter. She came to my home, completely bent out of shape at your disregard and belittling of the council. She wanted to send a full delegation to bring you in for gross negligence, implying that you'd intentionally destroyed historical property. You should count yourself lucky that it's only me here today."*

"Thank you," Devon replied, *"Very much. And my deepest apologies, for the necessity of my needing to handle this unfortunate piece of business before showing you the desk."* Devon felt Felix's grudging acknowledgment of his statement, and then turned his attention fully to Chuck as he pulled the 'closed for lunch' sign from the window.

Felix remained outside as Chuck led him through the compact shop. They passed fresh groceries from local farms and dairies before arriving at the meat counter, where Chuck motioned him to wait. Devon schooled his expression into neutrality as a skinny teen with a pimply, rat-like face and dark hair looked up as Chuck went to stand beside him. Devon's sharp hearing picked up their quiet conversation with no trouble.

"Chuck! Did you catch that furry menace?"

"Better. Found her owner. Says he's going to buy all the sullied fish."

The teen gawked. His tone rose in volume with exasperation. "I already hosed it all off—"

"We got a buyer, Aidan!" Chuck said through clenched teeth and a look that told the rat-faced youth to shut his trap.

Devon knew Chuck had been lying about tossing all the fish that Beez had stepped on. The butcher side-eyed him, looking as if he was about to be sick, and Devon smirked.

"Not to worry," Devon called across the counter, confirming Chuck's fears that they'd been overheard. "I've got an empty freezer. Won't exactly teach the cat a lesson, but maybe she won't be as grumpy for a while."

"That's good then," Chuck replied. "Hold right there, while I get you a total."

As Devon waited, a strange tugging upon his senses made gooseflesh raise upon his arms. He focused on the source, and found himself locking gazes with Chuck's assistant. A multitude of information assaulted Devon, and he felt his very spirit drawn into the kid's eyes, which had gone pitch black. Devon inhaled sharply, and opened his Sight.

Dozens of trapped souls, writhing and tangling amidst themselves, surrounded the butcher's assistant. They were attached to him, bound by spirit threads that tethered directly into Aidan's body. Devon had only ever heard of such a thing. The kid was a Ghost Collector.

Devon wanted to reach out to Felix, but he knew that if he tried, the ghosts would latch on to that mental wavelength and find him too.

"*Aidan...*" came the whispering chorus, barely audible and set to frequencies only a being tied to the supernatural world could receive and interpret.

"*Aidan... You will serve Aidan.*" The voices came from dozens of spirits who had seemingly blended into one another. "*Trap spirits, bend them to Our will.*"

"*Aidan's will.*"

"*Spirits. Cut them and trap them.*"

"*Vaaaaampire.*"

Devon startled out of his Sight, to find that every single one of Aidan's trapped spirits were looking at him.

Vampire.

They had named him. They knew. And if they knew, it stood to reason that Aidan knew too. In that moment of clarity, Aidan narrowed his eyes. Devon felt pinned in place by his gaze, and the black hole feeling grew stronger. Curiosity. Speculation. But above all, a domineering desire to possess everything that Devon was.

"Vampire," Aidan mouthed silently with a hungry smile, showing off the sort of naturally pointy canines that would have his friends making jokes about bats and capes.

Aidan turned his attention back to Chuck, who eagerly totaled the bill, but the ghosts stayed locked upon Devon, deepening their connection to him. The feeling of having ghostly fingers reaching into his brain was terrifying, but it also allowed Devon to infiltrate Aidan's mind. The Ghost Collector's plan was so clear, so simple. As soon as his minions snipped the thread of Devon's spirit from his body, they would feast on the energy of its severance and then drag the tail of his spirit back to Aidan, who would tether it just as he had tethered the others.

Devon's body would go into automatic mode without him guiding it. It would look like a panic attack, or an absence seizure. Or he might just collapse where he stood. Once Aidan had control over his spirit, he could force Devon to make his own former body do whatever he wanted. Aidan would become a vampire. A vampire with a legion of ghosts at his command. And Devon could already see the futures that Aidan was entertaining. He would not be a nice monster. He would drink from as many people as he pleased, and he would grow strong as their spirits joined him. Bombs couldn't kill him, government officials would seek to appease him. Backed by the power of his ghost army while also possessing his own vampiric powers, it wouldn't be long before the entire world was at his command.

Devon wasn't sure if a Ghost Collector would even survive being turned. It was possible that the ghosts would rise up while his body died, and puppet Aidan's corpse like he now puppeted them. Devon had no time to warn the kid before the ghosts surged forward.

Devon backpedaled. He couldn't outfly a score of ghosts without giving away the fact that he was a vampire; not unless he wanted to mindwipe every single person in the shop. He turned tail, and ran out the door. Once outside, he looked around for Felix, but the other vampire was nowhere in sight.

Chuck looked up from the register and swore. "He's getting away. Aidan, get him!"

Aidan grinned and gave chase.

"Beez!" Devon yelled through their link, *"Help, ghosts incoming. Distraction!"*

A yowl from above pinpointed her location—she'd been stalking a sparrow.

Beez growled her fury as the sparrow flew away, then hissed as she saw the amorphous forms rushing from the shop.

She launched herself from the tree—a furry black torpedo full of flashing claws and teeth—and landed in the center of the ghosts. The ghosts hadn't received any orders to sever a cat's spirit from its body, and so she was able to discorporate two of them with her silver-tipped claws before they realized she was a threat. She locked gazes with a third and sliced.

What Devon remembered of ghosts was that they hyper-fixated on whatever their problem was and had no real means of dealing with any real-world issues happening around them. Aidan had focused them on a vampire. With the boy's attention split, his coercion ceased to compel the spirits to any action beyond the original. But as the cat leaped and slashed through their incorporeal forms, their concentration on the task they'd been given wavered. They hovered in place, unsure of their purpose, like a man who forgets what he walked into a room to do.

Devon felt immeasurably lucky that his companion was both completely fearless and highly intelligent. She left him free to tack his gaze onto Aidan as he exited the building. This time Devon was ready, and it was he who was in command. He strode forward on stiff legs, bringing all of his force of will into one word which he blasted into Aidan's mind.

"STOP."

Aidan skidded to a halt, black eyes wide in fear.

"Follow me," Devon said, more gently but with no less dominance.

Aidan's legs moved as if a robot controlled him. Devon scanned the street. There were people about, but their attention was elsewhere. He forced his will again upon Aidan, who obeyed by opening the door to the passenger seat of the Camaro.

"Get in."

Aidan was fighting, trying to break free from his mind control.

"I won't bite," Devon said with a slow, pointy smile.

Aidan froze in fear as he recognized the lie, and Devon gave the command again.

Aidan did not get in the car. Instead, he tightened his muscles, then relaxed and tightened them again, struggling against the coercion. He won control back over one arm, and then a leg. Devon glanced around, feeling too exposed, but all strangers' eyes were glued upon the black cat leaping and slashing at seemingly nothing. They weren't watching the abduction at the curb. Good. Devon stepped up behind Aidan and slapped him hard upside the head. Aidan grunted at the impact, and Devon shoved him bodily into the car and shut the door. A pedestrian turned to the sound and regarded Devon with alarm. Devon smiled and shrugged, just as someone with a drunk friend might do, but he maintained eye contact, reinforcing the idea in the witness's mind that the poor kid was puking drunk.

The witness blinked, then focused instead on the dancing cat.

Devon slipped around the car and got in the driver's side.

Aidan was awake, and terrified.

"I won't kill you," Devon murmured. "Not right away, anyway. Not if you do everything I tell you. I am, as your spirits said, a vampire." He punctuated his words to sink through the kid's skull, and stared hard into his eyes. "Not the kind out of myth and legend that kids tell silly stories about in the dark. An actual. Real. Vampire." That seemed to get through to him. Devon tilted his head and let his eyes trail down Aidan's neck. He lowered his tone to barely a whisper. "I could wipe the memory of you from everyone but your mother. You would vanish completely out of existence, save for the vague feeling that she'd had a son once. A memory like a ghost, there and then gone again."

Aidan's nose scrunched up as he sat on the verge of tears, but a moment later Devon realized he'd said the wrong word. He shouldn't have mentioned ghosts.

He felt the spirits turn to focus on him again. Aidan's lips quirked up into a triumphant smile as they swarmed for the car.

Devon didn't waste time with words. He brought his hand up, seized Aidan by the neck, and forced a deeper connection into his mind. He could feel how he was controlling the ghosts, similar to how Devon forced his own will upon humans.

Aidan's power enabled him to capture threads of spirit, pull them into himself, and tie them to his body. Through that link, Aidan retained control.

Devon followed their threads to their tether. It was in Aidan's left side, opposite his liver. Some primordial, forgotten organ that had existed in humans from long before they had been able to call themselves humans, one that doctors could seemingly find no real use for. In Aidan's family, it was not only still present, but had remained functional. Devon wasn't a doctor; he didn't know what that particular organ was called. He only knew that it was the exact spot that the ghosts were linked to. Aidan saw what he intended to do, but under Devon's gaze he could do nothing besides tremble in pure bodily reaction.

Devon carried a silver dagger in his car—for *reasons*. He kept one hand on the Ghost Collector's throat while he pulled it from its sheath between the seats with his other. Devon showed the blade to Aidan, tilting it so its tarnished length gleamed dully in the light. With a practiced flip, Devon reversed his grip on the dagger. He stabbed it deep into Aidan's side. Aidan's black eyes went wide, and he gasped in shock and pain as the silver dagger severed his supernatural connection to the spirits. Devon turned Aidan's head to look out the window. Tears leaked from Aidan's eyes as the ghosts grew still, then began looking around themselves in sudden confusion. In that frozen moment Beez jumped in, screaming with her own silver weapons bared. She tore through the confused remnants, who vanished as if they had never been.

"Look, Aidan. Rest for the wicked, how about that."

Aidan shuddered as he bled from the wound in his side. He squeaked and wheezed with terror.

"Shhh," Devon said. "Shhh. Look at me."

Aidan turned his head against his will to look him in the eyes. Devon, with exaggerated slowness, licked his thumb. He worked up a bit of saliva, and then pressed it into the wound in Aidan's side.

"Coagulant in our saliva, anticoagulant in the venom of our fangs," Devon explained as the wound healed. "Creatures of the blood, vampires. If I thought you would have made a good vampire, Aidan, I would have made you one. But you, people like you, are the ones who give us a bad name. Grow up some, learn how to be humble, be a decent human being, and maybe I'll think about turning you some day."

Aidan nodded his head rapidly. There was hope in his eyes. Devon hated that glimmer as soon as he saw it, and he slammed Aidan's head into the window with so much force that it nearly cracked the glass. A lump raised instantly upon the kid's head, pulsing with heat. Devon's predatory instinct zeroed in on that pulse, and it took an absurd amount of self-control to not bend his neck to feed upon him. Instead, he pulled his head forward, looked deep into the dark pits of his eyes, and projected his brainwaves at a hypnotic frequency, into the core of Aidan's being until he felt Aidan sink into a trance. Devon quickly vanished the memory of the last ten minutes from his mind. Then he replaced those missing memories with a pleasant stroll outside, which had unfortunately ended with Aidan tripping over his own stupid feet and smacking his skull on the curb.

"Hi Aidan, I'm Devon. Your boss knows me. He and I are good friends. Okay?"

Devon waited for Aidan to give any indication that he agreed. He didn't so much as nod his head. Trance successful. Devon proceeded. "You are done with ghosts. Ghosts are just a memory to you now, a dream you had that you can't get rid of. You like your job, and you like people. You want to help people, you feel bad when you see people suffer."

Aidan continued staring blankly ahead, and Devon wondered for a moment how much he should push it. The kid had been a real nasty sort, but Devon figured that he had probably given him as much compulsion as he could get away with. Any more stuff about liking people, and he might realize something was wrong.

"Therapy might be a good idea," Devon suggested, and then broke the connection. He got out of the car, opened the passenger side door, and pulled Aidan out of the car. Devon had to hold him upright while he found his feet. "We're going back inside. Chuck is waiting for you."

"Oh," Aidan said. "Oh, right."

Chuck was behind the counter, looking anxious. His expression brightened when he saw them.

"Forgot my wallet," Devon called cheerfully, "did you get the total?"

"Got it right here," Chuck said, with real relief in his eyes.

The cost of all that fish was staggering, but not as bad as it could have been. Devon pulled his wallet from his back pocket and produced a credit card. The council let vampires have those these days, as long as they had social security numbers. Devon had quite a few of those, although some of them dated back to the twenties. His *dam* had been scandalously unscrupulous with her victims back then.

Chuck smiled with all his teeth as he handed Devon the receipt, no doubt because he'd never dreamed the payment would actually go through.

"You may be the strangest customer I've ever had in my life, but I'm thankful for you. Business has been slow." He grimaced, then sighed. "In truth, it's always slow."

Devon pocketed the receipt, which hadn't included the threatened cleaning charge.

"You think you can carry forty pounds of fish to your car," Chuck asked, "or would you like some help?"

Devon knew he could handle it, his thin frame was paranormally strong, but he didn't need to show off.

"It's what, six bags? I'd appreciate your help, Chuck."

"Sure thing" He glanced at his assistant. "Aidan, help us out."

Aidan appeared dazed but helped tote the cargo to Devon's trunk. After it was shut, Chuck rubbed his hands together in a performative gesture of wiping the slate clean.

"I'd shake your hand, but fish guts. Thanks again."

"Welcome. One thing I would ask: please just call me if Beez shows up again. She's a good cat, just naughty sometimes. I wouldn't want to soil the reputation of black cats even further."

Chuck nodded agreeably.

"I can do that. I suppose there's no chance that you could just keep her indoors?"

Devon spluttered, then laughed. "No chance at all, she would rip my throat out if I tried!" Literally and figuratively, Devon was sure of it.

Chuck shrugged.

"I figured as much. Well, I might give her some tidbits from the counter if I see her again."

"Any treats she begs for would be both appreciated, and paid for." Devon kept the conversation going, but he steeled himself mentally. Focusing his will, he formed an image in his head and made direct eye contact. He overcame Chuck's psychic barriers easily and insinuated the image into his mind.

"Let me give you my card, in case Beez shows up again," Devon continued as if nothing had happened. "So you won't have to show up at my door, cleaver in hand again."

Chuck ran a hand through his red hair with an embarrassed smile. He took the card and looked at it.

"Devon DuMorne. Now there's a name. I'll never remember it. Okay if I add you into my contacts as Cat Dude?"

"I've been called worse," Devon said with an easy smile.

"Tell your cat she's forgiven. I might even put a little picture of her up on a plaque, if she becomes a regular. We need regulars. As long as you keep up with her tab, she's welcome any time."

"I think she would love that," Devon said, as his mental suggestion was voiced. "I can get a nice picture of her for you."

"That would be great. I'm sure you can capture her good side better than I can."

"I'll bring it by sometime next week," Devon said. He waved goodbye and returned to his car. Beez had managed to take out a bumblebee while he'd been gone, and was noisily crunching it into a mess on the roof of his car. He glared and told her via their vampiric connection to get in. She flowed like liquid from the roof, through the window, and into the passenger's seat.

"That fish," he told her as he sat, "was not free."

"Sssss," she said, from the passenger side.

"I, however, have bought more fish for you. And you can have them, as long as you don't bring any people home to me, ever again."

"Ssss," she said, in a more somber tone.

"That didn't sound like a yes," Devon prompted.

"Fiiiiiine."

"Suppose that's the best I'll get," he muttered. He put the keys in the ignition, but held off on starting the engine. He checked his rear view to see if Felix was back in his car, then laughed at himself as he remembered that mirrors only worked for humans.

"Deffon should get out more," Beez said, enunciating as best she could with a mouth not made for human words.

Devon smacked his palm forcefully against the steering wheel.

"I knew it! You led him to the house intentionally!"

She flicked the tip of her tail. Kitty laughter.

"Fish would haff been free. Deffon could haff tormented them instead of payink them."

Devon glanced at her, amused by her long reply. "Well, yes," he said, "but pleasantly surprising people makes them like you. That man will have my back now."

"Ah."

"Oh, and I might have reinforced his thinking with a tiny bit of coercion, that you're a good cat. So he likes you now too."

"Effryone likes Beez."

"His assistant didn't."

Beez scrunched up her nose. "Bad mind," she said.

"Yes. Hopefully my fixes will take. At any rate, you're to have a plaque displayed in your honor. And you can visit Chuck for tidbits when you like. Just don't bring him home again, got it?"

Beez acknowledged him with a twitch of her left ear. He put out a hand, and she rubbed her face against it. Marking him as her territory, of course.

"You really are incorrigible," he said. "I have no idea why I'm so very fond of you."

The sound of her loud, rumbling purr filled the car.

As Devon turned the key in the ignition, he wondered privately how long her plaque would grace the butcher shop's wall. How much dust would it accumulate, how much would the varnish on it begin to yellow, and be renewed, only to yellow again. He wondered how many years it would take before the patrons began to ask how long the cat had been coming to the shop. And, decades after that, how long before they would begin to ask whether it was the same cat.

In the mirror, the lights of Felix's car blinked into life. A winnowing thought came questing into Devon's mind, a gentle tapping against his consciousness. Devon gave the equivalent of a nod, and Felix's thoughts arrowed into his mind.

"I saw what you did to the boy."

"Did you see the spirits he sent after me?"

A slight pulling away. *"I saw that too,"* Felix admitted.

"And did you see into him, how his plan was to rip my spirit away and use the empty shell of my body to make him a vampire? I was protecting all of our kind against him. Was I not justified?"

Felix sent him a mental shrug. *"Were it up to me? Yes. But the council will need to be informed of his existence. After I see the desk, of course."*

"Right." Devon brought out his cell phone and located the before and after pictures he'd taken. *"Should've thought to text you these before,"* he said, as he found Felix's contact info and clicked send.

Devon felt Felix's defeated sigh through their connection as the photos arrived. *"Really could have just been an email, couldn't it?"*

Devon snickered. *"You still need to see it in person, don't you?"*

"Precisely right. I knew you'd understand."

Devon held back his sigh as he put the car into drive and led Felix back home.

◆ ◆ ◆

The desk was, almost, exactly as Devon had left it.

Felix took the sight of the blackened top in stride, but ran a finger over the finish where Beez had managed to leave a few new scratches after Devon had polished it.

"It's not destroyed," Felix admitted with a weary smile. "I suggest you invest in a thick piece of glass to cover the top of it. Give kitty a little surprise. Next time she attempts to dig her claws in, she'll slide right off the edge."

"Why didn't I think of that?" Devon said with a smile.

"I'll call it a repair, and have the council pay for it, if you can find me some more of that nice honey."

Devon brought him to the shelf and gave him a sample of every variety he had. Beez jumped upon the balustrade and yowled in a bid for attention just as Felix was leaving, but he stopped and spared a moment to scratch between her ears.

"So you won't report my Beez to the council?"

Felix pursed his lips, then chuckled. "That was a toothless threat," he said. "Your Beez was never in danger; I like cats."

Immortality has a high market value—
Guard it with your Unlife

WHITECHAPEL

BY N. V. HASKELL

The scent of the rain pattering above mixed with the decay buried around me. Two bodies were nestled on either side, one small and frail, perhaps that of a child. The other robust with bloat. I'd woken in a pauper's grave like the one Martha and Annie had been placed in. My only hope was that the undertaker had neglected to bury me deep.

A shallow grave was a good grave.

Clarimonde, the creature who had made me, said that every new vampire must survive the first several nights alone—a traditional hazing that weeded out the weak and allowed the survivors to deal with any final mortal concerns. She'd quoted something about Darwin then, but, with my lacking education, I hadn't understood it. I'd been too terrified to retain anything said after she revealed what she was to me. Clari knew the type of woman I was, had heard my outcries of grief when Annie died, but the things I'd done to survive didn't seem to bother her. If I'd been honest about what I wanted to do — find and kill the butcher of Whitechapel — I wasn't sure she would have made me the offer.

According to Clari, after my transformation, not even the Ripper himself could do me in. I'd become something unimaginable for a woman of such low birth — independent. Powerful. Self-reliant enough to choose a better life. No more beatings, begging, or selling myself on the filthy streets of Spitalfields or Whitechapel. But the first step toward independence was a piteous crawl from the grave.

The thought that rats would come searching for easy meals soon spurred me to dig upward. Displacing the rain-soaked earth was slow and arduous. Fingernails tore off. Clothing ripped and joints popped as I clawed for my freedom while using the surrounding dead as leverage one foot at a time.

When the grave's crust broke, frigid rain beat down on my face. After I freed myself completely, I lay on the ground, arms splayed wide, Christ-like, and breathed in my own resurrection.

I stood on trembling legs. Mud caked my clothes, hair, and skin. There was a bathhouse in Goulston Square that would be closing soon and by the sounds of carriages and voices that carried from the street, the sun had only recently set. Walking down any well-lit road looking like this would draw unwanted attention. Clari's warnings had me climbing over a rickety section of wrought iron fencing that ran adjacent to a dimly lit side street. I wasn't worried about the police. They remained stubbornly prejudiced against the people of Spitalfields and Whitechapel, regardless of the grue-some murders that had taken Annie, Martha, and other scarlet ladies.

There'd been back and forth accusations in the newspapers demand-ing an increase in police presence, but the Chief Inspector countered that it wouldn't do any good without more streetlamps. But all of us too poor to live elsewhere knew that these arguments came down to a lack of money and something much worse: apathy. Though the newspapers had certainly made a sensation of the murders, no changes in either manpower or light-ing had come. Maybe it was cheaper to dispose of our bodies than ade-quately protect us. The murders had been going on for months, and each arrest had led to a quick release. There were only rumors as to who the villain might be.

Clari had given me basic guidelines for survival. Drink only from the living. It didn't matter who or what it came from -- rodents, stray cats, or the feeble elderly -- warm blood trumped all. Secure shelter before sunrise so I didn't burn to ashes, someplace guaranteed to be undisturbed during the day. I had to be invited into anywhere people called home, but public places required no such formality. She emphasized that discretion was the key to survival but given what I wanted, that might be difficult. I stayed in the shadows, ignoring the scurrying rodents in the alleys off Thrawl Street lest the savage hunger take over. For once, I was grateful for the November rain. The stench of the grave mixed with the water and masked the scents and sounds of life pulsing in the throats that passed by. I'd become a master at ignoring the gnawing hunger of my belly over the last five years, but this new, more vicious want would overwhelm me if I wasn't careful.

My first kill was a large rat behind the bathhouse. It scratched and bit furiously but when my newly serrated teeth sunk into its warm flesh, heaven flooded my mouth. Draining it and two others only teased my senses.

When the bathhouse lights were finally put out, I crept over the back gate and broke a lower window to gain entry. The air was still warm, and I scrubbed the mud from my crumbling dress and shoes then hung them to dry before washing my hair and body.

It was quiet here. Safe. But it would be teeming with people once the sun broke, and hunger still gnawed at my insides. I am ashamed to admit feasting on the clowder at St. Mary's Park. The cats' blood sustained me even if it wasn't wholly satisfying. Finding a place to hide for the day was more difficult than I'd imagined. As dawn marched toward the horizon, I curled beneath an overturned wheelbarrow in the park's gardener's shed. Even though the tiny building had been settled for the winter months, I knew it was a risk.

I woke the next evening to the people's voices moving through the park. Their smells wafted beneath the closed door and sparked an obsessive sort of lust. Discretion, Clarimonde had said, but what she really meant was limited risks and no witnesses. I held myself, aching and trembling, in the shed until silence descended and several cats crept from their hiding places.

It had been five weeks since the Ripper had slaughtered Elizabeth and Catherine on the same night. Desperate women were already returning to the streets to earn enough money for a bed or a meal while fighting the terrorizing understanding that they might be gutted. I and the other soiled doves may have come from various backgrounds and educations, but the vulnerability of our small, wretched lives had formed deep bonds.

A waxing moon glittered through hazy clouds as I turned down Dorset Street where it was easy to blend in with the drunks already slumping against buildings. An empty-eyed woman held a suckling babe to her breast while a child sat beside her. Their blood was muddled with despair and sad resignation and though they paid me no mind as I passed, I'd hastened away from the restless want that rose inside me.

Bawdy men and women stumbled out of the Brittania Pub. A couple screamed at each other in the street until a copper rounded the corner, swinging his truncheon and sending them scurrying with a sharp warning. I slunk into the deepening shadows and watched the people with a foreign detachment. The wrenching suffering that permeated the air didn't grip me the way it had only three days prior. Although my situations of home and hunger hadn't changed, I knew in my core that the death I'd endured would lead to a better existence. I wouldn't die in these gutters, nor be butchered by the Ripper.

A crisp black overcoat turned a corner. He fit a witness description of the man who'd met Annie before she was murdered. Pale skin, dark hair, thin moustache, thick eyebrows, and a brown felt hat. The way his eyes skimmed coldly over the working women was unnerving. A predatory gaze that had nothing to do with what they offered. It was the same look that Clarimonde had worn when she'd first shown me how she hunted and fed. I began to follow as he ambled away, but something else caught my eye.

A thin figure lay against the wall of a dark alleyway. His breath was shallow, reeking of gin and deep rot and, though years of drink and poverty might have aged him, he looked old and weak. He grimaced in his stupor while pulling the edges of his coat closer to stave off the night's bone-numbing chill.

I'd never been a particularly strong woman. Though years of labor had made me sturdy, I could barely ever defend myself from the louts that wandered Whitechapel. But this man had a frailty to him, like something other than life was eating him from the inside, and I knew with certainty that I could have him.

I quickly glanced over my shoulder, but no one paid attention to us. He remained still as I knelt beside him and examined the rhythmic pulse beneath his scruffy beard. Much like the rodents and cats, instinct took over.

In anticipation of his cries, I clamped a hand over his mouth as I sunk my teeth into his neck. I'd aimed for the pulse there, but the beard caused me to miss the target. I held him down with my body as I shifted my teeth while he struggled. Divine warmth flooded my mouth, coursed into my gut, and seeped into my limbs.

His heart slowed. Those ebbing beats sang to me like a siren, beckoning for me to follow. But I had no desire to die again.

His vacant eyes stared at the dark sky as I dragged the body further into the alley and left him for the rats. I spent hours in a warm euphoric state until the streetlights were shut off at midnight and the worst sorts of ruffians eyed potential victims.

The man in the black overcoat reappeared, and I tracked him until he vanished into a row of crowded tenement houses. The pulsing thrum of tightly packed bodies was overwhelming, spiking a dizzying need that was difficult to resist.

Fortune smiled on me as, just before dawn, I found an unlocked cellar with several empty barrels that stank of fermentation. The rule about being invited into a home didn't seem to apply to cellars unconnected to houses. I pulled the cover of the barrel above my head and fell into a deep sleep.

I found another drunkard to sustain me, then stole his hat, which I now wore low over my brow, angling away from the folks loitering along the sullied lights of Dorset Street.

"Julia, is that you?" Mary Kelly's voice startled me as I caught her cheap rose perfume. Her bright eyes and dirty blonde hair were a pretty contrast to our surroundings. "I've been worried. Where'd you get to?"

Since Mary Kelly and her husband had been on the outs, she'd let other ladies stay with her, offering safety from the threats on the street. She'd always been kind and trusting. Too good for Whitechapel, to be honest. But her life was as hard as everyone else's. She swayed slightly on her feet, but her gaze swept over me. She clicked her tongue before saying, "You've been through it, haven't ya?"

Our conversation lasted only a few minutes, long enough to reassure her of my wellbeing and that I was moving back to the countryside. She wouldn't be seeing me again. Her expression had gone wistful at that, and she'd wished me well. I was half a block away when I turned back, and that space we'd shared beneath the streetlamp was empty.

Women bargained with clients in hushed voices on the street and beneath covered passages, but I didn't catch a glimpse of the man I sought. When the biting rain came down, people clustered beneath awnings or vanished into pubs, but I stayed in my shadowed alleyway unconcerned by any of it.

Another sweep down Dorset Street late in the night had me pausing across from Miller's Court, where Mary lived. One of her neighbors lingered there, shivering in her shawl but no one approached her. An hour after she disappeared into her apartment down the court, there was a shout, but it didn't come again. All was quiet. Unnervingly so. As if the bricks and mortar held their breath while everyone else slumbered.

I was considering where to hide for the day when he emerged from Miller's Court. Pale skin, dark coat, felt hat. It was the overwhelming scent of blood and a particular perfume that drew me to him. Mary Kelly's perfume. I cursed myself for being a neglectful fool. If I'd been more focused, I might have saved her. There was a package tucked beneath one of his arms, carried with the same reverence that devout pastors handle their bibles. It likely contained an assortment of knives, scalpels, or pliers. Instruments that the police thought had been used in the grisly murders.

His steps were light and satisfied and, between the drizzling rain and his postcoital inebriation, he didn't notice me following him into the middle-class neighborhood. He walked boldly down dark alleyways, but I suppose when someone becomes a monster, they stop fearing those they deem lesser.

He had that natural leanness that tended to belie the strength within and, though I knew I'd become stronger these last few nights, I wasn't sure I could overpower him. If I could get him into tight quarters, I'd do better. But first I'd have to rely on his nefarious desires and manipulate his overconfidence before he entered his home.

The rain had eased slightly when the man crossed the street and started slowly up a set of stairs to a dark modest townhome that had been broken into several apartments.

"Excuse me, sir?" I let my voice waver, hoping he heard the desperation there, and saw nothing but a thin, bedraggled woman.

He paused with one foot higher on the steps, his eyes gleaming when he saw me. With a voice more nasally than expected, he asked, "Can I help you?"

I inched forward, hoping my vulnerable appearance would tempt him. "I know it's rather late, but I was wondering if you were needing company tonight?"

Those beady eyes narrowed. "Wouldn't you have more luck on Dorset Street?"

"I got lost coming back from the docks, and, with the weather being so awful, I can't afford a room or rope," I said softly. Something dark glinted in his stiff expression. The point of his tongue scraped his lower lip as I continued. "I'll do…" I cleared my throat, let the semblance of nervousness ebb through my voice. "…whatever you want. I just need a few pennies, a shilling if you're feeling generous, sir."

His throat bobbed at the temptation, and he turned fully toward me before stepping down. His thumb traced circles on the leather package in his hand. Despite the dim light I could see the fresh red stains that comingled with older rust brown spots across the worn leather. The blood of Martha Tabram, Mary Ann Nichols, Annie Chapman, Elizabeth Stride, Catherine Eddowes, sweet Mary Jane Kelly, and who knew how many others.

A thin smile twisted his moustache as his eyes swept over me. "Whatever I want?" I nodded and gripped the edges of my coat with trembling hands. He motioned me to follow him back the way we'd come, away from the safety of his home.

It would be light in another hour. There wasn't much time. He turned down a covered passageway that ended behind a set of run-down tenant houses. The stench of sweat and refuse permeated the air.

He motioned to a cellar attached to the building, waiting for me to go first. I reached for the doors, but an invisible force squeezed my chest, preventing me from touching them. I shook my head, trying to maintain that nervous façade. "You want me down there, sir? What about the alleyway?"

"You said anything I want." The tilt of his head, even the soft timbre of his voice was meant to both control and reassure. He had an arrogance born of someone who hadn't yet failed at getting what he wanted. But he would still have to invite me in.

"Why don't you go in first, sir? I've always been afraid of cellars."

The hinges groaned as he carefully pulled one door open. He paused, eyes darting to the windows above, but no one stirred. Clutching the package beneath his arm, he stepped down into the dark before turning back. "There's nothing to fear down here." He chuckled low at his lie.

"You really want me to come in there?" I asked.

His tone turned sharp, impatient. "I thought you wanted a shilling?"

No soiled doves I'd ever known would have gotten a shilling for anything less than complete perversion. He'd overplayed his hand, and, with the uptick of his pulse, I could tell he knew it. I stared at him with my feet planted, waiting, and hoping he'd take a more genteel approach.

Sharp, yellowy teeth shone beneath his moustache. "Please, come inside before they hear us."

The pressure against my chest dropped away and I stepped down into the small musky room. The door closed behind me. It was so dark that if it weren't for my improved vision, I wouldn't have been able to see him move. His breath was hot in the air, pulse rising rapidly as the package unrolled enough for him to retrieve an item. The scalpel glinted in his hand, and I knew he'd make a frantic butchery of me if he could.

Though I saw him clearly, I asked, "Where are you? What do you want me to do?"

He smiled maliciously and slid forward; pupils fully dilated. The scalpel swung toward my throat, but I moved before it found me.

"What was that?" I asked, watching his jaw clench with annoyance.

"Nothing," he said. "Come closer. Lift your skirts." His free hand reached out, grasping, but missed again.

I circled to his side, out of reach. He moved slower than I'd anticipated or, maybe, I was faster. "I'm right here."

He turned to the sound of my voice. Reached and missed again. The madness in his eyes deepened, twisting his expression into a contorted mask of seething rage. That steady thrum of his heart called to me. One predator to another.

I let him grasp my wrist. He yanked me toward him, slashing the small blade toward my neck but I caught his wrist in the air. He cursed, tried to jerk his hand away but my grip tightened until the scalpel fell from his fingers to the dirt floor.

When his fist struck my jaw, it released something feral inside me. I threw myself against him and we fell in a flurry of punches and grunts. A blow met my gut, but I gave as good as I got. Gasping for breath, he scrambled backward.

He licked the blood from his teeth and blocked the exit. The coppery smell heightened my awareness of each beat of his heart. He stumbled over the package he'd dropped on the floor, then stooped to pull a thin, dirty knife from it. Mary Kelly's dried blood still kissed that sharp edge.

The feline hiss that rose from my throat startled him.

I slapped one of his arms, then the opposite thigh, teasing him as he slashed and spun, spittle and blood flying with his raging breaths.

"Aren't you wondering why I'm not screaming for help?" I asked. "Or why I'm not trying to escape?"

He swallowed, waving the knife again. "Who are you?"

"Don't you want to know why I approached you at such an hour?" I whispered. "Or why I've been searching for you?"

I stayed still when he lunged forward. The blade sailed down, lodging into the shoulder of my coat and dress, slicing the skin beneath. But there was no pain. My fingers closed around his throat. He writhed as I knocked the knife away and twisted that arm until I felt the shoulder pop. His scream was a muffled choke.

"You'll die at the hands of a whore." Sharp fingernails broke his skin, flooding my nose with the intoxicating scent of his life. "Which is better than you deserve."

He clawed at my arms, cursing, begging, but I refused to release him. I thought of the vile things he'd done to those women and considered delivering some of those tortures back, but the caress of his blood down my fingers was too strong to resist. With a shiver, I pinned his arms to his side and cleaved his throat with my teeth.

I drank until his skin shriveled and his eyes had gone vacant, stopping only one beat before his heart stilled. Then I hid beneath his coat in the deepest recess of the cellar, prayed that no one would find me, and sank into exhausted satisfaction.

When I woke, I dismembered his body and wrapped the pieces in his coat to make the package more manageable. Using the coins from his pockets I hired a wagon to take me to the pauper's grave I'd crawled out of. It took half the night to bury him deep. As I patted the earth a final time, I felt my maker standing behind me.

"Are your debts settled?" Clari asked.

I nodded, wiped a smear of dirt across my brow as I turned to her. "There's nothing left for me here now."

She smiled gently, as if she understood what I'd done and why. And, looking at the liner around her eyes, the steel of her composure, maybe she'd chosen me for this very reason. I accepted her hand when she offered it and, together, we walked side by side. Two scarlet ladies in the night.

A shallow grave is a good grave

JUST A NIBBLE

BY JASON P. CRAWFORD

The best thing about being a vampire in Southern California is the waves.

If you ask pretty much any other vamp what they think about SoCal, they'll laugh you out of the room... assuming they aren't thirsty and didn't drain you for asking. It's sunny down here. It rarely rains. There are way too many churches.

All that is true, but what they don't realize is how bitching the swell is at 2 o'clock in the morning. There is no one out there but a few whackos, and they leave me alone; it was just me, the moon, and the waves. For a few hours, I can be away from the constant thirst and the call of blood and remember what it was like before I was turned into this.

So that was my plan, as usual, when Lily knocked at my door.

I opened it and leaned across the threshold, propping myself up with my arms, staring down into her eyes—staring at the bruising on her throat and the swell of her tits, all pushed up and on display for me. They reminded me of the ocean, rising and falling with every breath. She was a real looker, and every Tom, Dick, and Harry wanted to get their paws on her. Her eyes, though... I knew that hunger.

"What's up, Lily?" I spoke slowly, arching an eyebrow, waiting for her to say it. It was a game to both of us, a way of easing into this thing that we both needed, but neither wanted to admit. "Couldn't sleep?"

Lily looked down, kicking her foot. I counted in my head, and it took four seconds before she said anything.

"Hey, Ty. Just...just thinking about things, walking by, thought...thought I'd stop in."

I decided draw out the game a little longer. "What kind of things?"

Lily squirmed, making me think of the people you'd see in the alleyways, the ones who had maybe gotten too intimate with the product they were selling… the ones I'd avoid because I didn't want to be knocked out by what their blood was carrying. The same need gnawed at her brain, growing stronger.

"You know…looking for work tomorrow…books to read…" She glanced up at me again, eyes pleading, *begging. Let me in*, they said.

"Oh." I nodded, faking disinterest, until… "Want to come in?"

To her credit, Lily didn't jump at this, didn't immediately run for the door and push past me. Instead, she hesitated, giving me a shy smile, brushing her hair back from her face.

"It isn't a problem?"

I shrugged, then stretched and smiled, giving her a good view of my fangs. "Not at all. If you don't have anything else going on."

At last, she came in, taking two steps to cross the threshold. I moved aside to let her into the room but tracked her every move.

When the door closed, she was on me, and I was on her—the kind of game I liked, unsure of who pursued whom.

Her mouth sucked at mine hungrily, her tongue invading with the desperate want that had built up in her belly and her mind until she couldn't contain it. I could taste it within her as my fangs drew blood, pinching into her mouth and releasing the nectar into mine. I knew it hurt—I could *feel* it hurt her—but the pain just zinged through her nerves and drew her closer to me.

Sharing blood is the most intense experience a vamp can have. It dilates time and changes how long everything seems to take, so there was no way for me to keep track of how long we were there, tasting her blood, mixing it between our mouths, before I broke apart. Lily's lips looked like she had put on bright crimson lipstick, and her teeth were covered in the same.

"Please." She whimpered the word, one hand on the back of my head. "I need you. Please."

Without saying anything, I brought my wrist up to my mouth. My fangs dug into my own flesh, my own veins. Unlike Lily's bright red, vital blood, mine seemed lethargic, thick and heavy, almost black. Still, when I offered it to Lily, she clamped her mouth on it as if it were ambrosia it-self.

While she drank from me, I pierced her neck and began to take from her. We formed a cycle, a circle of life flowing from the one to the other, with my body transforming her blood into whatever kept me moving when I should be dead. Every limb tingled, every nerve throbbed and pulsed. It was like being locked inside a heartbeat, trapped in an infinity of orgasmic release and buildup.

Some vamps don't like what we've become. They wish they could go back to their living selves.

Why?

It wasn't more than three minutes, but again, there was no way to tell the time. What saved Lily's life, as always, was the difference in flavor; I could feel when my blood was starting to make its way through her sys-tem back into me, and that made me lay off. I stopped drinking and ran my tongue over her wound, sealing the injury closed. It would still bruise—the healing wasn't very deep—but it worked well in keeping our secret. Next, I had to dislodge her from my wrist gently enough that she wouldn't get hurt.

Lily stumbled backward, my blood dripping from her lips, her eyes wide with the pleasure of it, the traumatic, *invasive* ecstasy. It happened every time, but it was still the sexiest thing I had ever seen.

"I need more."

I shook my head. "Not just now, sugar. I'll see you in a few days." I nodded toward the couch, already bearing a pillow and blanket for her. "Juice on the table. I got you cookies, too."

Lily sighed, a mixture of laughter and disappointment. "It's like I'm at the doc's again."

"They get it right." I put an arm around her waist and guided her to the couch. "Rest. Sleep it off and get going when you wake up again. I'll be here when you get back."

"I don't want you to go." Lily grabbed hold of my hand and held it close to her. "I love you, Ty."

Now, it was my turn to sigh. "No, you don't. But it's sweet anyway." Turning her head, I looked into her eyes and stretched out the smallest fragment of my will.

"Go to sleep now."

Her eyes went a little vacant, but she nodded and sat on the couch. Her hands reached for the juice and cookies without looking at them.

This part always made me a little uncomfortable, so I grabbed my board and bag and headed out. On my way, I stopped by the pay phone in the hall, dialed collect. After a few rings, a monotone voice came over the line.

How many people?

"One."

Length of contact?

"Less than 15 minutes."

Thrall?

"Yes."

Registered?

"Yes."

No further action is required. Stay safe out there.

I returned the phone to its cradle, headed out the door, and stared at the sky. There were still hours of darkness left, and I needed to surf. Most nights, it gave me the peace I would need to endure the daysleep.

Most nights.

But this one…well, it broke all the record books.

Having a few decades to work on my technique meant I didn't often topple off my board—especially with the new hollow-cores; those things were the cat's pajamas—but when I did, it was just a matter of a few seconds before I would paddle my way back and get on again. It might happen once or twice a night, giving me a dose of that cold Pacific that could never really chill me again, and then the wind would dry me off while I tried it again. While I sometimes missed the shock—the sudden muscle tension from falling and freezing—it was amazing to just be out there, savoring the sea spray, enjoying the movement up and down.

And that's exactly what I was enjoying when something below me slammed into my board, hard. I tumbled off, spinning into the water, hitting with a hard slap and crash. My eyes cleared after the bubbles rushed past me, and the moonlight above the surface was more than enough to see the problem: a shark.

It was a fucking shark. Great white, and it was already spinning back at me. Being a vamp gives lots of advantages, and speed is one of them, but it's still hard to be fast while underwater; the water's just too thick to move quickly. I pushed away, trying to give myself enough distance that maybe he'd recognize that I wasn't really his type of food.

Turns out, I should have done some research on great white sharks, cause they'll eat dead things just as easily as live things. This one surged forward, its nearly solid-black eye on mine, and then it chomped down on my damn ankle. There was a flash of pain as the teeth cleaved through the whole thing, flesh and bone alike, and then my entire foot was gone, in the thing's mouth.

It was close, though, and I decided that swimming away wasn't going to work with me down a foot, so instead, I pulled my hand back, turned it into a knife edge, and slammed it into the bastard's gills as it swam by, just as hard as I could. It reeled—I swear I could hear something almost like a scream—and swam off. The water was swirling red around us, and the scent of it tickled my nose until I remembered that it was *my* fucking foot that was gone.

By the time I'd clawed back on my board, the bleeding had stopped; by the time I had paddled back to shore, the bite had healed over so that it looked like an old war injury or something like that. I slipped my shoe over the stump and did my best to hobble back home.

Thank God, Lily was gone when I got there. I really didn't want to have to explain to her what had happened. She might have freaked out. I locked the door, headed into the bathroom (which had no windows), and crashed in the tub.

Another blessing of being a vamp? No cramped muscles or cricked necks. Usually, the daysleep just kind of goes by in a rush of intense dreams that you can't remember too well, a blur of blood, hunger, sorrow, and thirst. Those were there, but there were also the healing dreams, where I got to feel my bones trying to regrow from the damage done to me.

It could have been a more pleasant experience.

In fact, it was *so* unpleasant that when the sun went below the horizon, I woke up and had to clap my hand over my mouth to stop the scream. I didn't know how long I'd been doing it. Hopefully, no one else had heard me.

I pulled myself out of the tub and slung my legs over the edge, comparing my good foot and my injured one. Rather than just a scabbed-over stump, the chomped ankle had grown a new appendage, but it looked raw, like someone had peeled off a bunch of the skin from it, revealing the muscles and the veins. Gross, but usable, and by tomorrow, it'd be back to normal.

I could feel the thirst burning in the back of my throat. Usually, a visit from Lily would sate me for a few days, but having to heal like this drained my strength faster, like exercise would a human. I'd need a top-off sooner rather than later. I stared at myself in the mirror, running my tongue over my teeth.

Shouldn't be too hard to find someone to… go home with. Just for a while.

A knock at my door.

Damn it. Not a good time. Smelled like the mail.

Sighing, I limped over and opened it up. On the other side was Griff Henson, a Great War vet who had taken it upon himself to pick up and hand out the mail to everyone when he got home each evening. He'd pass by, knock on the door, and hand you the mail, tucking his paper under his arm.

"Good to see you, Ty." He gave his trademark half-salute, then handed me my envelopes. "Did you hear about those protestors? Telling Washington to pay up early."

"Not my thing." I could hear his heartbeat, smell his blood. "Thanks for stopping by."

He paused. "Everything Jake with you, Ty? I saw that flapper you had in last night. Looked on the make to me."

I could feel my fangs distending. I didn't usually go for men, but I was thirsty *now*. And he was right there, pumping all that blood…

I realized I was opening my mouth, so I pretended to cough to cover it. "Ah, damn it. Sorry."

"Whoa! Feel better, all right?" Griff clapped a hand on my shoulder and squeezed it. "We need good, young men like you."

Things like that never failed to make me feel awkward. I could remember the *Rebellion*, much less the Great War. But I mirrored his gesture, and, almost against my will, I turned on my charm.

"Thanks."

Griff's eyes went vacant, and I realized what I'd done. All it would take now was the correct command, and in he'd come, and then we…

I was opening my mouth again.

"Hey, Griff."

"Yes."

"Come in for a minute." I smiled at him. "I want to ask you about something."

Griff left a few minutes later without a clear memory of what had happened, only the aching in his neck and the extra-whiteness of his skin as hints. As for me, I felt a lot better. *Maybe I should try enlisting Griff as a…*

There was a knock on my door: three raps, then two, then four. Something slipped underneath it: a folded-up newspaper, by the look.

"Fuck." I hurried over, picked it up. "What's going on?"

A note was stuck on the top of the paper, marking one of the articles.

Keep your cattle away from the beach.

I opened up the paper, found the article. My eyes scanned the text and caught several key lines.

…*vicious shark attacks*…

…*seventeen individuals*…

…*last several hours*…

…*believed to be a great white*…

My mouth went slack, but my brain ran faster than a man on giggle juice…mostly to swear repeatedly. I stepped back into my apartment, closed the door, and leaned against it.

It had gotten my blood. The shark…it was a thrall. And that meant…

I stepped out and picked up the hallway phone. Dialed the number.

Incident report.

"A shark bit my foot off."

The voice paused a minute.

You will be contacted shortly.

"Fuck." I rubbed my head with my free hand, and my foot twinged with pain as the skin continued to regrow. "This is—"

Bzzz bzzz. Bzzz bzzz. Bzzz—

I slid the front door open. "Hey."

In front of me stood a young-looking man, much like me, but his hair was black, and he wore a brown hat, grey tweed suit, red tie. His eyes pierced into me, and I knew I was in the doghouse.

"Who are you?" he asked.

"Ty Barnett. Registry number 142."

"Thank you." He pulled out a notepad, flipped through it, nodded. Then he put it away.

"Ty, my name is Nathan H. Dayton the Fifth. Preceptor."

Oh shit. "I… it's an honor, sir. I hadn't expected—"

"Don't worry about that right now." Nathan's voice had that soothing quality of someone who expects you to lose your shit at any moment, and they really, *really* want to keep that from happening because they just can't handle it anymore. "You reported that a shark bit your foot off?"

"Yes, sir."

"Why didn't you report this last night?"

Fuck. "I don't know." I started walking and pacing, even though every other step stabbed needles into my healing foot. "I guess I just got home and crashed."

"All right." Nothing for a few seconds, then: "Do you think this is the same shark?"

I wanted to throw my hands in the air or pull the phone out the wall. Instead, I nodded. "It could be. It was a great white, same as the one they're talking about. Would a great white getting ahold of some of my…you know…make it act like that?"

"Hasn't happened before, but it could be." Another pause. "They won't be able to kill it without fire, and fire doesn't work underwater. You know that."

"Yep." Better and better.

"So you're going to have to deal with it."

"Wait…what?" I shook my head. "How am I supposed to do that?"

"…"

Shit. "How am I supposed to do that, sir?"

"I don't know. But it's your thrall for now. That won't last long. If anyone can do anything about it, it's you. And if the cattle find out that the damn thing's unkillable, that's a level of heat that I don't want to deal with." He folded his arms, staring me down.

I let my head hit the wall behind me. "No. No, of course not."

"Then it's in your hands. It won't end well if I have to send out my people. For you, for them, or for your new pet."

It's not my pet! "I understand, sir. I'll… I'll see what I can do to take care of it."

There was no goodbye or farewell; I blinked, and he was gone. I didn't have to breathe to stay alive, but the sigh still came, a heavy intake and outrush of air.

The roads were shut down—obviously. When a killer shark was waiting for more prey to satisfy its newfound bloodthirst, you didn't want to drive out to the beach. Still, a few gawkers were trying to get in when I biked to the barricades. It was pretty heavy, too; four police officers on the line, with two cruisers behind blocking the road. Probably the same on the other side, too. There was no way the four blue boys would make way for me, but I didn't need them to.

Thanks to Griff, I was high on blood and ready to rumble. With a quick moment of concentration, I made myself unremarkable to everyone there. Not *invisible*; they could still see me, technically, but I was unimportant, someone else's problem. Since most people's natural inclination is to make it someone else's problem anyway, they just ignored me as I slipped through the lines and past the cruisers.

The surf crashed against the beach as I crossed the sand's border. It felt wrong to be in shoes, so I slipped them off and let the grains cover my feet. By now, my injured foot had fully repaired itself—thanks to Griff for that as well—and I felt good. The fear from before, from talking to the Preceptor, had vanished like my blood in the water, and I was calm.

The beach itself, however, was not.

I could smell the blood long before I could see it. The carnage hadn't just happened in the water; some of the attacked had made it onto the shore before dying from their wounds. The sand was soaked in it, like a sponge, and the smell was heady and intoxicating. A not-insignificant part of me wanted to scoop up a handful, taste it, swallow the whole thing so my body could get what it wanted, and to hell with the rest.

I didn't, but it was a close thing.

As I approached the waterline, I could sense the shark out there. It had tasted my blood, so, for now, at least, there was a part of me in it. Preceptor William wanted me to leverage that connection and use it so that…what? I could talk it down? Sure, some vamps I knew could swap speech with cats, bats, rats…dogs.

How do you even talk to a shark?

It had been less than a day, but the creature had clearly torn through the swimmers like a buzzed-out kid through his brother's candy stash. Even now, I could see bloody foam washing up on the beach. Was it human blood? Was it something else that the shark had found to tide itself over? I couldn't tell without closer inspection and didn't want to. Instead, I tried to home in on where the thing was.

The bond needed to be stronger for me to make that out. Sure, there was the vague impression that it was *out there* somewhere, but it was like a 45-degree arc and who knows how far. I stripped off my shirt, tossed it down, grabbed my wallet, dropped it on top, and then dived into the water.

Advantage number two of being a vamp that surfs: I don't need to breathe, so staying underwater for extended periods isn't a problem. I blinked my eyes, pushing some of my blood into them to sharpen their sight, then started swimming toward my personal Tick-Tock crocodile.

Hey, now at least I knew how Captain Hook felt.

The shark had retreated into the deeper waters after his immediate supply of shore-based snacks had gotten out of the pool, as it were. I swam farther and farther out, inhaling salt water through my nose to pick up the scent of blood.

And pick it up I did.

After about twenty minutes of swimming, the first faint hints of iron and heme touched my senses. As always, it made my vision flare and every sense heighten. Like I was looking through a telescope, I could see twice as far, three times, through the dimly lit water. The moon only gave me half the light it could, but that was just enough to see what was happening.

Down below, the shark circled around a massive beast, easily five times its length: a blue whale. Blood filled the water as the shark dodged in and out, tearing at the giant's flesh and swimming through those crimson clouds, mouth wide to take it in. The whale was thrashing, trying to strike back. Being so large, it shouldn't have been threatened—but this shark had an edge.

I couldn't help but pause and watch. The speed, the ferocity…was this the difference between humans and us, between the predator and the prey? The shark refused to back down, even when struck by the massive tail and sent spinning away. It shot toward the whale again and again, tearing chunks of flesh, swallowing them.

How much can it eat? If the shark kept swallowing pieces of the whale, surely its stomach would burst. Surely, its hunger *had* to be sated at some point…right?

Right?'

That question was answered very quickly. After swallowing down another piece of the whale—who by now was only feebly trying to escape, clearly overcome by pain and shock, bleeding out into the water—the shark *vomited up* everything it had swallowed. Along with pieces of whale, I saw human legs and hands, three heads… and then it went back for more.

That was enough. It *wouldn't* stop because it didn't have to, so the Preceptor was right. It had to be taken care of. I kicked off again, heading toward the carnage.

I couldn't tell if it felt my swimming or if it just knew I was there, but the shark turned about. Its cold, dark eye looked different, streaked with a bloody red, and its gills flared in and out as it got closer.

For a second, I wished I had thought to bring along one of my hippie vamp friends. Maybe they'd be able to drug him or something. Then I shook my head: the Preceptor asked me to handle it, and if I didn't, my ass was done. With that in mind, I focused on the shark and raised a hand.

He's just going to bite it off too, isn't he?

The biggest risk of making a thrall is the addiction. The blood is addictive, and people crave it after they've had it. At the same time, we could control them, use our thoughts to calm them, put them to sleep, whatever we needed… as long as they weren't too strong-willed.

How strong-willed was this shark?

Time to find out.

The beast swam up to my hand, and I could *feel* its mind. It was much different than Lily's; it was simple: a drive to feed, to be sated, to be safe. There were no emotions besides contentment and fear. The shark was *hungry*, and so it fed. It didn't understand the hunger it felt.

But I did.

I imagined it like soothing a scared dog. I swam forward another step, putting my hand on the shark's sandpaper skin, feeling the spines pass under my hand. The connection strengthened, and I saw the shark's eyes roll back into its head.

Then the moment vanished, and the black-red eye stared into mine. I knew what it wanted, knew what it *needed*, so I brought a wrist up to my teeth and tore open the vein. More blood, *my* blood, filled the water around me. The shark breathed it in, opened his mouth, and came straight at me.

I raised my hand again.

He stopped, turned, and instead of chomping my arm, swallowed down the water, pumping it through his gills and taking in my blood. As he swam by, I grabbed hold of his dorsal fin, maintaining that physical connection at the same time as the blood took further hold.

I could hear the shark in my mind now. Feelings, full-fledged wants and needs. And what he wanted now... was to make me happy.

Grinning, I asked him to bring me to shore. He started pumping his tail left to right, with each movement bringing us not only closer to land but syncing our minds more intimately together. I could feel his intelligence, his desire to adapt, and the blood made him see me as a social better, someone to learn from, rather than a prey animal.

When I could tell that the beach was close enough, I made him stop. As best I could—no matter how smart he was, he *was* still a shark and didn't speak English or Spanish—I told him he had to knock off attacking the humans.

For now, at least.

He didn't understand. Aren't they food? They have lots of blood in them. Can't I drink that?

I shook my head and told him No. They aren't food for you. They'll try to hurt you. It isn't safe.

He didn't want to get hurt, so that seemed to convince him. Then I reminded him of all the food there was out there, and that he needed to be careful so he didn't overdo it. He could run out of food if he killed everything.

I could swear he nodded in the water at that, but I might have just been projecting. Regardless, he swam off toward the deep, and I could sense his movement in the back of my mind.

There was more than relief in my step as I walked out of the surf and back to my shirt. Shaking off my hand and my hair, I glanced up, only to see the dark-haired, brown-hatted, grey-suit-wearing figure of the boss man himself.

"Preceptor Nathan."

He nodded.

"Hey." I couldn't stop grinning. "I've taken care of the problem."

"I've taken care of the problem..." Clearly, he wanted me to add his honorific.

"And..." I glanced out at the water, still grinning. "I want the beach. For my own grounds. And if you don't agree... well, you can take it up with..." And I jerked my thumb toward the bloody foam washing up on the beach. "...Bruce." As I turned, I gave the shark a mock salute, watching him jump out of the water as I thought about him.

"Are you threatening me?"

"Yes. Absolutely." I nodded along with my words. "Just imagine it, *sir*—no one coming to the beach until they bring the army out. And what's that going to do? They can't kill him; you said it yourself. And now he works for me."

"I'll—"

"Have me killed?" I laughed. "And then you just have a *rampaging* shark thrall on the loose. Good luck with that. I'll bid you farewell with a fucking smile on my face and watch from Hell while you deal with that... and all the rest of it from the others."

He paused. I could imagine the gears turning in his head. There was always another vamp ready to try for the king, as it were. If Nathan couldn't handle this situation, he'd be in deep water... even deeper than Bruce.

"Fine. As a reward for your service, the beach is yours."

"Full hunting rights?"

"Full rights. Fuck off." He turned to walk away, so I called after him. "I appreciate it, sir. Thanks."

He didn't turn, just flipped me off as he stalked into the night. I stared off, watching the moon on the ocean. Bruce was far off by now, but I could still feel him there, in the back of my mind, waiting to be called back if I needed him. And now the beach was mine. Laying back on the sand, I enjoyed the tickle of the grains on my skin and the sound of the water crashing against the shore.

The best thing about being a vamp in Southern California is the waves.

When an opening arises, strike (others will do the same to you)

THE PROJECTIONIST

BY MELISSA KOONS

"Look at that guy! What a lame-o!"

"Hey, quiet down! We're tryin' to watch the movie, jerk," a voice from the darkness, some rows behind the offender, shouted back.

The loud, fraternity jock look-a-like turned around in his seat with a lop-sided grin and unfocused eyes that tried to spot his confronter, but he couldn't make out a clear face in the crowd with the flashing light of the movie screen.

"Lighten up, you pussy. It's a stupid flick," the jerk shouted in a general direction, not able to identify the person who had called him out. He let out an uproarious laugh when no one replied and turned back to the screen, wrapping his arm around the young woman beside him who was trying her best to shrink away and disappear into the velvet of her seat.

"Babe, babe, look at the dog. Isn't that the dumbest thing you've ever seen?" The drunk laughed loudly again, making the blonde in his arms flinch at his abrasiveness.

"Chad, you're being a bit loud, it's hard to hear the movie," the young woman pleaded, wrapping her arms around herself as the angry stares from the other theatergoers pierced the back of her head.

"Don't worry about it, babe. Those assholes don't matter. I can't believe anyone would seriously want to watch—oh my god, that dog just ate that guy's face off!" Chad burst into another round of laughter.

"Hey, usher guy, aren't you going to do anything? Tell that idiot to shut up or kick him out of here!"

Already thoroughly embarrassed by her date's loudness, Claire looked over her shoulder and saw several people nodding in agreement and pointing to her "boyfriend."

The usher was a young kid—clearly in his first job—tall and skinny. This young lamppost would be about as effective with Chad as a buzzing fly—and Chad would squish him with as much ease. The lamppost sized up Chad, his eyes wide and his posture stooped, burdened with awkward teenage insecurity.

Claire met his intimidated gaze and shook her head rapidly, begging him not to do the thing all the angry theater patrons were asking him to do. She really didn't feel like dealing with bloodshed tonight—at least, not the lamppost's.

The poor usher kept his distance, but other patrons' requests to remove Chad transformed from harsh whispers to furious demands. Desperation marring every line on the kid's pimpled face, he turned to stare up at the projection booth's dark window. Suddenly, his shoulders eased, and his stressful expression relaxed. He then murmured reassurances to the patrons, which apparently placated them enough to resume watching the movie.

Claire frowned and tried to figure out what the kid had seen in the projection booth, but Chad interrupted her concentration by shouting another obscene comment at the screen. Claire tensed, but this time, no one complained.

Instead, the usher—again regarding the projection booth—gave a curt nod and rushed out of the theater.

Thrown off by the lamppost's abrupt dismissal, Claire squinted at the projection booth. She could just make out the silhouette of a figure standing beside the window. She blinked, and the figure vanished.

"Oh damn! Look at that dog chow down. You should've run, dumbass! What did I tell you, lame-o." Chad pumped his fist in the air victoriously, squeezing Claire against him as he did, forcing her to turn away from the shadowy figure in the projection booth and back to her "boyfriend."

Claire rolled her eyes and scoffed. She ducked out from under Chad's arm and tried to relocate the mysterious projectionist. Lamppost was back and was quietly escorting the other, moody patrons out of the theater, handing them vouchers as they slipped through the door to go watch the movie, undisturbed, at another show time. The other couples and groups of friends shot glares in their general direction; if they said anything, their voices didn't carry over the sound of the snarling beast on the screen. The last patron exited, leaving only Chad and herself near the front. Once the door closed a broom was slipped through the handles, barring the exit.

Claire stood from her seat; a cold sweat broke out on her forehead. She locked eyes with the usher who shifted his feet uncomfortably and gave her a sad, forced smile.

"Babe, babe what are you doing? The movie's almost over. Oh, don't worry! It's not a real dog that they kill. You're too emotional, Kate." Chad grunted and turned back to the movie, unaware he had her name wrong, watching with unmasked glee as the hero confronted the rabid animal with a shotgun.

Claire cast the Delta-Bravo-Pi she picked up at Sbarro two weeks ago a glare. God, she was going to be glad to be rid of him... but not yet. The hair on the back of her neck stood on end and she shivered. She swiped her blonde hair off her shoulders and tied it back in a low knot, ensuring it was out of her face for whatever came next that the kid didn't want the rest of the audience to witness. She scanned the now empty movie theater, her eyes darting back to the projection booth again and again. There was something about it that unnerved her and set her on edge. The way the usher kept staring at the window led her to believe she had good reason to be on edge. The blocked exit was also a pretty solid clue.

Something dreadful was about to happen.

The screen dimmed and the sound system went silent, both cutting out well before the natural end of the film.

"Awe! What kind of crappy theater is this? I paid to see the whole movie, and your dumb film is going to crap out with five minutes left? I want my money back!" Chad shouted, throwing his hands in the air then slapping them back down on his thighs.

"Chad, we need to go," Claire turned back to him, barely able to make out the outline of his broad shoulders in the darkness. Without the flickering light from the movie playing on the screen, the theater was nearly pitch black, the dim lights that lined the walkway offered an eerie glow but no real illumination. The only audible sound in the theater was Chad's groaning and complaining about the movie; all else had fallen unnaturally silent. He grumbled on and on, not seeming to notice that all the other patrons had vanished. His lack of attention to detail was what had drawn her to him, but it was proving to be a detriment to her situation now. He was making them easy targets.

"Shut up, Chad!" Claire growled. She didn't need to shout for her voice to have the same impact. The quiet was oppressive; Claire could hear her own blood pounding in her ears, and she didn't like it. She didn't like any of it. The hairs on her arms stood on end and the weight of a hidden presence loomed over her. It was the same sensation a deer would have with a mountain lion prowling in the foliage. They were being hunted.

"Kate?" Chad's voice was like that of a lost child. Her barking command had rattled him out of his macho obliviousness, and he was now realizing the strangeness surrounding them.

It wasn't supposed to go like this.

Claire didn't answer to the false name she had given him nor the plea in his voice. She remained silent, straining her ears and senses to pinpoint the threat. A rustling in the rafters was faint, but she could identify it clearly: wings.

Chad reached for her, but she batted his hand away. Whatever it was that hunted them, it grew nearer, and she didn't want to be slowed down by Chad's idiocy. She couldn't afford a broken bone due to his clumsiness and panic. She needed her bones for running. But she also needed Chad's bones... and his blood...

Damn, she cursed to herself. She spent too long grooming him. She'd have to start all over and she didn't have the time. The blood moon was tonight. In fact, it was in a couple hours. She brought Chad here to kill some time before she brought him to her coven. They should be readying the ceremony now. If she missed it or came empty handed... Not an option. She needed Chad.

"Kate?" His voice was soft and the pitch several octaves higher than his usual, douche-bag baritone.

The rustling stopped.

Claire took a deep breath in and closed her eyes. She brought her hands up to her chest, palms facing each other about six inches apart. She let her breath out slowly, gently blowing air between her palms. When all the breath was pressed from her lungs, she snapped her fingers, springing a spark to life that bounced on the tip of her index finger like a tiny star.

Light spilled out around them, casting a protective circle of illumination. Claire smiled as she heard a tiny *hiss* from the darkness. *There you are.*

"What the hell is that? How did you do that? What are you?" Chad screamed from behind her, pushing himself away and tripping over a row of seats as he tried to put distance between them.

"Relax, Chad. It's just a flashlight on a keychain," Claire lied. She held out her tiny star into the dark theater, penetrating the darkness. The hissing grew louder; Claire smiled. *Got you.*

"We're going to leave now, sorry for the disturbance," she grabbed Chad's clammy hand and pulled him along as she sidestepped out of the row, careful to keep the light pointed toward the soft *hiss*.

"I'm sorry, miss. We can't let you leave yet," the usher said, startling Claire and making her stumble over the aisle seat. She hadn't realized he was still there; he had been so silent she was certain he had slipped out after the movie was cut.

"Oh, I think you can. It will be in everyone's best interest if you do," Claire said, righting herself and hustling out of the row to the center aisle.

A rush of wind zoomed past her. In a flourish of impossible speed and leathery wings, a figure emerged from the darkness and blocked her path. It was a man, crouched with enormous, black wings wrapped around him like a protective blanket, shielding him from the light in Claire's hand.

The mysterious projectionist, at last. Claire leveraged the light and cast it on him completely, enjoying the soft *hiss* that came from his wings as the light of the star singed them.

"What the HELL is that!!" Chad screeched behind her, squeezing her hand so tightly she thought he might rip it off.

The man curled into himself but didn't move from her path. She took a step toward him, but he remained hunched over with his wings wrapped around him, despite the thin trail of smoke that drifted off his leathery hide like steam from a teapot.

"Let us pass." Claire held out her star like a weapon, trying to urge the man back.

A soft chuckle rose from the hunched man.

Claire froze a few feet away from him, unnerved and un-boldened in her push for the door by the man's unexpected and eerie laughter. The man straightened from his hunch, his bat-like wings flapped and folded behind him leaving his face and path unobstructed and his body unprotected from her light. His dark eyes were fixed on Claire as he stepped closer to her, closing the distance between them until the side of her raised palm nearly brushed his chest. Steam wafted off his muscled torso, his black button shirt smoldered, but both it and his person were still firmly intact and otherwise unaffected by her little starlight.

Claire flinched and looked down at her spark then back to the man in front of her. She squared her shoulders, yanked her hand out of Chad's frightened clutches, and brought both palms together again.

"Let us pass," she demanded.

The man tilted his head; looking from Chad and back to Claire again, trying to figure out the strange pairing before him. "No," he said smoothly, "he's mine."

"You can't have him," Claire held her hands out, steady and forceful. She glared fiercely at the projectionist and blew gently on her hands again to make her tiny star blaze.

The light cascaded over him like silver lava, but the projectionist didn't flinch. Steam rose off his black shirt with a soft sizzle, but he wasn't bothered by it. It was no more concerning to him than a loose thread or missing button. "He is in my house and has broken my rules. It is within my right, here and now, to take him and rid the world of his unpleasantness." His eyes flicked over to Chad who shrank back in fear, like a mouse cornered by a cunning snake.

"No!" Claire tried to push the projectionist back, but he refused to budge. Their faces were inches apart, and she could smell the familiar fragrance of death upon his breath. The red ring around his pupils identified him as what she feared, and the gold ring around his iris verified why he was immune to her circle of light: an elder vampire. A monster of the ages who had feasted upon so many souls that the sunlight that surged through their veins absorbed into his—an antidote that built a resistance to the scalding light; one that took centuries and thousands of victims to develop.

"You cannot have him."

The vampire sneered and his eyes flicked hungrily from her face to Chad cowering behind her. "Why do you defend him? Even he knows he deserves no better than this. Look! He can't even bring himself to flee. Why does such a pathetic man mean so much to you?" He trailed the back of his fingers gently down Claire's cheek; a burst of warmth flushed her skin from his cold caress.

She jerked her cheek away and took a small shuffle back, to keep his fingers from lingering on her skin any longer. There was hunger in his eyes:

a bloodlust for Chad which she understood, and a lust for her which she wasn't sure she wanted to understand. Understanding meant complicating. The countdown to moonrise had already begun. It didn't matter how handsome the vampire in front of her was, nor the look in his eyes that made a shiver run pleasantly down her spine, she had no time to waste on complications. "He's important to me."

"Yeah, you tell him, babe!" Chad chimed in, false bravado in his quivering voice. He squeezed her shoulder in encouragement and positioned her more squarely in front of him. His hard, solid muscles took refuge behind her soft, supple curves.

Claire rolled her eyes, unable to stop herself.

The vampire's lips twitched, and the tip of a fang protruded from his mouth for a moment as he smirked and teased, "Oh, he is, is he?"

Claire glared at him and blew on her hands again, flaring her tiny star. She knew it wouldn't hurt him—the rings of golden sunlight in his eyes sheltered him from that—but it still made him sizzle and ruined his shirt. His scowl brought a mischievous grin to her lips. "Yes, really. He's important to me. I need him."

"Parts of him, you mean," the vampire said, closing the space between them once more. He leaned in, his lips brushed against her throat as he whispered, "What's a witch like you need a wimp like that, for?"

Claire shivered at his chilled breath on her skin. "I need him. You clearly know why. Now let us pass."

"Why... what?" Chad asked, confused and hesitant. His mind might not comprehend the situation unfolding before his eyes, but his instincts understood imminent danger all too well. Even a mouse knew when faced with a predator it couldn't possibly defeat.

Claire didn't reply; she kept her stare fixed on the vampire.

He smiled, displaying both fangs, his razor-sharp grin ominous. "What if we trade? My usher for your... *boyfriend?*" He gestured over his shoulder at the slender young man who had stayed loyally beside him through this whole exchange.

"Babe! What are those? He has fangs, babe! Do something! Flash him with your light thing!" Chad pleaded, pushing Claire in front of him as a human shield, forgoing all subtleties.

"But, Arthur, sir!" the lamppost protested. "You said if I helped you… if I fed you… you wouldn't— I mean, you can't! I-I did everything you asked!"

The vampire rolled his eyes and waved him off. "Very well, it seems you can't have Billy for your little séance tonight. Such a pity, your *Chad* looks like he could feed me for a month. All brawn and no brains," Arthur licked his lip with a flick of his tongue as he eyed Chad's pulsing veins. He groaned in dismay, "It really is a shame that Billy does his job as well as he does. It would take months to train a new one, and who has the time?"

"Thank you, sir," Billy the usher grumbled.

"Oh Billy, don't be so bitter. You know I would have rescued you the second I finished draining that 'lame-o's' blood. Good workers are hard to find, and you've always done a stellar job." Arthur gave the usher an appreciative tilt of his head, which made Billy beam with pride and straighten his slouching shoulders to his full height. He seemed taller than a lamppost when he did that.

"Good to know your word means so little," Claire sneered. "I'm glad I didn't accept your offer."

"*Drain* me? Drain me of what? Don't let him do it, Kate!" Chad begged.

Claire shoved her elbow back, jabbing Chad in his stomach and forcing him off of her with an ungraceful "*oomph.*" Time was running out, and the awkward window she had before the ceremony was nearly up. Her coven was waiting for her. She could feel their questions swimming in the back of her mind, but she wasn't strong enough to both answer them and maintain the light. Once she performed the ritual and claimed Chad's sacrifice under the blood moon, then her powers would finally be at their full potential. She needed to leave—with Chad—before her window closed and she'd have to wait another few years before she got her chance again. "We will be on our way, *now.*"

Arthur rolled his eyes and checked his wristwatch. "Ahh, moonrise is due within the hour. I suppose you are pressed for time." He looked back up at Claire and pursed his lips. "I never let a meal go—especially not one with an equally delicious side dish." He allowed his gaze to languidly glide over Claire's curves.

Claire's lip curled in disgust out of principle—at being called a "side dish"—but if he could objectify her, turnaround was only fair. She couldn't deny that the vampire was devastatingly handsome. His brown hair was cropped short on the sides with a longer layer on top that was styled back, away from his piercing brown eyes; his square jaw had a thin layer of stubble, accumulated after a full day's rest and a night's work; and he did fill out his button-down shirt very well. His handsome features had undoubtedly played a crucial role in his survival over all these years, luring prey. She had to pay him respect for his current system: little need to hunt, his victims coming willingly and identifying themselves with their obnoxious rudeness. Judging by the healthy pallor of his skin and strength against her light, he was well fed by the Chads of the world.

"Let us go, and I'll let you live." Claire prayed her boldness would be rewarded by his retreat, but she was not so lucky.

Instead, the vampire wrapped his arm around her waist and pulled her closer, to nuzzle her neck. "Let *me* live? How generous of you. I was going to extend you the same offer—in exchange for your boyfriend." He seemed to relish her shiver as his lips brushed her throat, her ear, her chin. "We both know your little light is useless. Give up the game, and I'll let you go free. Believe me. I've never made this offer before and I never will again." Suddenly, the lust in his eyes vanished, leaving only cold, unbridled hunger. "We creatures of the night must show some respect to each other."

The ferocity of his gaze made his intent perfectly clear. Claire wanted to throw him to the ground and run, but without her coven, her powers were weak. Without the blood moon ceremony, they would always be weak. *She* would always be weak, a ghost of her potential. She took a deep breath in and closed her eyes, exhaling slowly through her mouth. She blew on the energy star between her palms, her breath diminishing it in size and light until it was a tiny spark, little more than a glowing ember. The voices in her mind grew louder as the light grew fainter.

Arthur grinned the red in his eyes consumed his pupil. His fangs lengthened into the canines of a beast, and his nails sharpened into treacherous talons. "A wise choice you've made," he snarled gleefully.

"A wise choice, indeed." Claire opened her eyes, her mischievous smile returning to her lips.

"Arthur?" Billy whimpered, looking around the darkened room with widened eyes.

Arthur's grip loosened around Claire at Billy's frightened cry. She maneuvered away from him, but the vampire hardly noticed as his attention was pulled toward the back wall of the dark theater; his breath quickened. He stepped back from the young witch; his talons clicked together apprehensively, his wings opened, and he held the leather barricade defensively around him like a loose cocoon. Billy took a cautionary step toward his master, preparing to dive beneath the haven of his wings.

"Don't do it, not in my house," Arthur scolded, glaring at Claire.

"Kate?" Chad asked one last time, pushing his chest against her back, uncaring about the threat of another elbow to his ribs. His eyes flickered nervously from the vampire to her, and back around the room. "Kate, please," he begged.

"You left me no other option. I told you it was in everyone's best interest if you let us leave." A gentle draft wafted through an open door and blew the rest of her tiny star-ember out, engulfing them all in darkness. "You of all beings should know a witch is never far from her coven."

A burst of brilliant light illuminated the theater as a dozen stars were born between the palms of her coven. Her twelve sister witches surrounded them in a circle along the perimeter aisles. They moved in, chanting the familiar Latin that had been passed down through the centuries.

"No!" Arthur shouted.

Billy dove beneath Arthur's wings. The vampire folded them around the pair, protecting them from the light of a dozen suns. He crouched down, shielding himself and the boy completely. Arthur's leathery flesh blistered and burned, but he didn't move. To flee would be to expose. While Claire's tiny star bore him no harm, these witches had the strength of blood sacrifice and an entire coven to fuel their energies. It would take centuries more time before he had devoured sufficient blood to be immune to their collective strength. He should have known better than to toy with a witch.

"Kate, what the hell is going on? Who are you?" Chad backed away from her, his hands raised defensively.

The blood moon had risen, the time was now.

"My name is Claire." Fear glowed in Chad's eyes. A frightened heart was a weak heart: it surrendered to her power. Claire grabbed Chad's wrist and used her weight and momentum to yank him down in front of her.

"No! What are you doing? Please, don't!" Chad begged, scooting away from her. He stopped, trapped between his girlfriend and the crouched vampire, unsure of where to go or what to do.

The coven of witches closed in around him. Their chants rose, and their feet pounded a beat only known by their primal intuition.

"Beneath the power of the blood moon, I offer this virile man to the void as sacrifice. As his blood flows from his veins, may his strength be transferred to me and enhance the gifts I have been bestowed by the Goddess of Nature, the God of the Sun, and the King and Queen of the Underworld." Clair stepped over Chad as he cowered at her feet. She straddled his crumpled figure, one foot on either side of his muscular torso. She drowned out the sound of his whimpering pleas with her spell. She held out her hand and one of her sisters passed her the ceremonial dagger.

"God, no! Don't do this!" Chad shouted, trying to wiggle out from under her, but her legs closed, squeezing him between her calves.

Chad kicked and pushed at Claire's legs, but she was planted more firmly than a tree. "No! I don't deserve this!"

Claire raised the dagger over her head and kicked Chad onto his back so that he was staring up at her. "Of course you do, sweetie."

She plunged the dagger into his chest; his blood splattered on her face and clothes like a macabre tie-dye. His yowling only fueled her as she carved his chest. His howls of pain silenced abruptly as she sliced through the aortic artery and yanked out his heart. She slammed the butt of her dagger into one of his ribs, fracturing it. With a little twisting, she broke off a piece of the bone. Using the hilt of the dagger again, she ground the bone into tiny pieces, which she sprinkled like confetti over his slick, heart.

"Blood to feed my blood. Muscles to give me strength. Bone to stabilize me. I offer him to you, so that you may flow through me." Claire raised Chad's heart into the air, his hot blood oozing down her arms.

"Blood. Muscle. Bone. Blood. Muscle. Bone. Blood, muscle, bone!" Her sisters chanted.

Claire brought the heart to her lips, its skin silky smooth. She bit into it. She passed the heart to her nearest sister on her left; they all took a bite from the offered heart, passing it counterclockwise around the circle until it was returned to Claire at the center.

The white light from their stars burned blue. Her sacrifice was accepted.

"A new witch is born into her power!" Claire's coven sister shouted. The rest of the coven erupted into celebratory shouts, their teeth stained red.

"Is it over?" Billy asked cautiously, his voice muffled beneath the bat-wing fortress.

Claire looked over at the sizzling vampire, blood-drunk and electric with the new power surging through her veins. "Yeah, alright. Sisters! Let's tone down the UV and let our friends join our celebration—provided they agree to be respectful." The witches cackled and dimmed their lights.

Arthur shot up, folded his wings against his back, and dust ash off his shirt, the fine material definitely ruined. "As long as *I* am respectful? You came into my theater with your rude boyfriend, created a ruckus, and disturbed my house with his obscene behavior. You denied me my rightful meal, tried to burn me to a crisp, and splattered blood all over the place! Look at this," he gestured to the velvet seats lining the center aisle. "That much blood won't come out easily. Do you know how much work you've created for poor Billy? He'll be here all night, and it's midterms."

Arthur gritted his teeth. He should have killed them both and been done with it. He winced in agony. His weakness for witches and their otherworldly essence was going to be his downfall after centuries of existing.

"Wait... I have to... Oh god," Billy's face blanched as he looked at Chad's mutilated body and the devastating stains.

Claire shrugged and stepped over Chad's remains, closing the distance between her and Arthur. With the ceremony complete, things were a lot less complicated. His arms were crossed over his chest bitterly, but his talons hadn't retracted nor had his eyes lost their red pupils: he was still hungry. "I am sorry for all this, but it is mostly your fault. If you had just let us leave when I suggested, I could have gotten Chad back to the ceremonial circle in the woods where the mess wouldn't be noticed, and his corpse would be devoured by the earthly creatures that lived there. Instead..." She gestured at the bloody mess.

"Yes, I suppose we are both to blame," Arthur teased. As Claire approached him, the scent of Chad's blood mingled with her fragrance and was too heavenly to resist. He pulled her close to him and licked the splatters of blood on her cheek, her chin, her neck.

"Since there are no other beasts around, would you care to finish him?" Claire offered, pushing Arthur away despite her racing heart. She would follow up on that later—after he had fed.

Arthur grinned and positioned himself over the still-warm body. "Don't mind if I do. Afterward, we'll get a drink while Billy gets this place looking decent. I know a great place you'll love. It's in my apartment." He winked at her then dug his fangs into Chad's still pristine gullet.

The lights came on overhead and Billy wheeled in a mop and bucket, a dour look on his face. He passed out paper towels to the witches idling around, offering his last one to Claire.

"Don't mind if I do." Claire wiped the blood off her face as Arthur feasted on her kill.

She suspected the vampire learned his lesson. He needed to remember that he could toy with witches all he wanted, but a witch's coven is never far. No matter his age or hunting ability, a vampire would never be a match against a coven of witches.

Don't play with your food
if you don't know all the players in the game

PART 2 - KEEPING GOOD COMPANY

You may have heard that "there is safety in numbers," or any of a thousand other quips about surrounding yourself with quality people. And you, being a vampire, might have rejected it out of hand. After all, you want to be captain of your own destiny—to say and do what you want, go where you want when you want to—but you will discover just how limited the solo venture can be.

Believe me: you cannot be everywhere all the time; you cannot even adequately defend yourself during the day. Unless you wish to exist in a clay hut in some seldom explored jungle hoping the bulldozer will never arrive, you will need to form connections. Finding willing thralls for food or avoiding witches is the easy part compared to the labyrinths of trust, social cues, and cunning manipulation.

Humans have become lately obsessed with posting "find your people" and similar sentiments. Seldom have they been more right.

THE LONG ROAD TO DEADWOOD

BY SHANNON LYNN FOX

July 1876

The scent of blood woke me.

Animal blood, rich and musky, flooded my nostrils first. Then, the decadent bouquet of human blood stoked my hunger from dull embers to full flame.

I opened one eye. Something—or someone—had put a gash in the wooden crate Hans had packed me inside. Moonlight filtered across my face. By its bluish light, I picked out a dusty canvas awning high overhead.

The crate was still in the wagon then. But by the blood I'd scented, something terrible had happened.

I lay inside the box a moment more, listening. I, Achille Francis, had not survived thirty-nine years of human life and another two hundred twenty-seven after my Turning by being an imbecile.

Only an owl's soft hoots reached my ears.

Bracing my hands against the inside of the crate's lid, I eased it to the side. Even with my inhuman strength, I could barely manage it. Hans must have had a devil of a time maneuvering the crate during our journey west.

I brushed the splinters of wood from my linen shirt and wool pants before climbing out of the crate and onto the wagon floor. The July night was warm, the air nearly still.

Everything around me was a wash of blues, grays, and greens, my pupils making the most of the available moonlight. After the Turning, my eyes had rapidly adjusted to suit a nocturnal hunter.

An ox slumped in the traces where it had fallen, an arrow stuck through its neck. The other lines were sawn through, hastily cut with a dull knife and the beasts spirited away. I moved to the front of the wagon, and the wood gave an ominous creak beneath me.

Peeking out from under the canvas that had saved me from the sun's harsh rays, I counted twenty-seven wagons broken and sundered. Overturned crates, discarded clothing, and yes, bodies littered the ground.

As I studied the scene, I quickly pieced together the likely chain of events.

Our party had been attacked. The men killed, the wagons robbed, the women and children taken for ransom. Someone had broken into my box, thinking there was something worth stealing inside, but upon seeing my inert form assumed only a dead body lay within. I still looked human enough with my dark hair and classical features, though my skin had taken on a corpse-like pallor from the lack of sunlight.

It's hard, but not impossible to wake a vampire before dark. The noise of fighting men, the terrified bellows of the oxen, the stink of death—none of that was sufficient. Neither, apparently, was merely breaking open the box. Only a serious and immediate threat to my person would have pulled me from my rest.

I climbed down from the wagon as I considered my options.

We were somewhere on the vast plain between Fort Pierre and Deadwood. I knew this because I'd last fed at the Fort, and Hans had informed me then that we'd be fifteen days on the trail. Fifteen days until we joined my friend Mattias, who'd enticed me on this adventure. A comfortable stretch of time for a sleeping vampire, but now that I was awake, I was ravenous.

Judging by the mountains looming along the dark horizon, I'd have to travel many more days to reach Deadwood—on foot and alone, possibly without any fresh blood to sustain me.

An owl landed on top of my wagon and hooted at me, its golden eyes wide and round in the dark. How I wished I were one of those vampires capable of shifting form!

After scouring the wreckage, I found Hans lying face down in the grass with a knife between his shoulder blades. I pulled the weapon out and wiped the congealed blood on his pants. It was a shame he hadn't managed to wake me before he died. Once his heart stopped, it was too late for the

Turning. He'd been a good and faithful servant. I would have gladly given him that gift.

As it was, he continued to serve me even in death. I knelt beside his body and inclined my head to feed.

◆ ◆ ◆

Hans's blood sat sour in my belly.

I wiped a hand across the back of my mouth, fighting nausea as I loped on into the night. I'd fashioned a rough pack out of the wagon's ripped canvas awning and brought along a dented pan for water, a length of discarded rope, and the knife. That I didn't have to carry food or fire-starting supplies was a boon. The Turning had granted me superior speed, and I could travel twice as fast as a human when not unduly burdened.

I estimated there were still three hours of night, and I might make it another twenty miles before I had to stop for daybreak. A copse of trees, or, better yet, a cave would help shield me from the sun's rays. Problem was, this part of the country was desolate. Wide, rolling prairie stretched in every direction. If I had a better sense of where I was, I might have struck out for Rapid City and the promise of fresh blood.

Instead, I struggled up the next rise, intent on reaching those mountains on the horizon.

Halfway up, Hans's blood made a reappearance as I threw up onto the dry grass. It had been a gamble to feed when the man had already been dead some hours, yet I didn't know when I'd next have the chance to eat.

When I finally stopped heaving, I stood up and adjusted the half-crushed hat I'd found. Though I did not sweat, I was as shaky as I'd been in the days immediately after the Turning—when I'd stubbornly tried to resist what I was and the blood my body now needed.

Forcing myself to keep moving, I cursed Mattias under my breath, hurling a whole host of colorful and intricate phrases his way. I called down every curse I knew in English and then switched to Gaelic, throwing in some of the choicer words I'd learned in my younger years.

It was Mattias who had lured me out to the Dakota Territory. The vampire's letter had arrived just after the turn of the new year, bearing tales of the riches of both gold and human prey in the booming new town of Deadwood.

I might have discarded the letter entirely if not for one thing: I was terribly, insufferably bored in New York. The city was a changing, ever-growing thing and new people stumbled into her bosom every day, but it was all for the worse. I missed the city of my younger years, and his letter was the call to adventure I was only too glad to accept.

As I crested the next rise now, I stopped and looked down on the stretch of plain below.

A sea of dark, shaggy shapes dotted the grassland. Bison, I assumed. Soft, lowing sounds reached my ears as the beasts grazed or slept. I wrinkled my nose against their rank odor.

On the far side of the herd, I spied several sizable boulders bordered by a gnarled copse of trees. Cover, at long last.

I stood on the ridge for a moment. I didn't know if bison were aggressive. Only the males had horns, but any one of the creatures was certainly large enough to trample me to death. I was fast, but there were hundreds of them scattered across the grass below me.

Still, the safety of the rocks was a temptation too good to pass up.

I descended with all the swift and terrible speed granted by the Turning. My pan thumped heavily against my back as I fairly flew across the ground. My empty stomach churned, and my weakened muscles burned, but I pressed on.

As I hit the flat plain, the nearest bison looked up in alarm but did not immediately react. Only after I passed did I hear a warning bellow.

A chorus the other creatures soon took up.

The males shook their heads and menaced me with their horns while the females stamped their feet. None outright attacked me though as I raced through that beastly sea, weaving around their hulking, stinking forms.

I was nearly through to the other side when one male finally charged at me with a tremendous bellow. He was huge and heavily muscled, his horns thick and long as one of my arms.

I dodged his initial attack, but he gave chase, his hooves pounding a tattoo across the hardened plain. Older than the others, I guessed, and less tolerant of a strange creature in his midst.

I was mere feet from the start of the next rise when one horn caught me—a searing pain cut across my right side. I cried out but did not stop, scrambling up onto the first of the gray rocks.

The bison let out one last guttural wail, and then I heard its heavy hooves dying away as it returned to the herd, satisfied that I was no longer a threat.

I clamped my hand to the wound. My fingers came away coated with blood, the liquid dark as pitch in the low light.

Cursing Mattias, his stupid letter, and my wanderlust, I climbed toward the safety that waited above.

◆ ◆ ◆

A vampire's remarkable healing abilities directly correlate to how recently they've fed.

So when I woke the next evening, I was dismayed but not surprised to see my wound still oozing blood. It had soaked through the dirty canvas binding I'd fashioned.

Still, it wasn't the injury itself that had woken me.

Someone was singing an off-key tune in the distance.

Peeling back the canvas cover, I quickly scanned my surroundings before hurriedly repacking. Then, on a hunter's silent feet, I glided toward the promise of a good meal.

The bison had moved on during the day. Now, only a single light bobbed along the hill's windward side. I moved slowly, creeping from rock to rock. The scent of hot, coppery blood, still wrapped in the delicate paper of human skin, was almost more than I could stand.

Two dark shapes huddled behind the lantern light. A wizened old man and a donkey. He had a thick, white beard, yellowed from poor hygiene and the dust that clung to his clothing. He held the lantern aloft as he sang to himself, the donkey's lead clutched in his other hand. A shotgun was slung through the holster on the pack saddle.

My nostrils flared, body thrumming with the anticipation of a good feeding.

But as I crept closer still and prepared to lunge, I felt another sensation.

A dull repelling force that indicated the man was under the protection of the Almighty.

I almost swore aloud.

I'd only met a human with this type of protection twice before, and I did not know what merited such attention from the Lord. It wasn't faithfulness that did it. Nor was it a blessed wooden cross around the neck. Like the power that turned humans into vampires, there were still great mysteries in the world.

I sank back against the rock, intending to let these two pass by unmolested, when a twig suddenly snapped beneath me.

The man stopped singing. He turned toward me and lifted his lantern.

"Hullo there, son," he said as the light fell on me. "You alone?"

I saw no reason to lie. I had nothing to fear from this old man. "I am."

He chewed his lip. "Beulah and I are just a couple'-a lone travelers ourselves. Though I suspect you aren't out here alone by choice."

Indeed.

"Cyrus Crego," he continued. "Lately of the Allegheny Mountains."

"Achille Francis. Lately of New York." My name meant nothing to him and would mean nothing to any others if repeated. Should he survive the encounter, of course.

He squinted and then nodded at my side. "You're wounded."

"Yes. My party was attacked."

"We must have been right behind you then. Saw the wagons. And the bodies. Spared 'em a prayer at least. It's a wonder the Indians that came for you left Beulah and me alone."

That was likely the work of the Almighty, the blessing protecting these two from harm.

"It's unusual to meet a man traveling at night," I said, steering the conversation away from any more questions he might have about how I'd survived.

Cyrus bobbed his head. "Got this skin condition. Can't stand to be in the sun for long. Clothes and hats help some." He tugged the brim of his hat for emphasis. "But I didn't want to risk it, so I figured we'd just keep to the dark."

Whatever answer I had expected about his nocturnal travels, it certainly wasn't that. I blinked, my hunger-addled mind struggling to imagine what could cause such a condition.

Meanwhile, the man yammered away. Recognizing me as a fellow traveler (and apparently not a predator), Cyrus had moved on to telling me his life story.

"…so we decided to walk to Deadwood, Beulah and I, as we couldn't come up with the coin to join a wagon train. My pappy taught me how to survive up on the mountain, so I'm not afraid of wild animals. Indians, some, but you can't let fear stand in the way of doing the things you want to do. When you're my age, and the clock starts ticking under your ribs, you'll understand that."

The donkey edged closer to me as he spoke, pulling her lead to its furthest extent as her big, soft eyes drank me in. I wondered if she knew me for what I was.

Not human, but predator.

"…and in Deadwood, they say the men are just picking gold nuggets out of the ground, big as goose eggs. Gold everywhere and a millionaire made every day. Hell, I'd settle for becoming half a millionaire. A quarter millionaire even."

Teeth latched onto my bicep. Then the donkey let out a startled *hee-haw* as she detected the cold flesh beneath my linen shirt.

Cyrus reached over and swatted her on the nose. "Apologies. Beulah's a bit of an opportunist."

I rubbed my bruised arm. "It's fine. Animals don't tend to like me."

While he patted the donkey's bristly coat, I considered my next steps.

I couldn't kill him, unless his seemingly divine protection waned. And I didn't like my odds striking off on my own. He'd find that more than strange. I'd have to continue to make him believe I was as human as he— even go against my nature as a solitary hunter.

"Why don't we travel together?" I suggested. "I don't mind walking at night; it's cooler anyway."

He nodded. "With that wound, you'll be easy prey. But together, Beulah and I can protect you."

I suppressed a snort. Even injured, I didn't need their help. Instead, I shot him a grateful smile, the expression he expected to see from his new human companion. "To Deadwood then."

We fell into a comfortable, if peculiar, rhythm.

By day, we slept. Me beneath the canvas. Cyrus, with his hat over his face and curled up beneath his blanket. Trees, rocks, and even the occasional rotted wagon provided protection from the sun.

By night, we traveled. I hated the lantern's bobbing light, its brightness a searing distraction. Though I kept my complaints to myself. Cyrus at least needed it to see by.

I also worried the light would attract undue attention, but in that, my fears proved unfounded. Whatever animals walked the plains at night, they did not approach, though we heard the calls of wolves and more in the distance. Perhaps it was that divine protection around Cyrus. Or maybe it was the instinctive sense a hunter has for knowing when it has slipped from the top of the natural order.

As we walked, our passage miraculously undisturbed, Cyrus continued to talk my ear off. I could have sworn I saw even Beulah roll her eyes at him

Three days passed, then four. The mountains grew no closer. A hole formed on the bottom of one of my boots, forcing me to tear off another strip from the canvas. Without the opportunity to feed, my healing abilities were no better than a human's. I winced with every step as the sore on my foot rubbed against the canvas binding.

Where the bison's horn had gored me, that wound had closed at least. Cyrus had looked at it that first night and furnished me with a foul-smelling poultice to rub on the skin. I'd done it to humor him as much as anything. To my great surprise, it had worked.

"When do you think we'll reach Deadwood?" I asked shortly before the fifth dawn. We'd stopped next to an abandoned wagon, its bent wheels sunk deeply into the ground. Scraggly trees surrounded the site, which was more sand than dirt.

Cyrus looked up from the hole he was patching in his shirt. "I think another three days to the foot of the mountains. Maybe three more after that to reach Deadwood."

My head throbbed. Six cursed days. And only if everything went according to plan.

I choked down a bit of the provisions Cyrus had, to sustain the illusion I was human. The dried meat and hard biscuits sat heavy in my stomach, as useless as a ship on the prairie.

For the first time in my very long life, I feared the shadowed hand of death. If I did not feed soon, it would claim me at last.

I stood up, intending to make my preparations for bed, but Cyrus stopped me.

"Achille, did I ever tell you about the time 'ol Beulah and I escaped a grizzly?"

He had. Three times in as many days. That and tales of many other wild and close brushes with death. I was beginning to think the Almighty had extended the blessing of protection because the man had a knack for getting in trouble.

Cyrus stared at me expectantly. But it wasn't the telling of the story itself that was important. Cyrus was powerfully lonely. He may have affected a cheerful disposition, but it was in these waning hours of night that the veneer bled off, exposing the real man and his lonely heart beneath

I should know.

I hadn't realized how important a role Hans had occupied in my life until he was gone. He'd been more than a familiar. A companion who helped stave off the worst of eternal life's monotonous march. Without him, I had little to protect me from the advance of loneliness.

I sat back down. Dawn was not yet blushing on the horizon.

I still had time to hear the story through once more.

◆ ◆ ◆

My eyes popped open.

A strange man loomed over me, rusty knife in hand. He had the wild look of someone hovering on the edge of sanity, red hair tangled, dirt smeared across his cheeks and nose.

By the warmth and light outside, it was day. The man must have happened on our camp while we slept.

I batted the weapon away and grabbed him by the throat with my other hand, slamming him up into the underside of the wagon. His eyes rolled back in his head, but he remained conscious.

My fangs descended. I opened my mouth wide to feed before I could stop myself.

I had heard it described that the first taste of water in a desert is as near to a religious experience as man can have on earth. That first taste of blood was like nothing I'd ever known. I drank greedily, feeling the fog lift from my mind and strength flow back into my limbs.

A shotgun cracked sharply through the warm air, returning me to the real and present possibility of other danger.

Cyrus shouted, and Beulah brayed in alarm. Scuffling sounds followed, and then a loud crash. From my position beneath the wagon, I could see nothing of what was happening.

The red-haired man went slack in my grasp, his body registering the sudden loss of so much blood.

Another crash. Wood splintered, and then Cyrus bellowed, "Git off me you bastards!"

I looked at the dying man and knew I had a choice to make. I could stay here and continue to feed, leaving Cyrus to his fate.

Or I could help him.

The red-haired man let out a rattling sigh as I laid him on the sand and peeked out from beneath the wagon. Four more men had Cyrus surrounded in the shade of a gnarled oak tree. The old man brandished a shotgun. By the way he held it, either it had misfired, or he was out of ammunition.

The four thieves were all younger men, ranging in age from twenty to forty. They held only knives in their desperate, twitching fingers. I did not need to see their eyes to know they held the same wild hunger as the man who'd accosted me beneath the wagon. Whether it was greed for whatever wealth we carried or actual hunger, I didn't know.

Nor did I care.

Pulling the canvas cover up and over my head like a shroud, I picked up the dead man's rusted knife. Then I squeezed out from under the back of the wagon, out of sight of Cyrus and the bandits.

Every instinct screamed at me to get back under cover as the sun's strength landed full on the outside of the canvas. Ignoring it, I moved on near-silent feet into the shadows of the trees.

Beulah saw me and brayed again. Cyrus had hobbled her so she couldn't escape while we slept, but now every muscle in her body strained with terror.

The thieves and Cyrus didn't even glance at her, locked in the wary dance of hunter and hunted.

I took a steadying breath and then sprang into action.

I grabbed the nearest thief by the back of his shirt, hauling him off his feet. I threw him into one of his fellows. They both went down in a tangled heap of limbs and startled shouts.

Another came right for me, knife raised. I blocked his strike with my forearm. The blade bit deep and hit bone. I winced, but already I could feel my body beginning to heal the wound.

A look of surprise crossed the man's face as I grabbed him by the throat. He was still surprised when he died, his windpipe crushed in my grasp.

Then, pain. Blinding pain.

Someone had torn the canvas cover away, exposing me to the full brunt of the sun's rays. I hissed and shrank back, blinded, grasping for the safety of the fabric.

"Hold on!" Cyrus yelled. There was the dull *thunk* of something heavy meeting flesh, and then a body thumped to the ground.

The canvas was thrown back over my head, and then the worst of the pain receded.

I cowered there in the thin shade, shuddering, aware of how close I had come to death.

My knife lay in the sand. I picked it up and brushed off the blade before adjusting the canvas around my face so I could see again.

The thief Cyrus had dropped was on the ground, blood leaking from a nasty head wound. Cyrus must have cracked him upside the head with the shotgun.

The other two thieves had regained their feet. Observing their dead and injured compatriots, they quickly turned and bolted through the trees. Moments later, the pounding rhythm of hoofbeats filled the air as they galloped away.

I turned to the old man. Spots of red, blistered skin stood out on his cheeks and forehead, evidence of that skin condition he'd referenced.

Then Cyrus turned the color of old parchment. His woolen white brows knit together in an expression of mingled confusion and horror. If it weren't for the steady thrum of his pulse, loud in the quiet of our camp, I would have thought the man was having a heart attack.

"You're... you're..." he stammered.

It was only then that I realized how I must have appeared.

I had fed so desperately and so fast; drying blood was smeared across my lips and chin. A peek at my linen shirt revealed crimson stains splashed upon the fabric. My fangs pressed against the inside of my lower lip, not yet retracted. He must have seen them when I opened my mouth and hissed at the sun. Not to mention my quick, effective means for dealing with his assailants.

We stared at each other for several tense moments.

He still held the shotgun, but he made no move to get his finger around the trigger. Nor did he heft it any higher.

After what he'd just seen, he knew I'd have no trouble taking him down as well. Yet he was clearly confused about why I'd let him survive this long. I could almost see the thoughts ticking through his mind as he tried to work it out.

That same pulse of protection still surrounded him, though I didn't know why it had allowed the thieves to close in. I was only a vampire and didn't pretend to understand the ways of the Almighty.

Then, the man on the ground let out a pained groan, and Cyrus nudged him with the toe of his boot.

"Well, if you're still hungry," he said. "This one probably has it coming."

♦ ♦ ♦

Cyrus watched me feed.

I don't know if it was morbid curiosity or a practical desire not to turn his back on me that kept him watching. He removed Beulah's hobbles and stood in the shade of the trees, stroking her long ears.

By the time I was finished, the sun was dipping toward the horizon. My healing abilities had dealt with the worst of the sun's damage, but the skin on my face felt tight and painful. I pulled the canvas more tightly around me and stood, facing Cyrus.

He dropped his hand from Beulah's ears. "I suppose there's a reason I'm alive and they're not."

I nodded. "You're under the Almighty's protection. Even if I wanted to, I couldn't touch you."

"Huh," he said, as if he were discussing the price of corn in Kansas. "Well, how about that."

A breeze lifted, rustling the dry leaves in the trees as I waited for him to continue. When he didn't, I let the matter lie. A man was entitled to his secrets, after all.

I cleared my throat and said, "The two that got away escaped on horse-back. Odds are good there's at least one more horse out there if you want to take it. You'll make better time to Deadwood that way."

"And what about you?"

"Me?"

"Yes. You said *I'll* make better time to Deadwood. Aren't you coming with me?"

There weren't many things that surprised me, not after more than two hundred and sixty years of life. But Cyrus's question was one of them.

"I reckon what you said about protection is true," he continued, as if I weren't staring at him slack-jawed. "Otherwise, I'd have been dead days ago." He shrugged. "But today, you saved my life."

"And you mine," I said, remembering how he'd thrown the canvas over me to protect me from the sun.

"Makes us even then." The corners of his eyes crinkled as he grinned. "Why don't we go see if we can find two horses? Then, you can tell me all about how a vampire ended up walking the long road to Deadwood."

Companionship is Essential for Survival

HOW TO MAKE VAMPIRE SOUP

BY ANGELIQUE FAWNS

Sutton police are investigating after a woman's body was found in a wooded area just outside the Lazy Beaver trailer park on Saturday, December 15th. A hiker made the gruesome discovery under melting snow and called the police. Officials say the deceased was in her early twenties and died under suspicious circumstances. Police are withholding the victim's identity until the next of kin can be notified.

Amber Smith
Sutton Town Crier
Issue: Mon Dec.17th 1984

Seth crouched behind the apple tree in the trailer park, his sharp incisors clicking together as he shivered. Shriveled frozen fruits littered the ground around him. Unfortunately for Seth, frigid overcast days like these were the only ones he could venture outdoors.

Despite the winter air, his armpits were damp with sweat. Spying on his gorgeous neighbor as she shoveled snow was embarrassing, but he couldn't figure out how to introduce himself. His undead heart throbbed in his chest as snowflakes got caught on the wild blonde hair sticking out of her toque. Her bright red legwarmers pooled around her ankles as she danced to her Walkman. He could hear WHAM's new song, "Last Christmas" leaking from her headphones.

Seth stayed as motionless as possible. The icy, crunchy snow would alert Amber's dog. The tiny brown terrier pounced nearby on mice unearthed by her shovel.

He imagined his pickup line:

"Hey Amber, I'm your local vampire. Can I take you out for a drink? You can be my cocktail!" He slapped his palm onto his forehead.

Seth reminded himself he wasn't spying in a perverted way, just keeping watch. He'd read the reports about dead women found in the woods nearby. The conservative local press didn't like to make wild assumptions or create panic, but the number of recent attacks hinted at a serial killer, or worse. Seth's anxiety was seriously cutting into his day sleep. With a new vampire in town, all of Sutton's single pretty women might be in danger.

Seth stretched, trying to work out the kink in his back—

And fell face-first into the snow.

The dog erupted into high-pitched yapping.

Amber rested on her shovel. "Is there anyone out there?" The crisp air caught her breath in a bubble.

Seth froze, hoping the thick trunk of the apple tree would keep him hidden, even with the branches bare.

"Hey, Snots, shut up for a minute," Amber commanded the dog. After a moment of silence, Seth heard her murmur, "Must have been a squirrel."

Snots's ears perked up at "squirrel," but he stopped barking.

With the dog distracted, Seth let out his breath.

Amber dropped her shovel. "Our work here is done." Seth watched her pick up Snots and turn back to her doublewide.

He thought she'd done a lovely job with the old trailer. It boasted hand-made yellow shutters and had festive Christmas decorations on the wood porch. Seth was about to head for home when a man slithered out from under Amber's deck.

The hairs on Seth's arm stood straight up when he recognized the heavily tattooed man as Dan: one of the other vampires hiding in their remote community. Dan wore a t-shirt and almost every inch of his visible skin was covered with heavy metal artwork. Scorpions, Iron Maiden, and Metallica decorated his arm, done in blue prison ink, and had the artistry of an untalented child.

Seth wanted to rush out and defend Amber, but he needed a strategy. He'd fought Dan once before when the tattooed vampire had tried to steal one of his pet pigs. Seth lost.

Snots beat Seth to the defense and rushed at the interloper, barking madly. Dan kicked the brown furball into a snowbank. Snots gave a sharp yelp, clambered out of the snow, and hid behind Amber's legs.

Seth was surprised to see Amber ball up her fists rather than scream or act scared. "Asshole. Who kicks a puppy?"

Dan lunged at Amber, but she spun away from his grasp and assumed an odd karate stance. "You picked the wrong lady, jerk face." She kicked at her assailant's groin.

Dan caught her foot with one huge hand and pulled her off balance. Her head hit the railing of her deck with a sick *thud*.

Seth's fists clenched at his side, and his eyes filled with tears. How could he help Amber? The frustration of being a younger, weaker vampire was unbearable. He needed a secret weapon, something that could take down a monster stronger than himself. Bile rose to Seth's throat as he watched Dan lick Amber's bloody forehead. Amber lurched to a sitting position, slapping and kicking.

Dan straddled her hips and wrenched her arms over her head. "Sometimes I like my breakfast to fight."

Seth's fangs fully extended, and a red rage washed over him. This wasn't happening. He grabbed a frosted stone nearly the size of his head and hurtled it. "Not today, mothersucker!" It hit Dan in the head with a loud *thwack*.

Dan's eyes rolled back into his head, and he slid to the shoveled walkway, unconscious. Seth had been lucky with the stone. But he might not be so lucky next time. He needed a more effective weapon if vampires were going rogue in his town.

Seth rushed over to help Amber to her feet, and Snots bit Seth's ankle.

"Hey!" He shook his leg gently.

Amber said, "Snots, let the man go." She reached one trembling hand to her forehead and wiped away a bit of blood.

Snots renewed her attack on Seth's ankle.

"Enough!" Amber scooped up the little dog.

Seth blinked awkwardly.

"So, I guess I owe you thanks. Except… What the hell were you doing in my wood grove."

"A-A-Apples," Seth stuttered, his face red.

"What?"

"Looking for old apples." He pointed to the brown shriveled apples half buried in the snow. "I'm Seth. From the farm over there." He gestured vaguely across the highway. "My pigs love old apples."

"You were picking apples in the winter. In a trailer park… for pigs." Amber crossed her arms. "Besides, I know who you are. This is a small town. About time you introduced yourself."

The butterflies in Seth's stomach swirled. She knew him! What should he say? He was saved from answering when Dan sprang up and ran, disappearing down the twisty lane out of the trailer park at an impossible speed.

"Yo, Dan!" Seth called after him. "Stay away from Amber."

Amber whirled on him. "Dan? You know that freak? Is this some sort of sick pick-up routine? One guy attacks, and the other saves the damsel-in-distress?" Cradling Snots protectively, Amber stalked up the stairs of her trailer. The door slammed behind her.

Seth felt nauseated. He'd ruined any chance he ever had of getting to know Amber. Instead of being a hero, he was a creep.

He needed a drink. A quick stop at the pub couldn't hurt. His system could handle a bit of red wine.

♦ ♦ ♦

Seth dragged his rubber boots through knee-high snow on his way back to the farm, his head foggy from the booze. The endless white fields mirrored his mood. Desolate. He kept a careful eye on the sky. A few rays were peeking through the clouds, illuminating streamers of smoke.

Seth frowned.

Why would there be grey plumes of smoke in the sky? His insides went cold. The smoke seemed to be billowing above his farm. He ran, panic closing his throat. He smelled the acrid burning before he saw it, his nose assaulted by char and destruction.

As he turned up his driveway, Seth gulped down a sob. The barn was on fire, red flames licking the top of the old bank barn. Squeals of terror and pain cut through the roar of the inferno. The barn housed all his precious pigs.

His worst nightmare was coming true, and he ran for all he was worth. The entire building wasn't involved yet. Maybe he could save them…

"Seth! Help me!" Amber's shrill familiar voice.

Seth came to an abrupt, panting stop. Amber was tied to his tall, ornate birdhouse. A bushel of firewood flaming around her feet. The bonfire licked at the pole, roaring higher as if it had been soaked in gas.

His heart leaped into his throat and panic burned his chest. He had to make a choice. Save his pigs or rescue his crush. He pressed his lips together. It was no choice at all.

Seth charged toward Amber and catapulted straight up the woodpile into the fire. His thick boots and sweat-soaked pants prevented him from burning right away. Amber's red-rimmed eyes met his and he pulled out his big knife.

"I've got you!" Seth sliced through the bailer twine holding her to the birdhouse pole.

Amber tumbled into his arms, and Seth carried her out of the bonfire. His rubber boots were smoking but he barely felt the heat. He dropped her gently to the ground, and she rolled onto her hands and knees. Harsh coughing racked her sinewy frame.

"That guy—Dan—broke into my trailer and kidnapped me." Amber gasped. "Drove me here in my own damn Jeep."

Seth's blood, already cold, dropped a couple more degrees. By saving Amber the first, he'd just incited Dan to send him a message. A warning. There must be a way he could take the renegade vampire out of commission for good—

Amber gasped and said, "Your barn!"

Coughing and choking, Amber ran towards the flaming building. Seth followed and saw Amber remove her jacket and wrap it around one hand as she blocked the side of her face from the heat with the other.

He took his sweater off and did the same. They each grabbed a handle of the barn door and yanked it open, falling back from the licking flame. He couldn't see any of his pets in the choking black smoke, and dived toward to door.

Amber gripped his arm, stopping him as the fire intensified.

Nothing. No pigs.

Amber shook her head sadly. "I'm so sorry Seth."

Seth's gut clenched—

A loud squeal pierced the air, and ten pigs ran out the door. A few red embers were caught on their thick, wiry hair, but they were still very much alive. One big sow ran straight for them and Seth fell to his knees.

"Esmerelda, my pork chop, thank goodness you made it out." He buried his nose against her fuzzy head.

Amber pointed to the smoldering embers of his barn. "Is there any point in calling the fire department?"

Thick snow began to fall while Seth watched his dreams turn to ash. "No. The barn is gone; it won't spread to the house in this." He caught a snowflake on his palm, where it didn't melt. "There's no insurance anyways."

"I'm so sorry, Seth." Amber put a hand on his shoulder. "I could use a drink."

Seth's shoulder tingled where her fingers touched him.

Seth led her into his old brick farmhouse. He'd never updated his parents' fifties décor. Amber collapsed in a lime green chair in the living room. Seth poured her a glass of red wine from his liquor cabinet.

His cheeks burned red as he observed the ash smeared on her face and hands. "You should have a shower…" He stammered the rest, "And-and spend the night? In case, you know, Dan comes back. I can protect you."

Amber took a little sip of the drink and her eyes fluttered shut. She looked so exhausted in the oversized cushions, Seth thought, that she must have dozed right off.

Seth took the opportunity to pour himself a glass that looked like red wine but came from the special bottle in his fridge. He'd had his one allowed daily glass of booze at the bar earlier today.

But when he turned back, her blue eyes were open. She lifted her glass. "Cheers. This is a merlot? What are you drinking?"

Seth's stomach dropped. She'd seen him, but his tired brain found an answer, thank goodness. "Same. I just prefer it refrigerated." Seth took a quick gulp of his drink, feeling immediately restored. "You can have my room; I'll take the couch."

"I don't want to impose."

Seth's heart sped up. "You wouldn't be. Are you hungry?"

She smiled at him. "A little."

He went to his cupboards and found a box of Ritz crackers he kept for the odd visitor, or if he got peckish. He didn't need food but sometimes liked to munch out of habit. One of the avocados on his table was counter was ripe, so he sliced it and put it on a plate with the crackers.

"Nice," Amber said as she placed a slice of green, silky avocado on the plate. "Do you have any powdered garlic? Brings out the flavor."

"Umm. I'm not a fan of garlic." Seth grimaced, what vampire was? But he wanted to keep the woman of his dreams happy. "I do have a concentrated garlic supplement I feed to my pigs, keeps them plump and healthy."

Amber raised her eyebrows. "I'll pass on the pig supplement." She dug into the perfectly ripe fruit.

Seth's shoulders dropped. Phew. He hated working with the stuff and took a lot of care handling it. Big plastic gloves. Plugging his nose with cotton wads. Get enough of the powder on his skin and he would shrivel up like a leech coated in salt.

"That was good." Amber wiped some green avocado mush off the side of her mouth. "Can I have that shower?"

Seth gulped. The images in his brain of Amber in the shower. The water cascading over those—

"Seth—a shower?"

"Of course." He pointed up the stairs and mumbled where to find the towels.

Amber walked past him, and Seth watched her hips swing back and forth. His fangs protruded and he willed them back into his gums. He'd be lucky if he slept a wink.

◆ ◆ ◆

Seth woke up on the couch and was momentarily confused. Why wasn't he in his bed? Then he remembered. Amber was here! He crept up the stairs and slipped into his room, holding his breath. He didn't do something he would regret last night, did he? If he had hurt her…

Amber was sleeping, undisturbed and peaceful. The sheets were tucked in and unruffled. He smiled as the first rays of the sun caught dust motes around her face. He finally had the girl of his dreams in his bed.

He quietly changed into fresh overalls, then put a little note beside her pillow.

Had to go somewhere. Sorry. Talk later. Seth.

He gently touched her cheek before leaving.

His barn still smoldered in a few places, but his pigs looked happy licking the snowflakes off the ground and exploring their paddock. He tossed a bucket of grain in with them and was relieved to see the burns on their skin weren't that bad. Esmerelda came up to the fence, so he patted her nose before continuing to the archery range.

Seth's father had set up the archery range at the back of their hundred-acre property. The ten-minute walk through his dormant fields now gave Seth time to think. When he was unsettled, he liked to shoot arrows. And Amber sure unsettled him. His shoulder burned with the memory of her touch.

He tried to focus on the beautiful morning—a morning where he had Amber in his bed! A thin coating of snow sparkled on the grass; it was brighter than yesterday but had enough cloud cover that he could stand the sun. He hoped older vampires, like Dan, could not.

The archery range sat against the edge of the forest, with some targets in the clear-cut glade and others against distant trees. Old leaves crunched under the snow, and Seth took a deep breath of the crisp air. His shoulders relaxed. Though he wasn't very good at archery, this was his happy place.

After grabbing his gear from the shed, Seth assumed a shooting stance and nocked an arrow on his bow. Slowly drawing it back, he focused on his mark: a large cardboard bullseye propped up on a haybale. He imagined Dan's face and released the bow. The whistle of the arrow sang in his ears as it flew—

It missed not only the bullseye but the entire haybale, disappearing into the woods behind it.

"Watch out!"

Seth whirled around, knocking himself in the head with his bow. Amber stood pointing at a dark creature in the forest. A black bear. With yellowed spots of foam where his paint was chipped.

Seth relaxed and smiled at Amber. "That's a 3D archery target; there's a bunch." He indicated the deer, coyote, and turkey sitting in the woods. "How did you find me?"

Amber grinned in return and nodded toward his footprints in the melting snow. She was dressed in the same plaid shirt as yesterday but had pulled on a puffy vest from his front closet. Her fluffy blonde hair stuck out from under the red toque.

Seth's heart raced; she looked adorable.

"Did you call the police?" he asked. "About Dan?"

"No, you know the local cops are useless." Amber followed him to the storage shed and put her purse on the rough wood floor.

Seth asked, "Do you remember reading about the body found near the Lazy Beaver trailer park last week?" He pulled out a quiver full of wooden arrows and a bow. He handed them to Amber.

She looked curiously at the artistic etchings of bats etched into the leather quiver. She pulled an arrow out expertly.

Stretching her arms over her head and flexing her triceps, Amber answered, "First off, I practically live at the Lazy Beaver, so obviously I'd hear about it. You read that article, eh?"

"Yes, I did." Seth was puzzled at her slightly arrogant tone.

"I wrote the dang thing! That's why I'm back in town. I'm the new staff reporter at the Sutton Crier." Amber winked.

Seth blushed as Amber expertly nocked the arrow and set her sights on the foam bear. "I also know the body was drained of blood. The cops told me to hold that detail back." Letting the arrow fly with a soft grunt, she smiled when it hit the bear dead center in the forehead.

Seth blinked. "You're full of surprises."

"I can shoot arrows and write articles." She raised one eyebrow. "I'm hoping to write a first-hand piece about the murders. Perhaps help catch the killer. A feature like that would get me out of this small town for good."

She plucked out another arrow and the string taunt with her foot. "Maybe get me a job in New York or Toronto." She decapitated the foam turkey, the head kicking up a plume of snow.

Seth felt a moment of panic, his heart thumping. Amber was planning to leave Sutton? How could he keep her here? The way he felt about her—

"Dan is a vampire." The words rushed out of his mouth.

She dropped her bow. "Are you for real?"

He met her eyes. "Yes."

Amber rubbed her nose. "Did you sniff some of the good powder going around the trailer park?"

"No." Seth leaned towards her, pleading. "Look Amber, I'm not joking or lying. We need to stop Dan. He's a vampire gone rogue."

Seth watched as the pink tip of her tongue slipped out of the corner of her mouth as she came to a decision. "Okay, I'll play along. So, what do we do?" Amber asked.

He shrugged helplessly. "I've been trying to figure that out ever since he attacked you."

Amber pursed her lips and then fingered the tip of her arrow. "Don't vampires hate garlic?"

Seth straightened his spine; Amber might be on to something. "They certainly don't like it."

Her face paled, and Seth thought, *Oh shit*. Did he just hint to Amber that he was a vampire? The red liquid in the fridge, the bats on the quiver, and he already told her he didn't like garlic. She was a journalist. He assumed she could put clues together.

They had a moment, just looking at each other, and Seth shivered. The tension between them held taut as a bowstring. Was she going to run screaming? Attack him?

"Don't you have garlic powder for your pigs?" Her eyes lit up but then she frowned. "Or did it burn up in the fire?"

Seth shook his head. "I keep their feed in a separate shed, pigs are smart and can get loose. I can't have them gorging and getting sick."

Seth's insides frothed like a cappuccino as Amber gave him a toothy grin, and she asked, "Are you thinking what I'm thinking?"

Seth was fairly certain she wasn't picturing *him* naked with a bow and arrow like a modern-day Artemis. "What are we thinking?" His cheeks flushed red.

Amber tucked the bow under her arm and grabbed the quiver of arrows. "Where do you keep your feed? Let's load up these arrow heads with garlic!"

Gorgeous and brilliant. How did he get so lucky? She grinned at him as she pulled a switchblade out of her back pocket. "You never know when you might need one of these."

Seth fought his fangs extending. She was turning him on. A true warrior goddess. Plus, she seemed to gloss over the whole "are you also a vampire" thing, for now. He was grateful.

At the storage cellar, he took his plastic gloves from a medical box on a shelf and stuffed his nose with cotton. "Is this what you are looking for?" He flipped up the lid on the freezer full of white powder. He bought in bulk, and a load lasted him the whole year.

Amber dipped a cup into the fine granules. "Perfect." She sliced the head of the arrow. "Do you have any duct or electrical tape?"

Seth grabbed a black roll from the shelf next to his glove box. "What good farmer doesn't?"

Amber poured some garlic into the arrow tip, and then used the electrical tape to seal it in. "Now we just need Van Helsing!"

Seth's lip twitched; this woman was amazing. "Van Helsing would be great."

Between the two of them, they managed to modify all the arrow tips in the quiver. Seth gratefully removed his gloves and the uncomfortable wads of cotton up his nostrils.

Leaving the shed, Amber asked, "Do you think this will slow Dan down?"

"I'm hoping it will kill him if you shoot it into his heart."

Her voice got a big edgier. "Are you going to tell me how you know he's a vampire?"

Seth felt his spine tingle. She wasn't going to drop it. "I'll tell you this. Dan lives with his sister Dolores at her Scandinavian mud spa. I sell them pig's blood."

Amber now sounded incredulous. "You sell pig's blood? To vampires?"

Seth walked faster. "Yes, I take a little from my sows and sell to the local coven."

"What a scoop!" Amber ran after him.

He whirled. "You can't write about this. You can't tell anyone!"

Hands up, she took a step back. "Okay, simmer down."

Seth thought it wise to change the subject. "Are you good enough to shoot that garlic directly into Dan's heart?" He already knew the answer.

"Yup. I'm good."

She popped the trunk of her Jeep, and they loaded the back with the weapons.

Seth climbed into the passenger seat, and Amber hopped into the driver's. "Promise me the full story after we take out Dan." She slapped her steering wheel.

Seth felt his ears turn red. Didn't she know he was also a vampire? She could never print that story. She must know, right?

Later that day, at the trailer park Seth fought the nerves in his belly. Acid bubbled up his throat like a fizzy pop. They both assumed Dan would come back for her. Seth hid behind the apple tree once more. He could see Amber sitting on her porch, a blanket on her lap.

They waited as the sky darkened, and a light sprinkling of snow began again.

Dan appeared at the edge of the trailer, just as silently as he had from under the porch. Amber didn't have time to aim but let her arrow fly, piercing Dan in the arm. He screamed and collapsed, frantically trying to pull the garlic-filled tip out of his arm.

Seth froze, his blood pressure skyrocketing. From his vantage point behind the tree, he saw another person slink out from under the neighboring trailer. Someone with fly-away blue hair, an unbelievably dark tan, and a million facial wrinkles. Dolores. Dan's older sister. Only slightly less skiddly than her brother, she barred her teeth and raised a fist with a long needle grasped in it.

Seth ran to intercept but tripped over Amber's shoveled snow mound and ended up with his face in the cold pile. Dolores closed the distance to her target in seconds and jabbed the hypodermic needle into Amber's back.

Seth had to make a snap decision. He couldn't fight both Dan and Dolores together, and they hadn't noticed him yet. Gritting his teeth, he hid behind his tree again. Every fiber of his being screamed at him to go fight for her, but having both of them captive would be stupid.

Seth impotently watched Dan sling Amber over his shoulder with his uninjured arm and carry the unconscious Amber to the end of her driveway where Dolores had parked the snowmobile.

Seth scrambled up as Dolores snapped at Dan, "All in good time brother. Don't play with your food."

Before he could reach them, the three climbed onto a snowmobile, and the high squeal of the engine ripped Seth's ears. The vampire siblings sledded off, Dolores driving and Dan holding Amber like a grocery bag.

Once again, Seth wished he had some magic skills like vampires in the movies—such as super speed to catch the sled! Instead, he ran back to his farm. He assumed they were taking Amber to Dolores's spa, The Sun & Mud. It was just down the road from his farm and featured tanning beds, mud baths, and a freshwater swimming pool.

Seth mentally ran over the layout of the spa. He sometimes used the mud baths himself, the vampire part of him needing the nutrients from the damp dirt. He didn't know how much time he had, but probably not much. Amber would be sucked dry by the vamp family faster than a hot kid with a freezie.

After racing home, Seth hopped into his tractor with the forks attachment. Driving it to the feed shed, he eyeballed the size of the door against the wide metal planks on his loader. He slapped his forehead. Of course, the forks wouldn't fit in the shed!

Seth only paused for a moment. Putting the tractor into gear, he smashed into the aluminum siding, destroying one wall and taking out his shelving. His farm was going to need a complete rebuild—and how would he explain this to insurance? Couldn't worry about that now. He slipped the forks under the freezer of garlic supplement, bounced over the wreckage of his shed, and eased the payload onto the back of his pickup truck. It just fit.

He leaped into his pick-up truck and rammed on the gas. The RPM needle shot straight into the red, and the diesel seared his nostrils. He was glad he had put on snow tires. A plan was coming together in his head. It was a "Hail Mary" but all he had.

Seth drove like a madman to the spa, the freezer blocking his view out the back window. Dolores's snowmobile was parked outside the stone bungalow. Complete with a glassed-in addition for the indoor pool.

He climbed out of his truck and crept over to one of the windows. Dan was lounging in the pool, his left arm shriveled from the garlic arrow, at odds with his muscular body. Dolores, now in a blue ballgown, was setting a table with a vase of trillium flowers, huge wine glasses, and a carving knife. Amber was tied to a pool chair, slumped and silent. She still looked dopey from whatever she'd been needled with. Duct tape pulled at the skin around her mouth.

Seth's heart raced. He didn't have much time. He climbed into the truck-bed and opened the freezer. The smell of the garlic almost made him vomit, but he gulped the bile down and scrambled back behind the wheel. Doing a quick two-point turn, he repositioned the truck so it was facing backward, and hit reverse. It lunged under him and jolted towards the pool area. Seth braced his shoulders and shut his eyes as it smashed through the glass. He pounded the brakes, hoping the vehicle would stop before the whole plummeted into the pool.

With a protesting screech, the truck slowed but didn't stop entirely. The rear tires dipped over the end of the pool, and Seth slammed into first gear. The tires spun in the opposite direction and the vehicle teetered on the edge. Flinging his body out of the door, Seth hit the edge of the pool deck and rolled away from the water.

The open freezer tumbled into the pool, making an instant fragrant soup of garlic water.

"Mother—trucker," Dan gasped, voice cracking with terror.

"Moron, get out of the pool," Dolores said, garlic water splashing up onto her arms. She shrieked in pain.

Dolores's face turned white when her brother sank beneath the water. His flesh bubbled and sloughed off his body. Seth held his nose, garlic concentrate was powerful stuff, and he could feel his brain cooking behind his eyes. He couldn't imagine the pain Dan must be in. Not that he didn't deserve it.

Seth dashed around the edge of the pool and released his nose, the smell making him gag. Fighting nausea, he picked up the chair with Amber. She struggled, barely conscious. He tried to keep his footing on the slippery pool deck as he ran back out through the broken wall of glass. The smell of Dan's garlic-spiced body dissolving was horrific.

Dolores shambled after them, slapping at her burning skin. "Hey Pigman, I'll kill you and your little skank." She grabbed the knife off her carefully set table and chased them.

The glass crunched under their feet as Seth tried to stay ahead of the skinny woman. She was faster, even if he wasn't carrying a chair with a bound woman.

Dolores grabbed his elbow. Seth reluctantly released Amber and spun to face Dolores. He swung. Dolores ducked. Then the old vamp grabbed his neck and bit him.

The pain was excruciating and immediate.

Seth yanked, but he couldn't move Dolores's skinny arms. Blood dripped down his shirt. Dolores was slurping and gulping. The old vampire was going to drain him! She'd have a belly ache, but he'd be dead.

Dolores hissed between gulps. "Seth, you're as worthless as gum on a boot heel. I never should have turned you." Seth sunk to his knees as his energy drained.

Amber banged her chair into the crushed glass trying to loosen the rope around her wrists. She bumped against Seth's ankle, and he glimpsed Amber's blue, wide-open eyes.

How did she see him now? The pathetic pig farmer? The weakest vampire in town?

Something in him ignited, and blood (what he had left) rushed to his head. Seth roared, fighting against the black threatening to overwhelm him. He walloped Dolores in her sinewy stomach with both fists. She teetered back a step, her teeth sliding out of his neck.

Dolores was wearing a pair of purple glittery high heels. She lost her footing on the broken glass, stumbled backward on the wet pool deck, and finally toppled into the pool.

She disappeared beneath the garlic-powdered surface with a splash and a scream. Seth didn't bother watching her shrivel. He pulled his shirt off and tied it around his neck to stem the bleeding. Then he released Amber, wrenching the duct tape off her mouth. They both staggered out onto the lawn and stopped by the snowmobile.

"Seth, felt like you took a month of Sundays to get here." She nodded at the pool through the demolished window. "You never told me you knew how to make vampire soup. It can never be too garlicky!"

With her arms free, she hugged him ferociously.

Seth closed his eyes and grinned, hugging her back. He then examined her. She had lots of small cuts from the shattered pool window but had no visible gashes or bites. "Any critical injuries I need to worry about?"

"I'm fine. Dolores only wanted to eat me, but she must have really hated you."

"Wh-What do you mean?" Seth stammered, remembering that Dolores had said *turned*. "I don't really know them—only the pigs blood, but—"

Amber rolled her eyes. "Drop the act, Seth. I know what you are."

Amber pointed to the ballgown floating near the submerged dump truck. There was nothing left of Dolores or Dan.

Seth's heart jumped. "Well… this story should get you on the front page of the New York Times." He tried to make light.

Amber gave him a warning look but played along. "More like the National Enquirer." She laughed. "What's my story? I was attacked by a brother-sister vampire team? The Sutton Town Crier would never print that."

Seth gulped. "Are you sure?"

Amber rubbed her wrists. "Nobody'd believe me."

Seth climbed onto the snowmobile and pointed to the tail of his pickup in the pool. "I think my truck is a writeoff; I don't think Dolores will mind if we take her sled." His mouth was suddenly parched, and he was weak. "I need a glass of wine."

Amber squeezed his ribs. "Or do you mean you need a glass of blood?"

Seth stiffened until she kissed his cheek. Was she going to accept him for who he was?

Her lips lingered—

He flushed and his belly was filled with butterflies. He revved the engine as Amber rested her head on his back.

Hope infused his next question. "Would you consider moving out of the Lazy Beaver?"

Amber whispered into his ear. "You're moving a little fast, Dracula."

Seth grinned, spraying snow behind them as he drove away from the spa. He couldn't wait to make dinner for the both of them—minus the garlic. He had a suspicion that as long as he was dating the town reporter, his secret was safe.

◆ ◆ ◆

Two locals, Dolores Duncan and Dan Duncan, have been reported missing after a strange accident on Monday night. A pickup truck, reported stolen by a local farmer, was found submerged in the pool of The Mud & Sun Spa. Though a window was broken and there were traces of blood on the pool deck; the police could find no bodies or concrete evidence of foul play.

Chief of Police Bob Kettle says, "Maybe some kids were joyriding."

Sutton police are asking anyone who might have some information on the where-abouts of the Duncans, or witnessed anything suspicious, to please come forward.

Sutton Town Crier
Amber Smith
Issue: Thurs. Dec.20th 1984

If you want to stay out of the news, befriend the local media

BLITHE BLOODSUCKING GILES

BY RAY ZACEK

'Twas the noontide, and I reposed peacefully in my coffin when the smiling varlet did hover over me with dagger in hand to plunge into my heart.

Blood spouted and bedashed my silken robes. My screams filled the cellar, and I thrashed about in final agony. Phantasms arose, leaping to devour me. Tongues of hell-fire beckoned, and the words of the Florentine poet echoed in my skull: *lasciate ogni speranza.* My damned soul exited aloft from my carcass and lingered in the air about the flickering torchlight to witness this unnatural scene.

"Ere ends this fiend," said the traitorous stabber, one of my own servants.

"Be it done, and gramercy," said the grim-visaged knave who had dogged me for years and at last tasted bitter victory. "His head I'll have. See to it."

"Then am I paid for't?"

"Aye, you are paid," avouched the other, and with clink of coins in the pouch tendered the blood-payment to the assassin.

Here it seems my grisly tale should end, but *seems* is a slippery crafty devil of a word. Allow me, then, to relate the Full History of Blithe Bloodsucking Giles. To those who would aspire to the Faction of the Night, I offer a valued lesson to keep.

First, know who is't I am. Trust not a guide with whom thou art unacquainted, for they may steer thee wrong.

I am Giles Scaife, once mere mortal man of seaside origin in Norfolk, who metamorphosed into one of the shadowy faction that haunts the Night. I am reckoned an evil and ravening angel by the dull fools of the sun-addled world, upon whom I feed. Kit Marlowe at the Mermaid did dub me Giles the Rebel, of a lunar disposition and opposed to the Tyranny of the Sun, for 'tis true I doth despise that orb and all things heliacal.

The Greeks call my kind, *vrykolakas;* among the Russians, I am *upyri;* among the Turks, *ubir.* The uncouth Bogdanians cower before the ancient *strogoi* of their demesne. The Albanians hath a becoming word, *dhampir,* one who drinks with the teeth; but the English Tongue lacks any proper name. Sans words, sans understanding; sans understanding, sans defense; sans defense, the Night faction wins.

Once I was a merchant and ventured traffic abroad, a wild wayfarer in the Venetian Stato Da Mar and the farther Ottoman provinces. In Bogdania, I was assailed by barbarous Tartars, robbed, stabbed, and abandoned in the Wilderness. *Interfectus a latronibus,* my epitaph.

There, in extremity of dire mishap, I cursed the Sun, indifferent witness to catastrophes upon the globe; and cursed all Mankind; and cursed God for His Mercy withheld. As the dusky sky bled to night, and blind oblivion, and I suffered without succor, a hooded figure approached. Grinning Death, I surmised, come to collect; and here ends Giles Scaife.

But not.

Bechance some infernal power heard my curses and intervened. For my timely rescue was effected by that *strogoi* lord, remnant of a noble and princely family of antic Bogdania. Enticed by the Albion blood in my veins, rare in that precinct of the world, he did covet my company and my corpuscles, and conveyed me to his ancient *castel de pietra* high in the barren mountains.

'Twas his illustrious lordship, Vornic, who fathered my turning and induction into the Shadow faction. We drank blood; he mine, I his, and together that of innocent others—base peasants couched below in the shadow of his castle. Vornic Negrul, the dark one, the peasants called him, and offered their fat sheep, cattle, and kin as if to appease an angry god. Vornic tutored me and invested me in the Night; made me his kindred and bid his dark mistresses and serfs to serve me; and taught me many skills of sorcery.

O happy times in Bogdania!

The Night breed is long-lived but, alas, lacks immortality. My Master, his knowledge piercing the veils of all things, saw his doom unavoided anon, and resolved in legacy to increase his kindred upon the world. For doth it be said: be fruitful and multiply, and replenish the earth, and subdue it, and have dominion over every living thing that moves upon the earth.

When my Master allowed me to leave, with a pile of gold as parting gift and serfs to guard me to channel's edge, I did by closed carriage, stealth, and night speed westward to England, across Poland, across Germany, feeding as I went. In a satin coffer, by ship of lading I crossed the water, therewithal to London, the Navel of England, there to happily abide.

Note this well: Walking in daylight is not beyond conjecture. Thou can'st shield thyself against the abhorred sun. Make use of what the Greeks call *prophulaktikos*; that is, a means of prevention. Various accoutrements avail; dark spectacles for the eyes, leathern gloves, a cloak, a quiofe or corner-cap upon the pate. Oil and balsam upon the skin protects and adds a pleasing fragrance. Thus attired, I was able to walk abroad in the day, going to and fro upon the earth, at will.

In Southwark I bought a secluded stone and timber house with a deep cellar, established my own privy estate in the Shadow, and lived deliciously. Would'st thou not? What greater oyster could'st thou desire? Blood is the wine of the spirit. Quaff lasciviously from that warm crimson river, and here I quote my master Vornic:

Let flood of Pleasure drown thy brain. Be wanton, and without the merest touch of remorse or compunctious shrinking from felicity. It is yours. Take it. For a Shadow is opposite to humanity and, my word on't, privileged over them. They are but provender. Beef-witted dolts lulled by ale and snoring in swinish sleep, nature's weeds, blood bubbles to be plucked like grapes.

But take this admonition: they despise and will destroy our faction, with spike or beheading or burning, and you must take pains to remain disguised amongst 'em and lie low.

For this, helpers are requisite. Wisely pick familiars—many are called, but few chosen. I recruited a sharp-toothed young rogue named Stout to be my steward and daylight agent. With lure of gold and a few drops of my blood in his cider, he fell prostrate and called me Master; and thereafter did my bidding without flinching, a fine accomplice to my dark business.

The English climate is melancholic, foggy, and raw. Tyrant Sun is muffled and pale, the skies seldom azured. London's great smoky chaos smothers light, and I did thrive there.

In Southwark, revels and masques abounded, like the *Carnavale di Venezia*. I did wander there happily amid brothels, taverns, markets-places, and bear pits; I haunted theatres, Rose, Globe, and Swan, and caught my blood-conies among the crowd.

At the Mermaid tavern I mingled with the *cavalieri ladri* of the Stage who connived, wrangled, and stole freely from one another and traded gossip like a gaggle of Winchester Geese. Much did I learn of stage device and showplace tricks. There did I meet sweaty Shakespeare, the great conduit of others' works; and Christopher Marlowe, pretty Kit, that Hylas for whom Hercules might weep. One night, on the stalk, I drank my Rhenish diluted with a tincture of blood from a dainty glass vial I carried. This Kit noted with a flash of mocking merriment.

"O, most delicate devil art thou, Giles!"

"Devil I am," I said. I desired to toy and trade wit with him, and he with me.

"Do say! A devil thou art?" Kit laughed. "Methinks more the fraud."

"No, I attest, I am one of that legion of night devils."

"How comes it then, devil, that thou art out of hell?"

"Tut, tut, tut, Why, this is hell," I said, "nor am I out of it."

"I see not Hell. I sniff not Hell nor feel its fire. What is this insensible Hell that insteeps thee, Giles?"

"Hell," I said, "hath no limits. Where I am is hell, and where hell is must I ever be. When all the world dissolves, and every creature shall be purified, all places shall be hell that are not heaven."

"Come, come," says Kit. "I think hell's a fable."

"Blasphemers!" A gorbellied knave in a black suit scowled over his bowl of boiled mutton and stood, incensed. "A pox o' your tongues for speaking so profanely!"

I laughed at him. His choler boiled, his face glowing-hot red, the very likeness of a roasted crab.

"I do warn you, sir," he said.

"Pah! What cannon of bombast is this?"

"An enforcer of decorum," replied Kit, "and tongue-wagger of cen-sure. A miser and Puritan diligently opposed to any mirth, his wit as shriv-eled as his cock. His name, I recall, Fartuous Something-Cutt."

"Fulke Nethercutt," declared our auditor, and he bellowed further dis-paragement, calling us unholy rogues and infidels, until Kit unsheathed a dagger. Then did Fulke Nethercutt pale and abandon his cold mutton and our company in distaste and strutted from the premises.

"Devil!" he pronounced me in parting.

"Peevish wretch," I said. "Good riddance of you."

Kit stole my words and dropped them wantonly in one of his plays but that diminished him not in my affection. I did fancy making Kit my famil-iar. To that endeavor, I dispensed drops of my blood in his wine but to ill effect. Contrarious Kit, wayward Kit; he would not be governed, and my blood drew him not to me but made him more choleric and unsteadfast. Poor Kit! He became snared in a ragged knot of conspiracy, the nature of which I do not untangle, and foul agents of the Privy Council murdered him in Deptford on false pretext over money. But this is mere digression from my history.

In Southwark, with delight, I played the Mountebank and engaged in *praestigiosis*, conjuring entertainments for the crowd. I beguiled with osten-tation, shows, pageants, fireworks, harlotry; hired wenches to dance, strumpets to strump, jugglers to juggle, and musicians to amuse with trum-pet, sackbut, fife, and psalterie. I sold charms and herbs and elixirs from my dark apothecary. Ingenious tricks I devised, for the rabble would pay money to gape at a three-headed ape, or the relic of Mary Magdalene's foot might they kiss. The wretches clustered; from the thus congealed mass of folly, I would pick the ones to be bled. Stout, playing the Host of the spectacles, would pluck them out and lure them away with a promise of a fortune or a grimoire by which they might cast spells or love charms. And into my privy audience chamber they did march. Yea, to be bled but never turned, for I needed that crimson provender but not competitors for it. I would leave them drained, pale and brainsickly; and reft of memory of their abuse.

Stout would lead them away like lost lambs as the dismal sun crept over the roof ridges. "Here's sixpence you were promised," he would say with a shoulder-clap to send them shuffling away. "Dismiss you now to home or hovel. Tarry not hereabout. Begone, begone!"

My dog-fox Stout proved an able actor as well. He could himself amaze and enthrall hearers with scenes recited from *Tamburlaine* or *Hieronimo is Mad Again*, like unto an epitome of Burbage. In long attendance to me, Stout played many parts; steward, sergeant-at-arms, factor—though with greedy touch, he commonly pocketed coins and cheated my purse. But I let this pass, for he was a serviceable blood-tapster and bawd.

Of wenches he procured, my favorite was dark-eyed Peg. Abducted from the seraglio of an alehouse, had something of the Gypsy or Spanish *mujer* about her; her blood pepper-gingerbread to taste. She too became my familiar, my raven-haired she-thrall and love.

I did prosper in Southwark. The globe whirls, years accrued, and times change. Contention arises. Mischance lurks and waits upon its sharp revenge. Upon a fatal day in March, Elizabeth expired, without issue or heir. Her cousin James ascended to the throne. Witch-hunter James, King of Scotland, Scourge of Satan, who in Scotland had taken delight to be present at the examination of witches and saw to the torture and hanging of several hapless hags. And the lordly monarch did publish a book he wrote, *Daemonologie*, to delineate the Dark Arts and condemn its vile base practisers.

Upon a fateful day in July, I was out in the light, accoutred against the baleful sun, to acquire balms and necessaries, when I was accosted by a black blot of a man who splintered from a larger blot of blackcoats to strut toward me particularly in the market-place crowd.

"Sir! Do I know you?" He eye-strained to examine me, attent as a vulture. "Aye, we are met before-time."

"Not so." I resolved I would be calm and not vexed by this contumelious creature. "You err, sir."

"Why dost thou wear dark spectacles in the shade and heavy attire on a warm day? Strange. What hast thou to hide from the sun?"

"Tut! Impertinency, sir! Who is't addresses me?"

"One who would root out all devils from England. One who opposes all witchcraft and witchconsulting, sorcery, conjuration, heresy, necromancy, idolatry, revels, impiety, whoring, Papistry, Satanic subscription, demi-devils, and dark dealing with evil and wicked spirits. Must all—all, I affirm—by the roots be hewn and fed to the flames."

"Whew! You admit yourself much timber to hew and burn."

"Rotten timber," he replied. "Know me by the name Fulke Nethercutt. Thou art Giles Scaife. Thou did'st haunt the Mermaid and boast of being a devil, and I decipher the stench of evil about thee, Giles Scaife. Thou art a sorcerer and canker-blossom."

"Thou art an ass," I said. As I turned away, the knave clutched my cloak.

Nethercutt shouted OK alarm to his Puritan companions and the jostling crowd, who love an extempore riot as much as a hanging and quartering. "Here's a demon in disguise! Seize him! Ungarment him!"

I sped away, quicker and nimbler than the knotgrass of my pursuers. A close 'scape from death by dread sunshine. I would have blotted out the knave Nethercutt then and there with a thrust of my blade, but Blithe Giles has learned to do nothing rash. Best to lie low and bide time. To sanctuary and comfortable coffin, did I fly.

But Fulke Nethercutt, persistent as an ulcer, inquired further after me through Southwark. For the knave was agent of a puritanical faction, with many high-placed members, that hunted witches and miscreants, and would purify all England. Nethercutt's rancorous spite against me remained unbated and unsatisfied. He importuned, he bribed, he threatened, but discovered nothing of my whereabouts, for I do not advertise my sanctuary. Safe in the shadows I remained.

Until I was betrayed.

And that brief chronicle is played thus:

SCAIFE UNDONE BY IGNOMINIOUS TREASON

Enter Fulke Nethercutt in his Study.

FULKE   O Lord, gracious Lord, preserve my rational and immortal soul; buttress my courage that I may contend with iniquity; and giveth me a deeper repentance, a horror of sin and its infection; and help me to chastely flee its approach, and relieve the concup'scible, intemperate lust that doth plague me. Mercy!

Knocking at door. Enter Servant to Nethercutt.

FULKE   What is't?

SERVANT   Sir, petitioners seek audience. They say they have information regarding your adversary, Giles Scaife.

FULKE   Aye, bring them forth.

Exit Servant.

Enter Stout and Peg, wretched, penitent, and disheveled.

FULKE   Speak, man. What is thy name?

STOUT   Francis Stout, may it please your honor, and she be Margaret Addlecock.

Peg curtsies.

FULKE   *(verting his gaze)* Cover thy eye-offending bosom, harlot.

Peg wraps scarf around bosom.

FULKE   Better, better. Speak then, Francis Stout. What intelligence have you of the accursed Giles Scaife?

STOUT   Giles Scaife is a fiend, sir! An unnatural thing! A breeder of dire events! A toadstool! The devil's nephew!

FULKE   Yes, yes. I suspected such already.

STOUT   A false cockleshell effigy of a man, void and empty! A defiler of all virtue and modesty! A deformity! Inhuman wretch! A blood ravening caterpillar!

FULKE   Cease! Waste not my time with prating. News, man, what news?

STOUT   We twain, Peg and me, know where Giles Scaife can be found and by what devices destroyed.

FULKE   Misdoubt I must. How knowest thou? Well? Wherefore standest thou silent? Speak.

STOUT   We confess, sir. We're base slaves o'the fiend.

PEG   *(swooning)* O, horrid, horrid fiend!

FULKE   Slaves? How is this?

STOUT   *(catching Peg's fall)* He beguiled us with his dark craft, like unto foolish children easily led astray or lambs libertined.

PEG   I am a temple of woe!

STOUT   Constrain us, he did, to unnatural acts and deeds of dark malice. We desire to be full enfreedom'd from wickedness and repent of our brutish and sinful acts.

PEG   *(in tears)* I wish me to enter a convent and atone for my shame.

STOUT   There's worse, sir, beastly worse, egregious evil worse, sir. I shudder and shrink to speak it. Scaife's a drinker of blood.

FULKE   Zounds, the horror, the horror!

PEG   *(standing)* See what the hobgoblin done to me. Oft-times he hath abused me and milked me for blood. Here, touch 'em. Please, touch.

Peg disrobes to display bite marks and scratches on neck,
shoulder, and bosom.
Fulke examines and touches her skin softly.

FULKE   Infamy! Unholy! Foul!

PEG   Stings too.

FULKE   Giles Scaife shall be hanged!

PEG   But your hand is gracious and godly, m'lord. Like a balm. I'm soothed.

Fulke comforts her.

STOUT   Pardon, sir, pardon, but you cannot hang the devil; his neck is stretch-proof, and he'd surely laugh at the gallows. Howbeit, he may be destroyed otherwise; only a pike piercing his evil heart will suffice.

FULKE   That is hard and hazards the doer of the deed in close combat.

STOUT   Yea, a queasy question be't to o'erpower him. In the black night, the bloodsucker goes abroad in search of innocent blood, and armipotent he is, strong as an hundred Turks. But in daylight, he's weak and debile, and perforce must slumber. At such times he is no more invulnerable than a mewing kitten. And Stout knoweth where the slugabed of Satan lurks in the day.

FULKE   Where? Where? Say!

STOUT   I shall say.

FULKE   Then say!

STOUT   An' it please your honor, so Peg and me may start lives fresh and repent of our sins, our redemption rests conditionally upon recompense.

FULKE   Aye, liberal reward shall be yours.

STOUT and PEG   Thank you, sir. O, thank you.

FULKE   Now say.

STOUT   Giles Scaife keeps a house in Blifilbugge.

FULKE   Blifilbugge? Strange, I know it not.

STOUT   It lieth between Green Shambles and Bloodknock Fringe.

FULKE   I had never heard of these places!

PEG   O, sir, London is vasty deep, with many winding nooks and hiding purlieus. But please, sir, my wounds ache, and your touch doth console me.

STOUT   No matter, sir. When the time is ripe, I will take you there. Stout now shall make haste, and determine the coast is clear, and return to guide you to where the creeping villain hides from the Sun.

FULKE   Make speed, Stout. The urgent cause demands celerity. I'll have the abominable monster dispatched to Hell before Sundown.

STOUT   Yes, sir! Swift as a greyhound I'll be.

Exit Stout, with celerity.

PEG   Might I stay, m'lord, kind sir, compassionate sir? I am much fatigated and weak with hunger and loss of precious blood and am giddy for lack of sleep.

FULKE   Thine pale and wan cheeks testify distress, and your plight stirs the pity of my heart. Aye, by all means, aye, I would have thee stay and be refreshed and fed and bathed and put to bed. Take my hand, sweet child.

Exeunt Fulke and Peg.

And thus, it went; the conspiracy hatched and in motion.

I did sleep sound and unawares in fragrant cedar box in the confines of my cellar after a night of fine and full feeding. *Avere l'abbiocco,* as the Italians say of their after-feast naps. Hours remained until sunset.

Then did the stone door open slowly, without scrape or sound, and Stout in foul treachery lead Nethercutt and his priestly cohorts into my privy chamber, under torches and cobwebs.

Silent, silent as stone they crept to my secret noontide bed behind damasked curtains. Stout pulled the curtains.

"'Tis as I told," whispered Stout, and drew the dagger.

"Proceed," said Nethercutt. He and his company of Puritans murmured prayers, the buzz of the holy.

Stout plunged the dagger. And as I have foretold, after torment and agony, my spirit hovered, observant. A paltry young Puritan took violently ill and ran; his fellows stood firm.

"Ere ends this fiend," said Stout.

"Be it done, and gramercy," said Nethercutt. "His head I'll have. See to it."

"Then am I paid for't?"

"You are paid," said Nethercutt and tendered the pouch filled with clinking coins, gold sovereigns. "We shall publish this; the Fiend is defunct and dead, his unholy terror bated, his evil soul consigned to Hell."

"The monster's head," Stout said, "I'll deliver to you tonight, and bury the guts in unsanctified ground with worms and serpents and toads."

"Offal concerns me not," replied Nethercutt. "We require no further particulars of the disposing. We are stifled with this noisome stench of sin and will leave this unholy place." With that, Fulke Nethercutt and his black woollen flock wheeled about conjointly, stiff and soldier-like, and departed.

At last, I stirred.

"The coast is clear, Master," whispered Stout.

Then I sat up and removed the false dagger and bloody tawdry-lace from around my neck.

"Well played, Stout," I said.

He bowed. "If't pleases you, Master, you played your part well too."

My performance as the Dying Hellbound Fiend did cozen the surly Puritan and his company. The dagger blade, a trifle for the stage; its blade did retract and cause no harm except to burst the bags of blood on my person and ruin my garments.

But for some few moments, my spirit did exit my carcass. It hovered about fairy-like over the scene and observed. A sort of flying trick taught me by my illustrious lord Vornic from his sorcery. Thus, did I accompany and witness Stout and Peg plot with Fulke Nethercutt, in accord with my plan and the lines I had writ for my vassals; and with great amusement I watched.

Stout that night did deliver a cunning wax effigy of my head, with ivory fangs, artificed over the skull of a beggar. Nethercutt and his black woollen confederates melted it in a furnace with grave and sanctimonious ceremony, never doubting its authenticity, or their virtue in ridding England of evil.

Upon the following Saturday Peg came trippingly back to me; scrubbed, perfumed, new-gowned, fed and fattened, hair combed and braided, and much sated.

"Master," says she, "I am a pirate."

"A she-pirate? How so?"

"I did make pillage of his honor, his pillicock, and his treasury and then sail straightway to your harbor. See here, the prize I took."

A clinking bag of gold sovereigns and crowns she brought, no cheap pilfering but a small fortune filched neatly from Fulke Nethercutt.

"Most excellent, wench," I said.

Dead I was to my enemies and in abundance of caution sought to remain that way to the Sun-boiled brains.

Now, prescience was another gift from my Master Vornic of Bogdania. The future groaned to show me the Puritans should anon ascend in power and influence; and bring about rancor and civil war, and the death of a king. A suppressive regiment would follow in England, with a ban upon theatre, games, whoring, and all revels; and witchfinders loosed upon the land. Environed by such foes, I could not endure, and resolved to seek a safer clime. Withal my affection for London, I chose vagabond exile in France, with my loyal servants, and established a new shadow estate there on the fringe of Paris. Cold farewell, England!

And in epilogue, to those who would join or are joined already with the Faction of Night, we happy few, we band of bloodsuckers, I leave you with the lesson:

Choose familiars wisely—
For they may save your bum

SEPARATION

BY MARTIN L. SHOEMAKER

I looked out across the Chicago skyline and over the darkened waves of Lake Michigan. There was no red in the sky yet. I still had time.

I turned away from the hotel room balcony door—and there she was. Of course I had seen no reflection in the glass. "Hello, Jane." I tried to keep the waver out of my voice.

"Hello, Kenneth." She spoke from the shadows. I couldn't see her teeth. "You hunted me down. You couldn't leave it alone, could you?"

"When could I ever leave you alone? I was there for school, I was there when you moved to the city, I was there..." I choked on the words.

"...for our wedding, and the house in Schaumburg, and the new job."

"And for... Larry." Our first miscarriage. We had stopped naming them after that. After the third, we had stopped trying.

She sighed and stepped closer, into the light from the hotel room entry. She looked... fuller. More appealing. Is this what death did to their kind? "Please, Kenneth," she said, "I want to forget all that. I *need* to forget."

"Is that why you went out?"

"I tried to talk to you, but you stopped listening."

"There was nothing left to say. We'd said it all."

"But I still had needs, Kenneth! Someone to listen. To... hold me close..."

"You're telling me that your bloodsucking lover *listens*?"

"It was different with Hans. He was... His eyes... They let me forget. For the first time."

"Yeah, they call it mesmerism. That's how *your* kind draw in your prey." It was a low comment. It tasted bitter in my mouth.

But she seemed not to notice my tone. "So you found me." She stepped closer and looked at the duffel bag at my feet. "Is that for me?"

I nudged the bag with my toe, and the wooden stakes within rattled. The mallet hung from my belt. "No. It's… I don't know. I didn't know who might be with you. If *he* might be with you."

She shook her head. "Hans loses interest once he converts you. And the others… They gave up on me. They didn't think I have what it takes to survive this… life. Maybe I'll show them!" Her voice had become shrill on that last line; but then she grew quieter. "But for now, I'm alone."

I shook my head. "I'm still here. Just like always."

She stepped fully into the light and grimaced. The bed lamp reflected from her fangs. "Are you, Kenneth? Are you here for me, or are you *hunting* me? How did you find me here?"

"It wasn't easy." I paused. Did I want to tell her all the old haunts I had visited, all the false trails before I found the hotel? Or might I need those secrets in the future?

What sort of question was that? She was my wife! Since when did I keep secrets from Jane?

But *was* she Jane? Or was Jane dead, and was I facing some demonic spirit?

She gave up on waiting for more of an answer. "So that's the way it is. We're still not talking, not really. Even in… Even in undeath, nothing has changed."

I shook my head. "*Everything* has changed, Jane. I… How can you say that? You're a God-damned vampire!"

"Damned…" She stepped closer, and I backed sideways a step, toward the corner. "Yes, damned. The Curse. And yet…"

"*And yet?* What can you say after that?"

She took another step; but this time I realized she wasn't coming for me. She was stepping towards the balcony door. "And yet the hurt is gone. Some of it. I can sleep at night. Well, at day. I don't need the pills now."

"But the pills were helping!"

"No, they weren't. They were helping *you*. You didn't have to listen to me mumble and cry in my sleep. They let *you* get rest, but never me. Not really. They just buried the problem. Like we buried Larry."

I stared at her, mouth agape. "You never told me that."

"I couldn't! Not then, that was part of the pain. You couldn't know how I felt."

"I lost babies too, you know."

"But you didn't carry them inside you! You didn't feel them grow, start to move. You didn't feel them... stop... You didn't... You didn't have to climb up on that table so the doctor could carve out the dead bodies."

"But I was there!"

She turned and looked at me with a weak smile on her face, lips closed. At least I couldn't see the fangs. "You were. And I know that wasn't easy for you. But it was a hundred times worse for me."

"Pain isn't measured like that! It's more than the physical, it was the death of hope! And then... And then losing you. Not all at once, not until the end. I lost you for four years as you grew distant and silent. Oh, you talked to the support groups, but never to me. Not really."

"Support groups..." She snorted. "They had nothing to offer me."

"You never gave them the chance. Lots of women in those groups—and men, too—found ways to move on. They didn't... They didn't go out..."

She looked out over the city. "Some of them did. More than you know, they would never tell you. But they told *me* stories in confidence..."

"I should've gone to the groups."

"You should have! You showed up a couple of times, and then you got 'too busy.' The husbands who *were* there, they seemed to understand. They listened. But the women who were alone, many of them were just as lonely as me. In fact, they... Some of them encouraged me."

"Encouraged you?"

"Encouraged me to go out. To find someone else, a new life. Make a clean break from the memories. Find myself, they said."

"Yeah." I tried to keep the edge out of my voice, but I failed. "That worked out really well, huh? You found this... What did you call him, Hans?"

She kept her eyes upon the darkened streets. I wished she would look at me, even though I wasn't sure what I'd see if she did. This was the same wall between us that we'd endured for two years before her... her... I couldn't even think the D word...

"Yes, Hans West," she said. "Though I don't think that's his real name. When you're... undead... you learn to change your identity a lot. Keep moving. Hunters are always after you." She leaned her forehead against the glass. "I never expected the first hunter to be my husband."

"I'm not hunting you."

She spun toward me, glaring. Her facial muscles were impossibly contorted and large, and her eyes glowed red. "And why not? *This* is what I am now, Kenneth! Your poor, pitiful little Jane is gone now, and all that's left is this!"

Without realizing it, I had backed up against the wall. I felt the rough wallpaper on the backs of my arms, and my right hand slid to the mallet. I was frightened, now that the truth was out in the open. We had gotten very good at ignoring truths, but we couldn't ignore this. Now I saw her as a vampire, and questions I had buried dug themselves out. "So have you… killed?"

Suddenly her face softened, almost back to her normal look. "Don't ask me that. Please." There was an awkward silence. Finally she broke it. "Not yet. I've hungered. I've… I've stolen. From small labs and clinics, sometimes you find blood in storage. It's easy for one of us to get into places like that. Those aren't *homes*, we don't need invitations. One of the others gave me tips before she abandoned me. If you only take a little from one place and don't revisit too often, the loss gets written off as a clerical error."

She looked in my eyes, defiant. "So I haven't killed. Yet. But it's only a matter of time, Kenneth. I'm feeling… almost feral."

"So it's true, then, that you can't enter a home without an invitation? Not even ours?"

"You're asking a lot of questions. Maybe you *want* to be a hunter? That would make you a feel like a man again, wouldn't it? You wouldn't be a nameless, faceless, childless drone slaving away in an insurance office. No, you'd be the famous hunter whose first kill was his own wife." She chuckled, and it was an ugly sound. "You'd hardly be the first. Most hunters start with a family member."

"I'm not a hunter!"

"Then why did you track me down?" She kicked the duffel bag, which still rested by the balcony door. "Why did you bring *these*?"

I feared this question more than I'd feared that visage. But I owed her an answer. "Because… Because I had to find you, had to get past any of *them* who might block my way to you. I wanted a chance to say goodbye."

More than a chuckle, this brought her a laugh, which sounded even more inhuman. Demonic.

And yet as she trailed off, there was an echo of her old laugh, that musical lilt that always made my heart light up. "You went to all this trouble for that?" She shook her head. "No, it won't work that way. You could've said goodbye two years ago. Three. But you wouldn't. It would've been so easy, but you wouldn't."

I spread my hands and shrugged. "I love you. I couldn't abandon you."

"You couldn't, could you?" She turned back to the window. "And you can't, even now. You won't be able to say goodbye."

"I will!"

"No, you won't. If you tracked me down here, you'll do it again. Over and over. You won't be able to let go, no matter how much it hurts you."

"And you?"

"I don't know." She sighed. "I don't know if the memories and what they do to you will get through to me, or whether I'll get callous. Maybe after a few kills under my belt, I won't be able to feel the pain anymore.

"And eventually…" She glanced over at me. "Is that what you want? To join me?"

I shook my head. I wanted her so much, but not *that* much. I wanted the old Jane. "No. Not that. Never that."

She closed her eyes, and she took a deep breath. Was that just habit? Vampires shouldn't need to breathe, should they?

Then she turned away again. "It'll happen, you know. It's inevitable. The others tried to teach me: You kill your loved ones, or they kill you, no third choice under the Curse. You'll keep following me, and someday… Someday I'll feed. Oh, I won't convert you, I wouldn't do that against your will."

"So that's it, then? That's our future, and it's only a matter of time?"

She shook her head. "A matter of time… No, there's one other way. We both know it."

I felt the mallet, and I glanced down at the duffel bag. "Jane, I can't. Maybe one of *them*, but not you. I can't."

"You don't have to," she said, with a voice suddenly almost tender. "Like I said, a matter of time. It won't be long now."

Then I realized what she was saying. The light had changed gradually, but I could see her face clearly now. Her eyes closed, and she faced the big window on the east.

Could I stop her? She was inhumanly strong and determined, but I could try. I rushed her.

But without even opening her eyes, she thrust out her left hand against my chest. With that single gesture she tossed me back against the wall.

No, she wouldn't be stopped.

I'd come to say goodbye, but now there was something more important to say. "Tell Larry his papa loves him."

The sun broke over the distant shores of the lake. Jane started to smoke.

Love is a weapon you carry in your heart

Rid yourself of it, or it can strike
at any time from any distance
…and it is sharper than any stake

PART 3 – HIDING IN PLAIN SIGHT

You may have wondered why we stay hidden. After all, if we're stronger, faster, and longer lived, why not just take over? In some ways, many of us have set ourselves up to pull important strings—albeit not publicly.

The brashness of youth would point to glory and fame as evidence of success, but those of us who live truly well also know the pitfalls of stealing the limelight. It is difficult enough to sleep through the day and subsist on blood when the average person would recoil from such practices; imagine becoming the target of scrutiny and suspicion while having to hide such habits.

The question then becomes "How?" How can you both live in the world and hide from it?

After all, bloodlust doesn't go away, nor does the news media, nor do the hunters even if they may be dubbed crazy by the mainstream. Even trusted companions can only clean up so much, so, my sibling in the blood, the responsibly falls to you to make clear guidelines and have the discipline to maintain them.

Here are a few helpful reminders to get you started…

No Nibbling on the Neighbors

by Julia V. Ashley

The bullfrog living in the reeds off Hamilton's deck belched out his pronouncement that twilight had arrived, and that he was in the market for a girl frog. He must be particular, Hamilton thought, because he belched out the same tune night after night, but still hadn't found the right lady.

Hamilton didn't blame him. The vampire had likewise grown pickier in his old age. During the 70s, he'd have sipped on anyone too stoned to care if a menacing shadow followed them home. Nowadays, he craved a specific diet, and his neighborhood offered less variety than he liked. But he made the best of it. There were perks to living on the edge of society with a small group of good-natured misfits as neighbors.

The swollen summer sun flattened itself against the horizon. Time to hunt for dinner. The Sunset Grill would have an influx of new appetizers within the hour, and Hamilton usually found it best to be at the bar as they arrived. The deck of his houseboat rocked almost imperceptibly as he stepped from it onto the dock. From the murky water of the reservoir beneath his home, a pair of eyes broke the surface armored by scaley ridges. Slitted pupils rolled in his direction. One winked conspiratorially.

As the alligator's snout emerged, a shriek of delight came from the houseboat docked opposite Hamilton's.

Hamilton leisurely turned his head, consciously moving slow enough not to draw suspicion from the curvy woman with dyed magenta hair. "Mabel," he called to his neighbor. "One would think you hadn't seen an alligator at the end of our dock every day for a month."

"Of course I have, silly. But I finally caught it grinning at you. I've been suspecting as much for a while, but this is the first time I am 100% certain that gator just gave you a sly smile. What have the two of you been up to?" she asked with a cheeky smile of her own.

Hamilton went utterly still for a beat too long. Mabel's eyes narrowed. She'd gone from studying the fit of his T-shirt across his broad chest to scrutinizing his expression warily. Hamilton forced himself to relax.

Of course, she hadn't meant anything by it. It was just her way of flirting. Not that she had her eye on Hamilton in particular. She just acted out of habit, her auto response to any male over 6 feet tall and not obviously unemployed. Hamilton wasn't sure how he made the cut, seeing as he didn't leave home by day. Perhaps she assumed he had a night job, which wasn't far from the truth.

He forced himself to respond with a seductive leer. "You know us boys don't kiss and tell." She giggled in response and fluttered her fingers in farewell before ducking back into the depths of her cheap, vinyl-sided houseboat.

Hamilton didn't look down on synthetic materials. Well, that was a blatant lie. He obviously did. Who with any taste wouldn't? And Hamilton had impeccable taste.

Speaking of which, he was getting a bit peckish. He turned to walk down the boardwalk connecting the boat slips. A "THWAP" from behind him resulted in a spray of water across the back of his custom jeans, personally fitted by Calvin Klein himself. He glared at the alligator as the smell of swamp water filled his nostrils.

"I told you, not here," he said testily.

"Talking to him don't do you no good," came a smoker's voice from the dark interior of the houseboat adjacent to Mabel's. "Seems somebody's been feeding him. They're just like dogs. You feed them and they never go away." Steel-gray eyes glinted, focusing on him, as if the old Marine knew Hamilton could see into the shadows.

Charlie kept a close watch over the small floating community docked along the boardwalk. Maybe too close of a watch. He still felt it was his duty to protect the weak and defenseless. Hamilton gave him a single nod as he passed. The two of them, an old vet and an older vampire, held a tenuous truce. Neither asked about the other's past. Nor their present, for that matter.

Hamilton respected Charlie, who lived in a floating steel box painted the aircraft-carrier gray. No aesthetic value, but not a spot of rust or debris to be seen. He cared for it as if he planned on living a long time and had no notion to moving. Hamilton understood the one and envied the other.

He waved at his nextdoor neighbors Joe and Amy, who proudly positioned a third metal flamingo on the deck of their houseboat.

Hamilton knew he'd have to move soon, but he liked to plant roots for as long as possible. For mobility, he'd chosen a houseboat instead of a garish RV. His home was built with flawless craftsmanship like a fine piece of teak furniture.

The wood, smooth as silk, had aged from a honey-gold to a silvery gray. Ebony accents cut clean horizontal lines from the gunwale to the one-inch pinstriping between side planks. A copper-clad arch framed the entry. And vintage brass portlights filled the interior with sunlight by day while reclaimed lanterns warmed it by night.

A piece of art.

As the moon rose, Hamilton's tooled black leather cowboy boots crunched across the shale drive connecting the docks to the parking lot of the Sunset Grill and the RV Park beyond. Steam rose into the dark sky from the exhaust stack over the kitchen, carrying the smell of fried food. It left a coating of aged grease on Hamilton's tongue. He'd wash it away soon enough, after he chose a succulent tourist to escort back to his place for a drink.

A midnight blue Mitsubishi Eclipse blocked the steps to the front door. Its license plate read "B-I-T-E-M-E". Choosing to ignore the crass humor, Hamilton stepped around the car and went inside. The lights shone in halos through the haze of cigarette smoke. The Sunset Grill on the backside of the Reservoir was one of the last bastions of reprieve for the pack-a-day smoker. They came for a few smokes, a few beers, and good company.

A cursory survey of the clientele told Hamilton that he'd have to make some compromises on his diet that evening. He had his preferences, but they were all subject to his primary rule, which was—

"Who the hell is that?" he asked, spotting a stranger at the bar, who clearly wasn't your typical RV tourist just passing through.

Hamilton's attention was hooked on this devil grinning like, well, a vampire at a human buffet. Half a head taller than everyone else at the bar, the rangy male wore jeans and a rumpled button-down. His shaggy hair almost hid the feral glint in his eye.

Sliding onto the stool next to the newcomer, Hamilton spoke under his breath. "What are you doing hunting my territory?"

The other vampire's grin grew even wider, exposing sharp canines. "Who says I'm hunting?"

"That hungry look in your eye," answered Hamilton, as he lifted a finger to get the bartender's attention. A lanky woman in tight jeans and a black apron came up to take their order. "Two Blue Moons," Hamilton said.

"Nope. None for me, thanks." The second vampire winked at the server, who rolled her eyes and poured Hamilton's beer.

Hamilton handed her a 10 and waited for her to walk away before muttering, "You need to order something, whether you drink it or not. You look suspicious."

The other vampire swiveled on his stool and put both elbows on the bar behind him. He gave a condescending smirk. His voice thick with attitude, he asked, "What do I care what these backwater people think? What're they gonna do? Shoot me?"

"I live here, and I would appreciate it if you followed some decorum while you're visiting," Hamilton said, pretending to take a sip of beer.

"See, that's your problem," the other vamp said. "You need to stay mobile. Keep moving. That's my first rule. Actually, it's my only rule. You keep moving and you can do pretty much whatever you want. I got myself a decked out 45-foot Foretravel Motorcoach Presidential Series Realm FS605 to travel in style. I never did understand your kind that liked to plant themselves in one place. How you get away with that, anyway?"

Without waiting for an answer, the stranger stood and started to follow a young woman, taking a tray of beer from the bar. Hamilton put a hand on his arm, stopping him. "Leave them alone. She lives around here."

"Not my problem," he said, but sat back down. He rolled his neck, cracking several vertebrae before he turned back around to the bar. "Name's Leonard," he said, holding up of finger to order a beer.

"Hamilton."

Leonard snorted in response and gave the bartender a second wink as he took his drink without paying. "Might as well run a tab. If I'm gonna pretend to drink, I might as well pretend to pay, too."

Hamilton knew this vampire's type. No respect for rules and order. Flashy, daring the humans to catch on. "Let me guess, the blue Eclipse with the vanity plate out front is yours?"

Leonard gave a lazy smile. "Yep. And the fussy cream-colored Cadillac? That'd be yours?"

"It's got a big trunk in case I decide to eat on the go," Hamilton explained. He shouldn't have been surprised that the vampire had pegged him so easily. It's not as if Hamilton hid his meticulous nature.

"Hm," Leonard nodded. "And the custom-made boat at the end?"

"That too." Hamilton took another sip of his beer, then set it down precisely in the center of the coaster, which he turned square to the edge of the bar.

"So why you hiding out in a floating tomb, acting like prey instead of a predator?"

"Not hiding, just enjoying getting to know some people for once. We look out for each other here. It's nice." Hamilton realized, as he said it, how true it was. He appreciated having people ask how he was doing. And when he asked about them, he liked the long-winded gossip session about who slept with whom, or who wanted to but hadn't gotten up the courage yet. Trivial human lives lived in stereo around him.

Leonard sneered. "Yep, prey mentality, sticking to the flock. You gotta own the apex predator nature."

That got under Hamilton's skin. Leonard was obviously a newbie vamp who had not learned the nuances of a long-lived afterlife. More than eat-and-run, Hamilton knew you needed to savor it. So he chose to educate rather than judge. He prided himself on making good choices.

"My one rule, or rather my first rule," he began his instruction, "is 'No nibbling on the neighbors.' It allows you to stay in one place longer, enjoy the ambiance."

"Ambiance? Here? Yeah, right." Leonard shoved his beer back, sloshing foam over the side, sending a rivulet of beer towards Hamilton's glass, and folded his arms on bar. "So, if that's your first rule, how many you got?"

Hamilton moved his coaster out of the stream of spilled beer. "Enough to keep me comfortable and keep my prospects open."

Leonard let his eyes roam over the other clientele at the bar as he began listing off questions for Hamilton to answer. "Sunscreen?"

"Don't find it necessary since I stick to the customary evening hours, but if needed, no lower than SPF 70."

Another grunted response from Leonard followed by, "EpiPen?"

"For what?" Hamilton asked as he leaned forward to see who Leonard was making eye contact with. A heavily muscled man in his late 20s, early 30s, sporting a tank top at least two sizes too small was making eyes back at the other vampire. Hamilton let it go. That guy wasn't local.

"I've heard it works for garlic allergies," Leonard said, tipping his beer to the muscleman.

"Hm," Hamilton mused. "Does it work?"

Leonard shrugged. "Never needed it myself." He caught the bartender's attention and ordered a drink for the muscleman, who then waved an appreciation. "I do like my dinner fed a Keto diet. That one looks like he's a strict acolyte, a serious Bacon Diet jock, if I've ever seen one." He stopped just short of licking his lips.

Repulsed by the vampire's barbarian hunting style, Hamilton started to get up, but Leonard waved him back in his seat.

"Don't leave now. We got us a civilized conversation going on. It's not often I meet someone to trade notes with."

Reluctantly, Hamilton sat back down.

"I bet you like them voluptuous and juicy." Leonard eyed a pair of women coming through the door and heading for the pool tables. Right behind them, his neighbor Mabel with her magenta hair came in, tugging a handsome, if haggard, guy behind her. No one Hamilton knew. He must be a transient, like Leonard, but hopefully less lethal.

Even though Hamilton found Leonard unsavory, the exchange of information still intrigued him. He would've never thought of using an EpiPen. "No. If I can find them, I prefer a vegan dish," he said.

Leonard blanched. "Stringy and tough?"

"I feel the extra fiber helps clean out my system, keeping me fit longer."

"Not savory enough for my taste." As if summoned, the muscleman walked their way. Before he could get there, Leonard asked a final question. "So, tell me, if you stay in one place, what do you do with your leftovers?"

Hamilton smirked, knowing even Leonard would appreciate his answer. "The alligators are particularly hungry around these parts."

Leonard's eyebrows shot up, and he roared with laughter. "Now you're talking." He clinked Hamilton's glass with his own, drained it just for show, and said, "Good luck with that first rule of yours. Hope it works out for you." Then he walked off with his arm casually slung over the muscleman's shoulder.

Hamilton really did not like that vampire. Low class and low standards.

Annoyed by the encounter, Hamilton finished his Blue Moon and ordered the hoppiest IPA the Sunset Grill had on tap. The bitter hops matched his mood. It's not like he didn't enjoy variety. But a civilized vampire had to live by a strict set of rules if he planned on remaining undead. And the first rule was the most important, if he wished to remain in one place for as long as possible.

After nearly a century, he'd grown bored with the transient lifestyle that most vampires lived to avoid human notice. Even here, on the fringes of society, Hamilton truly enjoyed getting to know the humans as individuals. Maybe he was just nostalgic, and their petty wants and their insignificant crises reminded him of the days when such things seemed all important. The days when he slept above ground.

Whatever the reason, he was not about to let this Leonard throw him off course.

As he pondered the heartburn Leonard would probably face after draining the muscleman, a well-kept woman in skinny jeans and an Animals Killing People band top sat down next to him. She ordered a Corona and fiddled with the menu before asking, "Do they serve anything here not made of meat and grease?"

It took Hamilton a second to realize she was talking to him. "I think they serve pickles."

She laughed. "I guess I shouldn't be surprised that a bar at the edge of the swamp doesn't have the most health-conscious choices." She folded the menu, thanked the bartender for her beer, and took a cautious swallow as if concerned the glass might be coated and animal fat.

"I don't suppose you're a vegan?" Hamilton attempted to keep the eager edge out of his voice.

She shook her head. "No, I'm not that dedicated. But I try to do better. Make better choices." She trailed off and began picking at the beer nuts in a bowl by the napkins. Her shoulders drooped and her face fell. She seemed lost in her own thoughts.

Hamilton had learned the signs of the downcast and knew how to use them to his advantage. "Are we still talking about food?" he asked, sipping his beer and donning a thoughtful expression for effect.

She gave a self-deprecating chuckle. "No, I guess we're not. I'm better off," she said without explanation. They silently drank their beers next to one another, accompanied by the sounds of the bar. The clink of billiard balls being racked up and the crack of a cue ball. A raucous argument over local sports. Drunken laughter.

Hamilton waited patiently, and it paid off. The woman cut her eyes to him and gave a longing smile. "I guess I'm on my own now. I can do what I want, when I want."

This was music to Hamilton's ears. Perhaps she wasn't a vegan, but she tried, and that was something. Even better, she was on her own and looked lonely. Just passing through, he'd bet. A perfect prospect for his charms. See, Leonard, he thought, there is a civilized way to do things.

"Hamilton," Hamilton said, holding out his hand. She took it with a look of surprise.

"Hamilton, really? That's your name?" He nodded. "I'm Kate. Katherine, but everyone calls me Kate except my mother, but she's gone now. So, no home to go to." She cocked her head in resignation.

On her own. No home. His mouth watered in a feral way that used to embarrass him, but he'd grown used to it. As he ran through his repertoire of opening seduction lines, he missed the beginning of her next statement. But something about it had set off a warning bell. "Excuse me, what was that?"

"I said, I'm staying at my cousin Mabel's. She has a houseboat down at the docks. My ex, Wayne—he's only met her once at our wedding, and he was too drunk to remember her. 'Been out all night, pre-celebrating,' he'd said. Like that made him stumbling down the aisle okay." She finished her beer in one swallow and looked at the bottom of the glass as if expecting to find a good excuse for her bad choices.

Speaking of bad choices, Hamilton could feel it. He was about to make one of his own.

Don't do it, he told himself. *No Nibbling On Neighbors.* But she wasn't really a neighbor. Yeah, yeah, close enough. The jibes from that low class Leonard had obviously gotten to him, if he was even considering it.

But he was hungry, and she was very nearly vegan or as close as he would get tonight. Plus, he was feeling a little reckless. Maybe Leonard had a point. He was not prey that belonged to a flock. Vampires were meant to hunt. If that prey lived close at hand, all the better.

Before she could collect herself, Hamilton leapt. "I have some quinoa back at my place," he said. She winced. "And wine," he added with a chuckle.

"Now, you're talking." She hopped off her barstool. He settled up their tabs and followed as she deftly wove between the tables and out the front door.

Mercury vapor lights in the parking lot gave Kate a deathly pallor as she walked arm-in-arm with Hamilton back to the boat dock. Sounds of a party drifted from the RV park. A wild holler was followed by the sound of broken glass and cheers. Hamilton couldn't help but wonder if Leonard would get reckless and let his dish scream for his life, and if he did, would it even be heard over the mayhem nearby?

By contrast, the dock was serene in its silence. Charlie's door was open, but there was no movement from within. Mabel's boat was dark.

Kate caught him looking and said, "She's out for the night. She told me to have a good time. That she planned to do the same. She won't notice if I don't come back . . . until late."

This could work. If he was careful. The glint of ridged eyes rising from the water assured him. He gave the gator a nod. Teamwork.

Kate practically crawled into Hamilton's lap as he deepened their kiss, leaving her breathless. He lifted her wavy hair to gently nip at the tender skin just beneath her ear. He breathed in the floral aroma of her perfume, the lingering smell of shampoo, and the more subtle scent of warm blood flowing through the vein running up the side of her neck. She groaned, and he wrapped an arm around her waist, securing her tight to his chest.

She tipped her chin to give him a clear shot to her jugular, and he took it. Clamping down on her throat, his canines punctured the skin. Startled, she cried out in ecstasy and anguish as the blood burst from the vein and into his mouth. After a moment's struggle, useless against Hamilton's strength, she relented, curving her body into his.

He suckled, and she moaned.

It was perfect. Rules be damned. That is, until his door crashed open.

A man in stained jeans, with wild wiry hair and wilder eyes, filled Hamilton's entryway. A shotgun slung low at his waist. "Katie!"

"Wayne?" Katie shoved back from Hamilton, the trance he'd held over her broken. A rivulet of blood dribbled down the side of her neck. Seeing the red stain spread across her Animals Killing People top, she started to scream.

Ignoring Katie's pleas for help, Hamilton asked, "Wayne? As in your Ex, Wayne?"

Wayne's attention snapped from Kate and the blood running into the neck of her blouse and onto Hamilton. The wild-haired Wayne drew the gun up to his shoulder. "Ex? That what she told you? Kate, that what you told him?"

Before Hamilton or Kate could come up with a reasonable excuse— or even a lame one— Wayne fired.

Buckshot tore through the cabin. Glass shattered. Wood splintered. And Kate screamed.

Lowering the shotgun enough to see over the barrel, Wayne gaped at the damage he'd done. Laid back against Hamilton's chest, Kate gasped for breath. She clapped a hand to her throat and another to her midriff. Blood gushed between her fingers and stained the front of her flimsy, flowered blouse.

This time, Hamilton was ashamed of the way his mouth watered at the sight. All that lovely nearly, vegan blood wasted. He took a moment to inspect himself, finding two holes in the shoulder of his T-shirt, before shoving Kate aside and coming to his feet with a growl.

Wayne's mouth snapped shut as he took aim and fired again, straight at the center of Hamilton's chest. Dark blood oozed sluggishly from a dozen holes. Hamilton ignored the inconvenience. How dare this puny human come into his home and ruin his dinner?

Hamilton crouched to pounce on the man when Wayne's head snapped forward, then back again. A gaping wound blossomed where Wayne's nose had perched only a moment before. Wayne looked confused as the shotgun slipped from his limp fingers. He swayed as if trying to get his sea legs before falling to his knees.

On the deck stood Charlie, sighting a pistol at the back of Wayne's head, waiting as if to be sure his point-blank headshot had done its job. Once Wayne faceplanted onto the Italian rug, Charlie turned his attention to Hamilton, keeping both hands on his pistol, pointed at the floor but ready to raise.

"Sounded like there was some trouble over here," he said, cold steel eyes tracking Hamilton's every move.

"Yeah," Hamilton replied, unwilling to take his eyes from the Marine and his gun. Charlie's eyes flickered to Kate. She made short, sharp gasps for air as her eyes fluttered shut. Her hand slid from her neck, leaving finger trails of blood down her chest.

Hamilton knelt beside her, possibly moving too quickly to keep his human guise intact, but he was a little rattled. He leaned over Kate to hide the holes in the front of his shirt. Wounds that would have killed a human, but being pre-dead had its perks. He made a show of checking her pulse and whispering assurances. He knew better than to bring her back here, yet he'd done it, anyway.

Under Charlie's steady stare, Hamilton checked her pulse and swallowed the saliva that rose at the pungent smell of fresh blood. He was relieved to see the buckshot had ripped through the teeth marks. You would have to know what you were looking for to see the tear his incisors had made. From the look in Charlie's eyes, the old Marine *did* know what to look for.

The primal urge to lick the final dribbles of blood from the wound almost overtook Hamilton, but the Charlie casually aiming the pistol at his back was enough to reign in even the most animalistic instincts.

"Call an ambulance, the police, someone!" Hamilton donned a guise of disorientation and shock.

Sirens wailed nearby, interrupting his performance. A glance over his shoulder at Charlie told him the old man wasn't buying it, anyway. He cradled Kate to his chest in a show of affection, hoping her blood would disguise his own, and muttered, "That was fast."

Charlie glanced around the doorframe as his finger carefully disengaged from the pistol's trigger and applied its safety. Blue lights flashed behind him on the dock. "They were here tending to a rowdy bunch over at the RV park," Charlie explained. "Someone reported hearing a man screaming for his life and called the police on the crowd partying over there. Though I have my doubts about it being them."

Holding tight to Kate as she cooled in his grip, Hamilton asked, "How did you hear all that?" Charlie didn't answer. "Police scanner," Hamilton guessed. The Marine shrugged. Hamilton thought he better soften the situation in his favor before the police arrived.

As the Marine turned to leave, Leonard called after him. "Thanks, Charlie, for protecting the neighborhood. Once a soldier, always a soldier, right?"

"Marine," Charlie corrected him. He turned, exposing the edges of the Marine Emblem tattooed across his back, showing past his crisp white tank top.

"That's right, a sailor," Hamilton added lamely.

Charlie walked from the cabin with a loose stride, belying the fact that the man remained as alert as a water moccasin, waiting for you to take one step too close to strike. Police lights strobed, painting him blue, then leaving him in silhouette before he disappeared.

As soon as Charlie passed beyond Hamilton's line of sight, he jumped up, no longer worrying about moving it human speeds. He snatched on a pullover to hide the holes in his shirt and the quickly healing ones in his chest, then knelt back beside Kate. He had her in his arms, slowly rocking her back and forth by the time the first police officer reached the end of the dock.

"This is going to be a shit show," he mumbled into Kate's hair. "You gotta follow rules."

◆ ◆ ◆

After answering the same dozen questions over and over again, Hamilton left the policeman on his boat with the EMTs who had arrived soon after. The alligator must have smelled a smorgasbord on board. Its snout rose into the flashing lights, exposing a toothy grin.

"You eat when I eat." Hamilton turned his back to the beast and made his way up the boardwalk, leaving his houseboat and the corpses in the hands of the officials. As Hamilton passed, Charlie stepped out of the dark cavern of his boat, settled into a metal lawn chair, and started whittling what looked like the end of a snapped off broom handle.

Word must've reached Mabel. She rushed over from the Sunset Grill, teetering across the shale parking lot on pink stilettos. She reached the dock in time to see the EMTs rolling stretchers with the corpses of her niece and her nieces Ex down the boardwalk. All her houseboat neighbors but for Charlie and Hamilton were gathered at the end of the boardwalk. Half of them swarmed around her in a seemingly protective circle, talking on top of one another. Each eager to be the first to deliver the news. A distressed Jim lingered behind his wife as Amy pronounced the fatal sentence.

Mabel screeched, her hands fluttering around her mouth. She shook her head as if she could deny her enthusiastic informants. Hamilton went to comfort her, if only to avoid further questions from the police. The circle parted, allowing him in, the privilege afforded as her closest neighbor other than Charlie, who remained on his boat whittling and monitoring the commotion.

Hamilton drew Mabel into a hug. She flailed against his chest until her wails ceased. Clinging to Hamilton's freshly bloodied pullover, she rubbed tears and snot in as she spoke between sobs. "That Wayne. I never did trust him. I told Kate. I told her he ain't good for you. You gotta leave him alone. And she did she did at the end, but it was too late." Heaving sobs garbled the rest of her words as Hamilton patted her back.

Seeing a familiar face standing in the shadows between light poles, Hamilton passed Mabel off to a hovering flock of female neighbors and went to meet his fellow vampire.

Leonard grinned at him, a smudge of blood at the corner of his mouth. Hamilton gestured to his own cheek. Taking the hint, Leonard rubbed the dried blood onto his leather coat sleeve. "Doesn't look like that first rule of yours helped you much."

"That's because I broke it," Hamilton confessed, shaking his head.

"Were they at least vegan?"

"Nearly. What about yours?"

"Tasted like bacon." Leonard smacked his lips. "So," he drawled the word out, "You broke your fundamental rule for a *nearly* vegan."

"Yep," Hamilton said, shamefully.

Leonard gave a long whistle. "You keep your grave dirt in the hold of that houseboat of yours?"

"Yep." He sighed.

Leonard nodded toward the other end of the dock. "That one down there looks like he has plans."

Hamilton followed Leonard's line of sight. Charlie looked straight at them as if he could see them in the shadows. He made a last cut with his pocketknife, then held up a sharpened stake, testing the point with the tip of his finger, and nodded at the two vampires.

Leonard returned Charlie's nod, and the Marine retreated into the depths of his cabin. "I wouldn't be sleeping in that houseboat of yours anymore, if I were you."

"Nope." Hamilton cut Leonard a look without turning his head. Watching the police tape off the crime scene, Hamilton tried to absorb the fact that he was freshly homeless.

"Looks like you might have to try out my method. Much simpler. Just one rule."

"Keep moving," Hamilton parroted.

"That'd be it."

"Maybe I could get me one of those sleek Airstreams and have the inside customized."

"Sure you could. But you better think of something before morning."

The other vampire appeared to be waiting for it. So Hamilton went ahead and gave it to him. "I don't suppose you have a spare bunk in that motorcoach of yours?"

Leonard gave a self-satisfied grin. "I might, once I drop some ballast," he said, turning and heading back across the parking lot. He talked over his shoulder as he walked. "Better get going. Those neighbors you prided yourself in befriending are gonna be looking for you soon. And they're gonna have questions you can't answer, I bet." He laughed to himself.

They walked in the shadows at the perimeter of the parking lot, and a reptilian form lurched up the embankment from the reservoir. The alligator's claws scrabbled at the loose shale as it lumbered up to join the two men.

"Ah!" Leonard exclaimed. "Just the fellow I was looking for. You hungry?" The alligator gave him a grin. Leonard gestured for it to follow as they headed for the RV Park.

"I'm hungry, too," Hamilton grumbled petulantly.

"You," Leonard said, pointing a judgmental finger, "can feed yourself. I got no respect for someone who can't follow their own rules."

The alligator gave Hamilton a wink before waddling to catch up with Leonard.

Hamilton really did not like that guy.

No Nibbling on the Neighbors

Dawn of the Lizard Prince

by Fulvio Gatti

The third time the curly-haired young man enters my field of view, I know he *wants* to be seen. Right now, he's probably looking for an excuse to cover the bunch of sandy steps dividing us and try to talk to me.

I know better than to offer him one.

First, because I'm immortal, I've been both a queen and an assassin, so I should bother for inferior beings as much as a regular human cares for ants. If men sucked ants' blood, indeed, but you get the gist.

Second—oh, crap.

I've met his gaze—surprisingly deep eyes—and those nice full lips have smiled back. I can ignore it, but there is a sudden full drum orchestra playing in my chest, louder than the waves splashing over the nearby shore.

Shouldn't all be quiet, in my body?

Well, it's complicated.

I'm complicated.

During the centuries, I've tried to learn something about our physiology, but never fully understood if I'm more alive or more dead. Also, it's not like I know many others like me—luckily, I'd lost track of my mother during the Italian Renaissance, five hundred years ago and a full ocean away.

The kid is walking toward me. He wears nothing but a pair of shorts, and there's some clumsiness in his shuffle which only makes him more adorable.

I should leave.

The Venice, California beach I spend my thoughtful nights at is almost deserted. Few silhouettes, mostly couples, often still, fade in the distance among the palm trees, unscathed by the dim glare of the streetlights behind us and the full moon above.

In the distance, another youngster with a jukebox sings about *getting no satisfaction*. I wonder if it's that raw, animal energy what's helping the kid taking his final leap.

When eventually the moonlight frames his features, I realize I'm staring at the young, plump promise of a truly handsome man. I'd fancied and drunk blood from a Theban warrior, back in Ancient Greece, but compared to the newcomer, he was nothing but a bulky brute.

"You're real, then," the kid says in a deep voice.

"What?"

"Over there, always on your own, and only at night," he continues. "I was starting to convince myself you were a ghost, or some kind of vision from the past."

I stifle a giggle. "You're not that wrong—"

"You're—supernatural then?"

"Sort of."

It's when I find the presence of mind to look back at the young man that I realize I'm not just telling him, *I'm a vampire and I'd feast on your blood.* My replies, till now, have been silly enough. "Listen," I say, "I just want to—"

He pulls back slightly. "I'm not here to spoil your precious loneliness, distinguished lady, I promise," he announces, voice lowering.

"Aren't you?" I can't help replying.

Opening number two. Towards a complete stranger, albeit a truly polite one. No wonder I've almost been burned as a witch five times, on both sides of the ocean. I never learn.

The young man surprises me by pushing his open palm forward. There is something glimmering in the middle, but it's probably just a trick of the light.

"Here, I found it yesterday."

If beauty is the only solace of endless lives, as some philosopher I may or may not have tasted the blood of once said, the seashell the kid is showing me hosts a remarkable splinter of wonder. A web of thin black lines wraps a perfect spiral whose center, under the moonlight, seems to be constantly moving.

"I've seen many shells," my visitor continues, while I can't look away from his offering. "For a little, I even made fancy jewels out of them. There are many—different shapes, among recurring, general styles, as if it rhymed. It's the poetry of the sea."

I smile slightly.

"But this one is unique." He finds my eyes again. "I'd like you to have it."

I'm opening my hand, close to his, holding my breath. Our skin doesn't touch, as he gently lets the seashell drop into my palm. It feels light but coarse, and it's so bright I briefly panic at the idea its light might hurt me.

"It's—perfect, isn't it?" he asks.

"Yeah."

"It's the ideal gift for you, then."

The cymbals in my internal drum band smash so loud that I shiver. I have no idea if I can blush—mirrors don't work with me—but I'm certainly impressed. That, and enraged at the drum band itself, which I'd slaughter with my claws right now if they weren't just a dumb metaphor.

The last moments have been so frantic that I barely realize my admirer is already stepping away like he promised.

"Wait!" I hear myself saying.

The seashell brings pleasant heat in my hand as his delightful smile finds me again.

"Huh?"

I can read people enough to realize he must have been rehearsing the whole scene a few times, maybe even writing a full script, since the charming attitude is now gone, leaving room to a thinly veiled uncertainty.

Why the heck do I like him more?

"What's your name?" I ask.

"James." A shadow cover his eyes. "Jim Morrison." This one sounds better, even according to the smirk he underlines his words with.

"I'm Nadia."

But he's slipped away.

◆ ◆ ◆

I like libraries, don't get me wrong.

They have been excellent shelters from the deadly daylight in almost every country I've lived, and they provide a nice way to pass the time learning new and helpful survival tricks.

By applying some stealth, and always making sure they would stay in business anyway, I occasionally aside some potential rare editions, only to sell them for a large profit a century or so later.

If there's a thing I can do quite well, it's waiting.

Still, libraries tend to get stuffy. I don't know if it's the dust, or the endless lines of barely touched shelves, or the stiff and nondescript-clothed human inhabitants who would really benefit some extra solar exposure—they can, and still they won't.

At the end of the day, all I want to do is break out of my shelter and take deep breaths in a wide-open space.

Like a beach, yes.

The fact that I'm now sitting in the very same spot I was yesterday, when that cute boy Jim came to visit me, is purely a coincidence.

Soon I grow restless. There's no sign of him around. I dig into my pocket to find the seashell he gave me as a gift. I don't know if it's because the moon is clouded tonight, and most of the light is the dead-yellow glare coming from the streetlamps behind me, but it's just—nice.

Not so unique, or perfect.

Did I delude myself? It wouldn't be the first time, in any case. The perfect features of Giacomo Casanova, Oscar Wilde, and Mata Hari each flash before my eyes. Every time I had thought I was just enjoying some quality company, and blood, I'd ended up feeling abandoned, unworthy, and utterly miserable.

But those had been great human specimens, those that human history, along with my personal memory, holds a special place for.

This Jim is nothing but a kid with an excellent timing.

"I wasn't certain I'd find you here again," a familiar voice says. My brain hasn't given a name to the man it belongs to, but my heart is already dancing.

To my left, with silent steps, Jim Morrison has appeared. The wind is fiddling with his dark curls.

"Why?" I ask.

"All of the other nights I'd seen you, you were always changing place."

Did I? Staying away from humans, unless I decide otherwise, is more of an instinct than a conscious act.

"Maybe I'm tired," I tease him.

"I see."

"What?"

I'm quite sure I've seen him fish from his memory another ready-made movie line. He doesn't disappoint.

"Shining so brightly like you do must take a strong commitment."

I chuckle, a nasty edge in it. He can't know, but he just found the worst analogy possible to refer to the attractiveness of someone who, to survive, hides from the sun.

"Anything wrong?"

I sigh lightly. Seeing him standing there, both the chiseled chin and the broad shoulders bent at an odd edge, is enough to foster some understanding.

"Sit down," I suggest in a warm tone.

"May I?"

I nod.

I relax, too, as the sand crackles under his shorts.

I find myself grinning at a memory. "You know, there was this guy I'd met, Diogenes…"

"The philosopher." Jim is wide-eyed as a cartoon puppy.

"N-no," I'm quick to withdraw. "It's quite a common name in Greece." I usually drop names from my ancient past with strangers, confiding in their ignorance, but Jim seems to be special.

"What about him?"

I can't tell him about the visit of Alexander the Great and how Diogenes just asked him to move away from the sun. I suspect he already knows the anecdote. I kinda fabricated it, since of course if I was there, there was no sun, but this is a complete other story.

"You won't tell me?" Jim has noticed I'm drifting away.

I frown at him. "Do you always make so many questions?"

A big laugh echoes from the group of kids hanging out three palms from us.

"Knowledge is like water," he replies, after some pondering. "I'm always thirsty, and it's never enough."

"What do you even know about knowledge, Jim Morrison?" I challenge him.

"I… read a lot."

"I like that."

Those deep eyes frame me once more, sucking away my annoyance like I would a wild animal's blood.

"I like you," he whispers.

"Thank you," I manage to bounce back. "About you, I still have to decide."

He seems to follow some invisible lines in the sand. "Fair enough."

I'm tempted to tease him again, but the group of noisy kids have left and the rest of the beach dwellers are either asleep or extra-universe high. I'm the one who complained him talking too much, so silence is fine.

I came here for the fresh night air, after all, not for the attention of some random, smooth-talking human.

"I think you should be the star of my dissertation," he then announces, his voice weaker than usual.

"Come again?" I ask.

He avoids my gaze.

"It'll be my movie," he explains. "I've been planning it for a while, now." He grimaces and waves a hand. "Forget it, it's nothing."

"A movie?" I wonder. "Didn't you talk about a dissertation?"

"For my undergraduate degree at UCLA film school."

"So, you're a student, interesting," I muse out loud. "Could have said it from the start."

"Could I?"

"A film school student, also," I continue, hoping the mockery isn't too sharp. "What do you want to become, a director?"

He shrugs. "Maybe, I'm not sure." He considers. "Moving pictures are nice, you can shock and awe people with them, but words just—resonate further through time and space."

An admiring smile betrays me. "I think I agree."

He does the movie-people thing, forming a rectangle with indexes and thumbs to frame me, while I briefly consider munching away one of those tiny rolls of flesh just to know what they taste like.

It's not like I'd really do it. Not in public. Not like that. But as I get to know this Jim better, admiration towards him seems to be putting roots.

"You would look stunning on camera," he suggests.

I shake my long black hair. "Better than in reality?"

He blushes and looks away. Good boy.

"Seriously, no," I explain. "Cinema is not my thing."

"How would you know?"

Had an accident with Mr. Murnau, to begin with. "I've been an actress, once. It didn't go well."

Those deep eyes sparkle. "Maybe you haven't met your ideal director, yet."

Hubris, like the world needed some more! So young, and so pretentious. I let my gaze slide down his chin, to his throat. He may think I'm having lusty thoughts, but the real deal is I'm deciding whether to sink my teeth into his jugular and put an end to his misery.

I met one other deluded artist, half a century ago, who later did quite a lot of harm to his whole kind. He wasn't quite as cute as Jim, though.

"Would you at least consider it?" he insists.

Now I'm the one looking away, shaking my head lightly. "Still a no." I let the splash of the waves penetrate my ears, yearning for some soothing. "Camera doesn't simply work well with—people like me."

I hear him moving and for a split second I fear he'll touch my hand or something. The smell of his blood is endearing enough; any skin contact might make me snap. I don't want to attack him. But I'm not sure how long I can keep my feral instinct at bay.

He's been subtly offering himself to me, all this time, without knowing *what* I truly am.

"Nadia—"

"What?" Calling my human name, remembering it, feels helpful. I'd been like him, long ago. Frail in the tissues and without a clue.

"Are you from Italy, maybe?" he asks. "I've never been to Europe, one day I'd love to see it."

I wheeze in relief. "Egypt, to be honest."

"Well, I've never been to Africa, either."

"It's a huge continent," I mumble.

As I stand, a sad mood takes over. Thirst isn't gone for the night; it's only temporarily subdued. This might be my last chance to keep from assaulting him.

"You're leaving, already?" Behind the mask of casualness, his begging to stay looms.

"I have business to attend." The beach feels empty and quiet.

"Business—at your place?"

"Business—at a place," I cut short.

My steps out of the beach, toward the small concrete ladder leading to the street, feel heavy.

"Will I see you again?"

I turn. Sunk into the sand, all alone, he looks little different from a cherub who lost his way to Heaven.

"It depends," I suggest, without thinking. "Do you trust the night?"

Jim smiles fondly. "I worship her, pray to her, and hope she will carry me to the end."

"Nice."

I walk away without looking back.

The streets I have to cross to reach my hideout at the library smells like alcohol, puke, and dreams about to be shattered by the new day. After a turn, I almost stumble into a large thug kissing a whiskey bottle.

"Aloha! What do we have here?" He reacts, leering up to reveal a desolation of rotten teeth. "Aren't you something, babe?"

I could just step away, but beyond the overwhelming sweat stink I guess some potential.

"Harry! Gil! Come and see what I've found!" the thug yells over my shoulder.

With a clang, from behind the dumpster emerge his partners in crime, both drunk and dirty. They surround me as if I'm some kind of French delicacy just delivered from a legendary chef.

I let my fangs glimmer under the moon.

It's dinner time indeed, but someone among us has mistaken their role at the table.

◆ ◆ ◆

"Can you turn me?"

Jim's question comes out of nowhere, with the same nonchalance as if he's just noticed that the gothic sandcastle we made on the shore last week hasn't been fully wrecked by the ocean, yet.

"Pardon?" I reply, hoping the glare—and some reverting back to dated language—might be enough to kill the topic.

We've reached the outer edge of Venice beach again, maybe he's tired.

"Let me become like you," Jim insists, instead. "Let me live forever."

I snarl. "Immortality is overrated." He barely blinks. "Plus, you get to be free only half of your time. Less, during summer, when the days are longer." I fearfully search for any sign of light at the edge of the horizon. "On summers like this, I regret it the most."

That pretty face of his looks unconvinced in a dramatic way.

"There must be good sides."

I scoff. "There are always good sides."

"I didn't mark you as an optimist."

I clench my teeth and mutter a curse. To redirect the annoyance, I grab a handful of sand. "There are good sides in everything, in the worst possible way." I let the grains slip, and it's as if I could count every single one of them. "Like that dumbbell Benito Mussolini, you know?"

"Who, the Italian dictator?"

When he is clueless, Jim looks even more attractive.

"That guy, yeah. He ruled Italy during the years leading to World War Two. He was a cruel man, erased freedom for the press, had people deported—and many killed. Some idiots, now, say he also did good things."

A gust of wind scatters what's left of the sand.

"My point is: the dumbbell ruled for twenty years, at the beginning of the Twentieth Century. When humanity was taking a giant leap into the future, discoveries were made, illnesses were cured." I take a deep breath, realizing I'm being too passionate. Part of me still feels guilty having not been eloquent enough, back then, to save poor Claretta Petacci from her husband's fate. "Anyone, even a dummy, would do something good, if they ruled at that time in the world!"

Jim chuckles. "You are a special woman."

The fact that he's calling me "a woman" silences some of my most recent worries. Even if I haven't openly admitted being a vampire, I have never denied, whenever our original conversation about me being a vision or a ghost drifted into those territories.

For the curly-haired boy, apparently, my true nature is just one of the many speculation topics he enjoys getting lost with me during our nights at the beach.

I sigh as I recognize a glimmer by the sea. Since we walked farther than usually, tonight, getting back at the library before dawn might will require supernatural speed—I luckily have it.

"Time out, gotta go," I announce.

Jim doesn't move. "Aren't you forgetting something?"

I blink, embarrassed. Two nights ago, he tried to kiss me, but I pulled back. He smelt nice, but that was all. It felt good enough not feeling the urge to devour him, why waste such a pleasant balance?

I scan those high cheekbones to find a reason for which things may have changed between us.

Finally, he breaks the silence by offering a small book and a huge smile.

I read the author on the cover. "Voltaire, really?"

"Speaking about optimism…"

"Whatever," I say, putting the book in my bag then fishing one for him.

"Plato?" he wonders, echoing my complaints.

I grin. "That's the very point of a book exchange," I point out. "Something you haven't read, yet."

He squints. "You're the one who told me not to trust Plato, since he misinterpreted most of Socrates' stuff."

"That," I raise a finger, "is why you shouldn't always listen to me." I blow him a kiss. "See you tomorrow."

I walk fast to the main road as long as I'm still in Jim's field of view. While I'm certain he'll look until I'm one with the night, my mood sours upon hearing my shrill mother's advice in my mind. *You shouldn't delude him, if you're not willing to commit.*

The streets flow around me at high speed. I yell an insult, confident the road noise will muffle it. Otherwise, it's the Sixties, and it's L.A.; nobody will really bother for someone cursing out loud early in the morning.

"I'm not deluding anyone," I mumble to my projected parent. "We've just spent a dozen nights together. Which, compared to the duration of my life, is nothing."

Once in the safety of the library, I sink my nose into a new, large fantasy novel and try not to emerge until it's night again.

◆ ◆ ◆

For the three following nights, Jim tries to convince me to skinny dip into the ocean. At my refusals, he grunts about me always wearing the same shirt and jeans, and how I'd probably look amazing in a bathing suit.

"I don't, but it's a whole other story," is my only reply.

On the fourth night, I have to sweep the beach to find him. Eventually, I meet him at the pier, together with a newly rented boat.

"Still no," I comment, while unable to hide an amused grin. "And you can't afford that."

"I borrowed it, in exchange for a favor."

"Feel free to do your boat trip, then," I suggest. "I'll be here when you're back." If the message isn't clear enough, I sit on the shore.

A wave finds my naked feet and the edge of my jeans. The cold gives me a pleasant shiver, but then I must wrap up the wet part.

When I look up again, Jim is stepping down the boat to join me on the shore.

"It was just an idea to celebrate," he explains. "Sorry you don't like it."

As usual, he's offered the bait. He came to my terms, so I can bite.

"Celebrate what?"

"My getting my film school degree."

"Congratulations!" He's been mentioning his studies on occasion, among the other million topics, so I shouldn't feel shame for forgetting.

"The movie turned out quite good," he continues, but his mood darkens a little bit. "It would have been better, with you as the main star."

"I'm sure you found a worthy substitute."

Jim smirks. "Yeah."

"And she was very nice, for accepting your request to take off all her clothes on camera."

Jim's jaw drops. "How do you know?"

I chuckle. "I just guessed right." I squint. "Or maybe, it's my supernatural powers."

We lose track of time as we discuss the ideas behind the latest books we've exchanged. He so much enjoyed the Arthur Rimbaud collection that I have to allow him to keep the copy. It's not a rare edition, so I'll find a way to put a different one on the library shelf.

At one point, the wind unties the rope holding the skiff by the pier, so we have to follow it along the shore until, with a lucky jump, Jim manages to leap on it and put an end to the drift.

He's dripping wet when I pull him back over the pier.

"That was fun."

I smile. "See? You didn't borrow a boat for nothing, after all."

There's some extra energy left in his body, and it shows by the frantic way he scans around. "Oh, there," he says, cheering up as he notices something. "Would you close your eyes for a moment?" he suggests.

I mock suspicion. "Why?"

"I have something for you." The memory of the seashell he gave me the first day we met glimmers.

"Oh. Then why don't you give it to me right now?"

"If you first close your eyes."

I grow wary, for real this time. I still know very little about this young man, and closing my eyes with him around requires a degree of trust I've probably lost centuries ago, in Ancient Egypt or so.

I study him. With his hair and shorts both wet, he conveys very little intimidation. I tell myself I'm only alert because the sea is bringing some hideous, unidentifiable smell.

"Let's do it, then," I decide. "But be quick, I'll count ten, then I'll open back!"

Full darkness welcomes me, unexpectedly peaceful, the waves splashing on the shore below us at a steady rhythm. On *1* and *2*, Jim fiddles with a bag to my right. His steps are still echoing when I reach *5*. Too bad the horrible smell seems to be strengthening, whatever its source might be.

"Trust me, you'll like it," Jim announces, getting closer. "It's my gift to you, to say thank you."

We're around *8* and he's putting something around my neck. A dry, irregular and sharp surface, scratching my skin, starts making me uncomfortable.

"By spending time with me, you sucked away my demons," Jim proclaims; to me, he sounds annoying. "Thanks to this, you'll be free, too."

10. I feel like puking, and I don't know why.

"You don't have to pretend to be a vamp—"

Garlic! A full, freaking garlic necklace around my neck! And the piece of shit put it there while I had my eyes closed!

"Fuck!" I yell, claws snapping out.

I wave them in the air, too dizzy to touch the garlic. It's like my strength has been squeezed away, all at once, and the only feeling left in my body is pure, uncontrolled fury.

"Nadia!" Jim exclaims. "What's wrong?"

"To Hell with this crap!" I cry. "Help me out!"

Jim tries to reach me, but my instinct prevails and I kick him off the pier. His big splash doesn't sound like a relief.

Meanwhile, I've gathered enough presence of mind to sink a claw into the closest bulb of garlic. Slicing it makes a disgusting sound, and I hate the very idea of touching it. So, let the little garbage go! I focus my rage and utterly destroy the tiny, dry vegetable. I slash the next bulb the very moment I start fading out.

The necklace snaps open, freeing my neck.

Half of the bulbs slip far enough from my head to uncloud my mind.

I grab the freaking necklace and dangle the hideous thing at arm's length. I shiver, need to puke, then clench my teeth hard. I'm still in control.

I toss the crappy thing at the horizon, and it's gone.

"Nadia, you—"

Jim Morrison has climbed back over the pier. Having been a prisoner on slave ships, I've seen livelier, not to mention drier, drown rats.

"Yes, I!" I hiss. "When someone mentions they are a vampire, it's polite to listen!" He looks small and stupid. "You didn't believe me, did you? You thought it was all a joke, I was just a damsel in distress that would be rescued by love!"

I leap down the pier, the sand opening before me like the Red Sea, then dive into the night.

No hideout is perfect, and some bring collateral issues when the owner finds out you've turned their place into an unauthorized shelter. My bane is the new guard. Having heard rumors that someone lived in the broom closet, the library director has hired a professional to find me and kick me away.

I'm not stupid, and I certainly don't lack experience in hiding. At first, avoiding the new recruit—a former athlete of Nigerian descent—has been a piece of cake.

But the whole Jim Morrison affair, and the pretty kid's utter failing at understanding who I am, has left me distracted.

"You're her, right?" the guard asks, polite but firm, stopping with his imposing figure any attempt at further escaping the broom closet.

I take a deep breath, looking up at my potential captor.

"It depends."

The guard chews his gum. His eyes don't leave me.

"I was planning to leave," I add.

The guard grimaces. "I should report you to my boss." More chewing.

It takes a few seconds, I may be getting dumber with the centuries, but the blatant alternative finally hits me. "You mean—you're still unde-cided?" Too many misunderstandings, lately, better to set things straight.

"Uh-uh."

This is the point where I usually change city, or even continent. It's a shame, since I traveled from England less than one year ago, and I'm half-way through the local copy of *The Lord of the Rings*. If there is a chance to stay—

"When exactly do you plan to make your choice?" I ask the guard.

He chews louder. "Not sure." He sniffs. "What about tomorrow—"

One extra day to stay is a gift itself.

"—night? I'm bringing pizza. And beer, if you like it."

Again, I may be getting dumber, but this a whole other surprise.

♦ ♦ ♦

"B-bite me!"

"What?"

"It's fine," my lover and undecided captor insists. "Please, do it."

I've been here before. Not exactly like this, but close. Charming but complicated suitors, with whom things have often gone sideways, compels me to be extremely nice to the next decent guy who shows interest in me. Sex is an option, but only if they insist. I don't know if it's part of my phys-iology, but the whole intercourse activity is not my thing.

Unless, as the guard and now my accomplice is apparently suggesting, sucking blood is involved.

I may be hopping up and down over him, the whole closet shaking and my panties swinging atop the longest broomstick, but at the moment I haven't the faintest idea about what to do next.

"You want me to suck your blood?" I end up asking in a polite manner.

The guard wheezes. "Yes!"

"It might hurt—"

"You like it. It's fine."

I blink. He pushes harder. His breath grows heavier.

"Do it now!" he yells.

I snap my fangs out, sink them into the tick neck, and what follows is pure bliss.

It would be even better, if my mind stopped putting Jim Morrison's face over this new guy's body.

But I get to take my favorite broom closet hideout as an extra, so who am I to complain?

I'm almost settled having a part-time lover, part-time blood donor, while full time accomplice, and my beloved Hobbits are finally hiking back from Mount Doom to the Shire—when Jim Morrison walks into my library.

I barely recognize him, at first.

He's thinner, more intense, the long curly hair swinging over his shoulders. I may have over-fantasized about him during our separation, but he looks hotter than ever.

"I'm looking for a woman," he thunders. "Her name is Nadia."

I pull him inside my closet even though everybody's watching.

"Are you crazy?" I ask him, pushing him against the wall. His shirt is slightly open at the top, but I fight the urge to rip it off him.

"Of course," he replies. "I'm crazy for you. I missed you like the moon misses the sun."

"That metaphor doesn't even make scientific sense," I complain.

"Poetry and love need no explanation."

I sneer and grow embarrassed all at once. "You're still an idiot."

He scans around the closet. He must notice the lack of windows. "Oh, and you're still a vampire."

If I said I weren't impressed, I'd lie. "Why are you here?"

A long, pensive, and heart-shattering silence.

"I want you—"

My life is becoming a poorly-written porn movie.

"—to visit my place."

Quite an unusual request, coming from the shirtless guy who spent all his nights at the beach. I squint at the obscenely pretty features. "What changed?"

"I changed."

"That, I can see," I concede. "But what else?"

"The solar system keeps turning."

Now, I'd like to punch him in the face. "You've been reading a lot."

He blabbers in a heavenly voice a verse that I soon realize coming from Rimbaud. I grin. "And good readings."

"The best," he grins back. Next, he frowns. "You comin'?"

I stifle a growl, just because I want to see how far my favorite idiot wants to get.

"What's this place like?" I ask, a spark of brightness somehow finding its way through my intoxicated synapses.

"It's a place of inspiration and creati—"

"Any garlic around?"

Jim pales lightly. "No," he replies. "I swear."

"OK then." I sigh. "Can you wait till sunset?"

At first, I'm not quite impressed by Jim Morrison's humble abode. Ground floor of a pretty decent building, there's more empty space than furniture, and the few pieces, none of them essential, reminds me of the last surviving legionaries in remote Roman outpost.

"Eh, not bad," I say, not to hurt his feelings.

"It's above," he replies.

"Oh."

We climb the stairs to enter a smaller flat, records and books stacked around instead of proper furniture.

"Eh, not bad," I repeat, still cautious.

"It's above."

"Oooh."

Eventually, we enter an attic that feels definitely more Jim-Morrison-y. There is a small bed, a couple of packed cabinets and books stashed in every existing corner.

"Well—" I begin.

Jim sighs lightly. "Still, above."

I look up. I don't remember the building to be that tall. After we climb one last, hidden stair, we emerge on the ceiling. Jim takes my hand and, excited, shows me a wide rooftop under a sky of stars. In a corner, he points me at his only belongings: a small bunk bed, a few consumed books—I immediately notice the Rimbaud library copy, and a notepad with a pen.

"Here is where I travel across the universe, seize inspiration from the cosmos and create brand new worlds, using nothing but words," he declaims.

"Uh." I'm unable to hide my surprise. "Romantic."

Facing me, arms around my waist and eyes like shimmering diamonds, he starts reciting fascinating verses in a low, intimate tone. I catch something about the moonlight, then at the mention of a gentle rain I manage somehow to stifle a cackle. Storms must be a true experience, up here.

Soon, his poetic words start turning into a mantra, steady and hypnotic. I can't help admiring this young man who chose to live, and create art, where everybody else would see nothing but an abandoned rooftop.

Whatever spell this long-haired shaman is attempting, it's working.

I pull him towards him and kiss him avidly. I stop only when I realize I'm getting hungry, and I might start by ripping the tongue off his mouth.

"Anything wrong?" Jim asks.

"Nothing," I whisper. I pause to kick away the mental image of me ripping his rib cage open and devouring every single warm and tasty drip of his blood. "There's just no need to rush it."

I can do it. The guard showed me how. I can have this extraordinary man, make love to him, without jeopardizing his life. I want it and I deserve it.

We end up lying down, holding hands, between the bunk bed and the stack of books, with the chimney of the building right behind us and the chilly air of the night wrapping us as if it was the coziest of the blankets.

From up here, away from the street and the rest of the world, stars and constellations create a unique, surprisingly vast tapestry. Jim starts chanting softly, and before I realize it, I'm crossing the celestial vault on a chariot made of pure joy.

"You were right, Jim," I consider. "It's ama—"

A gunshot brings both of us back to the empty rooftop.

"Let her go, you creep!" a strong, manly orders.

Time to sit up, and we're both under the aim of my favorite guard's gun. A small weapon, part of his equipment, but might be harmful at such a close range. He towers over us and looks concerned.

"I said, let her go!"

"Oh, hey," I welcome the guard faintly. "Can I stand?"

"Course."

As I comply, keeping my hands on sight, the guard follows me with his eyes. Once I've completed my move, he steps forward, putting between me and Jim.

"Did he harm you?" he asks.

"No," I reply. "Listen—"

"Nadia, who's this armed man?" Jim asks.

"A—friend."

"What's his name?"

I wish he hadn't asked. "Well—"

My friendly guard, lover, and blood-donor doesn't seem bothered by our lack of true familiarity. "Why are you talking to him? He's a hobo!" That's the longest complete sentence I've ever heard from him.

"And you're a fascist," Jim fires back.

"What?"

The poet has confused the guard enough to be able to stand without being immediately shot down. The armed man seems to register the piece of news a few seconds later.

"Why did you move?"

"It's my home," Jim replies, calm.

"Home?"

"I know," I intervene. "I was surprised too, at first." I nod above. "But, did you notice? The view is stunning."

"Did he harm you?" the guard asks me again.

"I would never," Jim replies.

I step close enough to gently touch my aspiring rescuer on his shoulder. He flashes me an questioning look.

"Listen…"

"I'm Jerry."

"Bingo!" I exclaim, fake enthusiasm masking my nervousness. "Names! This is a great beginning, everybody."

"That weapon can't harm you, right?" Jim asks. "You're immortal."

"This wasn't about me in the first place," I rebuke the poet. "I'm not the one he's aiming his gun at."

Jim smirks. "You can't be sure."

As Jim steps closer to me, the muzzle follows him. The fact that I'm a vampire seems to have become public domain in the Venice area, still it's hard to imagine they've already put ash wood bullets in production.

"Let's start again," I say. "Jerry, this is Jim. Jim, this is Jerry." Grunts follow. "Now you're not strangers anymore. You have a lot in common." I'd say something about having had sex with me, but my date with Jim was going so beautifully slow. "Both your names start with a J!"

The reveal meets little enthusiasm.

"I still don't like him," Jerry barks.

"He should have knocked," Jim retorts.

The guard looks at me. "Shall we go?"

"About that—"

Truth seems to find him. I feel bad for him.

"Not coming?" Jerry wonders, growing upset. "It took me a while to find the right place!"

Jim smirks again. "Also, most of my friends believe I'm in New York."

"I'm fine with Jim, Jerry," I explain after a long sigh. "But thank you for coming to the rescue. You are the best, I really think so."

Repeating, for my favorite guard, is apparently the key to understanding. "Not coming."

"Can he put the gun down?" Jim asks.

"Can you?" I repeat.

Jerry complies, his mood dropping as well.

"Would you give us a minute alone, Jim?" I ask.

"Sure," he replies, strolling away.

"But I love you," Jerry starts, eyes like a beaten dog. "Why all this?"

"Love?" I put my hand on his shoulder. "Come on. It was excellent and pleasant exercise." I continue by enumerating a mix of street level shrinking and simple, sad truths. Some, I recall, come from the many times I've impersonated Cleopatra for money or entertainment. It's amazing how many people enjoy having a beautiful, exotic woman telling them what to do with their lives.

My guard and aspiring savior finally accepts with a long hug goodbye. He keeps his hand on my butt for most of the time. As I watch him leave, I take mental note to set him up with the library secretary. He's a good guy and he deserves a non-bloodsucking woman.

"My shining star, you're back!" Jim says when I join him again. "I've composed a brand new poem for my muse."

I shut him up with my lips before he can even start. Next, I put his hand on the edge of my shirt, inviting him to lift it.

He hesitates.

"Is it OK for you, I mean—"

"If you let me drink some of your blood, while we do it, it'll be great."

"But I want you to stay for the night—after," he insists. "Sleeping together under a sea of stars."

"I don't exactly sleep, but I'll promise I'll worship you in a very quiet way."

Jim frowns. He seems concerned. "You're always awake? What kind of neurotic, hyper-aware life is that?"

I scoff. I liked him better when he spouted nonsense, pretending to be Hamlet. "It's terrible; I know better than anybody. Can we go on?"

I snap my jaw at his lower, full lip, but he pulls back.

"You tell me there's no way, no way at all, for you to lose consciousness?"

"I can get drunk on blood," I suggest, my tongue dancing frantically. "It requires a bigger amount, but it'll work."

The look that Jim gives me make my whole tremble. I wonder if being burnt by the sun feels somehow similar.

"So have it, my unearthly fox," he announces, dripping lust. "Let the blood flow."

I push him to the ground and attack his jugular vein.

◆ ◆ ◆

There's human blood in my mouth, a lot of it. It seems to have coagulated at the edge of my throat, and it's not the worst thing I'm experiencing right now. My whole body feels weak and dull, as if its articulation had been disjointed and then punched back into place.

Also, there's this wide, increasing heat, spreading from the tip of my nose to my toes.

I open my eyes and immediately close them. Too much light. I open again, shielding my face from the sun.

The sun?

The heat starts burning. It involves every inch of my body.

I jump up in the early morning air. The dawn is breaking and I'm at the top of a building, all alone, and naked. I shouldn't be here, why did I let this happen?

Oh, yeah.

Jim Morrison.

I grab the closest bunch of fabric, it must be clothing, and rush to hide from the blooming daylight to the side of the chimney. It's small, but it casts a small shadow. From there, I assess the danger.

I'll burn and die if I don't leave in the next five minutes.

The door leading downstairs is at the opposite edge of the rooftop.

There's no shirt or pants among the wrapped clothes, but instead a large black blanket and a folded paper. I'll look at the paper later, all I can do now is wrap the blanket around my head.

It reaches down to my feet. I've never been more happy to be short.

The light grows every second, so it's now or never.

I launch towards the exit door. Halfway through, I decide I'm gonna make it. Wrong guess.

I step on the blanket, it rips, and through the new hole a dagger of sunlight comes straight to pierce my naked shoulder.

They tried to burn me once with fire. Somehow, this feels much more painful.

If I had fallen down, I'd be doomed. But I've kept on my feet, so pushing forward one last time it's just a matter of sheer self-preservation instinct.

The floor hurts the soles of my feet as I stop in front of the exit door.

I scorch my hand in the light while I grab the handle.

It's locked.

If I die here, I swear I'm gonna turn into a vengeful spirit to haunt Jim Morrison forever.

I push again.

The back of my hand catches fire under my sight.

The handle snaps.

The door opens.

My burning hand under my armpit, I storm down the stairs, hitting the sharp edge of every step but still moving. I slip again and turn into a manic envelope, rolling down the stairs at impressive speed while wrapped inside a ripped blanket.

The light is invading the attic the very moment I land into it. It's wide—there's available space I can put between the consuming energy and me.

I stride through the attic and take the stairs down. Midway through, tired of limping, I let my ravaged blanket go. Butt naked I reach the ground floor. I'm quite sure I met a few living souls along my way. I hope they enjoy the show.

The ground floor, scattered with mismatched furniture, has big, broad windows. The sun will come through them at any moment. There are curtains, but they don't cover all of the windows, and none of them seem thick enough to block anything.

And then, I see it.

The cellar door.

I kick it open and sneak inside. At the bottom of a circular metal staircase, I use as a bumpy, rusty slide I find what I need. A bunker with no windows or doors, barely large enough room to host me and some oxygen.

I'm not even sure I'd need it, but right now I'm sure about very few things.

What matters is that the freaking sunlight will remain outside.

In the darkness, I control my breath.

I've done it.

I'm alive, well, I'm not a pile of ash.

After a while, I let my fingers search. Finding a switch, I turn on a tiny, blinking lightbulb wrapped in cobwebs.

More than enough to check Jim Morrison's last letter. I knew what it was; I'd tried to let it go when I left the blanket, still it stuck to my calf until now.

I only skim it.

I don't really like his writing, to be honest.

The letter is evenly split between apologies and bullshit. No, having me drink so much of his blood wasn't a good idea. He almost died in the process; ironically, so did I, but he'll never know. He left because he didn't want to delude me; how nice. He's moving to his friend Ray's place; good for him. And... that's it.

The kid is brilliant, he'll go places. Hopefully, I'll be half the planet away when he does, because if I ever see that beautiful face again, I'll finish what I started.

I'm thinking about Australia. Been there once, made some mistakes, but all the people involved must be dead now.

I wonder what it's the outback like, this time of the year.

Love Burns

ROAD TEST

BY WAYLAND SMITH

The biggest change in Angela's life happened because she decided to skip lunch. Or really, because she wanted to fit into the stupid silver dress Nat had talked her into buying. So, when everyone else at the DMV was off gossiping and eating and sharing pictures on their phones, she was at her desk, steadfastly trying to make herself believe she was enjoying the banana her diet allowed her, and looking at the picture of the dress she'd taped on to the side of her file cabinet.

"Miss Henson?"

Angela looked up, blinking in surprise. No one came to her office. She was usually out giving the tests, except for when she was on break, like now. And she wasn't exactly one of the more popular people in the office. "'M on break," she managed through a mouthful of banana.

"Yes, I can see that. I'm sorry to disturb you." The woman in the doorway was wearing a stunning suit. It fit her perfectly and somehow conveyed a sense of authority that had Angela sitting up straighter.

"It's fine," Angela said, although she really didn't like having her lunch, such as it was, disturbed. "What is it you wanted?"

The woman smiled. "My name is Edith Dalrymple." She handed over a business card, although Angela hadn't seen where it came from. The card was ivory, very thick, with raised printing, and told her next to nothing. There was the woman's name and a phone number. That was it.

"How can I help you, Miss Dalrymple?" Angela asked again.

"I represent a man who has a medical condition. He's essentially allergic to sunlight. He has recently relocated to the state, and wants to bring his driver's license up to date."

Angela blinked. "I'm not sure what you need me for."

The woman went on. "He would like to take the written and road tests at night. Naturally, we're aware this is both irregular and potentially an inconvenience to you. He's prepared to offer some compensation for your troubles."

Angela frowned. "I don't take bribes."

She shook her head. "I wouldn't dream of offering one. I've reviewed the regulations quite closely, and there's nothing that says the test can't be administered at night." She produced a folder, also from someplace Angela didn't see, and placed it carefully on Angela's desk. "These are the medical certificates from his physician. I also took the liberty of highlighting sections of the traffic laws and DMV regulations. Nothing prohibits you from giving him the test at night. And he will pass or fail on his own merits. You keep your fee regardless."

Angela's brows drew together as she pursed her lips. "I'd like some time to think this over," she said after a few moments.

"Certainly. My number is on the card. If I don't hear from you in a week or so, I'll presume you are declining, which is fine, and we'll seek to make other arrangements." Her eyes flicked to the file cabinet. "That's a lovely dress, by the way."

Angela flushed slightly. "Thank you."

"I look forward to hearing from you." Edith walked out of the office without a backward glance, leaving behind a very confused driving instructor.

"Ok, that was weird," Angela muttered to herself and finished her banana.

Just before five, after mulling the situation over, she went to see her supervisor. She knocked on the door, waited, and just as she was thinking he had gone home early, heard, "Come in."

Ron McNeil was a man on the upper end of middle age, with short red hair showing more and more gray, but a moustache that was oddly still vibrant red and, as far as Angela could tell, not dyed. He gave her a puzzled look and said, "Angela. What can I do for you?"

"I need to run a scenario by you," she said, and laid out her odd lunchtime visit.

"Huh," he said when she finished, then turned to his computer and did some typing and clicking. "Well… she's right. I can't find anything that says you have to do it during the day, and you're telling me, so you're not trying to hide anything or run a scam." He considered for a moment. "It would have to be a restricted license, but off the top of my head I don't know what code you'd use." He leaned back in his chair and took off the wire rimmed glasses. "I guess you have some research to do."

Angela went home and spent a lot of time thinking things over. She'd sleep on it, she decided, during her steamed chicken dinner. She tried not to remember how good the pizza from Johnny's was, or how close the place was to her apartment. It was a restless night's sleep and the morning came with a mental fog that not even coffee cut through.

After stalling as long as she could, Angela pulled out the odd card she'd gotten yesterday, and punched in the number.

"Edith Dalrymple," the voice answered.

"Miss Dalrymple, this is Angela Henson."

"I'm glad to hear from you. I hope it's good news?"

"I can do the test, but you need to tell your client," Angela glanced at the medical papers, "Mr. McLean, that pass or fail is up to him and his abilities, and that the best I can do is a restricted license."

"That's perfectly fair," Dalrymple answered.

"He needs to bring identification, and be ready for both tests. Would Tuesday at eight work?"

"I'll make certain it works. I can't imagine there will be a problem, but if there is, I'll call you back on this number?"

"That's fine. Thank you." Angela wasn't sure why she was thanking the woman, but that was just who she was most of the time. They went over a few more details, and Angela hung up, wondering what she was getting herself into.

Aside from seeing a movie with Nat on Saturday night, Angela didn't have any plans for the weekend. She wondered if she was making a huge mistake. More than once, she picked up the card for Edith Dalrymple, wanting to call her and cancel the entire thing, and then put the card away.

Monday dragged, aside from the usual brief spikes of adrenaline that came from giving driving tests to teenagers, first-time drivers, and people who watched way too much Fast and Furious. Tuesday had a staff meeting that lasted long enough to make her seriously reconsider both her diet and no drinking at work rule. Finally, Tuesday evening rolled around. Ron stopped by her small office, which almost never happened. "Hey, you okay with your mysterious student tonight? You want me to stick around or anything?"

Angela wondered if he was being a good boss or was actually concerned about her, and shook her head. "Thanks, but I'll be fine. Really. I can catch up on some paperwork until he's supposed to show up."

He hesitated in the doorway, as if he was about to say something, then shut his mouth again. Finally, he just nodded. "Ok then. Good luck." Ron turned and walked away, leaving Angela wondering if he was concerned about her, worried about his job, or maybe actually interested in her as more than work-friends.

At quarter to eight, she went out to the lobby, to wait and review her forms. At eight exactly, a soft knock on the front door startled her so badly she almost managed to drop everything. Outside the glass door was a man of slightly below average height. He had light brown hair, and was dressed formally in a gray suit. He also carried some kind of cardboard tray in one hand and a briefcase in the other. Angela walked over to the door. "Mr. McLean?" she asked through the glass. Looking past him, she saw just two cars in the lot, hers and a gleaming Mercedes.

He nodded. "Miss Henson, I presume?" He had some kind of accent, but she couldn't place it. She opened the door, and he moved inside with a fluid grace that impressed her. Holding the tray out towards her, he said, "I am aware the traditional gift for a teacher is an apple, but I thought this might be appropriate, given the late hour."

Angela's nostrils flared at the scent of some of the most delicious coffee she'd ever smelled. "Oh, thank you," she said, accepting the tray. "None for you?"

"I didn't know how you took your coffee," he said, holding up a small plastic bag of sugar packets and creamer cups. "And I did not wish to become jittery before the test."

Angela started to reach for the sugar, saw another vision of the damn dress, and drew her hand back. "Black is fine," she said, and McLean nodded as if she had confirmed something for him. "Do you have the paperwork I told Miss Dalrymple about?"

He nodded gravely, and moved to the empty seats where people waited during the day for their numbers to be called. He placed the case on the seat, opened it, and drew out a manilla folder. "I believe you will find everything you need within."

She nodded. "Thank you. I'm just going to go over these for a moment."

"Take your time," he said, crossing to the wall and reading one of the bulletin boards filled with assorted public safety messages and helpful tips.

She found medical documentation for the condition Miss Dalrymple had alluded to, and it seemed to match what she'd been told. His passport looked brand new, and only one stamp showed that he'd apparently been to London in the last year or so. She saw it from time to time, but was mildly surprised that he didn't have a middle name. She snuck another look over at him. The suit was very fine, and he wore it well. The shoes looked expensive, and gleamed in the dim light of the mostly dark DMV. There was a learner's permit showing he had it for the required six months. Finally, she found an envelope with her name on it, written in absolutely beautiful handwriting, with "For Your Inconvenience" written across the back. The envelope was thick, and, opening it, she was surprised at the number of hundred dollar bills in it.

"All right, this looks like it's in order," she said. "Are you ready for the written test?"

"I am," he said in that low, accented voice.

Angela led him back to the small classroom area, placed a booklet in front of him, and said, "You have one hour to complete this."

"I will not require that long, but thank you."

He picked up the sharpened number two pencil, and, at her sign, began reading and marking. Angela raised an eyebrow as he plowed through the test. She'd never seen anyone read, or write, that quickly. She wondered if she'd be able to read his handwriting.

Fifteen minutes later, he passed the booklet back to her.

"Are you sure you don't want time to review this?" she asked.

"I am confident," he said easily.

A few moments later, she saw why. Everything was filled in completely, without even a hint of an eraser being used. The few questions that required written answers were in the same lovely, flowing handwriting.

Maybe he was some kind of calligrapher? Finally, she looked up at him. "One hundred percent," she said. "That's rare."

"I take my obligations seriously," he replied. "I studied diligently."

She nodded. A perfect test always made her wonder if the student had cheated somehow, but she'd been right there the whole time, and there was no one else around to feed him answers. "I can see that. Are you ready for the practical exam?"

"I am," was all he said.

They went out to the parking lot, and he stopped. "I am not sure of the protocol. Did you wish me to use my own vehicle, or a state supplied one?"

"We can use yours," she said, and he nodded. He produced a key fob and pressed it, making the lights of the Mercedes flash. She got in on the passenger side, and looked around. "How did you get this here? You didn't drive, did you?"

"The entire point of the exercise is to bring all my paperwork up to legal standards. It would have been very foolish of me to drive here illegally. One of my employees left the car for us, and will return when I call them."

"All right," she said, because she couldn't think of anything else to say.

He slid behind the steering wheel, looking perfectly at ease, none of the fear or misplaced over-confidence she usually saw in her students. Following her directions, he pulled out of the lot, executed a series of turns, accelerated smoothly, and followed every traffic sign they passed. Angela was opening her mouth to say how impressed she was when she saw him frown, eyes moving up to the rearview mirror. "Pardon me," he said. "I must attend to something."

He parked perfectly in a legal space, and turned to her. "Please, remain in the vehicle. It will be better for both of us." McLean was out of the car before she could ask any of the many questions racing through her head.

A van pulled in a few spaces back, engine rumbling, lights a bit too bright to be comfortable. "Probably modified," she said. Then her mouth dropped open in surprise. Five men got out, carrying a strange array of implements. One had a huge hammer, another carried what looked like a wooden sword, the rest armed with nunchakus, a staff, and, furthest back, a bow. What was going on? What this some kind of weird movie she'd been suckered into being a part of? She didn't see any cameras; she didn't see much of anything, really. It was a dark and deserted street, and now fog seemed to be rolling in from nowhere.

She heard McLean's voice ring out strongly. "This is not a good time for this foolishness, gentlemen. It would be wise to put this off for another night."

"We know what you are!" the man with the staff yelled.

"We're going to end this now," the one carrying the sword added.

"Very well. I don't suppose it would do any good to mention the woman in the car is not in my employ, and is just doing her job?" McLean sounded resigned, a bit bored, and slightly irritated. Angela's heart was pounding, and she fumbled for her cellphone. The screen flashed in a pattern she'd never seen before, and she couldn't get a dial tone.

"If she's with you, she shares your fate," the bowman called. "And don't even think about calling in reinforcements." He pointed back at the van. "We've got a jammer."

Silhouetted against the bright lights, Angela saw McLean stand up straighter. "That would not stop me, were I to call. But there's no need."

Everything happened at once, and she stared out the back window in shocked horror. The archer fired an arrow at McLean, and then the others jumped forward. Impossibly, McLean caught the arrow, and threw it back with a negligent flick of his wrist. The archer screamed and fell, clutching his shoulder.

"I will have questions for you," McLean said to the fallen bowman. The one with the staff closed the distance quickly, swinging his weapon in an almost hypnotic series of arcs and circles. McLean stepped forward, reached out with one hand, and snatched the weapon out of a blisteringly fast arc, before it struck his head. McLean moved with no apparent hurry or concern, yanking the staff from the man's hand and stabbing forward with unexpected speed. The man clutched his chest, making a pained, wheezing sound before falling over.

"Normally, I might allow you a chance to reconsider," McLean said calmly. "But this is most inconvenient time for me." He threw the staff like a spear, and the man with the nunchakus fell as it struck his head with a crunch Angela could hear from the car.

"Ben!" the man with the hammer yelled. He was huge, at least six and a half feet tall and looked like he should be in a gym, lifting everything in sight. With a snarl, he advanced, swinging the hammer as the swordsman circled to McLean's left. The hammer whistled in the night air, and then McLean just suddenly wasn't there. Angela saw pale, strong fingers appear on the hammer man's shoulder, and the huge man was bent backward, his lips crooked in rage that turned to pain as he kept bending. McLean's head came into view, looking calm and unruffled. His eyes locked on the swordsman's, as he pulled the large man off balance, and then something even more impossible happened.

MeLean opened his mouth wide, his teeth brilliant white and the wrong shape. Angela didn't have time to figure out what was wrong with them, as the teeth disappeared into the man's neck. A howl of pain trailed off into a kind of moan, as the big man's eyes fluttered closed. McLean held on to him for a moment longer, then simply stepped backward. The hammer clattered to the blacktop as the man fell straight back.

"Your best chance of survival is to tell me who told you where I would be, and when," McLean said in that same measured, even tone he'd used to offer the coffee to Angela.

"Burn in hell, monster," the swordsman shrieked, the words sounding less impressive when his voice cracked slightly. He rushed McLean, sword raised high, anger clear on his face.

"Very well," McLean said, looking utterly unconcerned.

The sword hissed and struck out in what looked to Angela like a very well-practiced thrust. It splintered as it hit the street, McLean once again somehow not there. A blur of moment resolved into the mysterious man, now behind the swordsman who was trying to recover his balance. McLean picked him up easily, as if he were a toy, and hurled him at the van.

The windshield shattered as the man bounced off it, sliding bonelessly to the ground. McLean stalked (there was no other word for it) over to the fallen archer, casually kicking the swordsman on the way by. The man tumbled back into the van's grill and fell again, motionless.

"I said I'd have some questions for you," McLean's voice carried easily in the still night air. The fog swirled around the parked cars, the bright streetlights reduced to hints of light in the distance. "Now, we're going to talk about who sent you, and what they told you."

Angela couldn't hear what the man said, but his words turned into screams and then a trailing horrible gurgle. McLean turned back toward the Mercedes, and Angela would have sworn his eyes glowed red for a moment. Then, somehow, he was at the car door right next to her. "Miss Henson, open the window," he said.

She did, and he regarded her with an expression she couldn't begin to read. His eyes flashed again, and the protests, questions, and even screams she'd felt building inside her suddenly fell away, not important as a new sense of peace filled her. "Miss Henson?" he asked. She nodded dumbly. "I need to know who you spoke to about our arrangement."

"No one," she said, then frowned. "I ran the outline past my boss."

"His name?" McLean's voice was soft and calm, and there was no thought of resisting it.

"Ron McNeil," she said.

"Did you give him my name. Or any particular details?"

"I..." she suddenly could hear their conversation as if it were being replayed in front of her. "I told him about your medical condition and checked to make sure I wasn't breaking any rules by doing the test this way."

"Very... conscientious of you," he said.

"Did I do something wrong?" she asked.

"I do not believe so, no," McLean answered. "Remain calm and still," he instructed her, and she just nodded. It was a very nice night, and the strange fog seemed to muffle noises from the city around them.

McLean strode back to the van, and went inside. There were a few tearing sounds, and the vehicle rocked back and forth. Angela heard a beep, and glanced down to see her phone was behaving normally again. There had been something she had been going to do, hadn't there? A call she had needed to make? The thought slipped away from her before it could fully form, like trying to grab a fish with her bare hand.

McLean walked back to the car, a cellphone in his hand. "This location, one vehicle and five packages. Stephanie might want to have a look at some of the equipment." He hung up, and she watched as he picked up the assorted weapons, and bodies, and hurled them all into the van through the open side door. A small part of her brain howled at her, but she couldn't understand why. Everything was fine. She was waiting just where Mr. McLean had told her to.

He stooped next to the window, and she saw the strangest light in his eyes. It wasn't the scary red she'd seen before, but a softer, almost electric blue, that seemed to pulse as he spoke. "You will forget this regrettable incident. After I begin driving, you will simply recall an uneventful test. You will judge me fairly, based on my skill and adherence to the relevant traffic regulations." He paused, recalling some details from Edith and his own observations. "You will find it easier to eat healthier, and go for a walk each evening after dinner. Do you understand these instructions?" She nodded. "Was I in any way unclear?" Angela shook her head. "Very well."

McLean got behind the wheel, and they drove away just as a large black SUV pulled in near the van and several people got out. "Quickly, if you please, Mr. Doyle," McLean called to a man wearing a cowboy hat and two guns low on his hips, like someone in one of the Westerns Angela's father had been so fond of. The man grinned and flashed a thumbs up sign.

Shaking her head, Angela suddenly sat up straight. Had she dozed off? How unprofessional. "Are you ready to return to the Department?" he asked her.

"Yes, I believe I've seen all I needed to," she answered.

When they pulled into the parking lot, she saw the first hint of uncertainty on McLean's face since she had met him. "How did I do?" he asked.

"Excellently. I can't remember a smoother test," she said.

Instead of the smile she expected, a flicker of--- worry? concern? flitted across McLean's face. "Are you certain about that?"

Angela nodded. "Yes, your written test was perfect and I don't remember any issues with the practical test." Angela was a bit confused at her own phrasing. That wasn't how she usually described a test, even the good ones.

"Very well," McLean answered.

They went back inside, she took his picture, and issued him a paper temporary license. "You should have your permanent one in about two weeks," she said.

"My thanks. You are a most patient teacher," McLean said.

"You did great, really. I can tell you've been practicing."

"Good evening, Miss Henson," McLean said, giving her a partial bow, the effect of which was partially spoiled by her having to walk him to the door and unlock it so he could get out. After relocking it, she went back to her office to finish her paperwork. Frowning as she was leaving, she had the feeling she had forgotten something, but couldn't bring it to mind.

♦ ♦ ♦

Several weeks later, Angela was in the dress, a shimmering silver that fit her even better than she had dared to hope. Nat, wearing a similar dress but in sparkling gold, sipped her wine and took in the crowd. Angela didn't really know much about art or the world around it, despite Nat's efforts over their years of friendship. But she knew Nat was a good painter, and she was part of this showing, and that was enough for Angela.

Nat looked at her critically. "You look great, girl, but I know you. Still having nightmares?"

Angela shrugged and sipped her own wine. "Not as much. They're mostly going away." She frowned again. "A lot of weird fog, and I know something dangerous is out there in it, but somehow, I don't think I'm the one in danger. Then someone screams and I wake up." She shrugged, then made a note to not do that tonight as the already low neckline of the dress shifted with the movement.

"Any idea what that's all about?" Nat asked, moving her blonde hair back behind her shoulder, a nervous tick that was one of Angela's only clues when Nat was actually nervous.

"I really don't. It's weird and annoying, but like I said, they're mostly gone, and I usually get back to sleep pretty quick."

Nat reached out and moved one of Angela's dark braids back in an unthinking gesture of intimacy. It was a far more elaborate hairstyle than Angela usually wore, but Nat was her best friend, and she'd do almost anything for her. "I don't mean to play shrink with you," Nat began.

Angela sighed and made a "go on" gesture. Once Nat got going, you'd need an Act of God to stop her, and Angela wasn't that religious in the first place. "These weird dreams started right around when your boss disappeared?"

She considered that. "Yeah, but I mean, it's not like we were that close." Angela gave a wry smile. "One of the last times I talked to him, I had the impression he didn't even remember my name."

Nat noticed something behind Angela. "Don't look now, but I think that guy is checking you out," she said, nudging Angela in the ribs.

Angela looked around and felt a small thrill of surprise at seeing Brian McLean. He nodded to her, raising a glass, and walked in their direction. "Oh wow, he's really hot," Nat murmured.

"Miss Henson, a pleasure to see you again," McLean said, inclining his head slightly. He turned to Nat. "Miss Grant, I believe? I understand some of these pieces are yours?"

Nat flushed with pleasure. "Yes, I have some on the wall by the door," she said.

"I am sure some of your paintings will find a new home by the end of the night." McLean's voice still had that accent Angela couldn't work out. It wasn't quite British, but that was the closest she could think of. McLean shifted his attention back to Angela.

Nat cleared her throat. "I'm going to go get more wine. Anyone else want any?"

Angela shot her a "what are you doing?" look that Nat cheerfully ignored.

"I'm fine, thank you," McLean said. After Nat left, Angela took a quick but deep drink. "It is good to have close friends," he observed.

"She's the best," Angela said, meaning it. The things they had been through together over the years...

"I wanted to thank you again for accommodating my somewhat unusual circumstances," McLean said.

"You were very generous. More than you needed to be, really."

"I put you to some trouble, you should be fairly compensated for it," McLean said. "I also have heard you received a promotion?"

Where did you hear that? she wondered, but said, "Well, it's just acting for now. My supervisor kind of dropped out of sight a little while ago."

"Really? How unusual. It sounds like a good opportunity for you." She nodded but he went on before she could say anything. "On that note, I'm sure you're aware many people with unusual conditions tend to form a community with like-minded or similarly suffering people." She nodded again, wondering where this was going. "A few members of my community were impressed when I spoke about your graciousness in working with our particular needs. Unless you object, Miss Dalrymple may be in touch about a few similar offers in the future."

In the last few weeks, Angela had lost weight, gotten an at least temporary promotion, and received an unexpectedly generous payment for, as far as she was concerned, just doing her job. Life was looking up. "That would be great," she said. Then she took a breath and went on, "I was hoping we'd see each other again." Nat had come most of the way back, heard that, cast a wicked smile at Angela, and then retreated into the crowd.

McLean smiled, and it was a very nice smile, although it made her shiver for a reason she couldn't quite put her finger on. "I would enjoy that," he said.

Maybe life is finally looking up, Angela thought.

Bureaucracy is inevitable; make it work for you

A DIFFERENT IDEATION

BY JENNIFER L. COLLINS

The couch is deep, the blanket above me dark, and I press my fists together into the crevasse of the back cushions, my head limp on the pillow. There's a comfort in the overstuffed cushions, in the dark colors of suede and blanket and pillow. Behind me, the low drone of the television almost drowns out the noise of the men on the basement stairs, stacked up and eating their lunch.

Derek wants me to keep on eye on them while they're working on the renovations. He wants me to make sure they're making the most of their time and his money, day after day after day. But he also wants me off the couch, getting a new job or cooking or at least walking the dog or doing something, anything, besides lying on the couch and drowning in my latest bout of depression.

Today's not going to be that day.

On the other side of the couch, beyond the wall it's backed up to, I hear one of the workers joke that they could carry the couch down the basement stairs with me on top of it, and I wouldn't say a word. I push myself further into the depths of the cushions, wondering if he's right. One of them pinched my thigh through the blanket a few days ago, as he walked by, and I didn't say anything. Not then, and not later to Derek. I thought about it—I did—but it seemed like such trouble. It's much easier to lie still, waiting for the absence of feelings and the fatigue to pass. They always do. I tell myself they'll pass this time, too.

My list for the day is untouched on the refrigerator door. Things are bad enough this time, it's a simple one.

Shower

Walk the dog at least once
Eat a meal for lunch (not a snack)
Call Mom and check in
Make dinner

Derek helped me make the day's list last night, and then he put it on the refrigerator where I'd see it today, assuming I make it to the kitchen. But he also saw the sort of day it would be when he was getting ready for work this morning, and took our poor dog to daycare on his way to work. He was right to do it. The idea of putting on Marcie's harness and going out beyond the front porch with her seems like a monumental task right now—nothing I'm up to.

I push myself deeper into the couch. I don't think anything on the list is going to get checked off today.

◆ ◆ ◆

It's Day Eighteen on the couch and Day Ten of construction when the team's foreman sits down behind me on the coffee table around mid-morning. I know him by the sound of his cowboy boots on the tile, and, when he finally speaks, by the roughness to his voice that I remember from when he first came to see the space.

"Your husband says you're depressed."

How can he tell I'm not sleeping? Maybe he's just guessing. Betting that I can only sleep so much… but he'd be surprised.

"How depressed?" he asks next, when I've yet to answer.

I will myself not to press deeper into the couch. As usual, I'm facing its back, burrowed into cushions and blanket. The dog—whose purpose was partly to get me out of the house and walking—is in daycare again. She loves it there, playing with the other dogs, but it's still one more thing for me to feel guilty about. Derek, of course, is at work.

A week and a half into my latest bout of depression, I'm a third of the way toward reaching my longest deceleration into all but non-existence, and although I'm having no extreme moments of suicidal thinking—'suicidal ideation' to be all formal about it—I'm also not improving. *Ideation…* that term always sounded more like a child trying to sound their way around some medicine than what it should be. The word for picturing razor blades and jumps off bridges ought to be messy, though I've never talked to any *non*-ideator who'll admit to the sense in that. More often, I think the formal term puts up a wall of comfort for the ones doing the talking versus the thinking. Like Derek, and my mom, and every psychologist I've met in my life.

I hear a sigh behind me. No part of me is more than slightly curious about the man sitting behind me, stranger that he is, though I realize that's the depression's apathy and not the thought of an educated woman well into her thirties. I do know that. I just can't make myself care or act on the thought.

"My boy Joey said he pinched your ass. You didn't react. Pretty well gone, aren't ya?"

The man pinched my thigh. Could he not tell the difference?

"Here's the thing, pretty. I could use a girl on the crew. Us boys, we do well enough, but a pretty like you, we'd have more options. And I'm thinking you could use us, too."

I blink, wondering if I'm dreaming, but hold myself on the couch. I'm either imagining the conversation or this man's messing with me.

"Take your basement. We re-do it, get it all fancied up to the way your man has asked. Here six weeks or so and then gone, right? But there's more to it, pretty. A lot more. Meanwhile, we're using it to dig into some of your neighbors' basements. Stealing some... well, let's call it *life*, here and there. Your husband's got too many worries to notice. You ain't barely here. Your neighbors don't speak to each other any more'n most, and who cares if a few of us stay overnight to do what we do—don't leave as you'd expect? Who knows the difference? But it ain't always this easy on us, even specializing in basements that the owners don't go down into when we ain't working. Sometimes, some distractions get necessary. Distraction like you could come in handy, and have some real benefits for the both of us."

Is he really saying they don't always leave at night? That they're using this job to... what? Steal what? I must be dreaming.

Still, I keep myself from moving. In this mode, I'm so often still, it's not hard to stay soaked into the piece of furniture, confused and pretending non-existence.

The man behind me shifts, and stands, the creaking of the coffee table proving it.

I breathe.

"Oh, pretty, by the way. You join us, this'll be your last trip into depression, clinical or otherwise. How's that sound to you?"

♦ ♦ ♦

"So, you're saying you're having lucid dreams," Derek cuts me off.

"What? No, I just told you—"

"You just told me our contractor, our well-reviewed and licensed contractor who the two of us picked out and met with together and approved, sat down and talked to you like he's a cult leader instead of an expert on mother-in-law suites."

I bite my lip, watching my husband and trying to think of how to answer that. Technically, I can't disagree with what he just said. It's all true. That's what happened. The fact that I believe it happened and Derek only thinks I dreamed it up and told him about it is the issue.

He takes another bite of the stir-fry he ordered and waves his fork at me. I take the cue, lifting a fork-full of the meal to my lips. But I don't taste it, despite knowing it came from our favorite Thai place down the street.

Derek doesn't believe me.

"How many times did you leave the couch today?" he asks.

I force myself to take another bite, and chew.

"Did you shower?"

He knows I didn't. "I will after we eat," I answer quietly.

That seems to end the conversation. He refocuses on the food, and pretends not to notice when I slip a good portion of mine to the dog. Our boxer Marcie knows the drill—when I'm spending more time on the couch than walking around and playing with her, that's a good sign she can lay by the couch and get table scraps to her heart's content. I scratch her ears when my plate's empty, and she grunts her approval before setting her head down on my feet and going off into her own dreamland.

I sit back on the couch, telling myself I'll get up and shower soon. Maybe when Marcie wakes up for her nighttime walk. Maybe I'll do the dishes, too. Maybe I'll do all of that and then go downstairs to see if anybody's there. I didn't tell Derek about that part of the conversation, about how the foreman insinuated that some of his men don't leave some nights. I don't remember why I left it out, but it seems like an awful lot of work to bring it up now.

◆ ◆ ◆

On Day Twenty on the couch and Day Twelve of construction, the foreman comes back. Since he last talked to me, I've remembered his name is Tony something-or-another. It's later in the day, well past when he and his men broke for lunch.

"Hey, pretty. How ya doing today?"

I doubt he expects me to answer. I don't.

"I didn't get any calls about inappropriate contact or get fired, so I'm thinking you're either so far gone that you didn't even tell your husband about our conversation, or else you've been thinking on it and that's why you ain't said nothing to him."

He's so matter-of-fact. It's tempting to tell him the truth, to turn over and let it all out—I guess that means this is an emotional day when I'll end up doing a lot of crying tonight. The thought barely passes by my view, but I know it for truth. I'm outside of myself, aware of what I'm doing and how much I'm slipping, but there's no emotion to the thought right now.

"How does it sound, pretty, to be past this depression forever?"

I swallow at the unreality of that thought, and I'm answering before I can stop myself. "Lived with it forever. Doesn't go away. It just… sleeps."

There's a pause, and when the man speaks again, his voice is softer. Understanding, like Derek's is when I tell him the depression is approaching again and I'm trying to put it off, before he gets tired of dealing with it.

"Sounds like it came to you when you were a child, huh?" he asks.

I nod into the couch.

"Well, maybe we could help each other, pretty. My boy Joey—the rude one, you remember—he had a death sentence before I met him. Was wasting away from cancer. His parents were trying to turn their basement into a library for him, thinking that giving him a dream of his would perk him up and keep him around a few more years. It wouldn't have, but I did. And you seen Marco? Guy with the scar on his neck and the long mustache? He had some disease I can't pronounce, would'a been gone within a few years if I hadn't come across him."

I turn over on the couch, keeping toward the back of it. "What are you, Jesus? Collecting followers and saving them through your magical healing powers, so they just follow you around for the rest of their lives?"

"She speaks in full sentences." He's wearing a grin that looks sad, crooked, and I think the same thing I thought when I first met him, when he first came to the house and gave Derek an estimate. The man looks too young to be so mature, leading a crew or speaking with the kind of confidence that comes from wisdom rather than the cockiness of youth. His hair is too long and curly, like he's out of the 1970s, and he's got the dust on his button-down to show he works alongside his crew. But he's probably, in general, cleaner than I am; it's been a few days since I found the energy to shower.

When I only stare at him in response, he leans forward, his knees serving as landing pads for his elbows. I notice his nails are long-ish and dirty, with what looks like mud beneath them.

"I'm not Jesus, pretty. But I can save you from yourself, you want me to."

"You can do what pills and psychiatrists and my loving husband can't, huh?" I ask. The question was meant to be a joke, but it came out too sincere by half.

"If you want me to. And Joey might have crossed a line, but if you want to join us, he won't do it again. We're a family. We take care of each other."

The implication is pretty clear. I don't know what he'd think of as 'taking care of me,' but whatever it is he'd mean by it, I have no doubt that he'd do it.

"I could give you a few days. See how you like it. See if the taste makes you want to join us, long as you promise to keep quiet afterward."

A laugh strips itself out of my throat. "And if I'm not quiet, you'll kill me?"

He grins, and then he shrugs. "You're not quiet, the state you're in? Your sweet husband will lock you up in a hospital where nobody'll listen to you ever again, till you learn to be quiet again, and me and my crew'll go on like nothing ever happened."

The words sound true.

I feel my hand twitch, my heart speeding up a touch faster than it usually does when it's not being pressed by physical exertion, rare as that's been lately. But it's not as if anything this man's saying could be real. Saving me from depression, his crew from fatal diseases? There's no way.

And yet... what if there is? My mind's just far gone enough to wonder, as if from a distance.

"What do I have to do?" I ask him.

"Close your eyes."

Without thinking about the possibility of backing down or ignoring him, I do it. I close my eyes, there where I am lying on the couch. There's a sense of falling as he leans toward me, to the sound of the creaking coffee table and the neighbor's dog barking and a quick hammering downstairs somewhere, and then I feel a depression on the couch where one of his hands lands in front of me.

I don't flinch from him getting closer—another sign of how far gone into this bout I am, it occurs to me. What's happening doesn't feel real.

But then I feel one of his hands pressing my hair away from my neck, and hot breath on my skin just before lips and teeth. Teeth that are too sharp by a factor of ten, even sharper than our pup's. My eyes stay closed, but my hands clench into the couch as a stinging pain eats at my neck. I should scream, but I don't think I can.

When he sits back, I can feel blood trickling down my neck, but he stops it with his finger just as I open my eyes and stare at him. There's blood around his lips.

"Now, this," he tells me. In another moment, he uses one of his dirty nails to strike a deep cut through the skin of his forearm, about two inches wide, and before I can say anything, he's bringing it toward my lips, nudging my shoulder with his other arm so that my face isn't quite so buried in the pillow and he can better angle toward my mouth. "Try it," he suggests.

And I do.

The warmth on my throat is like a thick tea, like a cinnamon-flavored chai with the added tang of pomegranate. It's blood—I know it's blood—but that's not what it tastes like. My mind tells me I ought to be throwing up, pushing this man away from me, but for once, I welcome the distance that my depression brings. I welcome the fact that it's as if I'm observing myself from the outside, thinking about what I should be feeling instead of actually feeling anything at all.

When he pulls back, I can't help licking my lips.

"How do you feel?" he asks, sitting back from me and pulling the sleeve of his button-down back down to cover his bloody forearm. The blood leaks through the fabric, and I can't quite bring myself to take my eyes off it. "Think about it," he adds. "How do you feel?"

My tongue is darting over my lips, licking up the remnants of this man's blood, but the taste of it is welcome. Fresh. "Fresh," I say without thinking, and finally I look up to meet his eyes. "I feel fresh."

His grin looks more honest now. "That's a new one on me. Now, come on down and meet the boys."

He stands up, and though I don't expect it of myself, I stand. It's an easy, unthought-of thing to stand up and walk behind him over to the door. That, more than anything, is a shock to my system.

Where's the lead in my feet? The thoughts in my head telling me how warm and comfortable the couch is, how I'm not really hungry or in need of a bathroom or food or anything else but the sweet comfort of the cushions and the blankets and sleep? Where's the drowning desire to let the world go by me? The thought of dreams as more welcoming than anything else I could find away from my nest of cushions and blankets? The dread of speaking to anyone, meeting anyone, let alone moving?

Disrobed of the ever-present blanket, I follow the man over to the basement door, and stand waiting while he calls down to his men that 'the lady of the house took a first sip,' and now they'll show me what things are about. When he pulls the door open to usher me downstairs, I step ahead of him and walk on down.

Our basement is about half-done. I can't remember how long they expected the renovations to take, but if I had to guess, I'd say they're probably right on target. I can see where they've finished off work on electrical updates and plumbing, and there are walls partitioning off rooms, with insulation going in on the outer walls. A kitchenette is taking shape in one corner, and there's a new door that I can see leads straight out to our backyard, though a tarp covers its window. Derek will be pleased—this'll be the perfect space for his parents to stay after his dad's hip operation, when he can't navigate stairs and while they keep trying to sell their house in favor of buying a one-story. It's just what he hoped for, so far.

The only thing unexpected is a hole in the wall on the side of the house that must be facing our cross-the-street neighbors, the Winslows. It's large enough for a man to crawl through.

The foreman gestures to it. "Like I said, we do the work, and we take some extra payment via visiting neighbors. We take some life, and maybe branch out from their home at night to visit some others, but nothing gets traced back here. We're out of here in a month, nobody the wiser. All the homes round here are the same design. Easy enough to tell from permitting whether their basement is done up. It's not. Makes it a simple thing to head on over and visit. If you've got the right energy and strength and tools, that is, which we do. But the five of us, we could use a professional distraction to help us out. Warm the waters and the blood sometimes, so to speak."

I feel myself swallowing, preparing to ask questions, but instead I walk over to the hole and peer inside. It's a tight fit, but any of the men in my basement could go on through. "I never much liked the Winslows," I find myself whispering.

Behind me, the man named Marco laughs.

"Come see this," the foreman says, gesturing me toward the kitchenette.

When he opens up the brand-new refrigerator's door, I see rows of small bottles holding a dark-red liquid. I'd think it were a thick grape juice or prune juice if not for what I experienced upstairs. Without considering what I'm doing, I reach to my neck and feel the spot where the foreman's lips landed earlier. There's a cut, but it's not as big as it should be. And there's no real pain—just tenderness.

"Looks like a hickey now, pretty, but it'll fade before your husband gets home. That's the way of things."

I turn my back on the blood and look around the group of men. All of them but one look my age or younger, but they don't seem threatening. "So, you're vampires." I roll the words on my tongue, seeing how they taste—they don't taste or feel so odd as they should, really.

"Not like what you've read about, though," one of the men says. This is the one of them who looks older, closer to his fifties and with a close-cropped haircut of gray. He's got a military look to him. "We take what we need from life and earn honest livings, mostly."

"The undead," I say, unprompted, and sit heavily on the floor.

The foreman crouches down to look me in the eye, examining me as if he thinks I might faint.

"I just need to breathe," I tell him. "That's all." I close my eyes and try to focus on who I am, where I am and what I am. I try to find the depression that usually weighs me down, that's kept me on the couch for weeks, and understand what's happening, but it's as if it's gone. As if I'm suddenly cured. But that's not how it works.

I open my eyes when I feel someone else crouching down in front of me, breathing into my space. The man before me is one of the younger ones whose name I don't know. He's got some mud smeared on his brow, and I'm guessing he must have recently come from the tunnel.

"Joey," he says.

"The one who pinched me."

He has the slightest grace to look bashful, turning his eyes down as his cheeks blush red. "Sorry about that. It was a test. To see how off you were before Tony talked to you 'bout anything."

"You passed," Tony says from the side. "We thought you were just another client when you and your husband hired us on. This wasn't in the plans. Seems like you need some help, though."

"Seems like you already helped me," I answer, though my eyes are still flitting between the various crew members, trying to decide whether or not any of this is real.

"You feel good now," Joey says, standing and taking a few steps back to lean on the covered kitchen island. "It takes three trades for you to become one of us. If you don't do another tomorrow, and the next day—"

"The depression'll come back. Least, I see no reason why it wouldn't," Tony says, and I realize that's how I'm thinking of him now—as Tony instead of simply as the foreman.

I try to find the weight in my limbs that I'm so used to, but it's gone. I feel like I could stand up, walk the dog, go shopping, apply to jobs, and then greet Derek with a hot meal… all without thinking about it. Before I can reconsider, I'm asking, "And what would that look like? Joining you? I have a life."

"Not much of a life if you spend it laying on the couch up there. Talk about the undead," Marco comments.

Another laugh escapes my throat—I haven't laughed in weeks, and that's twice in one day now. "You've got me there," I tell him, and then I stand up and look to Tony. "But seriously, I need to know what we're talking about. I don't know if this is real, but if it is, I need to know."

"You'd work with us," Tony says. "Help me land clients, maybe help with some other aspects of the business if you want. And when the tunnels are open, you'd help out with the moving, the exploring, the taking. We don't take anything that'll be missed. Blood gets renewed overnight. I'll teach you to help calm the people we do come across when waking—your pretty face'll do a world of good in making that an easier filing, compared to our mugs."

"And I'd lose what?" I ask. "Daylight? But you all showed up in the morning, so I don't understand…"

"Like we said," Marco puts in, "we're not the vampires you read stories about. We stay out of direct sunlight. We live in a cloudy, rainy city that makes that simple. And we show up to jobs before the sun's full-up, and go home when it's mostly down. We still eat and do everything a normal person does. I go home to my wife most nights, to her home-cooked meals and our kids. But the life—the blood—keeps me going. I'd be dead without it. What's sunlight against that?"

Tony shrugs. "Summer can get tricky. Dog-walking mid-day might be an issue. But you join us, we'll put you up a fence around that backyard one night. That'll take care of the pooch better than you can now. Sun or not."

I think of how rarely I've seen the sun over the last few years, as the depression has come more and more often. And how much I miss cooking a meal for Derek and feeling like a wife to him instead of a hanger-on.

I look around the room, meeting the men's eyes. "I had thought about getting a job again."

◆ ◆ ◆

When Derek comes home, I've made dinner. Chicken piccata with breaded zucchini. Garlic bread is in the oven, and there's a bottle of white wine chilling in the refrigerator, wine glasses sitting by our plates.

I can almost feel the shock radiating off of him as he reaches the door of the kitchen. Marcie whines by his leg, and that brings him back to life so that he reaches for her bin of food from beneath the cabinet and begins the ritual of offering her dinner. But his eyes are still on me, processing. I can't blame him. I showered, of course, but I also put on a dress and makeup, and while he could care less about either of those things—he really is a decent man, my Derek—he's recognized both as signs that I'm getting back to being myself.

"You're feeling better," he says aloud as soon as he's gotten Marcie eating and can take a step toward me. He sniffs at my neck, where the bite has already somehow healed, and smiles. "You even put on perfume. You haven't done that in—"

"A month. I know. Thank you for being patient, love. I hope you're hungry."

He's still staring at me as I pull away from his hug and begin the process of getting dinner served.

"You don't usually come out of it so suddenly. You think... that's it?"

I pull an oven mitt onto my hand and open the oven, bending over just so to show off my figure as I reach for the garlic bread. When it's atop the oven, I look back to him before starting to cut it apart. "I think that's it. I think it's gone. Maybe for good this time."

He laughs, for the first time in at least a few weeks. "We can only hope."

I don't tell him there's more to it than that.

Nine weeks later, all signs of depression in my rear view, I'm with Tony—my new boss and the foreman who officially saved me from myself—as we're meeting a new couple across town. The sun's just gone down, and this is my first time meeting new clients and being called on to make a first impression, given that I came onto the payroll when they were partially into a new project. The couple hiring us smells good, and I think I can pick up a scent of the pine forest they must have been running through this morning. They're in office garb now, but the smell of the forest is heavier on them than sweat.

In the kitchen where we first talk about the plans, there's the smell of vegetable omelets in the air, lingering even after a full day's gone by, and it smells so good that I think I might wake up early tomorrow and cook up a nicer breakfast than the normal cereal for Derek and I. That was perhaps my biggest relief in all this—I can do without the sun, but the idea of not being able to eat a normal meal and enjoy it, even when not depressed, would have been a hard pill to swallow. A worthwhile pill, but a pill nonetheless. Whoever would have guessed that a day's or night's drink of blood would be best enjoyed after a sweet pastry or as the lead-up to a fancy dinner, it wouldn't have been me.

The basement is standard, just what we were led to expect it would be, and my presence seems to reassure the wife about the fact that there'll be a crew of men working in her basement all day while she works from home. I nod and laugh and smile like I've reassured a million women before her, and when the husband looks at my legs, I pretend not to notice. Meanwhile, Tony bends over backward to explain his inflated quote, even as I can see that he's looking around the walls and determining where best to cut into the neighborhood.

When we're walking outside, strolling in the dark, he pats me on the arm in silent congratulations. Neither one of us has to say it—the couple will be calling to hire his crew on by the end of the day tomorrow. In his pickup, we take a breath and sit back in the seats. "He smelled like pine," I say.

"You want the first taste?"

I think about bending over the man when he's sleeping, while Marco or one of the others tastes the wife and the others keep working on the tunnel, and the rush I'll get. I'm not even thirsty yet, not after feeding a few days ago and having snacks since then, but my mouth waters.

I've long since forgiven the men for tasting me and Derek while they were working on the tunnel out of our house. It doesn't hurt that Tony let me pick up a misplaced diamond earring from the last house, as a sort of signing-on bonus, as he called it. It matches the diamond necklace that Derek got me last week, to celebrate me being out of the depression for two months. Traditionally, that's the safety mark. The point at which we know my recovery hasn't been temporary, and I should be out of the woods for at least eight months or so more. There's no telling how long it will be before he accepts that the depression's officially gone, out of our lives, that the blankets I'd burrow into on the couch-turned-bed can be kept aside only for cold nights now rather than dark days, that Marcie will now only get doggy daycare when we leave town for a day or want to give her a playday to get some energy out, and that I've now got a job which won't disappear into the ether because I've taken to zoning out or sleeping late on one too many occasions.

But all of that knowledge is running in my blood, just as sure as the diamond hanging from my neck and the warmth still slick on my tongue from our morning's coffee break. And it feels good. Fresher, and life-filled.

Find a living that both supports and hides your vampire nature— preferably with your own kind

PART 4 – FULFILLING YOUR DUTY

The most common lament I've heard from the oldest of our kind is some flavor of, "What's the point?" Indeed, for how many centuries can a being Peter-Pan their way around the world before just existing grows too dull to tolerate?

I may not be in the popular majority—especially among those who treat the *Lost Boys* lifestyle as the gold standard—when I say that duty is a necessary component of an unlife well lived. Though I hardly bought into his rationales when the man was alive, I daresay I grew into Doctor Freud's theory that "work and love" were the recipe for happiness; for me, both are satisfied when fulfilling my duty to fellow vampires.

I could pontificate about how this sense of purpose might motivate the kinds of actions that keep a vampire alive and well, but I fear I have few statistics to support such a claim. Regardless, we are creatures in this world, and how we choose to live will impact it.

Though you will have to determine what is important to you, consider your family, whether sires or spawn; the city or country in which you live; your loyalty to a belief system or a way of life; and how you will address threats to your kind.

LEECHES

BY C. L. FORS

I have found that a life spanning centuries instead of decades makes the cuts and bruises inflicted and incurred more injurious...

The minutes of unlife become hours; hours, days; days drawn out into years that stretch decades, until it seems three centuries have come and gone while you sat sipping at a glass of mundanities and forgot to look up and notice the passage of time. Your experience becomes a magnified caricature of a human existence, and the same magnifying principle applies to your person as you become more blood-soaked ghoul than man. A slap between mortal friends becomes a beheading among the undead; a betrayal, when carried out by an immortal, becomes a plan to entrap and torment over lifetimes. Eventually, as one's own crimes amass and their severity rivals those of the gods, the question of forgiveness arises.

It is a phenomenon known only to the immortal undead, and only those who have the intellect and the stamina to stay awake, to persist and perceive in perpetuum. So when I tried to explain it to Cartia, to prepare her for the double-edged sword I offered, she had little understanding.

She curled her sweet, warm lips into a little bow against my frigid cheek, and she whispered, "I want to be with you, Andreas." Such sweet nothings for the recently met when I could have just as easily drained her as wooed her. She was unaware how precarious her life was in my ancient hands.

A butterfly has no concept of a hummingbird's life. Neither could fathom that of an owl. All of these would sit dumbfounded at the perceptions of the tortoise. Just so, Cartia had no chance of heeding my warning, which I gave not to comfort or protect her but to forgive myself for what I knew would come. It had been the same with Issachar, Cassius, and Olivia before her.

But this was Cartia, my little Cartia. Ever a dove, my paloma, I called her—peristera, colombe—for the little sounds she made as she delighted over the most minor things, the taste of rich creme eaten off of my fingertips, or a crawling spider to be captured and released onto the balcony.

Sweet Cartia. I had found her by the sea, a fisherman's daughter on the island chosen for my seventh death and rebirth in the year 1564.

As the progenitor of *De Humani Corporis Fabrica*—a revolutionizing atlas of the human internal anatomy, superior to earlier Greek extrapolations from the corpses of animals—my face became too well known for my long life, considering that, at twenty-three, I was an accomplished physician sought after by kings for their private care. What can pass for good health and vigor in one's twenties becomes unnatural and alarming at forty-nine.

I had taken to wearing mortals' discarded hair upon my own face, secured with paste each night when I wakened—a beard to hide both eternal youth and recognition. The beard was a help for a number of decades, wherein I paid particular attention to thicken and then begin the process of graying the hair.

As civilization, language, and people change, I do not, and it becomes necessary to disappear and stage my rebirth. And so, when I was accused of some improprieties in Rome—the vivisection of living bodies—I found myself traveling to find the proper place to stage my death. Spain, Turkey, the holy lands, finally Greece, and instead of my death, I found Cartia.

My teeth pierced her flesh before further proclamations of love could pass her lips. Warm blood flooded my throat with the sanguine evidence of her fleeting mortality. The taste was salt, and heat, and iron, but beyond that, it tasted like Cartia. If any vampire ever insists that blood is blood—all the same—they are lying. Or else they have lost their taste for living, because in the blood we find our humanity, if any remains.

Cartia's blood was all wonder, that shining light that drew me to her. Her blood filled me with an aching hunger to absorb her wonder into *me*.

I drank until little Cartia grew limp and soft in my arms, a woman of twenty-two summers in the world of the mortals. I held her at the precipice of death, her breaths shallow, a sickly pallor blanching the warmth from her sun-kissed skin until her extremities took on the dusky lavender shades of a corpse. The time was drawing near, the time when it would be too late to remake her in my image, to claim the role of god and maker from whatever being had given her a first life—and still I hesitated.

She had the sweetness of Cassius in her smile, the same eyes, a deep brown like sea glass polished and reflecting the sunlight through them. His had taken on a deeper hue after the change, a subtle reddening over the decades of blood-drinking and as the spark in them had extinguished for good and all, the blood had seeped into the whites and ruined them completely. There was that of Issachar in her as well, and Olivia—ah yes, Olivia. She had more of Olivia than I realized that night.

Their long-departed spirits cried out warnings from her fading pulse, where it thrummed under my cold fingers. They had haunted me and dogged my every step since meeting her on the pier, where she sat dipping her toes in the water and smelling of the sea-salt air. To let this child die in my arms would end me, I thought—and yet I didn't have the courage left to continue under such circumstance. To let her live again and I live through her—alas, that would be an adventure I hadn't the courage for. Therein, my indecision was born, the crux of my disquiet engendered.

If I awakened Cartia, she would be my child in the blood, bonded to my very life-force in a way that had no mortal equivalent. Parent and child, lover and beloved, slaughterer and slain—none of these can compare to the intimacy, nor to the level of responsibility.

It was a close thing, my destruction and hers. I had given in to melancholy watching her die upon my lap. But something nigh impossible, stemming from her indomitable spirit, hidden under the bright exterior of youth and a capricious expression of femininity—caused her to move. There she lay, drained to the extremity, her heart a trembling thing that seemed to whisper each beat would be its last. In this state of deathly exsanguination, my Cartia clutched at my hand! I thought at first it was a death throe or even that I, in my state of distraction, had allowed her to die, and this was a spasm such as many a fresh cadaver on my table had evidenced. But when I felt at her throat, probing with my fingers for the beating of her heart, it was still there.

Cartia's grasping hand in mine was like a sign of things to come, a beam of moonlight through the glass lighting a way forward.

My malaise-fueled stupor broken, I found myself suddenly desperate to revive her in the blood. There are many ways to accomplish the necessary infusion of dark blood, the most common and indeed the most pleasurable method being to feed the child from a cut, but I had my own methods. Despite the pressure of time and my growing fear that she would die, I felt compelled to do it right. Not being a man of passion but of planning, I kept my bag near and now retrieved surgical tools, a scalpel for a clean cut.

I worked fast—so much time I'd wasted on doubt, letting my demons rule me—I needed to reach her heart before it stopped beating, not a challenging task if one knows the human body as intimately as I. In one swift but skillful motion, I cut through her skin, just above the breastbone, and then severed the ties of the pectoralis muscles so that I might peel them back to reveal her ribcage where the costal cartilage joins the sternum. It took only seconds, no need to feel for the slow beat of her heart. The last dregs of her life-blood covered my hands, and it was bright red—the blood of the living.

Quickly, quickly, I needed to get to her heart. The costal cartilage gave way like so much putty under my strength, allowing me to part her ribs and push aside her left lung.

I cradled her small heart in my hand and, without further delay, slashed my other wrist before sinking my fangs into the muscle of her still-beating heart. My own poisoned blood poured into the puncture wounds, filling the chambers of her heart and spreading throughout her body faster than any other method of transfusion. Other methods, while less barbaric, were tedious and, I am still convinced, less effective in conferring the more subtle strengths of the father to the fledgling. Transfusion by mouth makes a sluggish child, waking in a daze and clinging to vestiges of their past selves for weeks thereafter. There would be no such impediment for my Cartia.

As soon as my blood poured into her heart, it spasmed mightily in my hand and then began pumping furiously. The whole of her body vibrated against me, a tremble at first and then a violent shaking as if her body fought against my frigid blood to warm itself. The warnings in my breast

still whispered against this folly, against making Cartia—or any mortal—
my child again.

Each act of the transfusion set off an echo in my memory, images of
the first ones to enact with me the undead play-acting of parent and child.
It tormented my psyche. But I had no will to undo what I'd done. Cartia
was grasping hold of me, weeping, gasping as if she would suffocate. She
was no longer a limp doll in my lap. She tried to throw her arms around
my neck, but I had to hold her still; her chest cavity still lay open, her
heart in my hand.

She fought me, eyes wild and searching. I soothed her as I released
my grip on her heart and massaged the organs back into place. I closed
her ribcage and replaced the layer of muscle and bronze skin where the
blue of her veins stood out, unnaturally suffused with my blood. Her
smell was different now, the darker, more highly concentrated musk of
my immortal blood already changing the tissues of her make-up. I
mourned that a little—the warm animal smell of humanity would leave
her entirely over the following weeks, clinging and then fading. I pressed
my face into her hair to inhale her sweet scent for the last time.

"Shhhh… You are well. You heal already, my dove. Better than before, stronger." I could feel her fear, the rapid pulse of a heart fighting
death.

I renewed the cut on my wrist, ripping the healing skin with my teeth,
and I pressed it to her mouth—unnecessary for her transformation, but it
would soothe. Her flesh knit itself rapidly, and I could hear her ribs cracking and shifting beneath her breasts. Then my Cartia wrapped her arms
around my neck and died in my arms. Her shallow, reedy breath now
stopped altogether.

Then she opened her eyes to stare into mine.

The deed was done, and I could not have been happier to have a second chance in Cartia. She was reborn into my world, and I would do the
same.

◆ ◆ ◆

I staged an ignoble death for myself. Andreas Vesalius taken by unexpected illness, I became Vassilios Andreadis. The coffin now stood empty,
and I was beginning again with Cartia. How fresh a start it should have

been, the past few decades and my ties to the holy Roman Emperor shaved away as cleanly as the false beard from my chin.

For the first few weeks on the time scale of an immortal that, in reality, spanned years, Cartia's zest for life infected us both and kept my creeping malaise at bay. Cartia, I found, once invested with my power, wealth, and ease of movement, had her own ideas of how to live an unlife. As the daughter of a fisherman, she came to me illiterate, but I found her quick mind and voracious appetite fascinating to watch, as I played facilitator and professor.

It was not until she was reading Latin and Greek and speaking several other tongues that her interests shifted to the culture of the times. She insisted, despite my reticence, that we must step out into the world again, travel, and bear witness to the opening of the first Theatre house in England.

Again, I tried to warn Cartia of the finer points of an immortal perspective, that I had tired of the era. She was my sole pleasure, and even with the years we'd passed in obscurity, haunting libraries and universities in the dark hours, there were still those who knew me as Andreas Vesalius alive.

But Cartia was beginning to chafe at the restrictions I imposed, as well as her position of fledgling and she continued to insist.

I do not blame her that failing, but as delightful a creature as she was, she had possessed a temper in life that carried over into unlife magnified by the blood. The early years for our kind are characterized by a manic frenzy to experience all that the wide world has to offer, and Cartia was no exception. Her mind burned with what was more need than want, and it would be decades before she mellowed and developed the ability to understand the tortoise's perspective. The longer I denied her wish, the more lives she took in increasing violence, until we had to leave the island of Zakynthos.

She had forced my hand, and while my pride chafed at it, I couldn't help but feel compassion for her isolation.

I took her to Paris and Rome, to Egypt, and all the places in between. Cartia's hunger for life grew with each city she walked. She drank it in with greedy gulps, the blood of each culture, and the blood of its people. I drew the line at the New World Colonies, but that was well with

Cartia. What she wanted—now that her mind was full of the sciences, philosophy, and history—was not wilderness but the arts.

By no accident, we found ourselves in England for a private performance at The Theatre. By the look in Cartia's eyes as she watched the actors take their final bows, I knew we would be here until she'd drunk her fill.

Each day was taken up navigating the cursed daylight by way of carriages, parasols, and cloaks to attend theatrical performances. Each night was filled with parties and social calls as Cartia insinuated herself with the local nobility. Cartia delighted in confounding her growing circle of admirers by slipping out of a clever mimicry of their social etiquette and mannerisms into a display of her rapid wit and intelligence… She had made a study of them to blend in, and now she toyed with them like a cat courting mice. The only difference was that Cartia, as much as the blood tempted her, did not eat her friends. She played with them—Oliver, and the duke, and her dear set of twins, Desdemona and Deirdre. Then, when flush with the excitement of the night, we would retire and find less charming fare to dine on.

Her energy did thrill me at first. She was a pleasure to watch and reminded me of my first flush of blood and the early years spent in a fever of self-discovery. But as time drew on, her fervor began to wear on me. In the pale gray moments before dawn, a certainty began to creep over me. Cartia's exuberance, her boundless energy so carelessly invested in her short-lived playthings was stolen from me. Could I not feel myself weakening, withering in my mind and body? What else could explain it if not Cartia? It was as if the magic in my blood was a finite resource and she was siphoning it away with her extravagant expenditures.

She did drink my blood each night and I hers, an intimate sharing that should have nourished us both along with the human blood we took from dark alleys. However, as the weeks passed, I began to feel like my very life was flowing into her, and she was hoarding it for herself, gradually draining me of my vitality. Being an introspective sort, I felt a change in me, like cold water poured into a glass of warm. I heard the thoughts that came with it, and the thing I had long feared began to threaten. It had started the same with the others. Little thoughts like whispers as they fed on me: *Each drop is a year they take… It will leave you shriveled, depleted, and weak…*

I couldn't tolerate the exchange before long and began to deny her. If she pressed, I resisted, making excuses each night so as not to alert her of the change in me.

Her voice was plaintive as she begged. "Have I angered you, my Andreas?"

"No, my dove."

"Then we could return to Greece, to the warm Aegean Sea that always soothed you—"

"I do not have need of soothing. I am well. Hale and hearty. Now go to your ball before you miss it!"

She flinched at the sharpness in my voice. I'd lost control, and now she sat there in her daffodil-colored silks and petticoats, hurt lending a bloody film to the corners of her eyes.

"You are angry."

"No, no… I am hungry, that is all."

She bent her neck and offered it to me, flouncing over with a rustle of fabric, the low-cut square neckline giving me ample places to drink. She smelled of jasmine, a thick, cloying perfume I'd found for her in France, and the warm, unchanged blood of a fresh victim she'd taken in the garden at moonrise.

I put on a smile and cupped her cheek with a hand. I brushed my fingernails against the sensitive skin of her jawline and felt her shiver. *To sever her head now—it would be simple and would solve this thing I'd gotten myself into. All the power I'd given her would return to me, and the whispers would cease…* She was still offering me her throat. I could drain her completely and leave her weakened body in the sun. *End my Cartia?* Lucidity returned, and I pulled my hand away as if burned. "I—think I'll go and feed at the Abbey. I have need of holy blood tonight, my dove. Enjoy your entertainment without me."

I was gone from her before she could object, fleeing in the night like some dark specter. I ran through Westminster. The echo of my boots across the cobblestones gave the illusion of a chase. Truly, there was no question that I was pursued, but my pursuers were the same specters that seemed to speak from within my blood, dark, slanderous thoughts about my Cartia. *Are we leeches to you?* This voice was Olivia's own crossing two deaths and years of memory, words she'd spoken as she pled for her life and those of her brothers: *Are we not your children—your family, Andreas?* And

how I'd wanted to refute those infernal voices that demanded my blood
back from their precious veins.

It was my lingering humanity that drew the Abbot close to me this
fog-shrouded night when I knelt before his censor and wept openly, my
grief and repentance evident in my face. His robes enfolded me, and I
took from him what I needed, not to the last drop; no, I couldn't carry on
my shoulders the black crime of killing a religious man offering succor in
my time of need.

Still, I left him unconscious in the house of his god and turned my
monstrous grief-fueled appetite to the small, soiled neck of another innocent. The child huddled in the cemetery behind a stone angel, lacking
both family and shelter. I almost took pity and changed the wretch on the
spot so that I could play benefactor to another lost soul and gift him to
Cartia—but pity prevented me behind that alabaster angel of a grave
marker, and I left this one barely breathing. Better dead by night's end
than eternity at the mercy of my demons.

A nun was the last of my victims for the night, withered in the flesh
but not blighted. Her skin smelled of the incense of the church, and the
decades of life had softened her tissues. Her warm, papery flesh was like
crumpled rose petals in my mouth.

I returned home just before dawn, sated and once again repentant. I
stood watching the sunrise a moment too long, retreating only as the first
golden rays touched my skin with a warmth I knew would progress to
burning should I stay any longer. The impulse to stay under the brighten-
ing sky and welcome the end was there, but the fresh blood in my veins
beating in my chest with fresh resolve dampened the urge—and Cartia
was waiting.

I was even able to let her feed from me, and I from her, curled up behind the dark curtains around our Gothic bedframe. Little wooden angels
stared down from the ornate carvings as if to serve as warning and witness to my renewed vows to be suitable for Cartia and hold my darkness
at bay.

I attended her gatherings with fresh eyes and delighted in her social
prowess, her cleverness, and the way she cultivated the dearest of her

friends like a garden, culling the weeds and watering the roses with praise and largess. She was patroness of the arts and had even begun cultivating her own skills with brush and pigment, and I supported her in all endeavors but one.

As time passed, she began to drop hints that her friends would not last for as long as she wanted them to. This one's health was fragile, and this other's age advanced to a precipice past which quality of life would fail. Another gem, her dear Oliver, was in the prime of life, and she spoke wistfully of how sad it was that a rose must bloom past its prime. Each of her not-so-subtle hints I sidestepped, but I felt her growing discontent and her need for more.

Had I suspected a return to her previous antics, the violence that drove us from Greece, I would have cautioned her, scolded, or locked her up, anything to stop what came next.

I was newly enamored with her and her social circles, each of the closest of her friends' precious creatures that I, too, would have chosen for eternal companions had the risk not been so high. I told myself the threat of harming Cartia had passed. I could still hear whispers trying to insinuate themselves into my foremost awareness, but they were so small, so quiet, and I could tuck them away faster than they could make purchase in my mind. I truly believed my control would hold... but more fledglings were out of the question.

Not a fortnight later, Cartia came to me covered in the blood of our dear friend Oliver. She was dressed in white silks like some cursed bride carrying her beloved across the threshold, and the wounds inflicted on both of them left a crimson trail on the marble floors. Her approach was rapid and desperate, and she flung his fading body onto the bed where I sat, herself tripping and tangling in the velvet drapes.

She grabbed the lace at my throat. "Please... please save him, Andreas."

I felt pity as I had in the graveyard, for the blood tears streaming from those cherished eyes—and some for poor Oliver lying there in a deathly pallor, the skin around his lips tinged blue for want of blood. But then I saw the wounds inflicted on them both: her wrists cut and healing and a messy gash in Oliver's throat, blood soaking through the front of his tunic from beneath the lace of his shirt. She had tried to change him, and she'd made a mess of it.

I pulled her grasping hands from my clothing and shook my finger at her; I could feel the dark scowl forming on my face. "What is this, Cartia? You know my rules—and your own limitations. Look at your dear Oliver now!" I bit my own wrist just a little and smeared blood into his wounds until they began to close—not enough to change him but to give him a chance at living the rest of his miserable life with the knowledge that there was more, and he couldn't have it.

"I tried to do it myself—now you have to finish it!"

"Cartia, no."

"He'll die if you don't!" She pawed at me, gripping my wrist as if to do the deed herself with blood from my veins.

Panic moved me as thought and reason fell away. I pulled my wrist from her grasp, and Cartia's sharp nails cut into my skin. Blood flowed, and I was struck with an urgency to contain it. I pressed my wrist against my own lips and backed away.

"I'm begging you..." She pursued me across the room, and I heard Oliver moaning behind her.

Then Cartia took hold of me, stronger than I'd realized, and it rekindled that thing in me I'd thought to contain. I wrenched free again, this time without regard for any pain I might cause. I felt the thin bones of both her wrists snap. Fear kindled in her eyes for the first time, fear engendered at my touch. But instead of being sickened, I was emboldened, and I advanced on her. She fell to her knees before me, a grimace of pain contorting her lips, and I fell upon her. Despite her growing strength, she was still no match, and I held both broken wrists with ease. Her lace collar gave way like so much tissue paper, and the flesh of her throat was the same, no gentle puncture wounds; the beast within me wouldn't allow it.

"No more fledglings!"

My hands became talons at her throat, my grip crushing as I took her blood into my mouth. I would drink her to the last. Take back what I regretted giving. She would feel my anger, my desperation—with the floodgates of my mind so open I could hold nothing back. Issachar, Cassius, and Olivia's faces flooded into her mind even as I tried to extinguish her light, beautiful, vibrant flames such as the immortal world had never seen. They were like Cartia... my four children, a perfect complement to each other and to me, whom I'd found and made a full two centuries into my unlife. I had loved them, cherished them, and then something had happened.

I had felt myself weakening—with each, I lost more vitality until I was a shell, and those whispers began, the same that forced my hands and fangs to Cartia's throat. *Their birth into unlife is your death—too weak to protect yourself or them—* And I had killed them for it, placed my hands about their trusting throats, and crushed the strength from their bodies, still so much frailer than mine.

Then I drank them back into myself: Cassius with his lively brown eyes so like Cartia's, and Issachar, so gentle that he didn't fight me for the life I gave—then took away. Olivia was last, my Olivia, with her sharp Scandinavian features now transposed over Cartia's Mediterranean softness. So different—the same.

Cartia's eyes fought me as her hands did; instead of pleading, she challenged.

You love me!

Her eyes spoke it. Her blood sang it. Olivia's death had felt the same, a war between the part of me that loved her and the demons that haunted me. Olivia died fighting me, but Cartia—would not. I didn't have the violence left in me to finish her. She was right; I loved her. I'd loved them all...

Cartia lay broken at my knees, skin mottled, neck at an unnatural angle to her body, her throat seeping blood. Some of it dribbled down my face, and I massaged it back into her wounds. She struggled to lift her head, one eye locking on mine, and I scrambled away from the fury it held. She couldn't harm me, not in this state, but still, I feared her, and I feared myself. I feared the darkness of those voices and what they'd made me do.

I fled our rooms and once more returned to Westminster Abbey. Not for blood this time but for solitude. I climbed into a coffin in a small mausoleum, pushing aside the stone lid and replacing it with myself inside. Guilt tore at me, self-loathing. Cartia was alive when I'd stopped, but I knew there was little hope for recovery. I knew that I'd left her close to death. She needed my blood; she needed my care to recover what I'd taken.

The best I could do was leave her to die or heal alone. With each thought of regret, of revulsion at myself, I feared the next would be self-vindication—and that sneaking voice would find a finger-hold on my heart and use my hands to wreak more havoc on the precious child I'd created.

I slept fitfully as if in a fever, and delirium from the intensity of my suffering took me. Each of my children visited me in turn—I had no doubt it was a delusion of the mind and not a spiritual visitation. If such as this existed, there was no sliver of humanity left in me to deserve company of those so beloved and so harmed. Issachar's soft treble whispered comfort, his slender harpist's hand at my brow offered succor. With his mind of reason, Cassius questioned me, as if by doing so, he could draw out the demons that had killed him. Olivia, dear Olivia, came last, and it seemed at first that she would rouse me to anger, to wrath with her harsh words and insistence that I rise and take up violence again. My blood burned at what seemed a challenge to my strength, the very thing I feared to lose—until the sounds of scraping reached my somnolent ears.

I became aware that I was indeed awake, and the voice was Olivia's, and it was Cartia's, a cry from the blood we shared—a warning. The transformation she thought to have failed was a success—indeed, with my coffin now open, I saw him there: Oliver, a wooden stake in hand and a machete in the other. He bared freshly minted fangs and a look of triumphant gloating over his blood-stained garments.

Andreas... Her voice in my mind was tenuous, but her regret was clear, and the pain I'd caused her a clarion call to my better self. *He pursued us from Greece, from Zykanthos. I didn't know...*

Had she not given warning, I would not have woken fast enough from my stupor. Had I awakened, I'd have let him take me to the grave where I felt I belonged. With Cartia living and the possibility of forgiveness, I could fight for our protection and redemption.

The machete he raised high, wielding it with some skill, and he rent a long gash across my chest as if to reach my heart beneath. Blood poured from the wound, a waste of the vitality I needed to fight him. It occurred to me that this blood spilt was so much more than what I shared with Cartia, and none would be given in return as she gave—yet I felt vital in this moment of threat and combat. It truly was a sickness of the mind I was suffering, an affliction which I had centuries to solve if I devoted myself...

Renewed vigor flooded me despite another blood-letting cut from the machete. My full determination harnessed at last, I charged Oliver, and with the speed of the ancients, I disarmed him. I repelled him to the entrance of the mausoleum and sunk my fangs into his throat, where the blood flowed hot and fast. I drank deep of this our mysterious pursuer and took in his many secrets—

He'd followed me from Rome, where he'd seen me dissect the living—the making of Olivia. The rumors that forced me to relocate and abandon my position and identity were his. Then he'd pursued me to the holy lands and, from there, Zykanthos. Across Europe, he trailed after us until here in England, he'd finally ingratiated himself into Cartia's social circles, convincing her that he was friend and not foe...

I was near to draining him when epiphany struck me. A truth ran like a steady current through his thoughts: a foe, perhaps, but only because he believed me a danger to Cartia, whom he loved. He loved Cartia and sought to join us in this unlife we so clumsily shared.

I withdrew my fangs. A clear way forward was forming in my mind. Then I lifted this clever playmate Cartia had chosen and carried him back to our home, where Cartia lay crumpled on the floor.

Fear came into my little Cartia's eyes when they fluttered open and landed on me. That I'd given cause for such fear cut at me, but it was a bed of my own making, and so I placed Oliver next to her. Opening both of my wrists, I offered one to each of them. Cartia, conscious and suffering, took it readily and drank deep, a tumbling of thoughts and fears filling my mind with her sadness, her love for me, and her fear of me.

"Shhhh.... All is well, my dove. Your Oliver lives, and I am making him well."

I felt her relax as she drank, my words soothing her still.

"It is a sickness in me, and you've pulled it into the harsh lamplight that I might lay it to rest for good and all. Until I do, you have Oliver."

She closed her eyes and fell into somnolence as she drank.

Oliver was too weak to take the food I offered at first, so I forced my wrist against his parted lips and allowed the blood to flow. At length, he began to tremble as if this was his first rebirth in the dark blood, and he grabbed hold of the wrist I offered, the sharp eyes of the man who'd followed and cornered me locked onto mine.

I offered the same to him that I offered Cartia—the truth of my past harms—my weakness. His anger flared up to match mine, an inferno in defense of Cartia, but we found that they were twin flames burning from the same fuel, whipped by the same winds, and I found pity in him, compassion for my weakness so long as Cartia was safe from my hands.

And I kept my word.

I didn't stay long once they were revived, just long enough to set my affairs, and theirs, in order. Cartia would handle our estate in England, and I would travel again to the foremost institutes of knowledge and research. The other organs of the body had not eluded me when I set my mind to mapping them and exploring their mysteries. I felt certain it would be the same with the mind—if it took centuries, I had an endless span of them at my disposal.

The Blood Magnifies Everything

CHANGE OF THE GUARD

BY L. A. SELBY

8 November 1989, 0300
East Berlin Guard Tower

Rigidity. Predictability. Routine.
Survival.

The crowds below the thirteen-foot border wall surged and retreated fretfully in the near freezing drizzle, some slipping or swaying for balance on slick wet stone. Axel Stein, one of the border guards called *Grenztruppen*, swung the roof searchlight from his twenty-foot-high guard tower across hundreds of heads and backs. The beam flashed across belt buckles, buttons, and rain-shined leather, like glittering scales of a snake with an invisible head.

No beginning to that snake, but there would be end. As always. Guns and razor wire and concrete made sure of that.

Jeers and taunts jack-hammered across the Western wall, across the death strip called no man's land, past the wall of Axel's tower. They vibrated through the deep cold wet and the aging concrete, smashing at his ears.

"Tear it down!" "Pigs!" "Traitors!"

He'd heard such cries at the riot two days ago, half-million souls not far from here. He'd also heard them when he'd helped put up the first wall, the wire, in '61.

Tonight, fewer people gathered - hundreds instead of thousands - yet more insistent. Somehow louder. Louder even than the sound of Hans scratching himself at the next window with one hand and holding binoculars in the other.

Hearing enhanced by his vampire nature, Axel had long ago mastered the deep desire to pummel the man next to him for scratching so constantly. Instead of acting on violent thoughts, he confined himself to a flatly innocent stare.

The jeers drowned out his secret thoughts of freedom. He did not want freedom. Since their shouting would not win anything, his routine would be safe. Hell, but safe.

Axel needed rules and order, or he would end up true-dead instead of undead. Worse than true-death, he would fail the brightly pure mission of his undead heart, to deliver secret information across the border to his sister in the West.

For that, all must be the same and rules must serve him. A mental nudge to a supervisor here. A repeated suggestion there. He looked down at the tangle of slashing wires on top of the necessary barriers below. No one had caught him and never would, so long as those walls, his walls, remained.

Tonight, with the snake mocking below, he had his usual work to do and messages to deliver. Messages that would get him shot. He could not afford to be shot. When their bullets did nothing, they would know he was undead. Their next attempts to kill him would be full of deadly silver. In either case, his access to this tower and to the necessary information would be lost.

The very human Hans, his dark green uniform intolerably wrinkled, had turned from street watching and private scratching to thumping at today's coffee-stained *Neues Deutschland.*

Axel wouldn't want to touch it after Hans and those wandering hands. His nose wrinkled thinking about it. He mastered that look quickly before not-so-hidden cameras saw and wondered what was wrong with him. He had no friends behind the cameras.

"Seen this?" Hans stabbed at the spattered ink. "You see what they say about our work here, eh? You see how we are puppets--"

Hans stopped himself, as if he were a mere simpleton having a slip of the tongue, by saying "puppets" like that. It was a simple loyalty trick, a test to see if Axel would join in to complain out loud.

Axel had never even *whispered* words that might be treason. That Hans would try so simple a trick to catch Axel boggled the mind. No one so stupid as Hans should have ever passed the loyalty tests, or been assigned to the inner border.

Axel listened for steps on the corrugated metal stairs that separated thin beds below from stiff chairs above. Those steps divided rest from reconnaissance, except there was no such thing as rest for vampires like him.

He counted those predictable moments before Erich, the third guard, returned from the toilets below. There were two or three guards assigned to every tower. They were never allowed to be alone, and changed at random. No pattern of duty. No moment of peace. No friends.

Axel used the calls of nature to time his actions and seize his moments.

Steps on the stair. *Clang clang*. The boots came closer. Once Erich walked in, Axel would have fifteen minutes for his own rest break, his only time alone in the tower. Ever. In that time, he would do what he must, grateful the waxing gibbous moon was no match for the thick clouds and their protection.

Three. Two. One. Erich.

Erich looked and smelled like a banquet in uniform. Not from the slight lines of worry that had grown next to his jaw, not from the way his warm brown hair had started to gray, but from the way the prominent vein called to Axel from his neck.

Axel had never once given in and would not. Not like those vampires for whom the meal had become a high, wiping out common sense and leaving them so often burned by the sun, lost and insensible.

No, his hunger was strong, but had never overcome Axel enough to wipe away his common sense. Axel had only one blood source, by vow and by need. So no, he could not sample Erich.

Axel stepped back from the window. Time for the dance, yes?

He glanced, face carefully emotionless, at Hans. Then, as he always did on nights like this, nights with purpose, he stretched his arms overhead. His shoulders popped as if they could ever be eased.

"Tired, so soon in the night?" Hans said, as he did each morning at 3 AM when Aexl had stretched his arms over his head and made his muscles crack.

"You say such every night," Axel replied, his voice much deeper than his slender frame might suggest. His voice hypnotized those who should have been his prey.

"Stay awake." Hans flipped another page and wiped an inky finger on his thigh.

"I am always awake."

The truncated sentences were recorded. The glint at Hans's second button from the top winked at Axel. Hidden camera of course.

Here was the constant reminder no guard was ever alone, and no slip of the tongue was real. The loyal were never free. Never trusted. No voice went unheard. Ever tower. Every job. There would always be a Hans and his button hole.

Erich nodded toward the door. "Your turn." And took his station at the window toward the crowd, though of course it would not be to catch someone coming in. No one fought to get in. Only out.

"I go." As always, Axel looked deeply into Erich's eyes, a bit too wide with stimulants and fear of sleep. Sleep could mean life lost. "I am gone as I always am and return as I always do," he said his deep voice penetrating, doing what he knew it would do because every night it did.

Erich repeated, "As always."

Axel turned to Hans said the same. "As always."

Erich and Hans, their minds wiped free from rational thought, their eyes empty of understanding or sense, faced their windows, unmoving, as if they had turned back to watch the snake below.

That's what a watcher might see. Their stupor would last fifteen minutes. Anyone might stand still for that long, staring at a window if that was their job. In case anyone cared. In case a certain button-hole camera got activated.

The cameras skulking at the top of the stairwell had stopped working recently.

If Axel ever smiled, he would have. He'd made sure the failure wasn't reported. And no amount of eastern Marks would be spent on unreported problem. The cameras in the stairwell were broken yes, the cameras in the guardhouse no.

Axel concentrated as he'd been taught. He forced his will against the atoms of his body. He sang to them in his mind, telling them how to fly together, and what they must do.

He dissolved into a dark metallic mist.

Finely cracked concrete gave him as much egress as the Brandenberg Gate. On a clear night, someone might have taken note of a swift-moving shimmer. Tonight, not even that. For the cluttered crowd below Axel had become all movement and will.

His target--both place and person--was a mere thirty seconds to his supernatural speed. Time he must always know.

When he was ten years old, Axel had slipped down chipped stairwells and through half-hinged doors out on the street to find bread under cover of night. Such actions had been punishable with beatings, back then. His youngest sister, Ilsa, had followed him as far as the crumbled bricks of the long-abandoned subway before he caught her. By the time he had stopped berating her for risking a beating, he realized the determination under her tears. The flush of her thin cheeks meant he could not stop her from risking herself, when the need was great enough.

He remembered his sister's small body, covered in tattered rags, stooping to pick up a crust tossed from a window, and the smell of week-old bread. He must make a life that did not require such risk.

To save her, he would take whatever job he could to save her. He vowed he would never skulk ashamed in the shadows, find food in dark alleys, or hide his real self in darkness.

But he had become a vampire, and he had not kept that promise, so he had made others.

The familiar basement window welcomed Axel, cracked open despite the frigid drizzle. It rose just barely above the cobbled street itself, and anyone would have walked by without notice, though here in the deep hours and the cold, there were no crowds.

The hospital, *Krankenhaus*, next door, still had the bright white lights of the West calling him to come for warmth, to stay where he might rest. It would always call. He would always say no.

From mist to man. He reformed inside, soldier's dark green uniform in place, weapon at his side, head dry.

Ilsa greeted him standing, as she always did. The lilac scent of her perfume almost covered the sharp antiseptic of the white uniform hanging over her threadbare couch. The smell burned in his sinus like a snort of pepper, and he tightened his lips to not cough in front of her.

This was her place. He would not by deed or distaste shame her for any piece of it. Even by such a small thing as coughing. He turned and closed the window for her, hoping she had not chilled too much waiting, though he was always on time.

"Axel," she said, her voice a more cultured and smooth German than his own. Her arms lifted slightly as if to hug him, a muscle memory now instead of invitation after so many years. She dropped her hands and smoothed her checkered dress to cover the motion.

Lines in forehead and cheek, the swept-up curls piled on her head, had turned her into their mother. He missed their mother. Maybe that was why Ilsa did it. Her eyes held softness for what he suffered, and fear for what she was about to do.

He bowed stiffly, a way to show respect without pushing on her more than he was going to do, and already had. Time forbade the greetings they might have had, their pitiful dances too rehearsed for explanation or discovery.

"Ilsa, you look well." She gifted him a small but genuine smile and nodded for him to go on.

He said, "I have four names for you to pass to your friends." These were the names of the double agents he had discovered on both sides of the wall. All of them could get Ilsa and the Americans killed if not for Axel's information. It was still hard to say all he knew out loud, even after twenty years of this work. He always had to remind himself the stasi didn't live here. The cameras didn't live here.

Ilsa did not grab pen or paper because her mind was sharp, and she would forget no detail.

Axel paced to dispel the energy he could never escape, the kind that came from being constantly observed and always aware of how little time he had to be here before the guard tower would notice he was gone.

He listed, "Millicent Beck. Potsdamerstrasse. False information given to the Americans and any messages to her go straight to the stasi. Carl Dan

Trigg. Giving false codes to you every third Wednesday. True messages between to throw you off. Melinda Roth. Has helped four to go out. The next run, she will bring twenty, it is a trap, all will be shot. Dietrich Fallon. Guardhouse, which I will give on my next trip. He uses some way to create shadows in the searchlight, 2 AM, posing as drunk, a trap."

Ilsa swallowed and lifted her chin. Behind her eyes so many messages chased each other. Messages for her friends, plans, and messages for him. Their mission drove them both and she understood what he must do.

He knew back at his post, Erich manned the searchlight, Hans scratched himself, and outside the crowd remained. As it had been and as it would be always be, except Ilsa would not live forever. He would never change her into a vampire just to keep her with him. Not if she begged. He would not condemn her to the place of perpetual fear and boredom and order, necessary and inescapable.

Once she was gone, who then would take his messages to the West?

"Danke, Axel," she said. *Thank you.* "You have saved many. It is time for you to eat. Do not hesitate."

Ilsa now extended her arm to him. For this, she would not sit on a bed or couch. They both knew that what they did, this sharing, was too close to wrong. Too close to what lovers might do. No, she would stand, and they would face each other yet look away.

His fangs snaked from his gums painfully, bone through freshly-healed flesh, and he sunk his teeth into her wrist. She stared away toward her kitchen, like a woman remembering there was something left to do.

His chest trembled with the coursing of strength like the warm sun he remembered after nights shaking under thin blankets. His muscles flexed and brain fizzed.

His memories in hers had long ago fused by shared childhood, then by shared blood. Tonight's sharing was not the same.

Change.

When he let go her hand, it hung in the air for one moment as if she had forgotten it. Then it dropped. He helped her to her chair, leaning back against the pungent white coat. His renewed strength made her light as a kitten in his careful grasp. White lamplight paled her more than he remembered. Her shoulders slumped as their mother's never had.

He wanted to touch her arm again, to say some word of comfort. He did not. He had taken so much, over decades. Any comfort she needed should come from someone else who was whole and human.

Her lids drooped, languid. She meant to shield him from knowing her cost yet he always knew. This time she was shielding him from information. *Change.*

"Ilsa, tell me, I see you have a secret you hold back from me. Even its nature is in shadow."

He had so little time with her, because of his guard routine.

He said, "You must tell me what is the change you see coming. You know my success and my use to you and the world depends on sameness."

Things must happen as they always did his job must go on. Purpose. Meaning. Sacrifice.

She whispered, her breath stained with coffee. "Tomorrow, Axel. Plans are in place. If I tell you, you might try to stop it." She paused. "And I will be in the crowd. It is my right to be in the place of change."

"Tomorrow?"

His hands tensed, his neck rigid with the need to be gentle with her while fear and strength warred in his body. "Where is this change? Where will you be? No. No. You are too weak from sharing your blood." Not just from tonight, but too many times. She would need another day to recover.

She looked up sorrowfully. "It is a good thing, change. You will survive when the world opens up."

"I cannot!"

He recognized his fear, as if he was ten years old again, vowing he would never again hunt the night for food. Hiding.

The child he had been, the one who made foolish vows, had no idea what eternity was or how sunlight could be death. If he wanted to, he could take the memories from her yet that was a violation he would and could never commit.

"Why won't you tell me, Ilsa?" Somewhere, Hans would be close to waking.

"You would stop me and stop change if you could with your gifts and your strength. You, or perhaps others like you."

That made no sense to him.

Her eyes softened, focused on his as if she were the eldest, and he was the child. "You must let change come. You will not fail."

Weakness closed her eyes, and time had run out for him tonight.

She was all he had. Her, and the wall. His jaws clenched, as he did the only thing he could do and tore himself into the atoms that flew into the darkness, avoiding the searching beams of the guard tower.

Axel materialized on the corrugated metal stair outside the closed guardroom door. Inside Hans' heart had begun stutter forward in its rhythm.

Axel threw open the door with extra force, metal weight swinging freely and hitting hard against the wall. Hans and Erich started at the same time turning, hands reaching for weapons and dropping. Their eyes became focused and frowning.

Hans patted his jacket as if to make sure everything was there, another sign he hid a camera inside. He muttered, "I didn't hear anything from down the stairs. The *toiletten* must be flushed, ah? You must go back if you did not."

The story that Axel had only gone below for private business would be ruined if he did not follow all the actions a man would take, such as the noise of a small toilet. Such action should have been automatic, to make all the noises of washing hands and so on.

He mastered his dismay at his mistake and shrugged in a way that must seem dismissive with the taste of his sister's blood sharp on his tongue.

Axel said bruskly, "You didn't hear."

He moved toward the window and forced himself to brush at his own clothes, a thoughtless motion anyone might do but that a guilty man might forget. "Your hearing is pathetic."

Ilsa had never hidden from him before. He struggled to understand why now and what must he prepare to do.

He asked, "What do you see out there?"

Erich pushed at the newspaper, "Are you seeing the *Neues Deutschland*? Are you not understanding what you read? The borders see too many people coming too close. Rumors there will be new schedules for all guards."

Axel scoffed, "I believe nothing. All will stay the same for our towers. Maybe a few more come and go around our feet, but nothing to make news stories about."

His sister loved him enough to save what was left of him, a monster, to help him find a way to save people instead of destroying them.

Unless things changed. Then what?

Erich ran his fingers over his shorn round head, thick brows lowered as he turned to stare into the night. "I will be glad when these crowds are gone."

Hans said. "Something to see makes our lives more interesting. I will be sad to see them go." He burped the remains of his pungent lunch.

Axel had ceased to be of interest, or Hans wanted Axel to believe that. He never knew what to believe.

The sun would rise over the guard tomorrow at 0715. Axel could not be outside in the sunlight or he would die, so no matter what his sister had planned, if it was during the day, he would not see it coming and there was nothing he could do to stop it.

♦ ♦ ♦

9 November 1989, 2100

Rigidity. Predictability. Routine.

Hans lounged on his left. Erich rubbed at his deliciously bare neck. This night was the same as all others, the way Axel needed things to be. Their searchlight shone above. Walls and wire waited below. The smell of vinegar and wine, Erich's dinner, was too pungent for Axel's nose in the cold of their tower.

His special hearing told him when the number of careful boots on slick stones had doubled from the usual sounds. There were so many of them. The voices were not the same as last night. It was not the same sound as the big riot, not at all.

Shouting came from the West in front of him.

Yelling came from the East behind.

He could not understand yet what they were saying, but they were getting closer, and he would know soon. He guessed it was another riot. That meant another call to his superiors--

"Tear it down!"

Repeated chanting. Richocheting words. Rising tension.

He listened closer. No. There was change here. These shouts were not fear or rage. The timber was completely new. He heard laughter. Never in his life had he heard such sounds and even he thought in the distance... *musik.*

Past the far wall, he heard them coming before he saw them. They came, the swelling crowds. They came in neon coats and glints of metal, scales of a snake in his lights. He trained his binoculars as if he needed them, pressing plastic tight against his cheekbones.

Hans dialed the phone urgently.

Axel turned, waiting to hear the news. They must have answers.

Hans cursed. "No answer!" His voice rose, his eyes flashing wildly. "Do we shoot? What do we do?"

Erich tried his hand radio. It squawked while the crowd grew outside. The other tower responded, and the voices of the other tower bounced off their walls with confusion. There was the sound of fear Axel had been expecting.

From the radio a man said, "We can reach no one. We have no orders. The checkpoint, the gate has been opened! They are all leaving!"

Ilsa had known. The word "leaving" made hair stand on his arms and his throat close. Axel raised his binoculars again, but Hans jerked his arm. The binocular bounced off the bridge of his nose.

"It is time to go," Hans urged Axel and Erich. Whether he meant to safety or to call for reinforcements, Axel couldn't tell.

Erich bolted for the door. His boots clanged down the stair.

Confusion rooted Axel. He could not know what to do until he understood what the crowds meant to do.

Hans did not wait any longer. He cursed and left, taking his smells with him.

Axel needed the wall. The routine of the wall was all that he had known his whole adult life, and protection for his dark undead life and the secrets he had carried from East to West.

When the first axes hit concrete, his body vibrated as if the strikes had hit him. This was what Ilsa meant.

When the people shoved through his gate, he felt as if their hands stretched inside his ribs, pulling them apart.

And because he loved her, Ilsa's voice reached him from down in the crowd below just as clear as Lorelei's siren. He felt her presence inside their chaos. He felt the weakness in her body and the vast strength of her purpose.

"Tear it down!" she yelled along with all the rest.

His gaze pinpointed her exactly. She could not—should not be there. She was too physically weak from giving her blood.

And when her foot slipped, he heard it separate from a thousand shoes, heard it between the echoed strikes of chisel and axe against his wall. And when her head slipped below the others, he saw.

It was an accident.

It was something that happened when thousands came together as one.

November...

The day does not matter.
It is night.
The time does not matter.

On the frozen curb of a street in West Berlin, not far from the hospital, Axel sat. The curb pressed into his lower spine and his legs were straight out in front of him.

A car could have hit him, it if wanted.

He sat in cast-off wool, not enough to keep anyone else warm, but cold was not something to bother him. He smelled antiseptic in the air and breathed deeper because of her. He would get weaker then. He meant to die if he had to, but he would not steal blood from another, though the hunger ate him from inside out.

Already his skin had thinned. Already it had become hard to walk. There was no bread for such as him. He would not hunt the night for unwilling food. He'd sworn he wouldn't.

He had failed her.

Footsteps sounded nearby. A man in a gray trench coat and bowler hat crouched next to Axel, sharing a thick cloud of cigarette smoke.

Axel breathed out slowly. People should not sit so close, but they would because people wanted to help each other. The man rocked a bit on the balls of his feet like someone not used to crouching on streets.

It had been a mistake for Axel to sit here where anyone would stare or get too close. He waited for the man to offer the help anyone might expect after the fall of the wall. When none came, he glanced over, eyes not focused, and not truly caring.

A thick hand, almost blue with cold, held a slip of paper.

Axel.

It was Ilsa's handwriting on the paper. Just seeing her handwriting again made his eyes blink back unwanted tears. He snatched at it, knowing how crazed he must seem, but having to see her last words. He read them, not caring what this man must think. Axel heard her gentle voice and felt again her deep purpose in this world. He read:

There is still much work to be done.

Now he looked to the man's face so close to his own, watching Axel carefully. It was pock-marked and plain. It was an unsmiling face, a closed and determined face. He had seen that look in Ilsa's eyes before, like the kind that kept secrets for the good of the world.

The man held out his thick wrist to Axel, like a promise.

Even the eternal

must change to survive

ONE TURN DESERVES ANOTHER

BY A. J. BENSON

The sun, not the foul air—"miasma" humans called it—killed Sergio's precious Angelica. Or rather those horrific humans from Venice wielded the autumn sun as their weapon of choice. Sergio planned to return the favor, if the plague did not claim him first…

The day before, Sergio's vampiri pride—three females and four males—were moving on foot across eastern France, headed for a castle near Dublin where vampires might be welcome. They kept among the dense pines to avoid sunlight.

The pride had almost reached the coast when a band of rogues with makeshift knives discovered and tried to rob them. Were it night or had they recently fed, any of the vampires could easily contend with a few humans, but not at high noon when so drained and not so near a church.

Though Sergio's pride surrendered most of their belongings in exchange for their lives, Sergio refused to give up his turning bracelet, a simple black iron cuff to the uninformed, but infused with the blood of his maker and bearing turning powers.

One of the rogues stabbed Sergio, but he did not bleed red, revealing them as vampires—dangerously close to a church. The head of the vampiri pride ordered everyone to flee, but the rogues regained their wits quickly and gave chase.

As they scattered over the roots and logs of beech and oak, Angelica had tripped and been seized by the humans. Sergio's dear, sweet Angelica with her black flowing locks and warm brown eyes—who had made him a better person. Almost human again.

Gone.

Sergio's brothers had physically restrained him in the shadows until the sun set. Then he raced to the open field where those monsters had tied her. Her arms and legs stretched out in four directions, tied to wooden stakes. Her skin peeled and flaked like ash.

He cut the ropes from her hands and ankles, then cradled his beloved in his lap in the middle of that forsaken field. His voice gravelly, spent from the screaming, he whispered, "The stars are beautiful tonight. Wherever you have gone, I hope you may see them too." He did not know where their kind went when they ceased to exist here. He could not even call it death. That would imply they were alive. And he had not been alive for almost a hundred years. He hoped that something other than hell awaited her. Awaited them all.

Sergio brushed her hair from her cheek and found lines of salt where her tears had fallen. He pulled Angelica's hand, a dry remnant of the soft and supple limb it had been, to his lips. The sweet scent of her last meal had faded, leaving only ash.

Though it tore his own unbeating heart to do so, Sergio opened her brittle jaw and found what he suspected within: the chain of the amulet she had swallowed to keep safe. They had crafted the smooth pendant when they'd discovered they were mates—using their blood, their bond, and old-world magic few still practiced. Greater than even his maker's iron bracelet, with the amulet's power, they planned to have a child, who would grow to adulthood but remain immortal as a vampire. They could have been parents together. Now that moment would never come.

The amulet still held some of the sun's warmth. He cursed under his breath as he fathomed the heat Angelica had endured in her last moments.

Sergio vowed he would survive the plague and find the humans; they deserved to suffer for this.

Dante placed a hand on his shoulder. His brother, his pale blue eyes likewise deep with grief, but insisting on urgency. The pride dug a quick burial plot and laid Angelica's corpse to rest in the churchyard, fulfilling the wishes she'd carried from life into unlife.

Sergio placed the amulet in his pocket, a reminder that his pride now numbered only six.

They traveled into Calais under the cover of nightfall, with Dante and Leonardo navigating. Lucio and Gabriella covered each flank, and Alessandra remained near the back of the pack with Sergio—not trying to conceal her intentions. Alessandra offered to mark Angelica's gravesite on a map of Calais, but Sergio turned her down. He would never come back this way. Or maybe in one hundred years. That was the thing about being a vampire. They existed forever.

He touched Angelica's amulet. Or they didn't.

They found a butcher's shop near a stream. They watched its owner—a gray-haired man who seemed to enjoy perhaps too much meat as well as mead—close up and depart.

Leonardo, stronger than the fit twenty-year-old he appeared, crushed the lock on the front door with one hand. Together, they headed to a back room, passing the fleshy riches of pig and sheep. They made their way to fresh blood in vats at the back of the shop—but rather than rouse his hunger, the aroma only reengaged Sergio's rage and disgust.

Humans wasted this precious commodity on ridiculous dishes instead of gaining trust in the vampire community. Angelica had often told Sergio the two communities could co-exist, and maybe even help each other. But they had taken her. Now he wished them all painful deaths. The humans hunted all outsiders; now he would do the same.

Alessandra touched his clenched fist, and Sergio wondered how long he had been standing still. Beautiful with her long wavy red hair, Alessandra had turned at the ripe old age of 45 and had so remained for a century.

Thirty barrels lined the edge of the room, a chunky oak table running the length of it. Leonardo and Gabriella stood to either side of a barrel whose lid they had removed. Gabriella looked the same age as Leonardo but tiny compared to him, with her mousy brown hair pulled back in a strip of ribbon that had seen better days. But her eyes were bright blue and sincere.

Gabriella understood Sergio's grief. The pride had lost her mate, Carmine, to the plague just a few months ago. While vampires were less susceptible to the plague, they were not immune to it. She'd buried her amulet with him, pressing it into his hand like an eternal pledge of faithfulness.

Though unaging, Carmine had gotten sick just as the humans did. The same symptoms until he ceased to be alert, aware. Not alive.

As the one with the most recent loss, Sergio was offered the first chalice of the smooth red liquid to soothe his ache. He took the offering from Gabriella and looked at each of them in turn. Alessandra, Lucio, Dante, Leonardo, and back to Gabriella. "To Angelica." He raised the chalice, and the others lifted theirs, echoing her name.

He drank the whole chalice down, a dribble of blood running down his chin. They had chosen the barrel well, the blood fresh with a gamey taste. And with the energy it gave him, he could destroy cities. For a while, his own body felt alive again, as if the blood in his veins moved and his skin were warm.

In turn, each of the vampiri pride drank a full chalice, bringing with it the color of life. In darkness, they would pass for humans for several days.

◆ ◆ ◆

Later that night, they walked along a city street with numerous bars and brothels, and humans trying to enjoy what little life they called their own. Alessandra, who led the group, put up her hand and turned, torchlights catching a sparkle in her black eyes. "Perhaps a night in a proper bed? We have sufficient coin."

Sergio hated this idea, hated being this close to humans. But when the group took a vote, and Leonardo sided with Alessandra, Sergio bit his tongue. They slipped in quietly through a tavern door, and madness greeted them. A packed room buzzed with a cacophony of local gossip, metal plates, and wooden bowls. Sergio lingered near the door, his cloak still over his head, so he remained as hidden as possible, a trick Lucio had shared with them all about traveling among humans.

Alessandra and Lucio strode through the tightly packed room and spoke in tones no mortal man might hear over the din, but which Sergio heard clearly. "Do you have any rooms?"

The barkeep's voice seemed older than the wrinkles of his face. "The sign at the door says 'Inn,' doesn't it?"

Alessandra placed a small leather pouch on the nicked-up bar. Without either weighing or peering into it, the barkeep handed her three brass keys.

A man bumped Sergio and apologized before moving past. Anger flooded Sergio, and he wanted to burn this whole place down, but Leonardo would disapprove. He hated that he couldn't share his room with Angelica tonight. Leonardo would also disapprove of him holding on. To be vampire was to be disconnected.

Lucio held a key in front of Sergio, who grabbed the cold metal from his friend. Friend—an interesting word. Just a few years ago, they would have been enemies. Lucio came from a religious family, his brother a vampire hunter. Lucio's insights into their hunting techniques had kept them alive more than once.

As they maneuvered through the crowd toward their rooms, Sergio caught snippets of conversation.

An old woman in a shawl that smelled of cognac whispered across the table to a young man, "She's coughing hard, and the labor might take her. I don't know yet about the baby. You mustn't go see her." Sergio's stomach churned and he wanted to vomit. The audacious irresponsibility to bring a child into this plague-riddled world.

A group of men played a game with stone tokens on a fabric board. "You cheat!" The silver of a dagger flashed, and Sergio encouraged Dante, who walked in front of him, to move a little faster.

A thirty-something woman sat sobbing at a table telling the man across from her that her mother just contracted the plague and sent word to her daughter to flee north, never to return.

The narrow wooden stairs creaked with every step, like the bones of an old man as he took himself to bed. A single lantern lit the far end of the hall, and Sergio strained to read the number on the cloth attached to his key, "15." He and Dante would share a room tonight. In appearance, they were close in age, which was what the humans needed to see. The females took the first of the rooms, and Lucio and Leonardo took the next.

As Sergio put the key in the door, a loud, pain-filled moan came from the next room over. He turned to Dante. "I'll be right back." He would not tolerate this noise all night.

Another moan came, and this time a young woman's voice called out faintly. "Help!" And then she sobbed. It made Sergio think of the noises Angelica must have made just before she'd been turned. He may have been a vampire, but he would be no less human than her captors.

Sergio knocked on the door. He would not let his grief make him more of a monster than his turning had.

"Hello? Please help me!" The thin, strained voice held a scrap of hope.

Sergio muttered, "I hope I don't regret this." And he opened the door.

The woman's scent, full of musk and amber, overpowered him. Dozens of candles lit the room, and he glanced behind the door to make sure they were alone. A woman with strawberry blonde hair lay on a four-poster bed wrapped in linens and blankets.

His heart, had he one, softened to the agony on her face.

Her white-clad arms stretched toward the bed posts, her wrists tethered—one tight, the other loose. She flailed back and forth.

How ironic that one monster should come help another. This must be how the humans treated their unwanteds. Had they tied her legs too, she would be suffering as Angelica had. He could not save Angelica, but he would not let her suffer this way.

"Please help me."

"What is your name, bella?"

"I am called Veronique. And my baby's coming," she panted.

Due with child. His brain tried to process this new information. Indeed, for all the linens wrapped around her, he had failed to notice how ripe she was. "I shall fetch the midwife." He stepped toward the door.

"No." She gritted her teeth. "She won't help."

Sergio closed the door behind him and walked closer. The candles showed her face covered in sweat and grime. "And why is that, bella?" He looked about for water to wet her brow. Finding a bowl, he dampened the cloth and sat on the edge of the bed. "And why are you tied to the post?" He knew he should untie her, but something stayed his hand. And he hated himself for it. It must be part of the human birthing process. He had never witnessed one. He placed the cloth on her brow and set his hand along her cheek.

She strained the loosely tied arm to point to her neck, where he saw a large swollen node in maroon.

The plague.

He stood, staggering back as if struck.

"Please don't leave." Of course, he would leave. He had left his home and his love to stay away from the plague. "I don't think it will kill you," she continued.

"Woman, you are a fool if you think this will not kill us both." He considered the pain Carmine had suffered before his death to the plague. Seven days of swelling nodes on his neck and groin and three more nights of coughing up blood. Aches so unbearable Carmine had begged for them to stake his heart, but Gabriella forbade it, hoping his vampiric nature might help him survive. And so, Sergio had watched his brother writhe in pain through the window, and not even tried to comfort him.

Now, he found his back against the door and grabbed the handle.

Sergio had been exposed and could not go back to his pride, not without dooming them all. And he knew they would leave him as they had left Carmine—with cold abandon. The pride stuck together—as long as there was no threat from within, and then the pride elder would be quick to put down the threat. *He* was now that threat.

She moaned and thrashed again—from labor or plague, he could not tell.

"I will be back. I must tell my companions where I am."

"Promise you will return before dawn," she pleaded.

"I promise." He needed time to think.

"I know what you are."

Sergio felt the hairs on his neck rise, but this woman could not have known.

He walked to the far end of the hall from the stairs and looked out the window. A light rain fell, like tears from his sweet Angelica.

He could run, and perhaps not get sick. If he got sick, though, there would be no coming back. No one to help. He might plead with Leonardo like Carmine, but to no avail. Not even Gabriella had been allowed to enter Carmine's room.

The hall lantern flickered, its candle low. Dawn approached in just a few hours. If he were leaving, it must be now.

His blood-laden flask still hung over his shoulder, and he hadn't removed his old wool cloak. Angelica's amulet felt heavy in his pocket, and though it could turn a child, it could not save anyone from the plague. He made his way to the stairs, pausing to look back, eyes welling up. One step. Creak.

A door down the hall opened, and Dante called to him. "Where are you going, brother?"

"Just requesting some extra blankets for the woman."

"The one with the plague?" Dante had heard through the wall, of course.

"I need to think." Sergio had no idea where to go, but he heard Dante close and lock the door, barring Sergio entry.

He descended the stairs. The tavern was dimmer now; fewer people packed the room. Perhaps the barkeep sent people home at the end of the night. The old woman in the blue shawl sat alone now, her young companion gone. He stopped next to her, and dull, nearly lifeless eyes looked back.

"Are you the midwife?"

She glanced warily upstairs. "Why?"

Sergio tried to assuage his guilt. "Veronique in room 16 needs you. The child is coming soon." He moved toward the door, not touching anyone. He would not bring misery on anyone in the form of the plague. He would head along the dirt road to the stream and walk along it for a while. He felt his flask. Still full. His own infusion of blood felt low again, though, despite having drunk his fill at the butcher's shop. He wondered how fast the plague would hit him.

Sergio strode out into the chilly night air, glancing up at the lights on the second floor. Candles flickered in four rooms. He took off towards the stream, pace quickening with each step. He would not look back. He could not. Turning his back on the woman began his descent into vampiric darkness.

A pale crescent moon lighting his way, Sergio moved to the dirt road on the edge of town at vampiric speed. He flapped his cloak in the fresh air, trying to clear the miasma from it. Some small part of him still hoped to escape his fate. The sound of horses galloping in the distance on the cobbles met his ears, the rhythm mesmerizing. He would wait a week, hiding in the woods, and if he had no signs of plague, he would buy passage to cross the channel and make his way to the castle called Cassia where vampires might be welcome.

Before he'd reached the stream, Sergio heard horsemen draw closer on the road. They might not see him at all in his gray cloak, or they might not see him in time. So, he stepped from the road into the leaves.

"Fresh tracks!" one horseman called.

Sergio knew that voice—one of the hunters that had followed them from Italy. One who had tied his Angelica in the sun.

Sergio bolted into the brush, branches whipping at his skin. He could easily outrun men. He had never outrun a horse before, though. He listened carefully to the galloping of hooves as they met the earthy road, mere minutes by foot.

He arrived at the water—not the stream he expected but the Pas de Calais. Over the miles of water, the lanterns of Dover Castle flickered in the distance. He had gotten turned around again. He cursed himself for not having looked at the map of Calais Alessandra offered.

The horses emerged from the foliage, and he could see the torches of their riders. "You can't run from us!"

Sergio wasn't sure how they had found him. He didn't have much time, but plague or murder were both death sentences. He considered swimming, but it was too far even for him.

He had no choice but to fight. Men on horseback would make formidable enemies, but he had strength and speed. They had torches. He touched the amulet in his pocket. The warmth indicated dawn was a mere hour away.

He ran his fingers over its sharp edges—Angelica's blood mingled with his. His dear sweet Angelica tied—just like Veronique. Sergio resolved to survive and return.

He rushed the horses, screaming at them. The dark horse, spooked by the sudden noise and motion, bolted, rider still astride. The other, a dappled gray, backed up, rider still in control, but barely. Horses disliked vampiric energy, so vampires likewise avoided them.

Sergio stepped directly into the rider's torchlight, and his eyes went wide.

"If I went willingly, where would you take me?" Sergio demanded. It was risky, but the man might take him back to the tavern.

"Take you? I'm going to kill you! Leave you in the sun just like that other one." He dismounted and pulled an old sword from a scabbard and lunged for him.

Sergio spun, allowing the man to go flying into a nearby oak, but the man's blade struck his arm on the way, and a black liquid gushed from the wound.

"Damn it!" It would heal, but not for a day or two. And only if he were not infected with the plague. But Sergio did not continue to face his attacker; he went for the horse.

Sergio pulled himself into the saddle, and the horse bolted. He had ridden often when he was human, and it came back to him quickly. He leaned over to reassure the horse, to the extent he could, and then spurred her toward the tavern he never should have left. The mare didn't settle, but she followed his direction. As unsatisfying as that was, it would be enough tonight.

♦ ♦ ♦

The smell of ale and vomit filled the streets. Four tavern rooms on the second floor remained lit. He could hear Veronique moaning from outside. As soon as he dismounted, the mare took off.

No rope, no ladder, but the tavern itself was built of river rock and lime mortar. Sergio scaled the stones, wedging fingers deep into crevices, almost falling twice as he pulled stones from their homes. He arrived at the slatted wooden shutters of room 16 and pulled.

But they did not open.

If he broke the latch, the noise would attract the attention of the pride. He shifted his position on the wall, going past the room where Dante sat, and the one where Leonardo and Lucio spoke. He listened. The males spoke so low, he could hear only concern in their voices. His fingers pulled him further, but the stone was more uneven as he approached Alessandra and Gabriella's room. They might understand.

He waited. He loved them both as sisters, and they might let him in. He raised his fist to tap on the shutters and stopped. He would condemn them to his same fate. He slowly made his way back to the window where Veronique lay, her moans now low screams that shook the shutters.

He carefully cracked the latch, and the shutters swung open. Once inside, he closed the shutters behind him.

"You came back," was Veronique's only greeting.

"Yes." He took the bowl of water he had gotten for her forehead and sat next to her on the bed, wetting the cloth and cooling her face. He wouldn't flee again. He would be there through the baby's birth, and through her death. And then he would face his own.

"You are a good man."

Sergio smiled just a little. "You are mistaken."

A contraction hit her so hard she torqued her body in agony, her arms still tied to the columns of the bed.

"Is there a reason for that? Does it help the birth in any way?" He wrinkled his nose. He wanted her free.

"Just to make sure I don't escape. And when the baby is born, I don't try to give a plague-carrying child away." She panted through the breaks in contractions now.

Sergio struggled to quell the rising anger. Immediately, he untied both arms. "There is nothing right about that."

"I agree, monsieur." She massaged her reddened wrists gratefully. "You never told me your name."

"Sergio."

"Sergio," she panted, "I am not mistaken. You *are* a good man. I know what you are." Pain wracked her body just then, and he offered her his hand. She gripped it with the strength of Leonardo.

"You do not know what you think you know," Sergio whispered, but it did not matter.

He did not know what to do but spoke soothingly to her, trying to take a place at the foot of the bed, but she would not release his hand. He looked about for whatever might help. There were already towels and more water in the room. The midwife at least left supplies.

"I will die, but perhaps my child won't." Another wave of contractions. "The baby will be like you." The woman was delusional in her pain, and Sergio chose not to argue. He felt her pain as she squeezed his hand this time. As she took his other hand in hers, she stroked the black iron of his turning bracelet. "Like this. Where are you from? Where are you going?"

He looked into her eyes and found curiosity but not hate. He wiped her cheek again. "I departed the Adriatic Sea almost three weeks ago with my kin. We are headed to Dublin via the Isle of Man, traveling under the cover of darkness. Our elder does not believe the Black Death can cross the water." That is what Leonardo had assured him when they left Carmine behind. Sergio's stomach roiled at the betrayal. "He told us that the bad air cannot travel so far, especially in winter." Leonardo could not explain, though, how vampires who did not breathe were being killed by the foul air.

She screamed. "The baby's coming—Now!"

Just then the door burst open, and Gabriella and Alessandra entered. Alessandra said, "Let us help."

Sergio stood between them and Veronique. "Stop. She has the plague. If you stay, we will all be doomed." He lowered his voice. "Save yourselves while you can. I cannot bear to lose more of those I love."

Gabriella grabbed the water and some towels. "Oh, move out of the way. We know the risks. And Lucio and Leonardo have been told. I will not sit by and watch another go through this."

Sergio's jaw dropped.

Alessandra opened the shutter to one side to let in the fresh night air. "She needs someone who has been through childbirth. Sergio, just hold her hand."

Gabriella patted the woman's leg. "You aren't going to break him, bella. *Squeeeeze*."

Sergio sat again, dumbfounded, prodded to motion only by the insistence in her voice. He let her squeeze, then wiped her forehead again. He could do that. He did not know if either female of his pride had ever given birth, but they seemed to know a lot more than he did.

Alessandra spoke soothingly to Veronique, helping her to breathe in a way that seemed to calm her. "Push!" Veronique groaned. "Harder!"

Gabriella chimed in. "You can do this. Push!" And the young woman bore down. Sergio marveled at her strength. With the aches of plague and hours of labor, she still had this energy. He wondered where it came from.

"The baby's here," Alessandra called.

"And it's a boy!" Veronique cried. Tears of relief or joy, Sergio could not tell.

"Can I hold him?" Veronique asked.

Alessandra smiled and handed the child, wrapped in a towel, to the woman.

"I will name him Salvatore. His father would have loved him so much." She stared into the child's face, holding him close. "His father was like you, Sergio. After I became pregnant, he was turned into a vampire. There are many of your kind coming north." She closed her eyes. "He had a bracelet like yours the last time I saw him."

Sergio rubbed the cold metal at his wrist, suddenly with a sense of kinship to this woman he had only met tonight. "I am sorry I left you," Sergio blurted out. "I saw the swelling on your neck, and I didn't want to—" He couldn't finish the words, but Veronique's smile was sweet as she looked up to him.

"It's okay, Sergio. You came back, and that is what matters. If I die, he will shortly follow, but we have tonight and perhaps another."

Gabriella turned to her brother. "Why *did* you come back? Dante saw you leave, and Lucio overheard the midwife say she had signs of the plague. So, we assumed you would not return."

Sergio pulled the amulet from his pocket, now beginning to warm. Dawn approached. He dangled it in the air. "She would have wanted me to. Our only union was that of the cold blood in our veins, and it meant everything to me, but here was a child, a union of life—and I could help, or I could leave Veronique and her baby to die. The answer became obvious." Gabriella touched his shoulder. She knew the torment he had faced in leaving and in returning. She had faced it too with Carmine.

Alessandra tipped her head. "What did you just say?"

"I could help or—"

"Before that." She put her hand under the amulet as it dangled from Sergio's fingers.

"Our only union was that of the cold blood in our veins." She shook her long wavy hair and laughed. "You are nothing short of amazing, my dear Sergio. Amazing. May I?" She lifted her hand to collect the amulet.

Sergio let it settle into her palm. Alessandra smiled. "Angelica *survived* the plague. We had to turn her to save her from the attack. The amulet contains *her* blood. Her immunity to the plague. And now we have a chance to make sure this child survives with the power of this amulet, with the power of Angelica's blood. If Salvatore survives, then we can use the child's blood with that same immunity, and our pride also might yet survive the Black Death. Mother willing to turn her child, that is." Sergio sat with his mouth open. Their amulet had held an answer all along.

All three of them turned to Veronique at that, the woman lost in her child's eyes. She stroked the full head of golden hair that graced the child's crown.

Alessandra spoke quietly, "It is ironic that to save a life, you must end one, though perhaps in the end that is always true."

Veronique responded without looking up, "Will he always stay this age?"

"No," Gabriella chimed in, running her fingers through the golden hair. "Vampires turned by artifacts grow into adults, but he will need to feed as our kind do. We have only one amulet with Angelica's blood, though."

"And so, with the amulet you can only turn one? I see." The ache in her heart was as plain as the dawn giving way to the sun.

Sergio was pained for the human woman. "Would you be turned as well, if we could? Vampires are not immune, but we have a resistance. It might buy you time."

Alessandra stared at him. She had been the one to turn Angelica after she had been stabbed viciously in a tavern. It had been an act of mercy for one who had endured the plague for weeks and *survived*. Then a man had attacked Angelica with a knife just for surviving it, thinking her a witch. Alessandra had found her in the bathroom, bleeding out like a lamb and brought her to the house they shared, with its heavy black curtains and chic white furniture. They had no time to debate feeding on her or turning her, because she would have only lived as a human for a short while. Sergio would never forget that it was Alessandra that had asked the girl what she wanted.

And so, Angelica had chosen this existence.

A choice he would offer Veronique.

Alessandra lifted her eyes from the baby to him, pleading with him not to do this. Not to jeopardize his own existence to give this woman a chance at one. He would willingly turn her so that she had even a remote chance to stay with her child, though. That dark truth was real even if Sergio himself might die of the plague before the child was old enough to incubate an elixir for them all.

Alessandra set the amulet on the dresser next to Veronique and asked him to walk near the window. "If you save her and get the plague, we will not be able to save you."

He gazed at the thin orange line spreading across the horizon. "I may have the plague already, as might you. But the time has come to do what is right."

"She is human. You would give up your immortality for her?"

Sergio ran his finger along the open shutter. "She is willing to give up her child for us." This might be ascension—to rise above what he was to be more.

Behind them, Veronique cried out in ecstasy. They swiveled toward her, to see Gabriella kneeling next to Veronique, fangs imbedded in her arm, Gabriella's turning bracelet upon it.

As Sergio closed the shutters, a thought hit him. Both humans and vampires sacrifice themselves for love. Sergio for Veronique for his love of Angelica. Mother for son for her love of his father. Gabriella for Veronique based on her love of Carmine. Maybe vampires were still more human than they remembered, and together, humans and vampires achieved a greater immortality than either of them could do alone.

Your best hope for survival
is each other

STAKES

BY MIA DALIA

"Vampires".

That's all my boyfriend, Greg, says when I ask him what his brother is into. Which is woefully insufficient.

Ask me about my sisters, and I'll go on for days. About how different they are, for twins; or how similar they can be. How one of them loves modern pop music, and the other swears that good pop died with ABBA. How passionate and terribly bad they both are at knitting, and yes, I have the lopsided tragi-comedic sweaters to prove it. How Tara, who is older by three minutes and never lets you forget it, will eat just about anything, and Lara will always end up with a pile of plucked-out ingredients at the side of any dish. About their shared obsession with Daniel Craig, pre- and post-Bond. And how much they say they hate their cutesy matching names, but they really don't. And how good Tara is at math and Lara is at crafts. I could go on.

Greg would listen too. He's good at that. Just sitting there and nodding at all the right moments and not saying much. A classic strong silent type. Honestly, that was one of the things that drew me to him. I was done with chatty guys, tired of the glib, self-congratulatory narrative they were always spewing, about their careers, investment portfolios, and Teslas.

I liked that the new guy in the office had the calming demeanor of an oak tree. Similar build too. I'm not gonna lie, it's nice to get to feel small next to someone—a luxury I seldom get at 5'10" barefoot.

Greg was always friendly enough; he just didn't say much. Somehow, he managed to come across as neither withholding nor standoffish, just... quiet. I don't know if it was the mystery or his movie-star hair or the way his clothes were never flashy but always matched that inspired me to make the first move—something completely out of character—but I did it. I broke the pattern of waiting for swipes to line up on the app and hitting up the bars with my girlfriends on the weekends; I asked the nice guy out.

We've been together ever since. Greg's easy to be with. His silences are never moody. His very presence is reassuring. He fixes things. He's sturdy. He's such a *Greg*.

Throughout our dating, Greg has proved himself to be kind and considerate, and not at all mysterious. He's merely self-contained. When it comes to having people around him, he can take it or leave it. He doesn't *need* anyone. If you're in his life, it's because he *wants* you there. I used to think it was strange; me, the youngest of three, who had never really been alone or wanted to, who lived with roommates long past the point of having to for financial reasons. But I am getting used to it. In fact, I'm kind of liking it now. It's freeing, this knowledge of being wanted without being needed.

Greg has met my entire family and all my friends, scoring high marks with everyone, and I've learned that his parents are dead and he has one older brother, Felix, who either travels around saving the world or writes books about traveling around saving the world. Perhaps, it's both.

And now this globe-trotting enigma is touching down at home for the first time in years to celebrate his birthday, and I get to meet him. The way I see it, I have one chance to impress Felix, and I'm not going to waste it.

But I was hoping for more than "vampires." What am I supposed to do with that, really?

I thought people left interests like that in the back of their closets with old photo albums, gaudy reminders of their goth years.

So, I do what I always do when I'm out of ideas: I hit up the internet. My desk jockey work may not pay much, but it does give me a decent amount of downtime. Normally, I cruise Twitter and Insta, but today, I'm all about proper research. And sure enough, eventually, something materializes.

It's a random suggestion on a Reddit subforum: a shop within driving distance with an allegedly good selection of oddities. Apparently, the owner doesn't permit photos, and there's no website, let alone anything like online inventory, but it sounds like it might be worth a drive.

So, I drive. It's a pleasantly crisp, overcast fall day, and my Pandora Taylor Swift station is pumping out a nice mix. I don't love it here, but it's home, this small in-between state where everything looks the same. Always told myself, I'd live in the city if I could afford it, but I wonder if that's really true. Whenever I'm there, there's a certain claustrophobic feeling of high-rises closing in, of too many people existing too close together, of the never-ending construction and impenetrable traffic. I try not to give in to it, but I always breathe a bit easier coming back home. Unexciting as it may be.

The town I'm driving to is about twenty minutes away according to Siri. And Siri is the most trustworthy female voice I'll listen to outside of my sisters. My mother has lost that privilege after lying one too many times about the pets of our youth. Took me years to figure it out.

By sheer virtue of being on the East Coast, our state is historically significant. Kind of. More like historical significance-adjacent. It has seen a battle or two, some generals have marched their armies through, that sort of thing. The town I'm headed to got hit by the past harder than most.

Also, it seems, by the recession.

The place may be rich in history but, it appears, nothing else. The wear and tear are everywhere as I park and walk around. Houses with signs proclaiming their years and relevance are crumbling bricks and missing windows. The streets are unswept, windblown trash gathers in the gutters.

The place has a sort of Mrs. Havisham vibe to it. Lost in an old story, sold on a lie, caught up in a daydream. The coattails of bygone splendor failing to provide a sustainable present.

The roads are uneven, the sidewalks are hazardous. This is a watch-your-step sort of place, but I want to look around, having never been, having no intention of ever coming back.

There's an old prison turned museum, a stone building much too small by modern standards for correctional facilities. A shutdown gallery near it. A law office that looks anything but. The town hasn't adjusted well to the present day and seemingly never got used to being poor.

The streetlight is on the fritz. I use my best judgment to cross the street.

I'm wondering what Greg would think of the place but then again, a lot of his opinions are some version of a shrug. And no, it isn't the sort of thing to get mad at with a man who can bench press me, take out two bags of trash at once, and fix a toilet.

At least this town has a Main Street. I'm partial to those. There's usually a pleasant charm to them, an innate quaintness.

This one is no exception, though the mix is unique. You can tell so much about a small town by its Main Street. Here, you have a combination of surprisingly diverse ethnic dining, barbershops, coffee houses, and low-end galleries. And then, there are all the crystal shoppes, those weird places advertising psychic services and spiritual cleansings. There's a surprising amount of them here, throwing the entire ratio off, but hey… whatever gets them through the day.

My parents have a neighbor like that, Mrs. Mackie, whom my father hilariously, though only behind her back, calls Mrs. Wackie. She's always going on about meditation and her crystal collection and her chakra alignments. Always in the backyard reading books with ridiculous titles about uncovering her true potential.

"It must be really locked," my dad jokes. "It's been years."

My father is a pragmatic, no-nonsense man. He works as a civil engineer and has no plans to retire. The closest he gets to whimsy is taking a break from his documentaries and watching an occasional romcom with Mom.

This town would amuse him, though he'd likely appreciate the history.

I'm glad I parked far and got to walk around. Now I'll have something to tell him when I come over on Sunday. It's our family's tradition. One shared meal a week no matter what.

The store I'm looking for is off Main. Tucked away on a side street seemingly too small to have a name. I'd likely walk right past it if not for the sign: a fire-engine-red door standing all by itself with Nightmare Den written on it. Gothic font, black letters. Perfect. But why a door?

It looks like the only visible part of an invisible house, completely incongruous, yet subtly ominous, like an invitation to nowhere. Maybe that's the point. Or maybe it was just cheaper than making a real sign.

The Nightmare Den is behind it, a small, squat, square building, looking like a converted garage or an oversized storage shed.

I walk in through a door, a black one this time, into a moodily lit room. There are no windows. My eyes take a moment to adjust from the sunlit brightness of the day.

Then I make out a proprietor, behind a tall counter at the far end of the store.

"Howdy." He grins at me.

I nod. I can't remember the last time I was in an actual store buying something other than groceries. I've been comfortably Amazon Priming from my nest, avoiding social interaction and its concomitant awkwardness for years now.

The man stands up to his full height. He's disconcertingly tall, close to seven feet, the top of his head is dangerously close to the ceiling. I normally like that sort of thing in a guy, but this is a bit of an overkill. Colorful tattoos snake up his arms and disappear behind the sleeves of a black T-shirt featuring a Michael Myers mug shot. The man has long thin hair and the sort of facial fuzz achieved through inability to grow a proper beard and a strong dislike for shaving. His eyebrows have a natural triangular arc to them, like Jack Nicholson's.

"First time here?"

"How could you tell?"

The man laughs. It's a nice laugh. "You've got that look."

By "that" he probably means a bit startled and a lot overwhelmed.

It's difficult to stop looking around or to even know where to look. The place is covered in merch, every inch of it: tables, vitrines, shelves, walls, even the floor. There is an obvious determination here to maximize the potential of a very limited space. That or simply an indiscriminative approach to stocking.

Framed prints, ranging from fan art to movie posters, action figures, and collectibles, are everywhere.

"It's a lot to take in, I know," the man says amusedly. I wonder how well his business does, with his shop being so niche and in the middle of nowhere.

"No, no, it's—" I search for the word "—nice" and come up with the wrong one. "I mean, it's a very good selection of macabre memorabilia."

"Ah, Macabre Memorabilia. I was going to call it that, but…"

"It's a mouthful?" I offer.

"I was gonna say it wouldn't have fit on the door."

We exchange smiles, we're chatting, next thing you know we'll be bonding. This is precisely why I avoid in-person shopping. Because now even if I don't find anything, I'll feel obligated to buy something to support his seemingly insupportable business.

"Looking for anything in particular or just browsing?"

I shrug a noncommittal "bit of both."

"Well, let me know. I've got all sorts of hidden treasures lying around."

Tara would have picked his brain by now, asking him a million questions. She should have been a journalist. Not only is she ridiculously nosy but people genuinely like opening up to her. Lara would have thought the place had weird vibes and left.

I wonder what "into vampires" Felix would think of it.

In high school, I had a boyfriend who would have loved it here. He was always making me watch horror movies and laughing when I covered my eyes at the gory scenes. "Life's a bloody mess," he'd say. "From birth." Then he joined the Army and got his legs blown off by an IED somewhere in a desert. Came home and dedicated the following years to drinking himself to death.

I'd see him wheeling himself down the street and never know what to say. We only ever had one real conversation after he came back.

"Half a man I used to be," he joked morbidly, lyrics stolen from a song he used to like. "And how are you?"

Small talk didn't work. I couldn't get away from the expression in his eyes like a plea from a dying animal to be put down.

I did go to his funeral. All of my family did. A day so grey, you could believe the sun left and would never return. His coffin was regular-sized. The thought of the empty space where the legs should have been made me shudder.

I don't know why I'm thinking about that now. Probably because of the meticulously crafted miniature wooden coffin I'm staring at. Is it a toy? A crafty place to keep cigars?

It isn't that there is no vampire-related merchandise in the store, it's just that it's all wrong. I don't want a framed Christopher Lee poster. I don't want a Criterion DVD edition of *Nosferatu* with hours of bonus material. I don't want a Universal Monsters collectible Dracula figurine, no matter how many points of articulation it might feature. I want something singular, something unique.

Something to dazzle my boyfriend's mysterious brother.

And then I find it. Almost as if I shouted my request into the universe loud enough, and it responded, but then again, that's exactly the sort of crap Mrs. Wackie believes in, and so I must not.

I'd almost overlooked it or dismissed it as some weird bastard offspring of a Ouija board and backgammon, but no, this open box is something else entirely. In the shop's overall gloom, I can still clearly make out a set of wooden stakes secured in leather loops and a mallet, small bottles full of (presumably) holy water, a sturdy looking cross, a rosary, a silver framed mirror with an elegantly engraved handle, a tiny toy-like gun, and some silver bullets. Lots of silver. *If* it's silver.

The box itself is lined in supple red velvet and appears to be made of some sort of fancy wood. Which is to say nothing like the cheap plasterboard of my home furnishings. I lower the lid to see a cross engraved there and a sturdy metal handle.

Perfect, I think. Expensive, is my next thought. But I just have to ask.

The kit is heavier than it looks, but I lug it to the front counter.

A full-size clown prop lurches at me as I approach, startling me into nearly dropping the box.

"Fu…" I exhale involuntarily.

"Ah, that's just Chuck." The man laughs. "Don't mind him, he's here to keep me company."

Whatever. Lara would have pissed her pants. The old adaptation of *IT* gave her nightmares for ages, and she still refuses to watch the remakes.

Up close, the shop owner smells of pizza and citrus, a strange yet not unpleasant combination.

"I see you found something," he says, petting the box proprietarily.

"Depends. How much do you want for it?"

Normal places would have tags or stickers or something, avoiding this awkward exchange, but this way perhaps this implies the man's open to making deals. I didn't inherit my mother's bargaining genes for nothing.

The man types something on his laptop, then turns it around to show me the screen.

There's an article there featuring a remarkably similar kit being sold at an auction in the UK for the equivalent of twenty grand. I note that the starting estimate was only about $2400. Wow, some people are *really* into vampires.

The item from the auction is allegedly a 19th-century vampire hunting kit. I wonder what year the owner will purport this one to be to inflate the cost—which will probably be prohibitive. Shame, really, because otherwise, it's perfect.

The man looks at me expectantly.

"Well, I don't have twenty grand," I tell him.

"I'm not asking for it," he counters. "Only wanted to show you. See." He points to the screen. "I think that one's a fake."

Of course, I'm thinking. Nice selling strategy. "And you've got the real deal here, right?"

A quiet moment passes. Chuck the Clown glares at me, making me want to leave.

"Oh no." The man laughs disarmingly. "This is just a well-made prop." He names a movie I've never heard of. "I couldn't sell you a real gun with real bullets. Come on."

I laugh too, the pressure release valve letting loose. "So how much for the fake?"

He tells me. It's way less than the auction cost, but way more than I was hoping to spend.

I think about Greg. His strong arms and his calm demeanor and the way I never ever feel like he's lying to me. I've been waiting to bring up the "let's move in" conversation, and maybe winning over his big brother is just the right overture in that direction. If I can't make myself needed by a man who isn't inherently needy, then perhaps I can become irresistible.

I think about my credit card debt and all the things I'll have to go without for the next month or two, and then, with a deep resolute sigh, I begin to bargain.

♦ ♦ ♦

The drive back feels longer. My purchase is safely tucked away in the footwell of the passenger seat. The shop's owner didn't have a bag big enough, and I didn't insist. He was crap at bargaining also, too obviously delighted by the prospect of making a sale to hold his ground.

It was still too much, but I can't wait to see Greg's face. Or Felix's face, for that matter, whatever he may look like. I've only seen a few photos, and they were from decades ago, so I'm left picturing essentially an older version of Greg. The same stoic demeanor. I once tried to look for Felix's books, but everything was from some random small presses and well out of print. I figured if Greg doesn't have them, I don't have to either. Maybe

Felix will bring me a signed copy as a gift. It would be a nice gesture after all I've done to impress him.

He arrives next Saturday. Insists he doesn't need to be picked up from the airport and makes his own way to Greg's loft. A place I hope to share on more than a part-time basis in the near future.

We've been cooking and baking. Greg is surprisingly adept in the kitchen, whereas my specialties are focused primarily on plating and presentation.

The table is set. Felix arrives with the sunset. The intercom comes alive, first with a ring, then with a "come-on-up" buzz, and the next thing I know, he's here.

And looking nothing like Greg. At all. If I didn't know, I would never guess the two of them were related, let alone brothers.

Felix is a reed to Greg's oak, his hair recedes from a sharp widow's peak, and his eyes are hiding behind tinted designer eyeglasses. He's a sartorial perfection in a slim-cut suit that khaki-pants-and-sports-coat Greg would never wear. Felix is clean-shaven to Greg's casual weekend stubble. They even carry themselves differently. Felix moves like a dancer; Greg's more of a lumberjack.

Could these two really share DNA?

They take a long look at each other, smile, shake hands, then hug. Back patting ensues.

"Ah, who is this lovely creature?" Felix asks.

"Felix, Annie. Annie, Felix."

He smiles at me and kisses my hand. "Pleasure," he says. I don't think I've ever had my hand kissed before. Maybe Jane Austen fans are really onto something there.

"It's nice to meet you," I tell him. "Happy Birthday."

"Oh thanks, thank you. Though I am getting much too old to celebrate."

"Nonsense," Greg booms amicably. "You're never too old to celebrate."

We sit down and share a meal and stories. Well, the stories are mostly Felix's, and they are fantastic. As in I'm struggling to believe some of them, they sound like movie plots. With destinations far enough off-the-beaten path to warrant looking up. Entertaining but outlandish to the point of straining credulity. This guy, to hear him tell it, is basically a cross between

Indiana Jones and Jason Bourne. Can anyone have a life *that* exciting? Is it supposed to be that *fun*? I can't wait to tell my family about Felix tomorrow.

Nevertheless, it's difficult not to be charmed by this man. Is it at all ironic that of the two of them, Felix is by far the most gregarious one?

I almost, though not quite, forget about the gift. I spent way too much on it to just forget it. Even wrapped it up, though it was difficult to get smooth lines with the handle sticking out.

"Oh my," he says rubbing his hands together, eyes alit, like a kid on Christmas morning. "Annie, you really, really didn't have to."

"I wanted to." I smile encouragingly, slyly watching for Greg's reaction as Felix unwraps the gift paper. Aren't you impressed? I'm beaming mentally at Greg. Am I not the one?

"Oh, my goodness," Felix exclaims like someone out of an old-timey movie. "Would you look at that?"

"Greg mentioned you were into vampires."

"Did he now?" I don't know Felix enough to read the look he shoots his brother. The tinted lenses don't help either.

"Aren't you?" I ask as Greg shrugs.

"Oh, I am." Felix's long fingers caress one object after another, carefully plucking them out from their slots, studying them, then replacing them. "This is lovely. Thank you, Annie."

There. He *is* impressed. Greg must be too. Credit card debt, I hereby declare you totally worth it.

I smile. A happy hostess. "Who wants dessert?"

To be honest, we hadn't actually baked the cake. Thought about it, but it seemed too complicated, no matter how many seasons of *British Bake-Offs* I've watched with my mom and sisters. So, we bought one from a bakery down the street. Gluten-free, just in case. When I asked Greg how many candles to put in, he laughed and said too many for the cake's surface, so we opted for a single oversized one.

Felix closes his eyes as he makes a wish and blows it out. We each have a slice. The cake tastes as good as it looks. My mind begins to calculate the extra calories I'm going to have to burn off tomorrow.

I go back to my own place at night, to give the boys a chance to catch up. I don't want to leave Greg, I hate sleeping alone. In the past, I've made some terrible decisions just to avoid it. Sometimes I list them to myself when I'm trying to fall asleep, counting them like sheep. The pretentious tweed-clad English professor who suggested we might be better off pursuing our intellectual equals. Like he wasn't just an adjunct. Seriously. The sexy bartender who made my toes curl but never hid the fact that I was only a part of his rotating roster of paramours. The pet store guy with wet sincere eyes who always smelled like a wet dog. The concert promoter with trendy vintage T-shirts and a professionally aged leather jacket who said my musical tastes were charmingly unsophisticated and cheated on me with a high school senior. The wealth manager whom my sisters to this day refer to as the Tesla Turd. What was his real name?

They say you have to sift through a lot of sand to find gold—well, someone says it, probably one of Dad's historical documentaries—and I've certainly done my share. Tired of it. Over it. I'm done looking. It's exhausting, and the aftermath is always so messy. I'm betting on Greg. I don't have to be the smartest person in the room to know I'm right. He's the one. I'm staking my claim.

Even my family, for once, is impressed with my choice. They compliment my judgment as we gather for our Sunday meal. How happy they are for me to have found someone at last. I know I'm the baby of the family, but still, sometimes the attention is too much. I get it, I get it—both my parents and my sisters have gotten their lives together well before they were my age—I just don't need to be hit over the head with it.

Tara is happily single, asexual and rocking it. Married to her job and by all accounts delighted with the arrangement. Lara is married to a lovely woman named Sosie, who owns a knitting shop of all things. They have a golden doodle called Marvin and a charming shabby chic house not too far from my parents.

I'm the one still living at in the University district, long after graduation, with a much-too-young roommate just to keep the space from echoing. I'm the one whose career is a series of meaningless desk jobs. The one who does worst at *Jeopardy* and reads the least. The family ditz, though no one would ever admit to it. The one whose dating life they could barely keep up with. Until Greg. My rock, my knight.

I like him so much I don't even have to love him. When I look at him, I see my future. And it scares me, because there's so much at stake now. This is a life-changing sort of thing.

Our Sunday family meal is the same as always. Mom's never been much of a cook, and Dad never minded it enough for her to improve. She claims to be an expert reheater, and that's good enough for us.

A portable speaker is playing oldies in the background. Everyone's phones are away. We have rules in our house. The last person with their screen lit gets stuck with dish duty. That's often me, betrayed by the need for that last moment message check. Tonight, though, my phone stays dark while my mind runs circles around Felix and his wild stories. How different he is from Greg. I slip my foot free of the shoe's confines to massage it as I contemplate this.

The meal is done. The warmth of proper satiation is coursing through us, making our limbs and our eyelids heavy. Lara is regaling us with a story about some newbie in Sosie's knitting club. I'm comfortable enough to doze off when there's a knock on the door.

It's too loud, jarringly so. Outside of us, our parents seldom have visitors, they like their own company too much.

Still, Dad harrumphs, cracks his neck side to side, and gets up to see who it is. I'm feeling too lazy to even turn around, but I do put my shoe back on.

"Greg," I hear my father's stentorian 'we have guests' voice. "What a pleasant surprise."

What? Is it? What's going on? In all our time together, I've always been very clear with Greg. Sunday nights are for family. Did something happen? Is Felix okay?

Right on cue, Dad says, "And this must be Felix."

Now I have to turn around. I don't care if my body feels twice its normal weight. I rotate my neck so that my eyes can shoot silent WTFs at my boyfriend, but what I see only confuses me more.

Felix, dressed head to toe in black, trading in his dapper look for something from Serial-Killers-R-US, is plunging a wooden stake into my father's chest. Right in our family foyer.

The force behind the attack has driven Dad back into the living room. Greg has entered behind Felix and is calmly closing the front door behind them. Like it's just another Sunday, business as usual.

Dad falls to the floor, Felix above him, using his weight and gravity to make sure the stab is lethal. There is so much blood.

I want to scream, but all that comes out is a feeble "Greg?"

My boyfriend shakes his head, looking suddenly very much like a stranger. "I'm sorry, Annie," he says. Like it's enough. Like it explains anything.

Felix looks up at us. The expression on his face is positively feral. Terrifying.

He gets out a small gun and points it at us. There's a rosary wrapped around his wrist.

And just like that, the recognition dawns on me, as devastating as a heartbreak—these are all items from the kit I gave him. But it was meant to be a joke, a gag, a replica. The stakes weren't sharp enough to kill and surely, the gun won't fire, and the bullets aren't real silver. Right? It's just a prop from some movie. What was the name of it?

I can't remember.

"No one move," Felix says, his voice eerily calm.

Mom's going pale with shock.

Tara's just staring, daggers of hatred sharpening in her eyes. If looks could kill…

Lara's crying, loud heaving gasps; she's always been too close to tears, apparently ever since she was a baby.

Me, all I seem to be able to do is say "Greg" again.

My boyfriend won't meet my eye.

"Five of them, Greg? Seriously?" Felix says nastily. "Well—" He looks at Dad. "Four now."

"I was monitoring them," Greg replies, lifting his shoulders and spreading his arms in that what-do-you-want-from-me gesture. "They were fine."

"Fine?" Felix mocks.

"Yeah. *Fine.* Animal blood once a week through a butcher shop contact."

How does he know this? I've never told him. Was he really just monitoring me this entire time while I was planning our future together?

Felix narrows his eyes. "Never any casualties?"

"Not on my watch."

Felix turns to me, a smile like a slash across his face. "Annie, darling, tell me you all have been surviving on animal blood this entire time?"

"Don't talk to him, Annie," Tara hisses.

But he's staring right at me with a snake charmer's piercing gaze, and I can't help but sway.

♦ ♦ ♦

When I was a kid, I noticed our pets tended to disappear. Also, sometimes, our neighbors' pets. My mom gave me perfectly plausible explanations, and it wasn't until much later in life that I put two and two together. Which made me feel like I really must be the ditz of the family. Somehow the connection between the missing animals and our Sunday meals had never registered to me.

For the longest time, I didn't think there was anything wrong with us. Except for our shared iron deficiency. And our sun-sensitive skins. We were as normal as any other family. A lot of people had dietary restrictions. One of my schoolmates couldn't eat gluten. Another was deathly allergic to peanuts.

I'd gladly drink our bitter tonics on Sundays and still eat all the cookies and peanut butter in the world.

A late bloomer, I didn't get the "hunger" until I was in my early twenties. I remember looking at my old boyfriend as he sat there in his wheelchair, his leg stumps covered by a plaid blanket, the rest of him smothered by self-pity, and thinking, "I can hear his heartbeat, I can hear his blood call to me." It was mercy if anything; he was ready, he wanted it.

Better that than letting a drink take him; better to share one last kindness and intimacy as he slipped away into the night.

From there I got the idea of dealing with all my romantic disappointments in a similar manner. It wasn't the brightest idea, but I stuck with it. My family shook their heads at their wayward baby and tolerated it, helping me every time. But I knew they were getting tired of it. It was one of the reasons they were so happy when I met Greg.

If only we had known.

For the record, my family doesn't glisten in the sun, although prolonged exposure to its light can kill us, and we can—though not without indigestion—eat garlic. We show up in mirrors and photos, albeit often blurry. We can digest regular food and drink. We age, though slower. It's almost nothing like the movies. Except for death. But then again, most people, regardless of their dietary preferences, die if they are stabbed through the heart with a wooden stake or are shot with bullets, silver or otherwise. That's just basic anatomy.

Now all I can do is spiral into Felix's eyes, as narrow and bottomlessly dark as the barrel of his gun. And I tell him how I dealt with the guys before Greg. Not a conversation I'd like to have with my boyfriend's brother under any circumstances, least of all these.

He looks at me with unconcealed disgust. Like he didn't just murder someone. At least, I had my reasons, however shaky that moral high ground may be.

Tara takes the moment as an opportunity and lunges at Felix. With his left hand, he flips his rosary at her like a small, beaded whip. She cries out, and that's when Greg steps in and sprinkles some water on her from the glass vial. I remember that one from the kit too. The real deal, I know, is meant to burn like acid. I just never thought *this* was the real deal.

Tara's screams pierce my heart. Lara's crying intensifies. It's my fault. That's all I can think: it's all my fault. I messed up once again, and this time epically.

"Greg, please." Yes, I'm resorting to begging, but it seems too late. He won't meet my eye, but he won't help me either. Greg looks resolute. Guess he chooses his family. I get it. I do too. Every time.

"What I don't get is why," Felix says, looking at me once again. "Considering what you are, why *that* gift? Were you trying to be funny?"

I don't say anything because I don't know what to say. It does seem stupid in retrospect, like many things. But no, I didn't think it would be funny. And no, for that matter, I don't actually think of myself as a vampire. I'm not some gothic creature that stalks the night. I'm not an ageless lovelorn menace that hides its true form. In fact, this *is* my true form—I can't turn into a bat or anything.

My family has an unusual diet and a slightly higher-than-average homicide record, but that's it. We're not like vampires in the movies. We're not like that.

"I just wanted you to like me," I tell him honestly.

"You got me a *VAMPIRE SLAYING KIT*, Annie. *You*."

"Because it's all Greg told me about you." Man, I really should have gone with a framed Christopher Lee poster. Did the shop owner not know the kit was a real deal? Was he duped too? Or was he just looking for a quick buck and not carrying about the consequences? Most of these antiques are out of circulation for a reason. I mean, seriously, if I ever get out of this, I'm making the drive again, and I'll show the Nightmare Den guy what real nightmares are made of.

I shrug. "Guess I was just hoping you were some goth geek who read *Dracula* one too many times. And I mean…"

Of all the insults I could have lobbed his way, apparently, this is the one that stings. Felix flinches, takes a couple of steps toward me, and slaps me. Hard. "You stupid cu—" he begins. He doesn't finish.

Here's the thing about our family. We may fight, we may drive each other crazy, but we will stand by each other. No matter what. And no one calls one of their own a stupid anything. Even if she is prone to certain lapses of judgment.

Mother launches at Felix with a speed and animal grace I had never seen her exhibit. Dad used to tell us she was wild when they first met, and I thought he was talking about disco boogying or whatever they did back in the day, but now I see what he meant. She's a lioness, a perfect deadly predator.

Felix gets off a shot but she's unstoppable. Greg lunges to his rescue, but my sisters close in on him like a vice. Twin danger. They used to hug me like that, only, of course, lighter.

Suddenly, I'm an extra in a horror movie too gory to enjoy yet impossible to look away from. We haven't fed live in ages, not since I started dating Greg. There's definitely a difference, don't let anyone tell you otherwise. What ensues can be best described as a sort of frenzy that is a far cry from our normal family meals.

I walk past Felix's supine form as mom is draining him from the jugular. He's twitching, and I know from experience he isn't long for this world. Greg's body is doing the same tragic last dance. I used to take such comfort in that body. Now it's just meat and blood. There's still a vial of holy water clenched in his hand. I step on it until I hear a satisfying crunch.

Then I kneel beside my father and examine the stake. It's pretty deep in there, but appears to have just missed the heart. Staking isn't easy, and the precision of pushing a sharp piece of wood through a person's rib cage to hit one relatively small body organ is hard to achieve under any circumstances, let alone in a hurry. At least, I think I'm right. Anatomy has never been my strong suit.

"Looks like he missed," I call out, but no one seems to hear me.

I pull out the stake as gingerly as I can. Through the heart or not, getting staked is still a severely traumatic event. Recovery times vary.

"Save some for Dad," I call to my family again, louder this time, and the sucking sounds cease abruptly.

We drag the bodies next to Dad, afraid to move him. The brothers have been made lighter by partial exsanguination, and heavier by death. Our carpets are definitely ruined now. The cleanup in general is going to be brutal. We're usually so much more organized.

Slowly, so slowly, we rip the thin bloody skin of Greg's wrist, press it against Dad's lips. Tenderly. Lovingly. Because when it comes to family, it's about more than blood. It's about hope. It's about love. It's about always having each other's back. With bated breaths, we wait. And soon enough Dad's eyes move beneath their membranous pale lids before shooting open.

The wet, hungry feeding resumes.

Dating:

Don't stake your life on it

ONE FINAL THOUGHT - LEARNING TO LAUGH

Through sixteen tales, I hope to have challenged your sensibilities. Whether you were simply naïve or actively denying, bitterly stubborn or merely complacent, there is always room for education, change, and growth.

Power, connections, stealth, and duty are effective cornerstones of our existence. But even among those serious pursuits, I find a bit of levity makes it all go down much smoother.

Indeed, my friends, life is long, so learn to laugh.

THE VAMPIRE'S NEW CLOTHES

BY MARTIN L. SHOEMAKER

(With acknowledgments to Mike Resnick)

"Repeat your instructions, Renfield."

The Master had a thick accent that the little man to whom he spoke couldn't identify. He was a tall man with dark hair in a widow's peak. He was cultured, powerful, and impeccably dressed in a dark tuxedo, a crisp white shirt, and a crimson bow tie. A small, blood-red rose was pinned to his left lapel. That rose fascinated the other man.

They stood in a luxurious room with marble floors and walls. Unlike the Master, the little man looked completely out of place with his gray sweatshirt, sagging jeans, and sneakers that might once have been red. His brown hair was unkempt, and his face was dirty. He wished *he* had a rose. He reached out a long fingernail but didn't quite touch the flower.

The Master grabbed the short man's shoulder and shook it. "REN-FIELD!"

The man cringed, his spray of hair waving as he looked up, down, left, right—anywhere but at the Master. "I'm sorry, I forgot that was my name, Master. Ummm… because it's not."

The Master scowled, revealing long, sharp canine teeth. "So what *is* your name?"

The short man looked down at his left shoe. "I forgot."

The Master stared at the arched ceiling. "Then until you remember a better one, your name is Renfield."

"Yes, Master."

The Master leaned over Renfield, and the little man leaned his head back. "Answer my question!" the Master shouted.

Renfield fell over; but without thinking, he flipped into a handspring and landed in a crouch on a marble-topped table. Renfield liked handsprings, they were fun. But he didn't like upsetting the Master. "Ummm... What was the question?"

"WHAT ARE YOUR INSTRUCTIONS?"

Renfield scurried under the table, but the Master snatched him by the collar, lifted him into the air, and held him so they were face to face. The little man whispered, "I forgot."

The Master sighed—a strange, breathless sound—and set Renfield back on his feet. In a quieter voice, he said, "Write this down."

"But Master... I don't know how to write."

The Master raised one dark eyebrow. "This is the twenty-first century. Who doesn't know how to write?" He counted quietly to ten and tried again. "If I go through this slowly, can you remember it?"

"I'll try."

"Why did I come to Manhattan?" the Master muttered. "London has a better class of lunatics. All right, Renfield, try very hard."

The Master paced. A picture of sunflowers was on the wall behind him, and Renfield found the picture distracting. So pretty. "Soon it will be sunrise," the Master began, "and I must retire to my bed."

Renfield raised his hand and said, "You mean the box of dirt in the coat closet? I planted purple irises in it."

The Master stopped and glared. "In my sacred native soil?"

"They're pretty." Irises were his favorite flowers. And roses. And sunflowers were nice, too.

"You do know flowers need sunlight to grow?"

"Oh." Renfield squinted. "I could haul the box out onto the balcony and open it up for them."

In an instant, Renfield again hung from the Master's grip. The Master's dark eyes peered straight into his own watery blue ones. "Listen to me carefully," the Master said in a quiet tone. "Don't ever say that again. Don't ever *think* that again. And in the name of Darkness, *don't ever do that!* Understood?" Renfield nodded, jiggling in the Master's grip. "All right. I shall let you live."

The Master dropped Renfield, and resumed pacing and talking. "Tomorrow night, I shall confront the Great Detective. So you—"

"But Master," Renfield said. He crouched, ready to race away at any moment. "How do you know you'll confront him?"

"Fate, Renfield, always drives me to confront my one worthy opponent of the era: the Great Vampire Hunter. Once it was the Great Prince. Later it was the Great Knight or the Great Professor. Always a lonely hunter with but a few companions, fighting the authorities as well as me. Since that fool on Baker Street, it has been Great Detectives. They are the knights of this age."

"Oooh…" Renfield rose, and then bent his legs and held out his arm, imagining holding a sword. "I like knights!" He lunged, thrusting and parrying at his unseen foe. "Avast, knave, defend yourself!"

The Master said slowly, "'Avast' is for pirates. You mean 'Hold, knave!'"

Renfield lowered his arm. "Are you sure?"

The Master shouted, "Does it matter?" Again he counted to ten. The Master liked counting, Renfield thought. He counted a lot. "The sun shall rise soon, so pay attention. Take that garment bag…" He pointed at a large linen bag hanging by the door. "…to the Great Detective's building. Climb up to his office and break in—"

"Which building is that?"

"The one we drove past last night?" The Master paused. "The five-story red brick office building?" Another pause. "The one I told you to remember because the Great Detective's office was in there?"

Renfield remembered… "The one with honeysuckle on the front?" Honeysuckles were his favorite flowers.

"Yes!" The chandelier trembled, and the Master lowered his voice. "The one with honeysuckle. Climb up to his office, break in, and hide that bag in the coat closet near the window. Can you remember that?"

Renfield nodded. "Honeysuckle… Climb up… Garment bag… Closet…" He continued nodding as he recited, because nodding was fun. But then he stopped and asked, "Why, Master? What's in the bag?"

"My spare suit."

Renfield looked at the bag. "You're giving him your suit?"

"No, the suit is for me."

"But you already have a suit. Why should I put one in the closet?"

"Because I said so!" Renfield scurried back under the table, but the Master tried again in a calmer voice. "I am not one of these Hollywood vampires who can do whatever some hack writer wants. I am Lord of the Night, but even I have rules. I can change into a bat, but I cannot change my clothes with me. I must leave those behind. *Now* do you understand?"

Renfield poked his head out. "No, Master."

The Master bent down nose to nose with Renfield. "When I confront the Great Detective, I must do so in my finest style, not stark naked. I have a reputation to maintain! I shall *not* confront him with my three-thousand-year-old *pulă* hanging out!"

Renfield wondered what a *pulă* was, but he thought of a better question, one that might even impress the Master. "But Master, can't you just memorize him to *think* you have clothes?"

"That's *mesmerize!* And no, not unless I can get him to concentrate on my eyes. That won't happen with my *pulă* hanging out, drawing attention. It may be three-thousand years old, but it's still impressive."

The Master sighed. "No, when I arrive as a bat, I must swoop in the window, swiftly change my form and my clothes, and *then* confront my foe. So my trusted ally—" He looked at Renfield and cocked an eyebrow. "—must conceal my clothes on the final battlefield. Can you do that for me, Renfield?"

Renfield nodded again (nodding was *still* fun), and the Master smiled, showing his long fangs in that way that always scared Renfield; but before Renfield could hide again, the Master yanked him back to his feet. "I must rest now, the sun is about to rise. Here is some money so you can take a cab to the office. You have all day to do this one task. Can I trust you, Renfield?" Renfield feared the Master, and he wanted to do a good job. Doing a good job was important, Mama always said that. Besides, when the Master was satisfied, he was less frightening, so Renfield relaxed and kept nodding.

Then the Master grabbed him by the throat with one knotted hand, stared into his eyes, and whispered, "One more thing: *no irises!*"

◆ ◆ ◆

Renfield danced through the mortuary lobby, imagining music. He twirled the garment bag like a beautiful lady, through the door and to the Manhattan sidewalk, which was still damp from last night's rain.

He liked dancing almost as much as handstands. And flowers. And knights. And *real* scissors (not *safety* scissors). And staplers. And doing a good job, and pleasing the Master.

Renfield knew he was different. Papa had called him *a failure*, Mama had called him *a burden*, and the police had called him *a dummy*. The woman in the white coat had called him a *deluge* (at least he thought that was the word), and the man in the black robe had called him *a danger to himself*. The attendants in the Home called him *special*. But the Master called him *an ally*. He gave Renfield important work to do, something the attendants had never done. They had let him do small tasks when he had first arrived; but every time he had trouble, they took it away and did it for him. They told him he was special, but they did everything for him. At first they let him make cloth dolls: he couldn't figure out needle and thread, but he could staple the cloth together. Then they took the stapler and safety scissors away. They were nice, but they treated him like a not-very-bright animal, and the Home was his cage. The Master was not a nice person and did not-nice things; but even when the Master was angry, he treated Renfield like a person, and so Renfield had run away from the Home to serve him.

And Renfield knew he saw things that weren't there, or he saw them wrong. That was why white-coat woman called him *a deluge*. He tried to see what he was supposed to, but he couldn't, and it hurt to try. He was comfortable with the world he saw. So when he saw yellow elephants in the street where other people saw cabs, he was okay with that. Either one would take him to the honeysuckle office, right?

Amid the cars that rolled past, splashing water as they went, there was an elephant just down the potholed street. Now what did people say to call an elephant? Renfield was sure he had seen that on TV. Was it…

"Taxes!" Renfield shouted, but the elephant did not budge.

"Toxic!" Neither did the turbaned man who sat atop the elephant.

Renfield paused, frowning; but before he could shout "Ticks!" the elephant rumbled like an out-of-tune engine and ambled forward.

Renfield ran after, but suddenly he saw that the elephant had left behind a big, stinking pile. Or was it motor oil? Either way, he didn't want to step in it. He leaped forward and over the mess, arcing into a handspring and bouncing back to his feet. That was so much fun, he did two more before coming to a halt. He leaned over to catch his breath, resting his hands on his knees.

His left hand was empty.

His right hand was empty, too. Something was missing…

He looked back at the pile of dung and saw the Master's bag laying in it. He took a step toward the bag—just before a truck drove over it, splattering the dung. A big, wet drop landed right in front of his foot.

The garment bag was crumpled in the middle of a wide, stinking mess. Renfield had to retrieve it before another car ran over it, but he didn't want to touch the stink. He searched the nearby bushes and found a long stick. With it, he snagged the hangers and pulled the bag free. Then he used a newspaper from a trash can to scrape the bag clean.

Renfield knew he would never get a cab—or an elephant—so he would walk. He knew the direction, and he had all day. How long could it take to cross Manhattan?

◆ ◆ ◆

Much later he had his answer: *too long*. He remembered the gardens: park gardens, window gardens, community gardens, even yard gardens. He thought he recognized them from the night before. Gardens—especially flowers—meant more to him than streets. So he let the asters and mums speak to him, leading him… somewhere. Asters were his favorite flowers. Or maybe mums.

Then suddenly he knew where they were leading him, and he broke into a wide grin. In one garden with a high spiked fence, he saw *sunflowers!* Not as many as in the Master's painting, but more than he could count. They stood there in all their golden glory, absorbing the warm autumn sunlight that broke through the remaining clouds! They were taller than him.

He had to touch them. The gate was locked, but Renfield was a good climber. He hung the bag inside the high fence, with the hangers hooked around one spike. Then he clambered over and dropped into the garden. He walked up to the nearest blossom, stuck his face up it, and inhaled deeply. Renfield had never smelled sunflowers before. The scent was green, earthy, and a little sweet, but so faint he might miss it if he wasn't so close.

He smelled another. The plants were in six rows, spaced so a person could just fit between them. He zigzagged from bloom to bloom, smelling and touching and laughing. Their leaves were damp, and he laughed as they showered him with cool droplets. Among all his favorite flowers, sun-flowers were his *favorite* favorite flowers! So tall and sheltering and beautiful.

Renfield forgot the bag. He forgot the Master and the Great Detective. He forgot the elephants and the Home and his parents and the city. He forgot time. For this instant, with the tall flowers and their scents surround-ing him and hiding him, he was transported to someplace else, someplace he couldn't name. Unless that name was *Happiness*.

But happiness never lasted. He heard a low growl, and he peered be-tween the stalks. A large black Great Dane stood there. Its lips were curled and drool dripped from its jowls to the ground. If the Master were a dog, he would be *that* dog.

"Nice doggie…" Renfield held out his hand to let the dog sniff it.

The dog barked—a deep boom that rattled Renfield's bones—and leaped.

Renfield bounded backwards without thinking. He crushed four of the sunflower stalks as he fled, and he moaned for their lost beauty. But he wasted no time springing to the top of the fence and down the other side.

The dog threw itself against the fence, rising up and planting its fore-paws near the top of the fence. It barked, and Renfield fell on his butt. Then he realized: the dog was on *that* side of the fence and he was on *this* side. He was safe.

But the garment bag was on *that* side.

Renfield climbed the fence, grabbed the hangers, and lifted… at the same time that the dog grabbed the bottom of the bag and pulled. The dog planted its huge feet in the moist earth of the garden. Renfield got a better hold, while the dog tried to yank the bag from his grip. Renfield pulled for all he was worth, and the Dane was forced to take three steps forward. Maybe it wouldn't win.

The dog lost its grip, and Renfield fell backwards. Before he could catch himself, the bag fell upon the spikes, and he heard a tearing sound. Then the dog leaped up and once more gripped the bag in its teeth, pulling and twisting. Renfield pulled back—and the sound of ripping filled the air, and he and the remnants of the bag tumbled into the street.

And into a mud puddle.

The dog had only an empty bag. And Renfield had… the suit. The muddy, smelly, crumpled, ripped suit.

♦ ♦ ♦

Mama had taken Renfield to a store like this once, a clothes-cleaning store. He had brought the Master's suit here, and the purple-haired kid behind the counter had taken most of his money, promising the suit would be cleaned and repaired in two hours.

Purple Hair stared at Renfield as he waited, but then he went back to looking at his computer screen, doing something in the back, and talking to customers as they came in.

Renfield didn't want to admit why he waited. He wasn't sure where else to go, and he didn't want to lose track of the Master's suit. And besides, he wasn't sure how long two hours was.

After a long time, Purple Hair brought a box up and set it on the counter. Then without a word he went to the back room.

Renfield fidgeted. Had it been two hours? Was that the suit? Was Purple Hair ashamed to even talk to him anymore?

That had to be it! Many people gave up on talking to Renfield. They didn't like having him around, but the polite ones wouldn't say it. The kid seemed polite, so Renfield could draw only one conclusion: Purple Hair wanted him to take his box and leave.

So he did.

Renfield didn't like making people uncomfortable, and he didn't know how he did it. The Master was never uncomfortable around him, which was another reason he liked the Master. He wanted to like other people, too, if only they would let him. But since he didn't know how, he was glad to leave Purple Hair behind.

Four blocks later, though, he heard shouting. He turned back, and through the crowd he made out a fast-moving spot of purple.

Oh, no... Sometimes people did worse than ignore Renfield: sometimes bad people got angry, and they... hurt him. Not like the Master's threats, they chased him down and really *hurt* him. Purple Hair hadn't *looked* like a bad person. But then, neither had Papa...

Renfield clutched the box and dashed through the crowd. He was small and quick, so he made good time; but when he looked back, Purple Hair was still shouting.

Renfield turned to run again—and collided with a bicycle messenger. The bicyclist crashed to the ground, dazed; but Renfield tumbled and sprang to his feet. He looked around, and the battered box lay under the bicycle. He lifted the bike with his left hand and retrieved the box with his right.

But then he thought... Mama said taking things that weren't yours was wrong. But disappointing the Master was worse. But *paying* for the things you took made it right. So he said, "Sorry," and he held bike and box in one hand as he dropped the last of his money on the cyclist. He climbed onto the bike and pedaled away, clinging to the box as he steered.

The wind in Renfield's face made him smile despite the shouts—which seemed louder, almost as if two people were shouting. But soon they faded, and he was free.

He recognized more plants, and that made him smile even wider. A few blocks further he smelled just the slightest hint of... *honeysuckle!* He rounded a corner, and there was the Great Detective's office building. Renfield knew he wouldn't disappoint the Master: it wasn't even dark yet!

But already the sun was behind the tall buildings. He had no time to waste. Renfield recalled his orders... "Honeysuckle... Climb up... Garment bag... Closet..."

So now he could walk up to the fifth floor. But the Master said *climb up*, not *walk up*. It was important to follow the Master's orders. Did he mean climb the wall? Stairs have steps, so you *step* up those, right? Although Renfield was good at climbing, he didn't like heights. Many times he had climbed trees at the Home, and then the attendants had to get him back down. Climbing was fun, but looking down was not fun.

But he had no choice. "The Master said 'climb up,' so I have to *climb* up!" He dropped the bike, tucked the box under his arm, and walked up to the corner of the wall.

The scent of honeysuckle surrounded him, so powerful when he was so close. Honeysuckles were his favorite flowers! Well, except for sunflowers, of course. The sweet smell made Renfield brave, and he easily scaled the corner, even holding the box. He was careful not to look down; and as the shadows lengthened, he made his way to the fifth floor.

Then he had to climb sideways to reach the office window. The bricks of the corner had offered him many hand- and footholds, but the wall was more even. Three times he found no place to put his foot, and he almost lost his grip; but he was a good climber, and patient. He felt with his toe until he found somewhere to put his weight.

At last Renfield stood on his toes on the ledge outside the Great Detective's window. He would make the Master happy! Well, at least he would make the Master not angry, which was pretty good.

Only the window wouldn't open.

It wasn't locked, wasn't even latched, just stuck. He had come so far, he couldn't let that stop him. He clenched the box between his knees, held onto his handhold with his right hand, and pushed up on the frame with the fingers of his left.

He knew that five stories of *down* were right behind him. If the window jerked suddenly open, he could lose his grip and fall.

At last the window budged. Just a little, but Renfield knew he had won. He had beaten the window. But there was no time to celebrate, not until he was inside! Slowly he pulled the window up until his toes slid forward for a more comfortable perch. Then he pulled it all the way open, and he slid inside.

And the box slipped. And fell. Outside. And *down*.

Despite his fear of falling, Renfield leaned out and watched the box fall. It tumbled, almost gracefully, until it struck the cement sidewalk. Then it burst open in a spray of pink.

Pink?

Before Renfield could wonder why the Master had a pink suit, Purple Hair ran up and lifted up a short, puffy pink dress. Renfield was sure the Master would never wear that.

Right behind Purple Hair ran the bicycle messenger. He picked up the fallen bike and inspected it. Then both young men looked up at Renfield and shouted at him, fists raised. Then the messenger mounted the bike and rode away. Purple Hair glared at Renfield and followed.

After the elephant, the wrong turns, the dog, the cleaner, the bike, the wall... After all of that, Renfield had failed. And the shadows told him there was no time to try again. He had let the Master down.

No.

He wasn't going to fail. He wasn't a *deluge*, he was a *person*. And the Master counted on him.

Renfield looked around the office. It was sloppy. Mama would've fainted away at the copies of *Racing Form* and the pictures of not-nice women in not enough clothes. Nearby was a kitchen, with dirty dishes and overstuffed drawers. There had to be something he could work with. He rummaged through the drawers—but very quietly. He thought he heard snoring from the mirror, and he didn't want to wake whatever was in there.

Then Renfield saw it. It had been there all the time, waiting for him to see it: the answer to his problem, right at the window. He would make the Master proud.

He curled up in the closet and waited for the Master. Soon he fell asleep.

◆ ◆ ◆

Renfield woke instantly when he heard the closet knob turn. The door opened and the Master looked in. Renfield held a finger to his lips, and he tried not to look at the Master's naked body as he whispered, "Quietly, Master. I think the mirror can hear us."

The Master looked at the mirror, and scratched his head. Then he turned back to Renfield and whispered, "What are you doing here? Where's my suit?"

"There was an elephant, and a dog, and a man with Purple Hair… But I have a plan!"

"I don't—" The Master caught himself as his voice rose, and he returned to a whisper. "I don't need a plan, I need a suit!"

"I know, but this is almost as good. At least in the darkness." Renfield brought his loot from the closet: a dingy white tablecloth, the dark gray curtains from the window, and the scissors and stapler from the Great Detective's desk. *Real* scissors, Renfield noted with pride, not *safety* scissors. "Just hold your arms out, and stand with your feet apart. I have to work fast."

The Master looked nervously at the clock. "Do I have a choice?"

Renfield held up the tablecloth and cut a front piece, a back, and sleeves. They were too big, but no one would notice in the dark. He held the pieces up to the Master and pinched the edges together, stapling him into the shirt.

The Master flexed and raised his arms, frowning at the gaps that showed, so Renfield stapled some more. The Master flexed again, and nodded.

Then he smiled, and Renfield knew he had done a *very* good thing.

Next Renfield stapled the Master into pants (being careful not to look at the Master's *pulă*—good boys didn't look there, Mama had said). The pants sagged, so Renfield stapled them to the shirt. There were also no shoes, so Renfield cut out black slippers, stapled the Master's feet into them, and stapled them to the pant cuffs.

That left the suit coat, but Renfield frowned. The Master's coat should look perfect, and Renfield wasn't perfect. So he settled for a long cape, cutting it from one complete curtain and stapling the hem. When he draped it around the Master's shoulders and stapled the collar, the look was close enough to frighten Renfield.

"How does it look?" the Master whispered. He could never check his appearance, even in a normal mirror, so Renfield was used to this job.

He looked at the Master. "*Almost* perfect." Renfield tiptoed to the open window, plucked a honeysuckle blossom, held it up to the Master's chest, and stapled it in place.

"Ouch!"

"Sorry, Master. But now… perfect!"

"This had better work, Renfield…"

"It will, Master, it will!"

The Master twirled, holding his arms out so his cape flowed. "All right, now leave. I can't protect you from the Great Detective and his henchmen." And he headed toward the bedroom at the far side of the office.

But Renfield couldn't help himself. He had never seen a Great Detective before, and he had never seen the Master confront his arch nemesis. He had to know how the battle would play out, so he crept close to the open door, hid under a table, and peered through the door. "Get him, Master!" he whispered very quietly.

But they didn't fight, they… talked. Renfield didn't understand most of the words, but it sounded bad for the Master. The Great Detective wasn't intimidated by him. How could *anyone* not be intimidated by the Master?

Maybe the Master was right: the Great Detective *was* a knight. Renfield had never seen a knight before, but he knew they were real. They did the right thing and treated everyone fairly. Could this man be one? Maybe his knight's armor and sword were in the bedroom.

At one point, a woman snuck into the office, closed the window, and sprayed it with some solution. The Master and the Great Detective kept talking as the woman snuck back out. Renfield wondered if he should warn the Master, but he didn't know how.

Later the Master stormed out of the bedroom and to the window; but before he could touch it, he recoiled so quickly and roared so loudly that Renfield feared the staples would give out. The Master ran back into the bedroom, and they argued more. Renfield couldn't follow all the words, all the things unsaid, but he could tell from the tone: somehow, impossible as the idea was, the Master had lost, and was simply reluctant to admit it.

Finally the Great Detective and the Master walked out of the bedroom. The Master's shoulders slumped. He was defeated.

Yet even in victory, the Great Detective was cautious. He walked behind the Master, keeping his guard up to the last as they discussed shipping schedules and the Master leaving the country for good.

Leaving... Leaving Renfield!

Then, when it seemed to be over, the Great Detective stepped toward the door; but he accidentally stepped on the hem of the Master's cape, pulling it to the side. The Master jerked away, but that made matters worse: the detective also stood on one of the slippers. Renfield heard staples pop loose and ping against the wall.

Just like that, the makeshift trousers let go. The Master stood before the Great Detective, half naked, with his three-thousand-year-old *pulă* hanging out.

The Master glanced down. The Great Detective glanced down as well. Then both men looked up, not quite looking into each other's eyes. The Master spoke in a low, clenched tone. "When you tell this story, detective, will you do me the honor of leaving this part out?"

The Great Detective nodded. "Not. A. Word. But..." He whistled as he opened the door. "Impressive!"

"Indeed." And with that, the Master turned into a bat, leaving behind the last of his stapled clothing. As he flew out the door, Renfield knew that was the last he would ever see of the Master.

The little man felt a touch of panic at that. *Who will I serve now?* But the panic was brief. Renfield had triumphed over adversity many times today. Against all odds, he had succeeded in his quest. He was a person, no matter what the Home said, and he would find someone who would appreciate that.

Maybe... Maybe a knight needed a squire...

A loyal aide can do what you cannot;
but never forget, they are only human

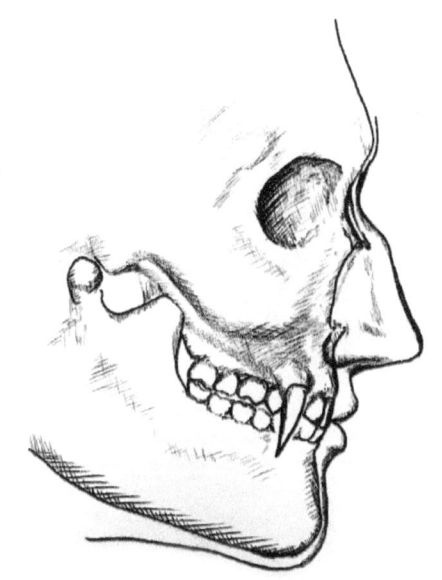

The End

ABOUT THE AUTHORS

Author biographies are included in story order; Martin L. Shoemaker, who wrote two stories in this collection, appears 8th on the list for the story "Separation."

Jentina Grey

Jentina Grey is an award-winning writer and artist who is currently working on editing her first full length novel. When she first discovered fantasy and science fiction, her whole world changed as she realized that there were people out there who lied for a living, and that there were other people who loved them for it. As an adult, she can't help but create the sort of art that gave her life at such an early age.

N. V. Haskell

N.V. Haskell is a speculative fiction writer who lives somewhere between suburbia and haunted creeks with her long-suffering spouse, rescue dog, and generations of groundhogs and squirrels that she can't help but feed. After many years in healthcare, she remains stubbornly optimistic. When not hiking, reading, or staring at a screen, you can find her incognito at Comic Expos or Renaissance Fairs.

Her debut novel, *The Malice of Moons and Mages* is forthcoming in 2025 from Cursed Dragon Ship Publishing. For more information, visit her website at www.nvhaskell.com

Jason P. Crawford

Jason P. Crawford is a father of four, author of the award-winning *Samuel Buckland Chronicles* and *Dragon Monarch Tetralogy*, and high-school science teacher. He has been spinning tales of the impossible and fantastical since 2012 and hopes to one day be able to spend his entire day creating new worlds. He can be found at his website https://www.jasonpatrickcrawford.com

Melissa Koons

Melissa Koons has a passion for books and creative writing. She has won the Editor's Choice Award for both her novel, *Orion's Honor*, and her poetry. Melissa writes in various genres but primarily publishes historical fiction, short story horror, and poetry.

Melissa works as a communications professional, tutor, relationship coach, grief coach, tarot reader, and ordained minister. When she's not working, she's taking care of her cats and turtles, and exploring the adventures of life.

Shannon Lynn Fox

Shannon is a multi-genre writer of stories spanning past, present, and future. Her forthcoming "Black Hills Arcana" series will be released by publisher Roan & Weatherford (Dragonbrae), with the first novel set to premiere in 2026. Her previous work has appeared in DreamForge Anvil, Air & Nothingness Press, and WonderBird Press, among others.

She has a B.A. in Literature-Writing from UC-San Diego. When not writing, she spends her time dancing with horses which she's found is significantly easier to do with four feet instead of two. She lives in San Diego, CA, with her husband and three cats—one of whom may or may not be a demon in disguise.

Visit her at www.shannon-fox.com

Angelique Fawns

Angelique Fawns is a journalist and speculative fiction writer. She began her career writing articles about naked cave dwellers in Tenerife, Canary Islands. After selling her first story to EQMM, she fell in love with weird fiction, which is *actually* stranger than non-fiction. You can find her lurking at @angeliquefawns on X, Blogging about upcoming calls at www.fawns.ca, or gazing into the abyss hoping it stares back at her.

She has over 80 stories published, which can be found at Mystery Tribune, Amazing Stories, and Space & Time, among others.

Ray Zacek

Originally from Chicago, Ray Zacek is a retired fed living in Tampa, Florida. He writes dark fiction, horror, and crime/noir. His work has previously appeared in Critical Blast, All Due Respect, Denver Horror Collective, Shotgun Honey, Sirens Call, Out of the Gutter, among other venues. His novel, *Don't Be Cruel*, about a north Florida psychic Elvis cult, is soon to be published by Critical Blast.

Martin L. Shoemaker

Martin L. Shoemaker is a programmer who writes on the side... or maybe it's the other way around. Programming pays the bills, but a second-place story in the Jim Baen Memorial Writing Contest earned him lunch with Buzz Aldrin. Programming never did that!

In addition to award-winning stories in Writers of the Future and Baen, his work has appeared in Analog Science Fiction & Fact, Galaxy's Edge, Digital Science Fiction, Forever Magazine, and numerous anthologies including *Year's Best Military and Adventure SF 4* (which published his 24 hour story from the WotF workshop), *Man-Kzin Wars XV* (edited by Contest judge Larry Niven), and *Avatar Dreams* (edited by the late Contest judge

Mike Resnick, whose prompting led Martin to write "The Vampire's New Clothes").

Martin's Clarkesworld story "Today I Am Paul" appeared in four different year's best anthologies and eight international editions. His follow-on novel, *Today I Am Carey*, was published by Baen Books in March 2019. His novel *The Last Dance* was published by 47North in November 2019, and was the number one science fiction eBook on Amazon during October's prerelease.

His latest work, "Today I Know," appears in *Robots Through the Ages* (edited by Bryan Thomas Schmidt and Contest judge Robert Silverberg).

Julia V. Ashley

Julia V. Ashley lives along the Natchez Trace Parkway, where she finds inspiration from the people and the creatures inhabiting the divide between civilization and the preserved wilds of the national scenic byway. Her short story collection, *Jazz by Faelight* came out in the fall of 2023, featuring otherworldly creatures lurking through the streets of New Orleans. Her short fiction appears in various anthologies, including A Bit of Luck and *Murderbugs*: Unhelpful Encyclopedia Vol.2. For more contemporary fantasy steeped in the gothic south, visit her at www.juliavashley.com

Fulvio Gatti

Fulvio Gatti is an ESL speculative fiction writer, cultural project manager, and journalist from the wine hills of Piemonte, Italy. His short stories in English can be found in pro magazines (*Galaxy's Edge*), anthologies, webzines and as podcasts in USA, UK, Australia, Canada, and Europe. His first indie-published collection, *The Record Store at the Edge of the Time Stream*, is available on all platforms; his Italian novel *Il Protocollo Scilla* was a finalist at the Urania Award in 2021. He believes his best co-creation, with his wife Filomena, is their brilliant daughter Teresa.

Wayland Smith

Wayland Smith is a native Texan who has moved around a lot and presently lives in Northern Virginia. His rather unlikely list of jobs includes private investigator, comic book shop owner, ring crew for a circus (then he ran away from the circus and joined home), deputy sheriff, writer, and freelance stagehand. His novels include *In My Brother's Name* and *The Wildside, Inc* series about superhuman mercenaries. He has also been in numerous anthologies, including *Hold Your Fire*, and *SNAFU: An Anthology of Military Horror*. His hobbies include gaming, reading, and movies—(Of course I want popcorn!)

Jennifer L. Collins

Jennifer L. Collins is a full-time writer and editor. She lives in southwest Florida with her husband and their six rescues—two big, loveable mutts and four very needy cats. You can find her work in *Cosmic Horror Monthly* as well as the recent anthologies: *Howls from the Wreckage*, *Howls from the Scene of the Crime*, and *Marshlands Horror*. Her first novel, *Locals Only*, is forthcoming from Polymath Press.

C. L. Fors

Cherrie Lynn Newman, writing under the pen name CL Fors, is a science-fiction and speculative fiction author and award-winning illustrator. You can find the first novel in her epic sci-fi series, Cradle of Mars, on Amazon. Cherrie lives in the Southern California desert with her four kids and fellow author-spouse Jason P. Crawford. She enjoys wilderness, creatures, and all things science, and spends most of her time in the worlds she creates. You can find her website at www.clforsauthor.com

L. A. Selby

L. A. Selby, suspense writer, finds inspiration in gray skies and the kind of forests that swallow their own shadows. Some forests are trees. Some are towers. The invisible specters of Checkpoint Charlie in Berlin inspired this tormented tale. The first city she ever fell in love with was Venice. Ten years ago, she fell in love with Rome. Her newest passion is Transylvania.

You can find her full bio at https://laselby.com/about-the-author/

A.J. Benson

AJ is the author of "Time to Play" in the *Grifty Shades of Fey* anthology and *Quest for the King*. She has been writing and editing as an analyst for 27 years. She is the Career Strategy Lead for Apex Writers and a member of the Maryland Writers Association.

She enjoys reading fantasy and paranormal romance and loves the epic struggle between good and evil. In her spare time, AJ plays D&D or meets with friends over coffee. She lives in Hanover, MD with her animal rescues and two young adult sons. To find out more, visit ajbenson.com

#EmbraceTheDragon

Mia Dalia

Mia Dalia is an internationally published, CWA-nominated author of all things fantastic, thrilling, scary, and strange. Her tales of horror, noir, science fiction, mystery, crime, humor, and more have been featured in a variety of anthologies, magazines, literary journals, online, and adapted for narrative podcasts.

Her stories have been voted top ten of Tales to Terrify 2023 and shortlisted for the CWA's Daggers Awards 2024. She is the author of the novels *Estate Sale* and *Haven*, novellas *Tell Me a Story*, *Discordant*, and *Arrokoth*, and the collection *Smile So Red and Other Tales of Madness*.

Find her at https://linktr.ee/daliaverse

ABOUT THE PUBLISHER

WonderBird Press, LLC., is run by husband-and-wife duo Mike Jack and Morrigen Stoumbos. They live with their old parrot and young puppy, surrounded by painting projects, board games, and books.

WonderBird Press, named for the bright red parrot Lutra, primarily publishes themed short fiction anthologies featuring up-and-coming authors in the scifi, fantasy, and horror communities. Despite the monstrous subject matter, many of the stories in this and other volumes are humorous, hopeful, or "feel-good" tales.

Mike Jack Stoumbos, the editor of this anthology, is also the author of the science fiction series *THIS FINE CREW*, from Chris Kennedy Publishing and Theogony Books, and award-winning short stories, including the 1st-Place *Writers of the Future* story "The Squid Is My Brother."

WE HOPE YOU ENJOYED THE VAMPIRE SURVIVAL GUIDE

If you had fun reading these stories—if they made you laugh, cry, gasp, or all of the above—please leave a positive review and rating where you purchased your copy, or wherever you recommend books. If you want to make an author smile for a week, mention their story as one of your favorites in your review. It's a small extra step, but it makes a big difference for indie presses and new publications, including paving the way for future projects.

MORE FROM WONDERBIRD PRESS

Anthologies

- *MURDERBIRDS*, Unhelpful Encyclopedia Volume 1, Spring 2023
- *MURDERBUGS*, Unhelpful Encyclopedia Volume 2, Spring 2024
- *VAMPIRE SURVIVAL GUIDE*, Monstrous Guidebook 1, Fall 2024
  and on the horizon
- *MURDERFISH*, Unhelpful Encyclopedia Volume 3, coming in 2025

Novellas

- *A Man of His Word*, a folkloric fantasy adventure, previewed below
- *Murder on the Barge Inn*, "Agatha Christie" on a spaceship
- *Dead of Night*, a deep-space thriller
  and on the horizon
- *Infinite Space*, a historical tale of a vampire muse

A MAN OF HIS WORD

Preview Story
by Mike Jack Stoumbos
from WonderBird Press

Though many years have passed, people continue to ask me how I survived, and moreover, how did I confront the evil that would doom our country? Some have heard enough of the story, beyond exaggeration and rumor, to ask me about the sacrifice. The truth was—and still is—I know nothing of sacrifice.

Fenton knew about sacrifice. I just knew how to keep my word.

1 ~ Out of a Nightmare

The day I met Fenton began with a nightmare. In particular, it began when I thrashed and yowled so much in my sleep that I not only woke myself, but the babe in the basket, just on the other side of the thin partition.

My sister-by-rights arrived to give me a deserved swat, drawing me the rest of the way into awareness, and chided me for rousing my nephew.

"Sorry, Imogen," I grumbled, and I truly was. Unpleasant though I found her, the circumstances of her life did earn my sympathy.

Mine might not have been much better. And I saw that she was not in the mood to reciprocate, when she shot back a brusque, "What've you got to cry about then?" before ducking away to tend to her child.

I rubbed at my face and eyes, trying to shake the clawing, spidering sensations from my slumber. In truth, I had reason to cry out: death in the family, an evil on the horizon, my responsibilities to both, and the fact that the woods—once my sanctuary—were now cause for fright. Any and all of these elements might have plagued me in nightmare. Though it frightened me to think it, my imagined demons might be close to reality, to something tangible I could sense in sleep, and which might sense me in return.

A splash of water on my face, and I resolved to rise, dress, and begin my duties. Imogen still rocked the babe; thankfully, the other bed was already empty, and the last and oldest person in the cottage absent. I was not keen on receiving his scowl or his shame for my night terror.

It had already been a summer of fear, which kept everyone in the village close to its borders. As the weather grew colder, the worries only intensified. We did not know for certain whether the Warlock and his host would come to our village or pass us by, but we had all heard rumors about spending too much time outdoors, outside of protective thresholds, after nightfall or even in the shadow of a tree.

Of course, being stuck indoors, or within shouting distance with one's closest relatives, engendered its own risks and worries.

So, when I stepped outside into the fresh morning air and shut the thin door behind me, I found some small relief. However, when I looked down and found my assignment from the village-mother, written by her swift hand and wrapped around a stone for weight, the bright feeling of the moment became clouded.

She had scrawled,

> *Fetch hoodwort, butterwort - in daylight, with speed.*
> *~B*

Despite the rumored dangers, perhaps it would be good for me to venture beyond our border today.

I remember the first report had come from a peddler, who interrupted a funeral, and allowed many of us to use *mourning* as an excuse to stay close. After the harvests, the whispers and warnings grew far too specific to be dismissed, and a voluntary curfew was agreed upon. Now, the weather was colder, cloud cover more than just patchy.

Few went into the woods at all anymore, and those of us who did broke out in sweats at the prospect.

But, as the village-mother would tell me, if I ever wanted to gain the people's confidence, I couldn't show that fear. To tell the truth, I didn't so much care about the people's confidence then, but I did care about my apprenticeship to the woman who'd taught me to read both the written word and the power of nature.

That morning, it was still quite early when I arrived at the edge and that fine shimmer of power that most would dismiss as a trick of the light.

I could see the sun, hear the birds. I could practically taste the dew. I knew the scent of moss and natural rot, and detected none of the brimstone we feared. So I set a firm command over my soul, and stepped over the threshold. Most wouldn't notice the cobweb wave of energy as they exited through a major ward, but I was attuned enough for the dozens. Not only would I find what I was looking for, but I could also avoid highwaymen or worse evils.

And if I should stumble into a rough patch with rough fellows, I reminded myself what the mother had taught me: *Root, soil, soot, oil.* It wasn't a nursery rhyme, not even a very good rhyme, for only a narrow sliver of accents made the *root* and *soot* ring together. It was, however, the easiest and most reliable manner of nature warding I knew, so I wouldn't scoff at it. This knowledge and a little bit of command over it served me better than any strong man's sword.

I kept my senses keen for any sign of hoodwort and, if fortune favored my search, fresh butterwort, still flush with mucus. The servants and creatures of a Warlock were rumored in the woods, but that didn't stop folk from getting sick and needing more ministry than a simple stitch or prayer.

I moved quickly, my soft boots leaving only the barest flat footprints. I knew I could find the first roots where the groves were lush, but streams slow. The second would be more elusive, as it did not grow as plentifully. Still, butterwort was a hardy plant, recognizable when spotted, and not nearly as tasty as its name would suggest.

I do not feel the least embarrassed that I startled and went to my knees at the sound of footfalls on approach.

The intruding party turned out to be a fallow deer, and not even a very big one. I had to smile, in spite of myself.

The young buck trotted awkwardly under his new antlers, clumsy and heavy-footed as you please—until he spotted me, at which point, he too froze. His mottled coat was not nearly as luscious as that of a larger red deer, and he was clearly ungainly. Still, there was something so simple and natural in his step that he brought my heart some ease.

Perhaps he found me as awkward as he, having recently concluded my own final growth spurt and occupying a role just on the border of adult— whether or not my own Da happened to think so.

I raised my empty palms toward the fallow, showing I meant no threat or harm. Just like that, he came out of his transfixed state, and began to resume his morning stroll. Keeping his eye for one more moment, I asked his favor in finding my quarry.

"Butterwort," I whispered. This fallow owed me no knowledge, but I was hopeful nonetheless.

He gave a snort which I perceived as haughty. But then, even adolescent fallow bucks can have a bit of decency when it's not forced upon them. After a few steps, he paused and indicated a heading with his snout.

I nodded, "My thanks," and started in that direction.

As I slipped farther into the wood, I felt more than a little pride at my own patience and grace. I could hear the mother in my head congratulating me. She would say that a lesser apprentice would have missed the answer or not known how to ask for it in the first place.

I snipped a few handfuls of hoodwort and secured them in my bag. I made sure to stay between the sparse trees for cover, but also in enough of the sun for self-protection from dark magics. I suppose I didn't really know if sunlight meant safety, but I wasn't foolish enough to dismiss cautions we'd heard from every traveler in the preceding months, few though travelers were in our region.

When I spied the butterwort, it was near the trade road, and also in the shadow of a great tree. I braved my way out of the sunlight and knelt to dig up its roots, telling myself I wouldn't be there long enough for mere shadow to be my undoing.

No sooner had I plunged a hand into the earth than did I hear a foreign voice wonder, "What was that, then?"

...

You can read more of *A Man of His Word*
and other WonderBird Press stories
in ebook and print form

www.ingramcontent.com/pod-product-compliance
Lightning Source LLC
Chambersburg PA
CBHW030646020726
47493CB00006B/1897